EVERYMAN, I will go with thee,

and be thy guide,

In thy most need to go by thy side

JOSEPH CONRAD

The Nigger of the "Narcissus"

Typhoon

Amy Foster

Falk

To-morrow

INTRODUCTION AND NOTES BY
NORMAN SHERRY
Professor of English, University of Lancaster

DENT: LONDON
EVERYMAN'S LIBRARY

© Introduction and Notes, J. M. Dent & Sons Ltd, 1974
All rights reserved
Made in Great Britain
at the
Aldine Press · Letchworth · Herts
for
J. M. DENT & SONS LTD
Aldine House · Albemarle Street · London
First included in Everyman's Library in 1945
Last reprinted 1974

No. 1980   Paperback ISBN 0 460 01980 5

INTRODUCTION

When Conrad's third novel, *The Nigger of the 'Narcissus'*, was published in 1897 it surprised both the reading public and the critics. He had until then been seen as the rightful heir to Robert Louis Stevenson's crown, writing about foreign places, about men such as Almayer and Willems, outcasts of the Bornean islands, ostensibly important but ultimately overcome by Malayan cunning and the tropical climate. According to Arthur Waugh (father of Evelyn Waugh), Conrad had annexed Borneo, 'a tract hitherto untouched by the novelist', and it must have appeared inevitable that he would continue to write about displaced white men in exotic settings. But in *The Nigger of the 'Narcissus'* the lonely trader is replaced by seamen, the jungle by the sea. Ignoring the tradition of the romantic naval officer and the kind of sea story that included a damsel in distress, Conrad produced a realistic account of the daily life of the ordinary seaman—indeed a 'Tale of the Forecastle'. *The Saturday Review*, 12th February 1898, catches for us the accent of contemporary amazement: 'Nothing in his earlier works . . . had hinted at the possibility of this *volte face.*' When the novel was published on 2nd December 1897, the day before Conrad's fortieth birthday, it received, as Garnett put it, 'a general blast of eulogy from a dozen impressive sources'. Four years later Henry James, in a letter to Edmund Gosse, summed up Conrad's achievement: '*The Nigger of the "Narcissus"* is . . . the very finest and strongest picture of the sea and sea-life that our language possesses—the masterpiece in a whole class.'

It is difficult to determine exactly to what extent this novel is based on Conrad's voyage in 1884 from Bombay to Dunkirk as second mate of the sailing ship *Narcissus* (see notes). There is evidence that he was trying to recapture the main events of this voyage, but his artistic intentions go further. Parts of his famous 1897 Preface to the novel suggest the determination of the historian to record with accuracy and precision times past: 'To snatch in a moment of courage, from the remorseless rush of time, a passing phase of life.'

To some degree, then, the novel is documentary, a realistic account of a journey from India to England in a sailing ship. Conrad considered himself to be 'the last seaman of a sailing vessel' and felt that his novel put 'a seal on that epoch of the greatest possible perfection which was at the same time the end of the sailing fleet', but it is also his testimonial to the loyalty and courage of the seamen who were his 'brothers' on a dangerous journey. The narrator ends the story with: 'Good-bye, brothers! You were a good crowd. As good a crowd as ever fisted with wild cries the beating canvas of a heavy foresail; or tossing aloft, invisible in the night, gave back yell for yell to a westerly gale.' Conrad wrote to Garnett as the novel grew in length: 'I must enshrine my old chums in a decent edifice. . . . There are so many touches necessary for such a picture.' He knew *The Nigger of the 'Narcissus'* was remarkable, and his letter to his friend Sanderson, serious and religious in tone, establishes his astonishingly dedicated approach to his work:

> . . . God knows,—but He also knows the spirit in which I approached the undertaking to present faithfully some of His benighted and suffering creatures; the humble, the obscure, the sinful, the erring upon whom rests His Gaze of Ineffable Pity. My conscience is at peace in that matter.

This double purpose, therefore, historical and personal, accounts for the abundance of factual detail in the story. For example, the preparing of Jimmy's corpse for burial at sea is as technically detailed as a nautical text-book—the arrangement of weights, 'two holystones, an old anchor shackle', broken links of a stream cable; the stitching of the canvas, the tarred twine, the grey sailcloth; the two planks nailed together; and the Union Jack with a white border to cover the corpse. But Conrad's philosophy of art also forced him, in this instance, to be emphatic and all-embracing. His aim was 'to hold up . . . the rescued fragments before all eyes . . . show its vibration, its colour . . . the stress and passion within the core of each convincing moment', which leads to an inclusive rather than an exclusive approach. He believed that art 'must strenuously aspire to the plasticity of sculpture, to the colour of painting and the . . . suggestiveness of music'. Thus we are given a brilliant collection of coloured canvases with scene succeeding scene. Conrad's contemporary, the novelist Arnold Bennett, made a valuable critical point when he commented on Conrad's 'extraordinary management of colour'.

Conrad had a further purpose in writing the story. In a letter to a Mr Canby written in the year of his death, he expressed it in this way:

> In the *Nigger*, I give the psychology of a group of men and render certain aspects of nature. But the problem that faces them is not a problem of the sea, it is merely a problem that has arisen on board a ship where the conditions of complete isolation from all land entanglements make it stand out with a particular force and colouring.

A year earlier he had recalled that his concern in the novel was with 'the crew of a merchant ship brought to the test of . . . the moral problem of conduct'. The crew, as the narrator in the story expresses it, are men who have 'together and upon the immortal sea, wrung out a meaning from [their] sinful lives'. This intention underlies all others, and is responsible for shaping the material and deciding emphases. It must have forced Conrad to move away from his actual experience of that voyage so as to 'wring a meaning' from it, to bring out 'the moral problem of conduct'. In order to present faithfully 'the humble, the obscure, the sinful, the erring', he gives us Singleton, Wait, Donkin, Belfast, the cook Podmore, the captain, the mate—a cross-section of mankind portrayed so as to bring out in each individual the fundamental moving spirit of personality when that personality is faced with particular problems. The problem that faces the crew of the *Narcissus* is threefold—there is the effect of James Wait and his illness, the threat of the storm and the possibility of mutiny. In dealing with these Conrad very skilfully demonstrates how such pressures bring about groupings and re-groupings among the crew and officers of the ship.

The human catalyst in the story is the Nigger of the title, James Wait: he is 'the centre of the ship's collective psychology and the pivot of the action'. He holds his position because he is dying or may be dying and because he is a final and difficult burden for men fighting a desperate battle with the elements. This 'black fraud', as the irrepressible and incorrigible Donkin calls him, had 'found the secret of keeping for ever on the run the fundamental imbecility of mankind'. The 'confounded dying man' makes himself master of every moment of the existence of the crew. 'He fascinated us. He would never let doubt die. . . . Invulnerable in his promise of speedy corruption he trampled on our self respect, he demonstrated to us daily our want of moral courage; he tainted our lives.'

Jimmy Wait is a man living with death. Death is seen as 'stalking' him, as an 'intimate companion', as an 'ever-expected visitor of Jimmy's'. He symbolizes the awareness of death in life, and although he holds his illness as a threat over the rest of the crew, he is himself afraid. The master's comment sums up his condition—he is 'three parts dead and so scared—black amongst that gaping lot—no grit to face what's coming to us all'. Ultimately it is fear that kills him, fear arising from Donkin's brutal account of what the future holds for him: 'An' ye're a thing—a bloody thing. Yah—you corpse! . . . Die, you beggar—die. . . . That's where yer bound to go. Feet fust, through a port . . . Splash! Never see yer any more. Overboard! Good 'nuff fur yer.' His last words repeat Donkin's like a terrifying refrain: 'Overboard! . . . I! . . . My God!' and his 'throat rattled faintly'.

How the crew, individually and collectively, react to the Nigger is of immense importance. At all points James Wait is the focus for the shifting relationships and the changing alliances in the novel and this is especially so in Chapter 4 where, using Wait as a symbol of unjust treatment (when in fact he is more properly a symbol of impending [Waiting] death), Donkin is able to bring about a near mutiny. Belfast first hates and then loves the Nigger, looks after him in sickness and in death, and his last words to the narrator are of Jimmy. And the crew come together in heroic action during the storm to rescue the Nigger, trapped in his cabin and 'screaming and knocking below us with the hurry of a man prematurely shut up in a coffin'.

Singleton alone of the crew is unmoved by Jimmy. It seems that only Singleton knows 'how to exist beyond the pale of life and within the sight of eternity' and his pronouncements upon Jimmy: 'You can't help him; die he must', 'Mortally sick men . . . linger till the first sight of land, and then die,' are prophecies the novel fulfils. The Nigger can be said, therefore, to bring out the fundamental nature of each member of the crew he influences.

If James Wait moves men on a personal and individual plane, Donkin moves them at the communal level, swaying them as a group through his ability to make propaganda out of events. Donkin is the fomenter of the mutiny, the true example of anarchism, a principle of persistent resentfulness, a 'votary of change' (this said by the author with his tongue in his cheek), and in his own mind 'a victim of injustice'. He does not understand his own nature. In answer to the Nigger's question, 'Why are you so hot on making trouble?', Donkin says:

> ''Cos it's a bloomin' shayme. We are put upon . . . bad food, bad pay . . . want us to kick up a bloomin' row; a

blamed 'owling row that would make 'em remember!
Knocking people about . . . brain us . . . indeed! Ain't we
men?' His altruistic indignation blazed.

Donkin has a 'fatal antagonism' towards all 'surrounding
existences . . . He had a desire to assert his importance, to
break, to crush; to be even with everybody for everything; to
tear the veil, unmask, expose, leave no refuge', and, of course,
a mutiny at that time (after the strains of the gale) allows
Conrad to be at his most caustic about the aspirations raised in
the heart of the crew by Donkin: 'We were oppressed by the
injustice of the world, surprised to perceive how long we had
lived under its burden without realising our unfortunate
state . . . [We] dreamed enthusiastically of the time when every
lonely ship would travel over a serene sea, manned by a
wealthy and well-fed crew of satisfied skippers.' But Conrad
draws our attention to the fact that: 'In the pauses of [Don-
kin's] impassioned orations the wind sighed quietly aloft, the
calm sea unheeded murmured in a warning whisper along the
ship's side.' The mutiny causes the helmsman to leave his post
and immediately the

> sails woke suddenly coming all together with a mighty flap
> against the masts, then filled again one after another in a
> quick succession of loud reports that ran down the lofty
> spars, till the collapsed mainsail flew out last with a
> violent jerk. The ship trembled from trucks to keel; the
> sails kept on rattling like a discharge of musketry; the
> chain sheets and loose shackles jingled aloft in a thin peal;
> the gin blocks groaned. It was as if an invisible hand had
> given the ship an angry shake to recall the men that
> peopled her decks to the sense of reality, vigilance, and duty.

Dereliction of duty cannot take place for long on a ship, for
the sea lies in wait for the unwary. The parallel with the social
order is obvious.

Donkin is deliberately contrasted, in word and action, with Singleton, the old seaman who spends thirty hours at the wheel in the storm. Coming off duty the old man 'suddenly fell forward, crashing down, stiff and headlong like an uprooted tree'. The 'venerable Singleton' who lived 'through half a century had measured his strength against the favours and the rages of the sea'—'monumental, indistinct, with his head touching the beam [he is] like a statue of heroic size in the gloom of a crypt' symbolizing Man's potential for nobility and heroic persistence in fulfilling his duty towards his ship. 'He is simple and great like an elemental force,' wrote Conrad of Singleton to his friend Cunninghame Graham. He represents an earlier generation of seamen celebrated by Conrad; 'they had been men who knew toil, privation, violence, debauchery —but knew not fear, and had no desire of spite in their hearts. . . . They were the everlasting children of the mysterious sea. Their successors [the Donkins] are the grown-up children of a discontented earth . . . if they had learned how to speak they have also learned how to whine.'

Set against Man is the Universe. The ship, sole protector of man from the warring elements, is seen as a 'fragment detached from the earth', 'lonely and swift like a small planet. Round her the abysses of sky and sea met in an unattainable frontier'. Chapter three deals principally with the storm (of which the critic of the *Pall Mall Gazette*, 20th December 1897, asserted, 'No finer or more vivid description of a storm at sea has been written') and here man, full of courage, is nevertheless dwarfed by the elements, and is increasingly described in collective terms at this point:

The men, knitted together aft into a ready group . . . stood admiring her valiance. Their eyes blinked in the wind; their dark faces were wet with drops of water . . . beards and moustaches, soaked, hung straight and dripping like fine seaweed. . . . Whenever she rose easily to a towering

green sea, elbows dug ribs, faces brightened, lips murmured: 'Didn't she do it cleverly', and all the heads
turning like one watched with sardonic grins the foiled
wave go roaring to leeward, white with the foam of a
monstrous rage.

Once the storm begins, the ship becomes the heroine and the
battle is her battle against the indestructible sea. The seamen
'looked wretched in a hopeless struggle, like vermin fleeing
before a flood'. And man's decline in hierarchy is underlined by
the fact that the 'model' chief mate has to move during the storm
'on all fours with the movements of some big cautious beast'.

Given man's capacity for good and evil, Conrad yet stresses
that set against the perspective of the universe, he is insignificant (like vermin before a flood) and indeed, not even worthy
of attention or notice. Speaking of the Singleton generation,
Conrad writes that they 'were strong and mute; . . . bowed and
enduring, like stone caryatides . . . They are gone now—and it
does not matter. The sea and the earth are unfaithful to their
children: a truth, a faith, a generation of men goes—and is
forgotten, and it does not matter.' In a letter to R. B. Cunninghame Graham, written eighteen days after the publication of
The Nigger of the 'Narcissus', Conrad spoke of the universe as
an 'infamous' knitting-machine which 'knits us in and knits us
out', and in another letter to the same friend on 14th January
1898 he returned to this theme, seeing man's reasonable attitude in the face of such a universe as one of 'cold unconcern';

Of course reason is hateful—but why? Because it demonstrates . . . that we, living, are out of life—utterly out of it.
The mysteries of the universe made of drops of fire and
clods of mud do not concern us in the least. The fate of a
humanity condemned ultimately to perish from cold is not
worth troubling about. If you take it to heart it becomes
an unendurable tragedy. If you believe in improvement
you must weep, for the attained perfection must end in

cold, darkness and silence. In a dispassionate view the ardour for reform, improvement for virtue, for knowledge, and even for beauty is only a vain sticking up for appearance as though one were anxious about the cut of one's clothes in a community of blind men. Life knows us not and we do not know life.

Donkin, having stolen from Jimmy Wait, having brought about his death, leaves the Nigger's cabin:

Donkin closed the door behind him gently but firmly. Sleeping men, huddled under jackets, made on the lighted deck shapeless dark mounds that had the appearance of neglected graves. Nothing had been done all through the night and he hadn't been missed. He stood motionless and perfectly astounded to find the world outside as he had left it; there was the sea, the ship—sleeping men; and he wondered absurdly at it, as though he had expected to find the men dead, familiar things gone for ever: as though, like a wanderer returning after many years, he had expected to see bewildering changes. He shuddered a little in the penetrating freshness of the air, and hugged himself forlornly. The declining moon dropped sadly in the western board as if withered by the cold touch of a pale dawn. The ship slept. And the immortal sea stretched away, immense and hazy, like the image of life, with a glittering surface and lightless depths. Donkin gave it a defiant glance and slunk off noiselessly as if judged and cast out by the august silence of its might.

But, of course, as Conrad sadly insists, the 'august silence' does not judge men.

The voyage of the *Narcissus* is obviously carefully contrived by Conrad to present a microcosmographical picture of human society as he saw it. The dangers of such a symbolic intention draining a story of life and vividness are avoided by Conrad's devotion to the details of reality which we emphasized earlier, so that the symbolic interpretation of man's existence, although it determines the shape of events, does not affect the quality of the life described.

An early reviewer of the *Typhoon* volume, in *Truth*, 28th May 1903, recommended that these stories should be read backwards, 'beginning with the last story or sketch, and ending with the superb description in the eponymous tale', and there might be some point in this since one would begin with the lesser stories and end with the best. *T.P.'s Weekly* of 15th May 1903 suggested that the stories here reveal three distinguishing characteristics of Conrad and his race—'a certain capacity for silent endurance, an intense determination to survive, and the restlessness of a race whose home is the wide world'. MacWhirr in *Typhoon* certainly demonstrates silent endurance, Falk the determination to survive, and Harry in 'To-morrow' the restlessness that prevents a man settling down. But these stories reflect other aspects of Conrad's life and deeply held beliefs: his knowledge of the effects of the foreign and bizarre on the settled and conventional—of Falk on the community in an eastern port, of Yanko on Amy Foster; his recognition that in the settled and conventional there can also be bizarre elements—Amy Foster's rejection of Yanko, and MacWhirr's defiance of the storm; and his awareness of a grotesque and macabre quality in life that his short stories particularly bring out.

Typhoon is another sea-piece, sharing some characteristics with *The Nigger of the 'Narcissus'*. Both celebrate man's stand against the sea, both celebrate a ship, evidence of man's skill in invention and craftsmanship, in her battle with the elements, though one is a sailing ship and the other a steamer. Indeed there are some odd duplications of incident: both stories have helmsmen on duty for thirty hours, both have cowards on board their respective ships. But *Typhoon* is a slighter story: it attempts and achieves less, it is less complex in its story-telling techniques, does not experiment with a narrator figure, and is in many ways the more traditional sea story told from the point of view of the Olympian author. Whereas the influence of Wait, Donkin and the storm in *The Nigger of the 'Narcissus'* is traumatic and revealing, the sub-plot of *Typhoon*, dealing with the fighting Chinese coolies locked in the ship's hold, has no significance in the revelation of character, unless it is to put the mate, Jukes, on his mettle and give us a further insight into MacWhirr's mind. For MacWhirr settles the problem of how to re-distribute the coolies' scattered dollars:

> He told me afterwards that, all the coolies having worked in the same place and for the same length of time, he reckoned he would be doing the fair thing by them as near as possible if he shared all the cash we had picked up equally among the lot. You could not tell one man's dollars from another's . . . and if you asked each man how much money he brought on board they would lie . . .

Conrad originally had in mind simply the story of the coolies and their scattered dollars, a magazine story in terms of plot, which he thought of calling 'Equitable Division'. It is in the character of MacWhirr, which Conrad treats with a lightness of ironic humour, that the success of the story lies.

MacWhirr is well summed up by Conrad: 'the past being to his mind done with, and the future not there yet, the more general actualities of the day required no comment'. In the early part of the story the verbal images belittle MacWhirr effectively: 'MacWhirr's honesty . . . had the heavy obviousness of a lump of clay.' And MacWhirr's literalness is the source of much of Conrad's humour:

> 'It's the heat,' said Jukes. 'The weather's awful. It would make a saint swear. Even up here I feel exactly as if I had my head tied up in a woollen blanket.'

Captain MacWhirr looked up. 'D'ye mean to say, Mr. Jukes, you ever had your head tied up in a blanket? What was that for?'

'It's a manner of speaking, sir,' said Jukes, stolidly.

'Some of you fellows do go on! What's that about saints swearing? I wish you wouldn't talk so wild. What sort of saint would that be that would swear? No more saint than yourself, I expect. And what's a blanket got to do with it—or the weather either. . . . The heat does not make me swear—does it?'

This is all in line with the strict view the author has of his hero and his life before he is tested by the sea. 'Captain MacWhirr had sailed over the surface of the oceans as some men go skimming over the years of existence to sink gently into a placid grave, ignorant of life to the last, without ever having been made to see all it may contain of perfidy, of violence, and of terror.' His limitations are obvious—his failure to understand the behaviour of others:

'I can't understand what you find to talk about! . . . Two solid hours. I am not blaming you. I see people ashore at it all day long, and then in the evening they sit down and keep at it over the drinks. Must be saying the same things over and over again. I can't understand.'

his simple hatred of profanity which interferes with his judgement of the second engineer: 'That's a very violent man, that second engineer. . . . A profane man. . . . If this goes on, I'll have to get rid of him the first chance'; his perverse rejection of book knowledge: 'Running to get behind the weather! Do you understand that Mr. Jukes? It's the maddest thing. . . . You would think an old woman had been writing this'; his rejection of Captain Wilson's 'storm strategy': 'It was like listening to a crazy man.' But for all his limitations he has powerful virtues. With only 'just enough imagination to carry him through each successive day, and no more' he is nevertheless a curiously moving figure once he has confronted his destiny. Fundamentally he is unable to change. Even his phrases remain with him throughout: 'A gale is a gale, Mr. Jukes . . . and a full-powered steam-ship has got to face it. There's just so much dirty weather knocking about the world, and the proper thing is to go through it,' and this is exactly what he does. After the ship has gone through the first typhoon and during that awful pause before the gale returns, MacWhirr rests alone in his cabin, his defences finally penetrated, and he comments simply, as befits the man: 'I shouldn't like to lose her.' Back on deck, he repeats his simple but effective philosophy to Jukes because he feels that he might be swept overboard leaving Jukes alone: '"Don't you be put out by anything. . . . Keep her facing it. . . . Facing it—always facing it—that's the way to get through. You are a young sailor. Face it. That's enough for any man. Keep a cool head."'

Conrad deliberately put all he could into creating a character who had little of the romantic and heroic about him and yet carries the burden of command, and though Jukes can turn to MacWhirr for moral and physical support, MacWhirr 'could expect no relief of that sort from anyone on earth'—'Such is the loneliness of command.'

In his Author's Note to *Typhoon*, Conrad writes that 'it was but a bit of a sea yarn after all' and this is a correct placing of it. Conrad's friend Garnett, at the time of the publication of *The Nigger of the 'Narcissus'*, inscribed in a copy of Constance Garnett's translation of Turgenev's *The Torrents of Spring* the following words: 'I see the Nigger is out at last. I drink its luck though its life is assured for ever.' Edward Garnett was being truly prophetic here.

1974   NORMAN SHERRY

JOSEPH CONRAD

Born at Berdiczew, in the Ukraine, of a Polish family, 3rd December 1857; christened Jósef Tedor Konrad Nalecz Korzeniowski. Travelled to Marseilles, 1874, and became a seaman, first reaching England in 1878. Became a naturalized British subject and obtained Master Mariner's Certificate, 1886. Married Miss Jessie George, 1896; two sons: Borys (*b.* 1898), John (*b.* 1906). Died at Bishopsbourne, Kent, 3rd August 1924.

SELECT BIBLIOGRAPHY

JOSEPH CONRAD'S WORKS

1895 *Almayer's Folly—A Story of an Eastern River.*
1896 *An Outcast of the Islands.*
1897 *The Nigger of the 'Narcissus'—A Tale of the Sea.* (First edition to include Preface, 1914.)
1898 *Tales of Unrest.* (Contents: 'Karain' a Memory', 'The Idiots', 'An Outpost of Progress', 'The Return', 'The Lagoon'.)
1900 *Lord Jim—A Tale.*
1902 *Youth: A Narrative; and Two Other Stories.* (Contents: 'Youth', 'Heart of Darkness', 'The End of the Tether'.)
1903 *Typhoon, and Other Stories.* (Contents: 'Typhoon', 'Amy Foster', 'Falk', 'To-morrow'.)
1903 *Romance—A Novel.* (In collaboration with Ford Madox Hueffer.)
1904 *Nostromo—A Tale of the Seaboard.*
1906 *The Mirror of the Sea—Memories and Impressions.*
1907 *The Secret Agent—A Simple Tale.*
1908 *A Set of Six.* (Contents: 'Gaspar Ruiz', 'The Informer', 'The Brute', 'An Anarchist', 'The Duel', 'Il Conde'.)
1911 *Under Western Eyes.*
1912 *A Personal Record.* (First published as *Some Reminiscences.*)
1912 *'Twixt Land and Sea—Tales.* (Contents: 'A Smile of Fortune', 'The Secret Sharer', 'Freya of the Seven Isles'.)
1913 *Chance—A Tale in Two Parts.*
1915 *Victory—An Island Tale.*
1915 *Within the Tides—Tales.* (Contents: 'The Planter of Malata', 'The Partner', 'The Inn of the Two Witches', 'Because of the Dollars'.)
1917 *The Shadow Line—A Confession.*
1919 *The Arrow of Gold—A Story between Two Notes.*
1920 *The Rescue—A Romance of the Shallows.*
1921 *Notes On Life and Letters.* (Essays, mainly from periodicals; 13 in Part I on Letters, 13 in Part II on Life.)
1923 *The Rover.*
1925 *Suspense—A Napoleonic Novel.*

1925　*Tales of Hearsay.* (Contents: 'The Warrior's Soul' 'Prince Roman', 'The Tale', 'The Black Mate'.)
1926　*Last Essays.* (19 essays, uncollected in book form at the time of his death.)
1923–8　Uniform Edition of the Works of Joseph Conrad. Re-issued as Collected Edition, 1946–54, 21 volumes, containing all the works listed above. All published by J. M. Dent & Sons.

CONRAD'S LETTERS

The Life and Letters of Joseph Conrad (2 vols.), edited by G. Jean-Aubry, 1927. *Letters from Conrad, 1895–1924,* edited, with an introduction, by Edward Garnett, 1928. *Letters from Joseph Conrad to Richard Curle,* 1928. *Letters of Joseph Conrad to Marguerite Poradowska,* New York, 1940. *Joseph Conrad: Letters to William Blackwood and David S. Meldrum,* edited by W. Blackburn, 1959. *Conrad's Polish Background: letters to and from his Polish Friends,* ed. by Zdzisław Najder, 1964. *Joseph Conrad's Letters to R. B. Cunninghame Graham,* ed. by C. T. Watts, 1969.

BIOGRAPHICAL AND CRITICAL WRITINGS ON CONRAD

Joseph Conrad, A Study, by Richard Curle, 1914. Essay in *Notes on Novelists,* by Henry James, 1914. *Joseph Conrad,* by Hugh Walpole, 1916. Essay on Conrad in *A Book of Prefaces,* by H. L. Mencken, 1917. *Joseph Conrad, a Personal Remembrance,* by Ford Madox Ford, 1924. Essays on Conrad in *The Common Reader,* by Virginia Woolf, 1925. *Joseph Conrad as I knew Him,* by Jessie Conrad, 1926. 'Reminiscences of Conrad' and 'Preface to Conrad's Plays' in *Castles in Spain* by John Galsworthy, 1927. *The Last Twelve Years of Joseph Conrad,* by Richard Curle, 1928. *The Polish Heritage of Joseph Conrad,* by Gustav Morf, 1930. *Joseph Conrad's Mind and Method,* by R. L. Mégroz, 1931. *Joseph Conrad and his Circle,* by Jessie Conrad, 1936. *Joseph Conrad, Some Aspects of the Art of the Novel,* by Edward Crankshaw, 1936. Introductory Essay by Edward Garnett to *Conrad's Prefaces to his Works,* 1937. *Joseph Conrad, the Making of a Novelist,* by John D. Gordan, 1940. *Joseph Conrad, England's Polish Genius,* by M. C. Bradbrook, 1941. Introduction by A. J. Hoppé to *The Conrad Companion,* 1946. *The Great Tradition* (George Eliot, Henry James, and Joseph Conrad), by F. R. Leavis, 1948. *Joseph Conrad,* by Oliver Warner, 1951. *Conrad, a Re-assessment,* by D. Hewitt, 1952. *Six Great Novelists,* by Walter Allen, 1955 (Conrad is the sixth subject). *The Mirror of Conrad,* by E. H. Visiak, 1955. *The Sea Dreamer: Life of Conrad,* by Jean-Aubry, 1957. *Joseph Conrad,* by Thomas Moser, 1957. *Joseph Conrad, A Study in Non-conformity,* by Osborn Andreas, 1959. *A Reader's Guide to Joseph Conrad,* by Frederick R. Karl, 1960. *The Art of Joseph Conrad: A Critical Symposium,* ed. by R. W. Stallman, 1960. *Joseph Conrad, A Critical Biography,* by Jocelyn Baines, 1960. *Conrad's Heart of Darkness and The Critics,* ed. by Bruce Harkness, 1960. *Joseph Conrad, Giant in Exile,* by Leo Gurko, 1962. *The Political Novels of Joseph Conrad,* by E. K. Hay, 1963. *Joseph Conrad and the Fiction of Autobiography,* by E. W. Said, 1966. *Conrad's*

Eastern World, by Norman Sherry, 1966. *The Sea Years of Joseph Conrad*, by Jerry Allen, 1967. *Conrad: A Psycho-analytic Biography*, by B. C. Meyer, 1967. *Conrad's Politics: Community and Anarchy in the Fiction of Joseph Conrad*, by A. Fleishman, 1968. *Conrad the Psychologist as Artist*, by P. Kirschner, 1968. *Joseph Conrad*, by J. I. M. Stewart, 1968. *Joseph Conrad's Fiction: A Study in Literary Growth*, by J. A. Palmer, 1968. *Conrad's Short Fiction*, by L. Graver, 1969. *My Father: Joseph Conrad*, by Borys Conrad, 1970. *Conrad's Western World*, by Norman Sherry, 1971. *Conrad: The Critical Heritage*, ed. Norman Sherry, 1973. *Conrad and his World*, by Norman Sherry, 1973. *Joseph Conrad: The Modern Imagination*, by C. B. Cox, 1974.

BIBLIOGRAPHIES

A Bibliography of the Writings of Joseph Conrad 1895–1921, by T. J. Wise, 1921. *A Conrad Library*, collected by T. J. Wise, London, 1928. *A Conrad Memorial Library*, collected by G. T. Keating, New York, 1929, with 'Check List of Additions', 1938. *Joseph Conrad at Mid-century, Editions and Studies, 1895–1955*, by K. A. Lohf and E. P. Sheehy, 1959. *A Bibliography of Joseph Conrad*, by Theodore G. Ehrsam, 1969. *Joseph Conrad: An Annotated Bibliography of Writings About Him*, compiled and ed. by Bruce T. Teets and Helmut E. Gerber, 1971.

PREFACE

A work that aspires, however humbly, to the condition of art should carry its justification in every line. And art itself may be defined as a single-minded attempt to render the highest kind of justice to the visible universe, by bringing to light the truth, manifold and one, underlying its every aspect. It is an attempt to find in its forms, in its colours, in its light, in its shadows, in the aspects of matter and in the facts of life what of each is fundamental, what is enduring and essential—their one illuminating and convincing quality—the very truth of their existence. The artist, then, like the thinker or the scientist, seeks the truth and makes his appeal. Impressed by the aspect of the world the thinker plunges into ideas, the scientist into facts—whence, presently, emerging they make their appeal to those qualities of our being that fit us best for the hazardous enterprise of living. They speak authoritatively to our common-sense, to our intelligence, to our desire of peace or to our desire of unrest; not seldom to our prejudices, sometimes to our fears, often to our egoism—but always to our credulity. And their words are heard with reverence, for their concern is with weighty matters: with the cultivation of our minds and the proper care of our bodies, with the attainment of our ambitions, with the perfection of the means and the glorification of our precious aims.

It is otherwise with the artist.

Confronted by the same enigmatical spectacle the

artist descends within himself, and in that lonely region of stress and strife, if he be deserving and fortunate, he finds the terms of his appeal. His appeal is made to our less obvious capacities: to that part of our nature which, because of the warlike conditions of existence, is necessarily kept out of sight within the more resisting and hard qualities—like the vulnerable body within a steel armour. His appeal is less loud, more profound, less distinct, more stirring—and sooner forgotten. Yet its effect endures forever. The changing wisdom of successive generations discards ideas, questions facts, demolishes theories. But the artist appeals to that part of our being which is not dependent on wisdom; to that in us which is a gift and not an acquisition— and, therefore, more permanently enduring. He speaks to our capacity for delight and wonder, to the sense of mystery surrounding our lives; to our sense of pity, and beauty, and pain; to the latent feeling of fellowship with all creation—and to the subtle but invincible conviction of solidarity that knits together the loneliness of innumerable hearts, to the solidarity in dreams, in joy, in sorrow, in aspirations, in illusions, in hope, in fear, which binds men to each other, which binds together all humanity—the dead to the living and the living to the unborn.

It is only some such train of thought, or rather of feeling, that can in a measure explain the aim of the attempt, made in the tale which follows, to present an unrestful episode in the obscure lives of a few individuals out of all the disregarded multitude of the bewildered, the simple and the voiceless. For, if any part of truth dwells in the belief confessed above, it becomes evident that there is not a place of splendour or a dark corner of the earth that does not deserve, if only a passing glance of wonder and pity. The motive then, may be held to justify the matter of the work; but this preface, which is simply an avowal of endeavour, cannot end here—for the avowal is not yet complete.

Fiction—if it at all aspires to be art—appeals to temperament. And in truth it must be, like painting, like music, like all art, the appeal of one temperament to all the other innumerable temperaments whose subtle and resistless power endows passing events with their true meaning, and creates the moral, the emotional atmosphere of the place and time. Such an appeal to be effective must be an impression conveyed through the senses; and, in fact, it cannot be made in any other way, because temperament, whether individual or collective, is not amenable to persuasion. All art, therefore, appeals primarily to the senses, and the artistic aim when expressing itself in written words must also make its appeal through the senses, if its high desire is to reach the secret spring of responsive emotions. It must strenuously aspire to the plasticity of sculpture, to the colour of painting, and to the magic suggestiveness of music—which is the art of arts. And it is only through complete, unswerving devotion to the perfect blending of form and substance; it is only through an unremitting never-discouraged care for the shape and ring of sentences that an approach can be made to plasticity, to colour, and that the light of magic suggestiveness may be brought to play for an evanescent instant over the commonplace surface of words: of the old, old words, worn thin, defaced by ages of careless usage.

The sincere endeavour to accomplish that creative task, to go as far on that road as his strength will carry him, to go undeterred by faltering, weariness or reproach, is the only valid justification for the worker in prose. And if his conscience is clear, his answer to those who in the fulness of a wisdom which looks for immediate profit, demand specifically to be edified, consoled, amused; who demand to be promptly improved, or encouraged, or frightened, or shocked, or charmed, must run thus:— My task which I am trying to achieve is, by the power of the written word to make you hear, to make you feel —it is, before all, to make you *see*. That—and no more, and it is everything. If I succeed, you shall find there according to your deserts: encouragement, consolation, fear, charm—all you demand—and, perhaps, also that glimpse of truth for which you have forgotten to ask.

To snatch in a moment of courage, from the remorseless rush of time, a passing phase of life, is only the beginning of the task. The task approached in tenderness and faith is to hold up unquestioningly, without choice and without fear, the rescued fragment before all eyes in the light of a sincere mood. It is to show its vibration, its colour, its form; and through its movement, its form, and its colour, reveal the substance of its truth—disclose its inspiring secret: the stress and passion within the core of each convincing moment. In a single-minded attempt of that kind, if one be deserving and fortunate, one may perchance attain to such clearness of sincerity that at last the presented vision of regret or pity, of terror or mirth, shall awaken in the hearts of the beholders that feeling of unavoidable solidarity; of the solidarity in mysterious origin, in toil, in joy, in hope, in uncertain fate, which binds men to each other and all mankind to the visible world.

It is evident that he who, rightly or wrongly, holds by the convictions expressed above cannot be faithful to any one of the temporary formulas of his craft. The enduring part of them—the truth which each only imperfectly veils—should abide with him as the most precious of his possessions, but they all: Realism,

Romanticism, Naturalism, even the unofficial sentimentalism (which like the poor, is exceedingly difficult
to get rid of,) all these gods must, after a short period
of fellowship, abandon him—even on the very threshold
of the temple—to the stammerings of his conscience
and to the outspoken consciousness of the difficulties
of his work. In that uneasy solitude the supreme cry
of Art for Art, itself, loses the exciting ring of its apparent immorality. It sounds far off. It has ceased
to be a cry, and is heard only as a whisper, often incomprehensible, but at times and faintly encouraging.

Sometimes, stretched at ease in the shade of a roadside tree, we watch the motions of a labourer in a distant field, and after a time, begin to wonder languidly
as to what the fellow may be at. We watch the movements of his body, the waving of his arms, we see
him bend down, stand up, hesitate, begin again. It
may add to the charm of an idle hour to be told the
purpose of his exertions. If we know he is trying to
lift a stone, to dig a ditch, to uproot a stump, we look
with a more real interest at his efforts; we are disposed
to condone the jar of his agitation upon the restfulness
of the landscape; and even, if in a brotherly frame of
mind, we may bring ourselves to forgive his failure.
We understood his object, and, after all, the fellow has
tried, and perhaps he had not the strength—and perhaps he had not the knowledge. We forgive, go on our
way—and forget.

And so it is with the workman of art. Art is long
and life is short, and success is very far off. And thus,
doubtful of strength to travel so far, we talk a little
about the aim—the aim of art, which, like life itself,
is inspiring, difficult—obscured by mists. It is not
in the clear logic of a triumphant conclusion; it is not
in the unveiling of one of those heartless secrets which

are called the Laws of Nature. It is not less great, but only more difficult.

To arrest, for the space of a breath, the hands busy about the work of the earth, and compel men entranced by the sight of distant goals to glance for a moment at the surrounding vision of form and colour, of sunshine and shadows; to make them pause for a look, for a sigh, for a smile—such is the aim, difficult and evanescent, and reserved only for a very few to achieve. But sometimes, by the deserving and the fortunate, even that task is accomplished. And when it is accomplished—behold!—all the truth of life is there: a moment of vision, a sigh, a smile—and the return to an eternal rest.

1897.   J. C.

THE NIGGER OF THE "NARCISSUS"

To
Edward Garnett
this tale
about my friends
of the sea

THE
NIGGER OF THE "NARCISSUS"

CHAPTER ONE

MR. BAKER, chief mate of the ship *Narcissus*, stepped in one stride out of his lighted cabin into the darkness of the quarter-deck. Above his head, on the break of the poop, the night-watchman rang a double stroke. It was nine o'clock. Mr. Baker, speaking up to the man above him, asked:—"Are all the hands aboard, Knowles?"

The man limped down the ladder, then said reflectively:—

"I think so, sir. All our old chaps are there, and a lot of new men has come. . . . They must be all there."

"Tell the boatswain to send all hands aft," went on Mr. Baker; "and tell one of the youngsters to bring a good lamp here. I want to muster our crowd."

The main deck was dark aft, but halfway from forward, through the open doors of the forecastle, two streaks of brilliant light cut the shadow of the quiet night that lay upon the ship. A hum of voices was heard there, while port and starboard, in the illuminated doorways, silhouettes of moving men appeared for a moment, very black, without relief, like figures cut out of sheet tin. The ship was ready for sea. The carpenter had driven in the last wedge of the main-

hatch battens, and, throwing down his maul, had wiped
his face with great deliberation, just on the stroke of
five.   The decks had been swept, the windlass oiled
and made ready to heave up the anchor; the big tow-
rope lay in long bights along one side of the main deck,
with one end carried up and hung over the bows, in
readiness for the tug that would come paddling and
hissing noisily, hot and smoky, in the limpid, cool
quietness of the early morning.   The captain was
ashore, where he had been engaging some new hands
to make up his full crew; and, the work of the day over,
the ship's officers had kept out of the way, glad of a little
breathing-time.   Soon after dark the few liberty-men
and the new hands began to arrive in shore-boats rowed
by white-clad Asiatics, who clamoured fiercely for payment before coming alongside the gangway-ladder.
The feverish and shrill babble of Eastern language
struggled against the masterful tones of tipsy seamen,
who argued against brazen claims and dishonest hopes
by profane shouts.   The resplendent and bestarred
peace of the East was torn into squalid tatters by howls
of rage and shrieks of lament raised over sums ranging
from five annas to half a rupee; and every soul afloat
in Bombay Harbour became aware that the new hands
were joining the *Narcissus*.

Gradually the distracting noise had subsided.   The
boats came no longer in splashing clusters of three or
four together, but dropped alongside singly, in a subdued
buzz of expostulation cut short by a "Not a pice more!
You go to the devil!" from some man staggering up the
accommodation-ladder—a dark figure, with a long bag
poised on the shoulder.   In the forecastle the new-
comers, upright and swaying amongst corded boxes
and bundles of bedding, made friends with the old hands,
who sat one above another in the two tiers of bunks,

gazing at their future shipmates with glances critical
but friendly. The two forecastle lamps were turned
up high, and shed an intense hard glare; shore-going
round hats were pushed far on the backs of heads,
or rolled about on the deck amongst the chain-cables;
white collars, undone, stuck out on each side of red
faces; big arms in white sleeves gesticulated; the growling voices hummed steady amongst bursts of laughter
and hoarse calls. "Here, sonny, take that bunk!
. . . Don't you do it! . . . What's your
last ship? . . . I know her. . . . Three
years ago, in Puget Sound. . . . This here berth
leaks, I tell you! . . . Come on; give us a
chance to swing that chest! . . . Did you bring
a bottle, any of you shore toffs? . . . Give us
a bit of 'baccy. . . . I know her; her skipper
drank himself to death. . . . He was a dandy
boy! . . . Liked his lotion inside, he did!
. . . No! . . . Hold your row, you chaps!
. . . I tell you, you came on board a hooker,
where they get their money's worth out of poor Jack,
by——! . . ."

A little fellow, called Craik and nicknamed Belfast,
abused the ship violently, romancing on principle, just
to give the new hands something to think over. Archie,
sitting aslant on his sea-chest, kept his knees out of the
way, and pushed the needle steadily through a white
patch in a pair of blue trousers. Men in black jackets
and stand-up collars, mixed with men bare-footed,
bare-armed, with coloured shirts open on hairy chests,
pushed against one another in the middle of the forecastle. The group swayed, reeled, turning upon itself
with the motion of a scrimmage, in a haze of tobacco
smoke. All were speaking together, swearing at every
second word. A Russian Finn, wearing a yellow shirt

with pink stripes, stared upwards, dreamy-eyed, from under a mop of tumbled hair. Two young giants with smooth, baby faces—two Scandinavians—helped each other to spread their bedding, silent, and smiling placidly at the tempest of good-humoured and meaningless curses. Old Singleton, the oldest able seaman in the ship, set apart on the deck right under the lamps, stripped to the waist, tattooed like a cannibal chief all over his powerful chest and enormous biceps. Between the blue and red patterns his white skin gleamed like satin; his bare back was propped against the heel of the bowsprit, and he held a book at arm's length before his big, sunburnt face. With his spectacles and a venerable white beard, he resembled a learned and savage patriarch, the incarnation of barbarian wisdom serene in the blasphemous turmoil of the world. He was intensely absorbed, and as he turned the pages an expression of grave surprise would pass over his rugged features. He was reading "Pelham." The popularity of Bulwer Lytton in the forecastles of Southern-going ships is a wonderful and bizarre phenomenon. What ideas do his polished and so curiously insincere sentences awaken in the simple minds of the big children who people those dark and wandering places of the earth? What meaning their rough, inexperienced souls can find in the elegant verbiage of his pages? What excitement?—what forgetfulness?—what appeasement? Mystery! Is it the fascination of the incomprehensible?—is it the charm of the impossible? Or are those beings who exist beyond the pale of life stirred by his tales as by an enigmatical disclosure of a resplendent world that exists within the frontier of infamy and filth, within that border of dirt and hunger, of misery and dissipation, that comes down on all sides to the water's edge of the incorruptible ocean, and is the only thing

they know of life, the only thing they see of surrounding land—those life-long prisoners of the sea? Mystery!

Singleton, who had sailed to the southward since
the age of twelve, who in the last forty-five years had
lived (as we had calculated from his papers) no more
than forty months ashore—old Singleton, who boasted,
with the mild composure of long years well spent, that
generally from the day he was paid off from one ship
till the day he shipped in another he seldom was in a
condition to distinguish daylight—old Singleton sat
unmoved in the clash of voices and cries, spelling
through "Pelham" with slow labour, and lost in an
absorption profound enough to resemble a trance. He
breathed regularly. Every time he turned the book
in his enormous and blackened hands the muscles of
his big white arms rolled slightly under the smooth
skin. Hidden by the white moustache, his lips, stained
with tobacco-juice that trickled down the long beard,
moved in inward whisper. His bleared eyes gazed
fixedly from behind the glitter of black-rimmed glasses.
Opposite to him, and on a level with his face, the ship's
cat sat on the barrel of the windlass in the pose of a
crouching chimera, blinking its green eyes at its old
friend. It seemed to meditate a leap on to the old
man's lap over the bent back of the ordinary seaman
who sat at Singleton's feet. Young Charley was lean
and long-necked. The ridge of his backbone made a
chain of small hills under the old shirt. His face of a
street-boy—a face precocious, sagacious, and ironic,
with deep downward folds on each side of the thin, wide
mouth—hung low over his bony knees. He was learn-
ing to make a lanyard knot with a bit of an old rope.
Small drops of perspiration stood out on his bulging
forehead; he sniffed strongly from time to time, glancing
out of the corners of his restless eyes at the old seaman,

who took no notice of the puzzled youngster muttering
at his work.

The noise increased. Little Belfast seemed, in the
heavy heat of the forecastle, to boil with facetious fury.
His eyes danced; in the crimson of his face, comical
as a mask, the mouth yawned black, with strange
grimaces. Facing him, a half-undressed man held his
sides, and, throwing his head back, laughed with wet
eyelashes. Others stared with amazed eyes. Men
sitting doubled up in the upper bunks smoked short
pipes, swinging bare brown feet above the heads of
those who, sprawling below on sea-chests, listened,
smiling stupidly or scornfully. Over the white rims
of berths stuck out heads with blinking eyes; but the
bodies were lost in the gloom of those places, that resembled narrow niches for coffins in a whitewashed and
lighted mortuary. Voices buzzed louder. Archie,
with compressed lips, drew himself in, seemed to shrink
into a smaller space, and sewed steadily, industrious
and dumb. Belfast shrieked like an inspired Dervish:—
". . . So I seez to him, boys, seez I, 'Beggin'
yer pardon, sorr,' seez I to that second mate of that
steamer—'beggin' your-r-r pardon, sorr, the Board of
Trade must 'ave been drunk when they granted you
your certificate!' 'What do you say, you——!' seez
he, comin' at me like a mad bull . . . all in
his white clothes; and I up with my tar-pot and cap-
sizes it all over his blamed lovely face and his lovely
jacket. . . . 'Take that!' seez I. 'I am a sailor,
anyhow, you nosing, skipper-licking, useless, sooper-
floos bridge-stanchion, you!' 'That's the kind of man
I am!' shouts I. . . . You should have seed
him skip, boys! Drowned, blind with tar, he was!
So . . ."

"Don't 'ee believe him! He never upset no tar;

I was there!" shouted somebody.   The two Norwegians sat on a chest side by side, alike and placid, resembling a pair of love-birds on a perch, and with round eyes stared innocently; but the Russian Finn, in the racket of explosive shouts and rolling laughter, remained motionless, limp and dull, like a deaf man without a backbone.   Near him Archie smiled at his needle. A broad-chested, slow-eyed newcomer spoke deliberately to Belfast during an exhausted lull in the noise:— "I wonder any of the mates here are alive yet with such a chap as you on board!   I concloode they ain't that bad now, if you had the taming of them, sonny."

"Not bad!   Not bad!" screamed Belfast.   "If it wasn't for us sticking together. . . . . Not bad! They ain't never bad when they ain't got a chawnce, blast their black 'arts. . . ."   He foamed, whirling his arms, then suddenly grinned and, taking a tablet of black tobacco out of his pocket, bit a piece off with a funny show of ferocity.   Another new hand—a man with shifty eyes and a yellow hatchet face, who had been listening open-mouthed in the shadow of the midship locker—observed in a squeaky voice:—"Well, it's a 'omeward trip, anyhow.   Bad or good, I can do it on my 'ed—s'long as I get 'ome.   And I can look after my rights!   I will show 'em!"   All the heads turned towards him.   Only the ordinary seaman and the cat took no notice.   He stood with arms akimbo, a little fellow with white eyelashes.   He looked as if he had known all the degradations and all the furies.   He looked as if he had been cuffed, kicked, rolled in the mud; he looked as if he had been scratched, spat upon, pelted with unmentionable filth . . . and he smiled with a sense of security at the faces around. His ears were bending down under the weight of his battered felt hat.   The torn tails of his black coat

flapped in fringes about the calves of his legs. He
unbuttoned the only two buttons that remained and
every one saw that he had no shirt under it. It was
his deserved misfortune that those rags which nobody
could possibly be supposed to own looked on him as
if they had been stolen. His neck was long and thin;
his eyelids were red; rare hairs hung about his jaws;
his shoulders were peaked and drooped like the broken
wings of a bird; all his left side was caked with mud
which showed that he had lately slept in a wet ditch.
He had saved his inefficient carcass from violent destruction by running away from an American ship where,
in a moment of forgetful folly, he had dared to engage
himself; and he had knocked about for a fortnight
ashore in the native quarter, cadging for drinks, starving,
sleeping on rubbish-heaps, wandering in sunshine: a
startling visitor from a world of nightmares. He stood
repulsive and smiling in the sudden silence. This clean
white forecastle was his refuge; the place where he could
be lazy; where he could wallow, and lie and eat—and
curse the food he ate; where he could display his talents
for shirking work, for cheating, for cadging; where he
could find surely some one to wheedle and some one
to bully—and where he would be paid for doing all
this. They all knew him. Is there a spot on earth
where such a man is unknown, an ominous survival
testifying to the eternal fitness of lies and impudence?
A taciturn long-armed shellback, with hooked fingers,
who had been lying on his back smoking, turned in his
bed to examine him dispassionately, then, over his
head, sent a long jet of clear saliva towards the door.
They all knew him! He was the man that cannot steer,
that cannot splice, that dodges the work on dark nights;
that, aloft, holds on frantically with both arms and
legs, and swears at the wind, the sleet, the darkness;

the man who curses the sea while others work. The man who is the last out and the first in when all hands are called. The man who can't do most things and won't do the rest. The pet of philanthropists and self-seeking landlubbers. The sympathetic and deserving creature that knows all about his rights, but knows nothing of courage, of endurance, and of the unexpressed faith, of the unspoken loyalty that knits together a ship's company. The independent offspring of the ignoble freedom of the slums full of disdain and hate for the austere servitude of the sea.

Some one cried at him: "What's your name?"—"Donkin," he said, looking round with cheerful effrontery.—"What are you?" asked another voice.—"Why, a sailor like you, old man," he replied, in a tone that meant to be hearty but was impudent.—"Blamme if you don't look a blamed sight worse than a broken-down fireman," was the comment in a convinced mutter. Charley lifted his head and piped in a cheeky voice: "He is a man and a sailor"—then wiping his nose with the back of his hand bent down industriously over his bit of rope. A few laughed. Others stared doubtfully. The ragged newcomer was indignant—"That's a fine way to welcome a chap into a fo'c'sle," he snarled. "Are you men or a lot of 'artless canny-bals?"—"Don't take your shirt off for a word, ship-mate," called out Belfast, jumping up in front, fiery, menacing, and friendly at the same time.—"Is that 'ere bloke blind?" asked the indomitable scarecrow, looking right and left with affected surprise. "Can't 'ee see I 'aven't got no shirt?"

He held both his arms out crosswise and shook the rags that hung over his bones with dramatic effect.

"'Cos why?" he continued very loud. "The bloody Yankees been tryin' to jump my guts out 'cos I stood

up for my rights like a good 'un. I am an Englishman,
I am. They set upon me an' I 'ad to run. That's
why. A'n't yer never seed a man 'ard up? Yah!
What kind of blamed ship is this? I'm dead broke.
I 'aven't got nothink. No bag, no bed, no blanket,
no shirt—not a bloomin' rag but what I stand in. But
I 'ad the 'art to stand up agin' them Yankees. 'As
any of you 'art enough to spare a pair of old pants for
a chum?''

He knew how to conquer the naïve instincts of that
crowd. In a moment they gave him their compassion,
jocularly, contemptuously, or surlily; and at first it
took the shape of a blanket thrown at him as he stood
there with the white skin of his limbs showing his human
kinship through the black fantasy of his rags. Then
a pair of old shoes fell at his muddy feet. With a cry:—
"From under," a rolled-up pair of canvas trousers,
heavy with tar stains, struck him on the shoulder.
The gust of their benevolence sent a wave of sentimental
pity through their doubting hearts. They were touched
by their own readiness to alleviate a shipmate's misery. Voices cried:—"We will fit you out, old man."
Murmurs: "Never seed seech a hard case. . . .
Poor beggar. . . . I've got an old singlet.
. . . Will that be of any use to you? . . .
Take it, matey. . . . " Those friendly murmurs
filled the forecastle. He pawed around with his naked
foot, gathering the things in a heap and looked about
for more. Unemotional Archie perfunctorily contributed to the pile an old cloth cap with the peak torn
off. Old Singleton, lost in the serene regions of fiction,
read on unheeding. Charley, pitiless with the wisdom
of youth, squeaked:—"If you want brass buttons for
your new unyforms I've got two for you." The filthy
object of universal charity shook his fist at the young-

ster.—"I'll make you keep this 'ere fo'c'sle clean, young feller," he snarled viciously. "Never you fear. I will learn you to be civil to an able seaman, you ignerant ass." He glared harmfully, but saw Singleton shut his book, and his little beady eyes began to roam from berth to berth.—"Take that bunk by the door there—it's pretty fair," suggested Belfast. So advised, he gathered the gifts at his feet, pressed them in a bundle against his breast, then looked cautiously at the Russian Finn, who stood on one side with an unconscious gaze, contemplating, perhaps, one of those weird visions that haunt the men of his race.—"Get out of my road, Dutchy," said the victim of Yankee brutality. The Finn did not move—did not hear. "Get out, blast ye," shouted the other, shoving him aside with his elbow. "Get out, you blanked deaf and dumb fool. Get out." The man staggered, recovered himself, and gazed at the speaker in silence.—"Those damned furriners should be kept under," opined the amiable Donkin to the forecastle. "If you don't teach 'em their place they put on you like anythink." He flung all his worldly possessions into the empty bed-place, gauged with another shrewd look the risks of the proceeding, then leaped up to the Finn, who stood pensive and dull.—"I'll teach you to swell around," he yelled. "I'll plug your eyes for you, you blooming square-head." Most of the men were now in their bunks and the two had the forecastle clear to themselves. The development of the destitute Donkin aroused interest. He danced all in tatters before the amazed Finn, squaring from a distance at the heavy, unmoved face. One or two men cried encouragingly: "Go it, Whitechapel!" settling themselves luxuriously in their beds to survey the fight. Others shouted: "Shut yer row! . . . Go an' put yer 'ed in a

bag! . . . " The hubbub was recommencing.
Suddenly many heavy blows struck with a handspike
on the deck above boomed like discharges of small
cannon through the forecastle. Then the boatswain's
voice rose outside the door with an authoritative note
in its drawl:—"D'ye hear, below there? Lay aft!
Lay aft to muster all hands!"

There was a moment of surprised stillness. Then
the forecastle floor disappeared under men whose bare
feet flopped on the planks as they sprang clear out of
their berths. Caps were rooted for amongst tumbled
blankets. Some, yawning, buttoned waistbands. Half-
smoked pipes were knocked hurriedly against wood-
work and stuffed under pillows. Voices growled:—
"What's up? . . . Is there no rest for us?"
Donkin yelped:—"If that's the way of this ship, we'll
'ave to change all that. . . . You leave me
alone. . . . I will soon. . . . " None of
the crowd noticed him. They were lurching in twos
and threes through the doors, after the manner of
merchant Jacks who cannot go out of a door fairly, like
mere landsmen. The votary of change followed them.
Singleton, struggling into his jacket, came last, tall and
fatherly, bearing high his head of a weather-beaten
sage on the body of an old athlete. Only Charley remained alone in the white glare of the empty place,
sitting between the two rows of iron links that stretched
into the narrow gloom forward. He pulled hard at the
strands in a hurried endeavour to finish his knot.
Suddenly he started up, flung the rope at the cat, and
skipped after the black tom which went off leaping
sedately over chain compressors, with its tail carried
stiff and upright, like a small flag pole.

Outside the glare of the steaming forecastle the serene
purity of the night enveloped the seamen with its sooth-

ing breath, with its tepid breath flowing under the
stars that hung countless above the mastheads in a
thin cloud of luminous dust. On the town side the
blackness of the water was streaked with trails of light
which undulated gently on slight ripples, similar to
filaments that float rooted to the shore. Rows of
other lights stood away in straight lines as if drawn
up on parade between towering buildings; but on the
other side of the harbour sombre hills arched high their
black spines, on which, here and there, the point of a
star resembled a spark fallen from the sky. Far off,
Byculla way, the electric lamps at the dock gates shone
on the end of lofty standards with a glow blinding and
frigid like captive ghosts of some evil moons. Scattered all over the dark polish of the roadstead, the ships
at anchor floated in perfect stillness under the feeble
gleam of their riding-lights, looming up, opaque and
bulky, like strange and monumental structures abandoned by men to an everlasting repose.

Before the cabin door Mr. Baker was mustering the
crew. As they stumbled and lurched along past the
mainmast, they could see aft his round, broad face
with a white paper before it, and beside his shoulder
the sleepy head, with dropped eyelids, of the boy, who
held, suspended at the end of his raised arm, the
luminous globe of a lamp. Even before the shuffle of
naked soles had ceased along the decks, the mate began
to call over the names. He called distinctly in a serious
tone befitting this roll-call to unquiet loneliness, to
inglorious and obscure struggle, or to the more trying
endurance of small privations and wearisome duties.
As the chief mate read out a name, one of the men
would answer: "Yes, sir!" or "Here!" and, detaching
himself from the shadowy mob of heads visible above
the blackness of starboard bulwarks, would step bare-

footed into the circle of light, and in two noiseless strides pass into the shadows on the port side of the quarter-deck. They answered in divers tones: in thick mutters, in clear, ringing voices; and some, as if the whole thing had been an outrage on their feelings, used an injured intonation: for discipline is not ceremonious in merchant ships, where the sense of hierarchy is weak, and where all feel themselves equal before the unconcerned immensity of the sea and the exacting appeal of the work.

Mr. Baker read on steadily:—"Hansen—Campbell—Smith—Wamibo. Now, then, Wamibo. Why don't you answer? Always got to call your name twice." The Finn emitted at last an uncouth grunt, and, stepping out, passed through the patch of light, weird and gaudy, with the face of a man marching through a dream. The mate went on faster:—"Craik—Singleton—Donkin. . . . O Lord!" he involuntarily ejaculated as the incredibly dilapidated figure appeared in the light. It stopped; it uncovered pale gums and long, upper teeth in a malevolent grin.—"Is there anythink wrong with me, Mister Mate?" it asked, with a flavour of insolence in the forced simplicity of its tone. On both sides of the deck subdued titters were heard.—"That'll do. Go over," growled Mr. Baker, fixing the new hand with steady blue eyes. And Donkin vanished suddenly out of the light into the dark group of mustered men, to be slapped on the back and to hear flattering whispers:—"He ain't afeard, he'll give sport to 'em, see if he don't. . . . Reg'lar Punch and Judy show. . . . Did ye see the mate start at him? . . . Well! Damme, if I ever! . . . "

The last man had gone over, and there was a moment of silence while the mate peered at his list.—"Sixteen, seventeen," he muttered. "I am one hand short, bo'sen," he said aloud. The big west-countryman at his elbow, swarthy and bearded like a gigantic Spaniard, said in a rumbling bass:—"There's no one left forward, sir. I had a look round. He ain't aboard, but he may turn up before daylight."—"Ay. He may or he may not," commented the mate, "can't make out that last name. It's all a smudge. . . . That will do, men. Go below."

The distinct and motionless group stirred, broke up, began to move forward.

"Wait!" cried a deep, ringing voice.

All stood still. Mr. Baker, who had turned away yawning, spun round open-mouthed. At last, furious, he blurted out:—"What's this? Who said 'Wait'? What . . . "

But he saw a tall figure standing on the rail. It came down and pushed through the crowd, marching with a heavy tread towards the light on the quarter-deck. Then again the sonorous voice said with insistence:—"Wait!" The lamplight lit up the man's body. He was tall. His head was away up in the shadows of lifeboats that stood on skids above the deck. The whites of his eyes and his teeth gleamed distinctly, but the face was indistinguishable. His hands were big and seemed gloved.

Mr. Baker advanced intrepidly. "Who are you? How dare you . . . " he began.

The boy, amazed like the rest, raised the light to the man's face. It was black. A surprised hum—a faint hum that sounded like the suppressed mutter of the word "Nigger"—ran along the deck and escaped out into the night. The nigger seemed not to hear. He balanced himself where he stood in a swagger that marked time. After a moment he said calmly:— "My name is Wait—James Wait."

"Oh!" said Mr. Baker. Then, after a few seconds

of smouldering silence, his temper blazed out. "Ah! Your name is Wait. What of that? What do you want? What do you mean, coming shouting here?"

The nigger was calm, cool, towering, superb. The men had approached and stood behind him in a body. He overtopped the tallest by half a head. He said: "I belong to the ship." He enunciated distinctly, with soft precision. The deep, rolling tones of his voice filled the deck without effort. He was naturally scornful, unaffectedly condescending, as if from his height of six foot three he had surveyed all the vastness of human folly and had made up his mind not to be too hard on it. He went on:—"The captain shipped me this morning. I couldn't get aboard sooner. I saw you all aft as I came up the ladder, and could see directly you were mustering the crew. Naturally I called out my name. I thought you had it on your list, and would understand. You misapprehended." He stopped short. The folly around him was confounded. He was right as ever, and as ever ready to forgive. The disdainful tones had ceased, and, breathing heavily, he stood still, surrounded by all these white men. He held his head up in the glare of the lamp— a head vigorously modelled into deep shadows and shining lights—a head powerful and misshapen with a tormented and flattened face—a face pathetic and brutal: the tragic, the mysterious, the repulsive mask of a nigger's soul.

Mr. Baker, recovering his composure, looked at the paper close. "Oh, yes; that's so. All right, Wait. Take your gear forward," he said.

Suddenly the nigger's eyes rolled wildly, became all whites. He put his hand to his side and coughed twice, a cough metallic, hollow, and tremendously loud; it resounded like two explosions in a vault; the dome of

the sky rang to it, and the iron plates of the ship's bulwarks seemed to vibrate in unison, then he marched
off forward with the others. The officers lingering
by the cabin door could hear him say: "Won't some
of you chaps lend a hand with my dunnage? I've got
a chest and a bag." The words, spoken sonorously,
with an even intonation, were heard all over the ship,
and the question was put in a manner that made refusal impossible. The short, quick shuffle of men carrying something heavy went away forward, but the tall
figure of the nigger lingered by the main hatch in a
knot of smaller shapes. Again he was heard asking:
"Is your cook a coloured gentleman?" Then a disappointed and disapproving "Ah! h'm!" was his comment upon the information that the cook happened
to be a mere white man. Yet, as they went all together
towards the forecastle, he condescended to put his head
through the galley door and boom out inside a magnificent "Good evening, doctor!" that made all the saucepans ring. In the dim light the cook dozed on the
coal locker in front of the captain's supper. He
jumped up as if he had been cut with a whip, and dashed
wildly on deck to see the backs of several men going
away laughing. Afterwards, when talking about that
voyage, he used to say:—"The poor fellow had scared
me. I thought I had seen the devil." The cook
had been seven years in the ship with the same captain.
He was a serious-minded man with a wife and three
children, whose society he enjoyed on an average one
month out of twelve. When on shore he took his family
to church twice every Sunday. At sea he went to
sleep every evening with his lamp turned up full, a
pipe in his mouth, and an open Bible in his hand.
Some one had always to go during the night to put out
the light, take the book from his hand, and the pipe

from between his teeth. "For"—Belfast used to say, irritated and complaining—"some night, you stupid cookie, you'll swallow your ould clay, and we will have no cook."—"Ah! sonny, I am ready for my Maker's call . . . wish you all were," the other would answer with a benign serenity that was altogether imbecile and touching. Belfast outside the galley door danced with vexation. "You holy fool! I don't want you to die," he howled, looking up with furious, quivering face and tender eyes. "What's the hurry? You blessed wooden-headed ould heretic, the divvle will have you soon enough. Think of Us . . . of Us . . . of Us!" And he would go away, stamping, spitting aside, disgusted and worried; while the other, stepping out, saucepan in hand, hot, begrimed and placid, watched with a superior, cock-sure smile the back of his "queer little man" reeling in a rage. They were great friends.

Mr. Baker, lounging over the after-hatch, sniffed the humid night in the company of the second mate.— "Those West India niggers run fine and large—some of them . . . Ough! . . . Don't they? A fine, big man that, Mr. Creighton. Feel him on a rope. Hey? Ough! I will take him into my watch, I think." The second mate, a fair, gentlemanly young fellow, with a resolute face and a splendid physique, observed quietly that it was just about what he expected. There could be felt in his tone some slight bitterness which Mr. Baker very kindly set himself to argue away. "Come, come, young man," he said, grunting between the words. "Come! Don't be too greedy. You had that big Finn in your watch all the voyage. I will do what's fair. You may have those two young Scandinavians and I . . . Ough! . . . I get the nigger, and will take that . . .

Ough! that cheeky costermonger chap in a black
frock-coat. I'll make him . . . Ough! . . .
make him toe the mark, or my . . . Ough!
. . . name isn't Baker. Ough! Ough! Ough!"

He grunted thrice—ferociously. He had that trick
of grunting so between his words and at the end of
sentences. It was a fine, effective grunt that went well
with his menacing utterance, with his heavy, bull-
necked frame, his jerky, rolling gait; with his big,
seamed face, his steady eyes, and sardonic mouth.
But its effect had been long ago discounted by the men.
They liked him; Belfast—who was a favourite, and
knew it—mimicked him, not quite behind his back.
Charley—but with greater caution—imitated his rolling
gait. Some of his sayings became established, daily
quotations in the forecastle. Popularity can go no
farther! Besides, all hands were ready to admit that
on a fitting occasion the mate could "jump down a
fellow's throat in a reg'lar Western Ocean style."

Now he was giving his last orders. "Ough! . . .
You, Knowles! Call all hands at four. I want . . .
Ough! . . . to heave short before the tug
comes. Look out for the captain. I am going to lie
down in my clothes. . . . Ough! . . . Call
me when you see the boat coming. Ough! Ough!
. . . The old man is sure to have something to
say when he gets aboard," he remarked to Creighton.
"Well, good-night. . . . Ough! A long day before us to-morrow. . . . Ough! . . . Better
turn in now. Ough! Ough!"

Upon the dark deck a band of light flashed, then a
door slammed, and Mr. Baker was gone into his neat
cabin. Young Creighton stood leaning over the rail,
and looked dreamily into the night of the East. And
he saw in it a long country lane, a lane of waving leaves

and dancing sunshine. He saw stirring boughs of old trees outspread, and framing in their arch the tender, the caressing blueness of an English sky. And through the arch a girl in a light dress, smiling under a sunshade, seemed to be stepping out of the tender sky.

At the other end of the ship the forecastle, with only one lamp burning now, was going to sleep in a dim emptiness traversed by loud breathings, by sudden short sighs. The double row of berths yawned black, like graves tenanted by uneasy corpses. Here and there a curtain of gaudy chintz, half drawn, marked the resting-place of a sybarite. A leg hung over the edge very white and lifeless. An arm stuck straight out with a dark palm turned up, and thick fingers half closed. Two light snores, that did not synchronise, quarrelled in funny dialogue. Singleton stripped again—the old man suffered much from prickly heat— stood cooling his back in the doorway, with his arms crossed on his bare and adorned chest. His head touched the beam of the deck above. The nigger, half undressed, was busy casting adrift the lashing of his box, and spreading his bedding in an upper berth. He moved about in his socks, tall and noiseless, with a pair of braces beating about his calves. Amongst the shadows of stanchions and bowsprit, Donkin munched a piece of hard ship's bread, sitting on the deck with upturned feet and restless eyes; he held the biscuit up before his mouth in the whole fist and snapped his jaws at it with a raging face. Crumbs fell between his outspread legs. Then he got up.

"Where's our water-cask?" he asked in a contained voice.

Singleton, without a word, pointed with a big hand that held a short smouldering pipe. Donkin bent over the cask, drank out of the tin, splashing the water, turned round and noticed the nigger looking at him over the shoulder with calm loftiness. He moved up sideways.

"There's a blooming supper for a man," he whispered bitterly. "My dorg at 'ome wouldn't 'ave it. It's fit enouf for you an' me. 'Ere's a big ship's fo'c'sle! . . . Not a blooming scrap of meat in the kids. I've looked in all the lockers. . . . "

The nigger stared like a man addressed unexpectedly in a foreign language. Donkin changed his tone:— "Giv' us a bit of 'baccy, mate," he breathed out confidentially, "I 'aven't 'ad smoke or chew for the last month. I am rampin' mad for it. Come on, old man!"

"Don't be familiar," said the nigger. Donkin started and sat down on a chest near by, out of sheer surprise. "We haven't kept pigs together," continued James Wait in a deep undertone. "Here's your tobacco." Then, after a pause, he inquired:—"What ship?"—"*Golden State*," muttered Donkin indistinctly, biting the tobacco. The nigger whistled low.—"Ran?" he said curtly. Donkin nodded: one of his cheeks bulged out. "In course I ran," he mumbled. "They booted the life hout of one Dago chap on the passage 'ere, then started on me. I cleared hout 'ere.—"Left your dunnage behind?"—"Yes, dunnage and money," answered Donkin, raising his voice a little; "I got nothink. No clothes, no bed. A bandy-legged little Hirish chap 'ere 'as give me a blanket. . . . Think I'll go an' sleep in the fore topmast staysail to-night."

He went on deck trailing behind his back a corner of the blanket. Singleton, without a glance, moved slightly aside to let him pass. The nigger put away his shore togs and sat in clean working clothes on his box, one arm stretched over his knees. After staring at Singleton for some time he asked without emphasis:—"What kind of ship is this? Pretty fair? Eh?"

Singleton didn't stir. A long while after he said, with unmoved face:—"Ship! . . . Ships are all right. It is the men in them!"

He went on smoking in the profound silence. The wisdom of half a century spent in listening to the thunder of the waves had spoken unconsciously through his old lips. The cat purred on the windlass. Then James Wait had a fit of roaring, rattling cough, that shook him, tossed him like a hurricane, and flung him panting with staring eyes headlong on his sea-chest. Several men woke up. One said sleepily out of his bunk: "'Struth! what a blamed row!"—"I have a cold on my chest," gasped Wait.—"Cold! you call it," grumbled the man; "should think 'twas something more. . . . "—"Oh! you think so," said the nigger upright and loftily scornful again. He climbed into his berth and began coughing persistently while he put his head out to glare all round the forecastle. There was no further protest. He fell back on the pillow, and could be heard there wheezing regularly like a man oppressed in his sleep.

Singleton stood at the door with his face to the light and his back to the darkness. And alone in the dim emptiness of the sleeping forecastle he appeared bigger, colossal, very old; old as Father Time himself, who should have come there into this place as quiet as a sepulchre to contemplate with patient eyes the short victory of sleep, the consoler. Yet he was only a child of time, a lonely relic of a devoured and forgotten generation. He stood, still strong, as ever unthinking; a ready man with a vast empty past and with no future, with his childlike impulses and his man's passions already dead within his tattooed breast. The men who could understand his silence were gone—those men who knew how to exist beyond the pale of life and within sight of eternity. They had been strong, as those are strong who know neither doubts nor hopes. They had been impatient and enduring, turbulent and devoted, unruly and faithful. Well-meaning people had tried to represent those men as whining over every mouthful of their food; as going about their work in fear of their lives. But in truth they had been men who knew toil, privation, violence, debauchery—but knew not fear, and had no desire of spite in their hearts. Men hard to manage, but easy to inspire; voiceless men—but men enough to scorn in their hearts the sentimental voices that bewailed the hardness of their fate. It was a fate unique and their own; the capacity to bear it appeared to them the privilege of the chosen! Their generation lived inarticulate and indispensable, without knowing the sweetness of affections or the refuge of a home—and died free from the dark menace of a narrow grave. They were the everlasting children of the mysterious sea. Their successors are the grown-up children of a discontented earth. They are less naughty, but less innocent; less profane, but perhaps also less believing; and if they had learned how to speak they have also learned how to whine. But the others were strong and mute; they were effaced, bowed and enduring, like stone caryatides that hold up in the night the lighted halls of a resplendent and glorious edifice. They are gone now —and it does not matter. The sea and the earth are unfaithful to their children: a truth, a faith, a generation of men goes—and is forgotten, and it does not matter! Except, perhaps, to the few of those who believed the truth, confessed the faith—or loved the men.

A breeze was coming. The ship that had been lying
tide-rode swung to a heavier puff; and suddenly the
slack of the chain cable between the windlass and the
hawse-pipe clinked, slipped forward an inch, and rose
gently off the deck with a startling suggestion as of
unsuspected life that had been lurking stealthily in
the iron. In the hawse-pipe the grinding links sent
through the ship a sound like a low groan of a man
sighing under a burden. The strain came on the windlass, the chain tautened like a string, vibrated—and the
handle of the screw-brake moved in slight jerks.
Singleton stepped forward.

Till then he had been standing meditative and unthinking, reposeful and hopeless, with a face grim and
blank—a sixty-year-old child of the mysterious sea.
The thoughts of all his lifetime could have been expressed in six words, but the stir of those things that
were as much part of his existence as his beating heart
called up a gleam of alert understanding upon the stern-
ness of his aged face. The flame of the lamp swayed,
and the old man, with knitted and bushy eyebrows,
stood over the brake, watchful and motionless in
the wild saraband of dancing shadows. Then the
ship, obedient to the call of her anchor, forged ahead
slightly and eased the strain. The cable relieved,
hung down, and after swaying imperceptibly to and
fro dropped with a loud tap on the hard wood planks.
Singleton seized the high lever, and, by a violent throw
forward of his body, wrung out another half-turn from
the brake. He recovered himself, breathed largely, and
remained for awhile glaring down at the powerful and
compact engine that squatted on the deck at his feet
like some quiet monster—a creature amazing and tame.

"You . . . hold!" he growled at it masterfully, in the incult tangle of his white beard.

CHAPTER TWO

Next morning, at daylight, the *Narcissus* went to sea.

A slight haze blurred the horizon. Outside the harbour the measureless expanse of smooth water lay sparkling like a floor of jewels, and as empty as the sky. The short black tug gave a pluck to windward, in the usual way, then let go the rope, and hovered for a moment on the quarter with her engines stopped; while the slim, long hull of the ship moved ahead slowly under lower topsails. The loose upper canvas blew out in the breeze with soft round contours, resembling small white clouds snared in the maze of ropes. Then the sheets were hauled home, the yards hoisted, and the ship became a high and lonely pyramid, gliding, all shining and white, through the sunlit mist. The tug turned short round and went away towards the land. Twenty-six pairs of eyes watched her low broad stern crawling languidly over the smooth swell between the two paddle-wheels that turned fast, beating the water with fierce hurry. She resembled an enormous and aquatic black beetle, surprised by the light, overwhelmed by the sunshine, trying to escape with ineffectual effort into the distant gloom of the land. She left a lingering smudge of smoke on the sky, and two vanishing trails of foam on the water. On the place where she had stopped a round black patch of soot remained, undulating on the swell—an unclean mark of the creature's rest.

The *Narcissus* left alone, heading south, seemed to

stand resplendent and still upon the restless sea, under
the moving sun.   Flakes of foam swept past her sides;
the water struck her with flashing blows; the land
glided away slowly fading; a few birds screamed on
motionless wings over the swaying mastheads.   But
soon the land disappeared, the birds went away; and
to the west the pointed sail of an Arab dhow running
for Bombay, rose triangular and upright above the
sharp edge of the horizon, lingered and vanished like an
illusion.   Then the ship's wake, long and straight,
stretched itself out through a day of immense solitude.
The setting sun, burning on the level of the water,
flamed crimson below the blackness of heavy rain
clouds.   The sunset squall, coming up from behind,
dissolved itself into the short deluge of a hissing
shower.   It left the ship glistening from trucks to water-
line, and with darkened sails.   She ran easily before
a fair monsoon, with her decks cleared for the night;
and, moving along with her, was heard the sustained
and monotonous swishing of the waves, mingled with
the low whispers of men mustered aft for the setting
of watches; the short plaint of some block aloft; or,
now and then, a loud sigh of wind.

Mr. Baker, coming out of his cabin, called out the
first name sharply before closing the door behind him.
He was going to take charge of the deck.   On the
homeward trip, according to an old custom of the sea,
the chief officer takes the first night-watch—from eight
till midnight.   So Mr. Baker, after he had heard the
last "Yes, sir!" said moodily, "Relieve the wheel and
look-out"; and climbed with heavy feet the poop ladder
to windward.   Soon after Mr. Creighton came down,
whistling softly, and went into the cabin.   On the
doorstep the steward lounged, in slippers, meditative,
and with his shirt-sleeves rolled up to the armpits.

On the main deck the cook, locking up the galley doors, had an altercation with young Charley about a pair of socks. He could be heard saying impressively, in the darkness amidships: "You don't deserve a kindness. I've been drying them for you, and now you complain about the holes—and you swear, too! Right in front of me! If I hadn't been a Christian—which you ain't, you young ruffian—I would give you a clout on the head. . . . Go away!" Men in couples or threes stood pensive or moved silently along the bulwarks in the waist. The first busy day of a homeward passage was sinking into the dull peace of resumed routine. Aft, on the high poop, Mr. Baker walked shuffling and grunted to himself in the pauses of his thoughts. Forward, the look-out man, erect between the flukes of the two anchors, hummed an endless tune, keeping his eyes fixed dutifully ahead in a vacant stare. A multitude of stars coming out into the clear night peopled the emptiness of the sky. They glittered, as if alive above the sea; they surrounded the running ship on all sides; more intense than the eyes of a staring crowd, and as inscrutable as the souls of men.

The passage had begun, and the ship, a fragment detached from the earth, went on lonely and swift like a small planet. Round her the abysses of sky and sea met in an unattainable frontier. A great circular solitude moved with her, ever changing and ever the same, always monotonous and always imposing. Now and then another wandering white speck, burdened with life, appeared far off—disappeared; intent on its own destiny. The sun looked upon her all day, and every morning rose with a burning, round stare of undying curiosity. She had her own future; she was alive with the lives of those beings who trod her decks; like that earth which had given her up to the sea, she had an intolerable load of regrets and hopes. On her lived timid truth and audacious lies; and, like the earth, she was unconscious, fair to see—and condemned by men to an ignoble fate. The august loneliness of her path lent dignity to the sordid inspiration of her pilgrimage. She drove foaming to the southward, as if guided by the courage of a high endeavour. The smiling greatness of the sea dwarfed the extent of time. The days raced after one another, brilliant and quick like the flashes of a lighthouse, and the nights, eventful and short, resembled fleeting dreams.

The men had shaken into their places, and the half-hourly voice of the bells ruled their life of unceasing care. Night and day the head and shoulders of a seaman could be seen aft by the wheel, outlined high against sunshine or starlight, very steady above the stir of revolving spokes. The faces changed, passing in rotation. Youthful faces, bearded faces, dark faces: faces serene, or faces moody, but all akin with the brotherhood of the sea; all with the same attentive expression of eyes, carefully watching the compass or the sails. Captain Allistoun, serious, and with an old red muffler round his throat, all day long pervaded the poop. At night, many times he rose out of the darkness of the companion, such as a phantom above a grave, and stood watchful and mute under the stars, his night-shirt fluttering like a flag—then, without a sound, sank down again. He was born on the shores of the Pentland Firth. In his youth he attained the rank of harpooner in Peterhead whalers. When he spoke of that time his restless grey eyes became still and cold, like the loom of ice. Afterwards he went into the East Indian trade for the sake of change. He had commanded the *Narcissus* since she was built. He loved his ship, and drove her unmercifully; for his secret ambition was to make her accomplish some day a brilliantly quick passage which would be mentioned in nautical papers. He pronounced his owner's name with a sardonic smile, spoke but seldom to his officers, and reproved errors in a gentle voice, with words that cut to the quick. His hair was iron-grey, his face hard and of the colour of pump-leather. He shaved every morning of his life—at six—but once (being caught in a fierce hurricane eighty miles southwest of Mauritius) he had missed three consecutive days. He feared naught but an unforgiving God, and wished to end his days in a little house, with a plot of ground attached— far in the country—out of sight of the sea.

He, the ruler of that minute world, seldom descended from the Olympian heights of his poop. Below him—at his feet, so to speak—common mortals led their busy and insignificant lives. Along the main deck, Mr. Baker grunted in a manner bloodthirsty and innocuous; and kept all our noses to the grindstone, being—as he once remarked—paid for doing that very thing. The men working about the deck were healthy and contented—as most seamen are, when once well out to sea. The true peace of God begins at any spot a thousand miles from the nearest land; and when He sends there the messengers of His might it is not in terrible wrath against crime, presumption, and folly, but paternally, to chasten simple hearts—ignorant hearts that know nothing of life, and beat undisturbed by envy or greed.

In the evening the cleared decks had a reposeful aspect, resembling the autumn of the earth. The sun was sinking to rest, wrapped in a mantle of warm clouds. Forward, on the end of the spare spars, the boatswain and the carpenter sat together with crossed

arms; two men friendly, powerful, and deep-chested.
Beside them the short, dumpy sailmaker—who had
been in the Navy—related, between the whiffs of his
pipe, impossible stories about Admirals. Couples
tramped backwards and forwards, keeping step and
balance without effort, in a confined space. Pigs
grunted in the big pigstye. Belfast, leaning thoughtfully on his elbow, above the bars, communed with
them through the silence of his meditation. Fellows
with shirts open wide on sunburnt breasts sat upon the
mooring bits, and all up the steps of the forecastle
ladders. By the foremast a few discussed in a circle
the characteristics of a gentleman. One said:—"It's
money as does it." Another maintained:—"No, it's
the way they speak." Lame Knowles stumped up with
an unwashed face (he had the distinction of being the
dirty man of the forecastle), and showing a few yellow
fangs in a shrewd smile, explained craftily that he "had
seen some of their pants." The backsides of them—
he had observed—were thinner than paper from constant sitting down in offices, yet otherwise they looked
first-rate and would last for years. It was all appearance. "It was," he said, "bloomin' easy to be a gentleman when you had a clean job for life." They disputed
endlessly, obstinate and childish; they repeated in
shouts and with inflamed faces their amazing arguments; while the soft breeze, eddying down the enormous cavity of the foresail, distended above their bare
heads, stirred the tumbled hair with a touch passing
and light like an indulgent caress.

They were forgetting their toil, they were forgetting
themselves. The cook approached to hear, and stood
by, beaming with the inward consciousness of his faith,
like a conceited saint unable to forget his glorious reward; Donkin, solitary and brooding over his wrongs

on the forecastle-head, moved closer to catch the drift of the discussion below him; he turned his sallow face to the sea, and his thin nostrils moved, sniffing the breeze, as he lounged negligently by the rail. In the glow of sunset faces shone with interest, teeth flashed, eyes sparkled. The walking couples stood still suddenly, with broad grins; a man, bending over a washtub, sat up, entranced, with the soapsuds flecking his wet arms. Even the three petty officers listened leaning back, comfortably propped, and with superior smiles. Belfast left off scratching the ear of his favourite pig, and, open mouthed, tried with eager eyes to have his say. He lifted his arms, grimacing and baffled. From a distance Charley screamed at the ring:— "I know about gentlemen morn'n any of you. I've been intermit with 'em. . . . I've blacked their boots." The cook, craning his neck to hear better, was scandalised. "Keep your mouth shut when your elders speak, you impudent young heathen—you." "All right, old Hallelujah, I'm done," answered Charley, soothingly. At some opinion of dirty Knowles, delivered with an air of supernatural cunning, a ripple of laughter ran along, rose like a wave, burst with a startling roar. They stamped with both feet; they turned their shouting faces to the sky; many, spluttering, slapped their thighs; while one or two, bent double, gasped, hugging themselves with both arms like men in pain. The carpenter and the boatswain, without changing their attitude, shook with laughter where they sat; the sailmaker, charged with an anecdote about a Commodore, looked sulky; the cook was wiping his eyes with a greasy rag; and lame Knowles, astonished at his own success, stood in their midst showing a slow smile.

Suddenly the face of Donkin leaning high-shouldered

over the after-rail became grave. Something like a
weak rattle was heard through the forecastle door. It
became a murmur; it ended in a sighing groan. The
washerman plunged both his arms into the tub abruptly;
the cook became more crestfallen than an exposed back-
slider; the boatswain moved his shoulders uneasily;
the carpenter got up with a spring and walked away—
while the sailmaker seemed mentally to give his story
up, and began to puff at his pipe with sombre determination. In the blackness of the doorway a pair of eyes
glimmered white, and big, and staring. Then James
Wait's head protruding, became visible, as if suspended between the two hands that grasped a doorpost
on each side of the face. The tassel of his blue woollen
nightcap, cocked forward, danced gaily over his left
eyelid. He stepped out in a tottering stride. He
looked powerful as ever, but showed a strange and affected unsteadiness in his gait; his face was perhaps
a trifle thinner, and his eyes appeared rather startlingly
prominent. He seemed to hasten the retreat of depart-
ing light by his very presence; the setting sun dipped
sharply, as though fleeing before our nigger; a black
mist emanated from him; a subtle and dismal influence;
a something cold and gloomy that floated out and settled on all the faces like a mourning veil. The circle
broke up. The joy of laughter died on stiffened lips.
There was not a smile left among all the ship's company. Not a word was spoken. Many turned their
backs, trying to look unconcerned; others, with averted
heads, sent half-reluctant glances out of the corners of
their eyes. They resembled criminals conscious of
misdeeds more than honest men distracted by doubt;
only two or three stared frankly, but stupidly, with
lips slightly open. All expected James Wait to say
something, and, at the same time, had the air of know-

ing beforehand what he would say. He leaned his back against the doorpost, and with heavy eyes swept over them a glance domineering and pained, like a sick tyrant overawing a crowd of abject but untrustworthy slaves.

No one went away. They waited in fascinated dread. He said ironically, with gasps between the words:—

"Thank you . . . chaps. You . . . are nice . . . and . . . quiet . . . you are! Yelling so . . . before . . . the door. . . ."

He made a longer pause, during which he worked his ribs in an exaggerated labour of breathing. It was intolerable. Feet were shuffled. Belfast let out a groan; but Donkin above blinked his red eyelids with invisible eyelashes, and smiled bitterly over the nigger's head.

The nigger went on again with surprising ease. He gasped no more, and his voice rang, hollow and loud, as though he had been talking in an empty cavern. He was contemptuously angry.

"I tried to get a wink of sleep. You know I can't sleep o' nights. And you come jabbering near the door here like a blooming lot of old women. . . . You think yourselves good shipmates. Do you? . . . Much you care for a dying man!"

Belfast spun away from the pigstye. "Jimmy," he cried tremulously, "if you hadn't been sick I would——"

He stopped. The nigger waited awhile, then said, in a gloomy tone:—"You would. . . . What? Go an' fight another such one as yourself. Leave me alone. It won't be for long. I'll soon die. . . . It's coming right enough!"

Men stood around very still and with exasperated

eyes. It was just what they had expected, and hated
to hear, that idea of a stalking death, thrust at them
many times a day like a boast and like a menace by this
obnoxious nigger. He seemed to take a pride in that
death which, so far, had attended only upon the ease of
his life; he was overbearing about it, as if no one else
in the world had ever been intimate with such a companion; he paraded it unceasingly before us with an
affectionate persistence that made its presence indubi-
table, and at the same time incredible. No man could
be suspected of such monstrous friendship! Was he a
reality—or was he a sham—this ever-expected visitor
of Jimmy's? We hesitated between pity and mistrust,
while, on the slightest provocation, he shook before our
eyes the bones of his bothersome and infamous skeleton.
He was for ever trotting him out. He would talk of
that coming death as though it had been already there,
as if it had been walking the deck outside, as if it would
presently come in to sleep in the only empty bunk; as
if it had sat by his side at every meal. It interfered
daily with our occupations, with our leisure, with our
amusements. We had no songs and no music in the
evening, because Jimmy (we all lovingly called him
Jimmy, to conceal our hate of his accomplice) had managed, with that prospective decease of his, to disturb
even Archie's mental balance. Archie was the owner
of the concertina; but after a couple of stinging lectures
from Jimmy he refused to play any more. He said:—
"Yon's an uncanny joker. I dinna ken what's wrang
wi' him, but there's something verra wrang, verra
wrang. It's nae manner of use asking me. I won't
play." Our singers became mute because Jimmy was a
dying man. For the same reason no chap—as Knowles
remarked—could "drive in a nail to hang his few poor
rags upon," without being made aware of the enormity

he committed in disturbing Jimmy's interminable last
moments. At night, instead of the cheerful yell, "One
bell! Turn out! Do you hear there? Hey! hey! hey!
Show leg!" the watches were called man by man, in
whispers, so as not to interfere with Jimmy's, possibly,
last slumber on earth. True, he was always awake, and
managed, as we sneaked out on deck, to plant in our
backs some cutting remark that, for the moment, made
us feel as if we had been brutes, and afterwards made us
suspect ourselves of being fools. We spoke in low tones
within that fo'c'sle as though it had been a church. We
ate our meals in silence and dread, for Jimmy was ca-
pricious with his food, and railed bitterly at the salt
meat, at the biscuits, at the tea, as at articles unfit for
human consumption—"let alone for a dying man!"
He would say:—"Can't you find a better slice of meat
for a sick man who's trying to get home to be cured—
or buried? But there! If I had a chance, you fellows
would do away with it. You would poison me. Look
at what you have given me!" We served him in his
bed with rage and humility, as though we had been the
base courtiers of a hated prince; and he rewarded us
by his unconciliating criticism. He had found the
secret of keeping for ever on the run the fundamental
imbecility of mankind; he had the secret of life, that
confounded dying man, and he made himself master
of every moment of our existence. We grew desperate,
and remained submissive. Emotional little Belfast
was for ever on the verge of assault or on the verge of
tears. One evening he confided to Archie:—"For a
ha'penny I would knock his ugly black head off—the
skulking dodger!" And the straightforward Archie
pretended to be shocked! Such was the infernal spell
which that casual St. Kitt's nigger had cast upon our
guileless manhood! But the same night Belfast stole

from the galley the officers' Sunday fruit pie, to tempt
the fastidious appetite of Jimmy. He endangered not
only his long friendship with the cook but also—as it
appeared—his eternal welfare. The cook was overwhelmed with grief; he did not know the culprit but he
knew that wickedness flourished; he knew that Satan
was abroad amongst those men, whom he looked upon
as in some way under his spiritual care. Whenever
he saw three or four of us standing together he would
leave his stove, to run out and preach. We fled from
him; and only Charley (who knew the thief) affronted
the cook with a candid gaze which irritated the good
man. "It's you, I believe," he groaned, sorrowful
and with a patch of soot on his chin. "It's you. You
are a brand for the burning! No more of YOUR socks
in my galley." Soon, unofficially, the information was
spread about that, should there be another case of
stealing, our marmalade (an extra allowance: half a
pound per man) would be stopped. Mr. Baker ceased
to heap jocular abuse upon his favourites, and grunted
suspiciously at all. The captain's cold eyes, high up
on the poop, glittered mistrustful, as he surveyed us
trooping in a small mob from halyards to braces for the
usual evening pull at all the ropes. Such stealing in a
merchant ship is difficult to check, and may be taken
as a declaration by men of their dislike for their officers.
It is a bad symptom. It may end in God knows what
trouble. The *Narcissus* was still a peaceful ship, but
mutual confidence was shaken. Donkin did not conceal his delight. We were dismayed.

Then illogical Belfast reproached our nigger with
great fury. James Wait, with his elbow on the pillow,
choked, gasped out:—"Did I ask you to bone the
dratted thing? Blow your blamed pie. It has made
me worse—you little Irish lunatic, you!" Belfast,

with scarlet face and trembling lips, made a dash at
him. Every man in the forecastle rose with a shout.
There was a moment of wild tumult. Some one
shrieked piercingly:—"Easy, Belfast! Easy! . . ."
We expected Belfast to strangle Wait without more ado.
Dust flew. We heard through it the nigger's cough,
metallic and explosive like a gong. Next moment we
saw Belfast hanging over him. - He was saying plaintively:—"Don't! Don't, Jimmy! Don't be like that.
An angel couldn't put up with ye—sick as ye are."
He looked round at us from Jimmy's bedside, his comical mouth twitching, and through tearful eyes; then
he tried to put straight the disarranged blankets. The
unceasing whisper of the sea filled the forecastle. Was
James Wait frightened, or touched, or repentant? He
lay on his back with a hand to his side, and as motionless as if his expected visitor had come at last. Belfast
fumbled about his feet, repeating with emotion:—
"Yes. We know. Ye are bad, but. . . . Just
say what ye want done, and. . . . We all know ye
are bad—very bad. . . ." No! Decidedly James
Wait was not touched or repentant. Truth to say, he
seemed rather startled. He sat up with incredible
suddenness and ease. "Ah! You think I am bad, do
you?" he said gloomily, in his clearest baritone voice
(to hear him speak sometimes you would never think
there was anything wrong with that man). "Do you?
. . . Well, act according! Some of you haven't
sense enough to put a blanket shipshape over a sick
man. There! Leave it alone! I can die anyhow!"
Belfast turned away limply with a gesture of discouragement. In the silence of the forecastle, full of interested men, Donkin pronounced distinctly:—"Well,
I'm blowed!" and sniggered. Wait looked at him. He
looked at him in a quite friendly manner. Nobody

could tell what would please our incomprehensible invalid: but for us the scorn of that snigger was hard to bear.

Donkin's position in the forecastle was distinguished but unsafe. He stood on the bad eminence of a general dislike. He was left alone; and in his isolation he could do nothing but think of the gales of the Cape of Good Hope and envy us the possession of warm clothing and waterproofs. Our sea-boots, our oilskin coats, our well-filled sea-chests, were to him so many causes for bitter meditation: he had none of those things, and he felt instinctively that no man, when the need arose, would offer to share them with him. He was impudently cringing to us and systematically insolent to the officers. He anticipated the best results, for himself, from such a line of conduct—and was mistaken. Such natures forget that under extreme provocation men will be just—whether they want to be so or not. Donkin's insolence to long-suffering Mr. Baker became at last intolerable to us, and we rejoiced when the mate, one dark night, tamed him for good. It was done neatly, with great decency and decorum, and with little noise. We had been called—just before midnight— to trim the yards, and Donkin—as usual—made insulting remarks. We stood sleepily in a row with the forebrace in our hands waiting for the next order, and heard in the darkness a scuffly trampling of feet, an exclamation of surprise, sounds of cuffs and slaps, suppressed, hissing whispers:—"Ah! Will you!" . . . "Don't! . . . Don't!" . . . "Then behave." . . . "Oh! Oh! . . ." Afterwards there were soft thuds mixed with the rattle of iron things as if a man's body had been tumbling helplessly amongst the main-pump rods. Before we could realise the situation, Mr. Baker's voice was heard very near and a little impatient:—"Haul away, men! Lay back on that rope!" And we did lay back on the rope with great alacrity. As if nothing had happened, the chief mate went on trimming the yards with his usual and exasperating fastidiousness. We didn't at the time see anything of Donkin, and did not care. Had the chief officer thrown him overboard, no man would have said as much as "Hallo! he's gone!" But, in truth, no great harm was done—even if Donkin did lose one of his front teeth. We perceived this in the morning, and preserved a ceremonious silence: the etiquette of the forecastle commanded us to be blind and dumb in such a case, and we cherished the decencies of our life more than ordinary landsmen respect theirs. Charley, with unpardonable want of *savoir vivre*, yelled out:— "'Ave you been to your dentyst? . . . Hurt ye, didn't it?" He got a box on the ear from one of his best friends. The boy was surprised, and remained plunged in grief for at least three hours. We were sorry for him, but youth requires even more discipline than age. Donkin grinned venomously. From that day he became pitiless; told Jimmy that he was a "black fraud"; hinted to us that we were an imbecile lot, daily taken in by a vulgar nigger. And Jimmy seemed to like the fellow!

Singleton lived untouched by human emotions. Taciturn and unsmiling, he breathed amongst us—in that alone resembling the rest of the crowd. We were trying to be decent chaps, and found it jolly difficult; we oscillated between the desire of virtue and the fear of ridicule; we wished to save ourselves from the pain of remorse, but did not want to be made the contemptible dupes of our sentiment. Jimmy's hateful accomplice seemed to have blown with his impure breath undreamt-of subtleties into our hearts. We were disturbed and cowardly. That we knew. Singleton seemed to know nothing, understand nothing. We had thought him till then as wise as he looked, but now we dared, at times, suspect him of being stupid—from old age. One day, however, at dinner, as we sat on our boxes round a tin dish that stood on the deck within the circle of our feet, Jimmy expressed his general disgust with men and things in words that were particularly disgusting. Singleton lifted his head. We became mute. The old man, addressing Jimmy, asked:— "Are you dying?" Thus interrogated, James Wait appeared horribly startled and confused. We all were startled. Mouths remained open; hearts thumped, eyes blinked; a dropped tin fork rattled in the dish; a man rose as if to go out, and stood still. In less than a minute Jimmy pulled himself together:— "Why? Can't you see I am?" he answered shakily. Singleton lifted a piece of soaked biscuit ("his teeth"— he declared—"had no edge on them now") to his lips.—"Well, get on with your dying," he said with venerable mildness; "don't raise a blamed fuss with us over that job. We can't help you." Jimmy fell back in his bunk, and for a long time lay very still wiping the perspiration off his chin. The dinner-tins were put away quickly. On deck we discussed the incident in whispers. Some showed a chuckling exultation. Many looked grave. Wamibo, after long periods of staring dreaminess, attempted abortive smiles; and one of the young Scandinavians, much tormented by doubt, ventured in the second dog-watch to approach Singleton (the old man did not encourage us much to speak to him) and ask sheepishly:—"You think he will die?" Singleton looked up.—"Why, of course he will die," he said deliberately. This seemed decisive. It was promptly imparted to every one by him who had consulted the oracle. Shy and eager, he would step up and with averted gaze recite his formula:—"Old Singleton says he will die." It was a relief! At last we knew that our compassion would not be misplaced, and we could again smile without misgivings—but we reckoned without Donkin. Donkin "didn't want to 'ave no truck with 'em dirty furriners." When Nilsen came to him with the news: "Singleton says he will die," he answered him by a spiteful "And so will you—you fat-headed Dutchman. Wish you Dutchmen were all dead—'stead comin' takin' our money inter your starvin' country." We were appalled. We perceived that after all Singleton's answer meant nothing. We began to hate him for making fun of us. All our certitudes were going; we were on doubtful terms with our officers; the cook had given us up for lost; we had overheard the boatswain's opinion that "we were a crowd of softies." We suspected Jimmy, one another, and even our very selves. We did not know what to do. At every insignificant turn of our humble life we met Jimmy overbearing and blocking the way, arm-in-arm with his awful and veiled familiar. It was a weird servitude.

It began a week after leaving Bombay and came on us stealthily like any other great misfortune. Every one had remarked that Jimmy from the first was very slack at his work; but we thought it simply the outcome of his philosophy of life. Donkin said:—"You put no more weight on a rope than a bloody sparrer." He disdained him. Belfast, ready for a fight, exclaimed provokingly:—"You don't kill yourself, old man!"—"Would you?" he retorted with extreme scorn—and Belfast retired. One morning, as we were washing decks, Mr. Baker called to him:—"Bring your broom over here, Wait." He strolled languidly.

"Move yourself! Ough!" grunted Mr. Baker; "what's the matter with your hind legs?" He stopped dead short. He gazed slowly with eyes that bulged out with an expression audacious and sad.—"It isn't my legs," he said, "it's my lungs." Everybody listened.—"What's . . . Ough! . . . What's wrong with them?" inquired Mr. Baker. All the watch stood around on the wet deck, grinning, and with brooms or buckets in their hands. He said mournfully:—"Going—or gone. Can't you see I'm a dying man? I know it!" Mr. Baker was disgusted. —"Then why the devil did you ship aboard here?"— "I must live till I die—mustn't I?" he replied. The grins became audible.—"Go off the deck—get out of my sight," said Mr. Baker. He was nonplussed. It was an unique experience. James Wait, obedient, dropped his broom, and walked slowly forward. A burst of laughter followed him. It was too funny. All hands laughed. . . . They laughed! . . . Alas!

He became the tormentor of all our moments; he was worse than a nightmare. You couldn't see that there was anything wrong with him: a nigger does not show. He was not very fat—certainly—but then he was no leaner than other niggers we had known. He coughed often, but the most prejudiced person could perceive that, mostly, he coughed when it suited his purpose. He wouldn't, or couldn't, do his work—and he wouldn't lie-up. One day he would skip aloft with the best of them, and next time we would be obliged to risk our lives to get his limp body down. He was reported, he was examined; he was remonstrated with, threatened, cajoled, lectured. He was called into the cabin to interview the captain. There were wild rumours. It was said he had cheeked the old man; it was said he had frightened him. Charley

maintained that the "skipper, weepin,' 'as giv' 'im
'is blessin' an' a pot of jam." Knowles had it from the
steward that the unspeakable Jimmy had been reeling
against the cabin furniture; that he had groaned; that
he had complained of general brutality and disbelief;
and had ended by coughing all over the old man's
meteorological journals which were then spread on
the table. At any rate, Wait returned forward supported by the steward, who, in a pained and shocked
voice, entreated us:—"Here! Catch hold of him, one
of you. He is to lie-up." Jimmy drank a tin mugful of
coffee, and, after bullying first one and then another,
went to bed. He remained there most of the time,
but when it suited him would come on deck and appear
amongst us. He was scornful and brooding; he looked
ahead upon the sea, and no one could tell what was the
meaning of that black man sitting apart in a meditative attitude and as motionless as a carving.

He refused steadily all medicine; he threw sago and
cornflour overboard till the steward got tired of bringing it to him. He asked for paregoric. They sent him
a big bottle; enough to poison a wilderness of babies.
He kept it between his mattress and the deal lining of
the ship's side; and nobody ever saw him take a dose.
Donkin abused him to his face, jeered at him while he
gasped; and the same day Wait would lend him a warm
jersey. Once Donkin reviled him for half an hour; reproached him with the extra work his malingering gave
to the watch; and ended by calling him "a black-faced
swine." Under the spell of our accursed perversity
we were horror-struck. But Jimmy positively seemed
to revel in that abuse. It made him look cheerful—
and Donkin had a pair of old sea boots thrown at him.
"Here, you East-end trash," boomed Wait, "you
may have that."

At last Mr. Baker had to tell the captain that James
Wait was disturbing the peace of the ship. "Knock
discipline on the head—he will, Ough," grunted Mr.
Baker. As a matter of fact, the starboard watch came
as near as possible to refusing duty, when ordered one
morning by the boatswain to wash out their forecastle.
It appears Jimmy objected to a wet floor—and that
morning we were in a compassionate mood. We
thought the boatswain a brute, and, practically, told
him so. Only Mr. Baker's delicate tact prevented an
all-fired row: he refused to take us seriously. He came
bustling forward, and called us many unpolite names
but in such a hearty and seamanlike manner that we
began to feel ashamed of ourselves. In truth, we
thought him much too good a sailor to annoy him will-
ingly: and after all Jimmy might have been a fraud—
probably was! The forecastle got a clean up that
morning; but in the afternoon a sick-bay was fitted up
in the deck-house. It was a nice little cabin opening
on deck, and with two berths. Jimmy's belongings
were transported there, and then—notwithstanding his
protests—Jimmy himself. He said he couldn't walk.
Four men carried him on a blanket. He complained
that he would have to die there alone, like a dog. We
grieved for him, and were delighted to have him removed from the forecastle. We attended him as
before. The galley was next door, and the cook looked
in many times a day. Wait became a little more
cheerful. Knowles affirmed having heard him laugh
to himself in peals one day. Others had seen him
walking about on deck at night. His little place, with
the door ajar on a long hook, was always full of tobacco
smoke. We spoke through the crack cheerfully,
sometimes abusively, as we passed by, intent on our
work. He fascinated us. He would never let doubt

die. He overshadowed the ship. Invulnerable in his promise of speedy corruption he trampled on our self-respect, he demonstrated to us daily our want of moral courage; he tainted our lives. Had we been a miserable gang of wretched immortals, unhallowed alike by hope and fear, he could not have lorded it over us with a more pitiless assertion of his sublime privilege.

CHAPTER THREE

Meantime the *Narcissus*, with square yards, ran out of the fair monsoon. She drifted slowly, swinging round and round the compass, through a few days of baffling light airs. Under the patter of short warm showers, grumbling men whirled the heavy yards from side to side; they caught hold of the soaked ropes with groans and sighs, while their officers, sulky and dripping with rain water, unceasingly ordered them about in wearied voices. During the short respites they looked with disgust into the smarting palms of their stiff hands, and asked one another bitterly:—"Who would be a sailor if he could be a farmer?" All the tempers were spoilt, and no man cared what he said. One black night, when the watch, panting in the heat and half-drowned with the rain, had been through four mortal hours hunted from brace to brace, Belfast declared that he would "chuck the sea for ever and go in a steamer." This was excessive, no doubt. Captain Allistoun, with great self-control, would mutter sadly to Mr. Baker:—"It is not so bad—not so bad," when he had managed to shove, and dodge, and manœuvre his smart ship through sixty miles in twenty-four hours. From the doorstep of the little cabin, Jimmy, chin in hand, watched our distasteful labours with insolent and melancholy eyes. We spoke to him gently—and out of his sight exchanged sour smiles.

Then, again, with a fair wind and under a clear sky, the ship went on piling up the South Latitude. She passed outside Madagascar and Mauritius without a

glimpse of the land.   Extra lashings were put on the
spare spars.   Hatches were looked to.   The steward
in his leisure moments and with a worried air tried to
fit washboards to the cabin doors.   Stout canvas was
bent with care.   Anxious eyes looked to the westward, towards the cape of storms.   The ship began to
dip into a southwest swell, and the softly luminous sky
of low latitudes took on a harder sheen from day to
day above our heads: it arched high above the ship
vibrating and pale, like an immense dome of steel, resonant with the deep voice of freshening gales.   The sunshine gleamed cold on the white curls of black waves.
Before the strong breath of westerly squalls the ship,
with reduced sail, lay slowly over, obstinate and yield-
ing.   She drove to and fro in the unceasing endeavour
to fight her way through the invisible violence of the
winds: she pitched headlong into dark smooth hollows;
she struggled upwards over the snowy ridges of great
running seas; she rolled, restless, from side to side, like a
thing in pain.   Enduring and valiant, she answered to
the call of men; and her slim spars waving for ever in
abrupt semicircles, seemed to beckon in vain for help
towards the stormy sky.

It was a bad winter off the Cape that year.   The
relieved helmsmen came off flapping their arms, or
ran stamping hard and blowing into swollen, red fingers.
The watch on deck dodged the sting of cold sprays or,
crouching in sheltered corners, watched dismally the
high and merciless seas boarding the ship time after
time in unappeasable fury.   Water tumbled in cata-
racts over the forecastle doors.   You had to dash
through a waterfall to get into your damp bed.   The
men turned in wet and turned out stiff to face the
redeeming and ruthless exactions of their glorious and
obscure fate.   Far aft, and peering watchfully to wind-

ward, the officers could be seen through the mist of squalls. They stood by the weather-rail, holding on grimly, straight and glistening in their long coats; and in the disordered plunges of the hard-driven ship, they appeared high up, attentive, tossing violently above the grey line of a clouded horizon in motionless attitudes.

They watched the weather and the ship as men on shore watch the momentous chances of fortune. Captain Allistoun never left the deck, as though he had been part of the ship's fittings. Now and then the steward, shivering, but always in shirt sleeves, would struggle towards him with some hot coffee, half of which the gale blew out of the cup before it reached the master's lips. He drank what was left gravely in one long gulp, while heavy sprays pattered loudly on his oilskin coat, the seas swishing broke about his high boots; and he never took his eyes off the ship. He kept his gaze riveted upon her as a loving man watches the unselfish toil of a delicate woman upon the slender thread of whose existence is hung the whole meaning and joy of the world. We all watched her. She was beautiful and had a weakness. We loved her no less for that. We admired her qualities aloud, we boasted of them to one another, as though they had been our own, and the consciousness of her only fault we kept buried in the silence of our profound affection. She was born in the thundering peal of hammers beating upon iron, in black eddies of smoke, under a grey sky, on the banks of the Clyde. `The clamorous and sombre stream gives birth to things of beauty that float away into the sunshine of the world to be loved by men. The *Narcissus* was one of that perfect brood. Less perfect than many perhaps, but she was ours, and, consequently, incomparable. We were proud of her. In

Bombay, ignorant landlubbers alluded to her as that
"pretty grey ship." Pretty! A scurvy meed of com-
mendation! We knew she was the most magnificent
sea-boat ever launched. We tried to forget that, like
many good sea-boats, she was at times rather crank.
She was exacting. She wanted care in loading and
handling, and no one knew exactly how much care
would be enough. Such are the imperfections of mere
men! The ship knew, and sometimes would correct
the presumptuous human ignorance by the wholesome
discipline of fear. We had heard ominous stories
about past voyages. The cook (technically a seaman,
but in reality no sailor)—the cook, when unstrung by
some misfortune, such as the rolling over of a saucepan,
would mutter gloomily while he wiped the floor:—
"There! Look at what she has done! Some voy'ge
she will drown all hands! You'll see if she won't."
To which the steward, snatching in the galley a moment to draw breath in the hurry of his worried life,
would remark philosophically:—"Those that see won't
tell, anyhow. I don't want to see it." We derided
those fears. Our hearts went out to the old man when
he pressed her hard so as to make her hold her own,
hold to every inch gained to windward; when he made
her, under reefed sails, leap obliquely at enormous
waves. The men, knitted together aft into a ready
group by the first sharp order of an officer coming to
take charge of the deck in bad weather:—"Keep
handy the watch," stood admiring her valiance. Their
eyes blinked in the wind; their dark faces were wet with
drops of water more salt and bitter than human tears;
beards and moustaches, soaked, hung straight and
dripping like fine seaweed. They were fantastically
misshapen; in high boots, in hats like helmets, and
swaying clumsily, stiff and bulky in glistening oilskins,

they resembled men strangely equipped for some fabulous adventure. Whenever she rose easily to a towering green sea, elbows dug ribs, faces brightened, lips murmured:—"Didn't she do it cleverly," and all the heads turning like one watched with sardonic grins the foiled wave go roaring to leeward, white with the foam of a monstrous rage. But when she had not been quick enough and, struck heavily, lay over trembling under the blow, we clutched at ropes, and looking up at the narrow bands of drenched and strained sails waving desperately aloft, we thought in our hearts:—"No wonder. Poor thing!"

The thirty-second day out of Bombay began inauspiciously. In the morning a sea smashed one of the galley doors. We dashed in through lots of steam and found the cook very wet and indignant with the ship:— "She's getting worse every day. She's trying to drown me in front of my own stove!" He was very angry. We pacified him, and the carpenter, though washed away twice from there, managed to repair the door. Through that accident our dinner was not ready till late, but it didn't matter in the end because Knowles, who went to fetch it, got knocked down by a sea and the dinner went over the side. Captain Allistoun, looking more hard and thin-lipped than ever, hung on to full topsails and foresail, and would not notice that the ship, asked to do too much, appeared to lose heart altogether for the first time since we knew her. She refused to rise, and bored her way sullenly through the seas. Twice running, as though she had been blind or weary of life, she put her nose deliberately into a big wave and swept the decks from end to end. As the boatswain observed with marked annoyance, while we were splashing about in a body to try and save a worthless wash-tub:—"Every blooming thing in the ship is going overboard this afternoon." Venerable Singleton broke his habitual silence and said with a glance aloft:— "The old man's in a temper with the weather, but it's no good bein' angry with the winds of heaven."   Jimmy had shut his door, of course.   We knew he was dry and comfortable within his little cabin, and in our absurd way were pleased one moment, exasperated the next, by that certitude.   Donkin skulked shamelessly, uneasy and miserable.   He grumbled:—"I'm perishin' with cold outside in bloomin' wet rags, an' that 'ere black sojer sits dry on a blamed chest full of bloomin' clothes; blank his black soul!"   We took no notice of him; we hardly gave a thought to Jimmy and his bosom friend.   There was no leisure for idle probing of hearts. Sails blew adrift. Things broke loose. Cold and wet, we were washed about the deck while trying to repair damages.   The ship tossed about, shaken furiously, like a toy in the hand of a lunatic. Just at sunset there was a rush to shorten sail before the menace of a sombre hail cloud.   The hard gust of wind came brutal like the blow of a fist.   The ship relieved of her canvas in time received it pluckily: she yielded reluctantly to the violent onset; then, coming up with a stately and irresistible motion, brought her spars to windward in the teeth of the screeching squall.   Out of the abysmal darkness of the black cloud overhead white hail streamed on her, rattled on the rigging, leaped in handfuls off the yards, rebounded on the deck—round and gleaming in the murky turmoil like a shower of pearls.   It passed away. For a moment a livid sun shot horizontally the last rays of sinister light between the hills of steep, rolling waves.   Then a wild night rushed in—stamped out in a great howl that dismal remnant of a stormy day.

There was no sleep on board that night. Most seamen remember in their life one or two such nights of a culminating gale. Nothing seems left of the whole universe but darkness, clamour, fury—and the ship. And like the last vestige of a shattered creation she drifts, bearing an anguished remnant of sinful mankind, through the distress, tumult, and pain of an avenging terror. No one slept in the forecastle. The tin oil-lamp suspended on a long string, smoking, described wide circles; wet clothing made dark heaps on the glistening floor; a thin layer of water rushed to and fro. In the bed-places men lay booted, resting on elbows and with open eyes. Hung-up suits of oilskin swung out and in, lively and disquieting like reckless ghosts of decapitated seamen dancing in a tempest. No one spoke and all listened. Outside the night moaned and sobbed to the accompaniment of a continuous loud tremor as of innumerable drums beating far off. Shrieks passed through the air. Tremendous dull blows made the ship tremble while she rolled under the weight of the seas toppling on her deck. At times she soared up swiftly as if to leave this earth for ever, then during interminable moments fell through a void with all the hearts on board of her standing still, till a frightful shock, expected and sudden, started them off again with a big thump. After every dislocating jerk of the ship, Wamibo, stretched full length, his face on the pillow, groaned slightly with the pain of his tormented universe. Now and then, for the fraction of an intolerable second, the ship, in the fiercer burst of a terrible uproar, remained on her side, vibrating and still, with a stillness more appalling than the wildest motion. Then upon all those prone bodies a stir would pass, a shiver of suspense. A man would protrude his anxious head and a pair of eyes glistened in the sway of light glaring wildly. Some moved their legs a little as if making ready to jump out. But several, motionless on their backs and with one hand gripping hard the edge of the bunk, smoked nervously with quick puffs, staring upwards; immobilised in a great craving for peace.

At midnight, orders were given to furl the fore and mizen topsails. With immense efforts men crawled aloft through a merciless buffeting, saved the canvas and crawled down almost exhausted, to bear in panting silence the cruel battering of the seas. Perhaps for the first time in the history of the merchant service the watch, told to go below, did not leave the deck, as if compelled to remain there by the fascination of a venomous violence. At every heavy gust men, huddled together, whispered to one another:—"It can blow no harder"—and presently the gale would give them the lie with a piercing shriek, and drive their breath back into their throats. A fierce squall seemed to burst asunder the thick mass of sooty vapours; and above the wrack of torn clouds glimpses could be caught of the high moon rushing backwards with frightful speed over the sky, right into the wind's eye. Many hung their heads, muttering that it "turned their inwards out" to look at it. Soon the clouds closed up and the world again became a raging, blind darkness that howled, flinging at the lonely ship salt sprays and sleet.

About half-past seven the pitchy obscurity round us turned a ghastly grey, and we knew that the sun had risen. This unnatural and threatening daylight, in which we could see one another's wild eyes and drawn faces, was only an added tax on our endurance. The horizon seemed to have come on all sides within arm's length of the ship. Into that narrowed circle furious

seas leaped in, struck, and leaped out. A rain of salt,
heavy drops flew aslant like mist. The main-topsail
had to be goose-winged, and with stolid resignation
every one prepared to go aloft once more; but the officers
yelled, pushed back, and at last we understood that no
more men would be allowed to go on the yard than
were absolutely necessary for the work. As at any
moment the masts were likely to be jumped out or
blown overboard, we concluded that the captain didn't
want to see all his crowd go over the side at once.
That was reasonable. The watch then on duty, led
by Mr. Creighton, began to struggle up the rigging.
The wind flattened them against the ratlines; then,
easing a little, would let them ascend a couple of steps;
and again, with a sudden gust, pin all up the shrouds
the whole crawling line in attitudes of crucifixion.
The other watch plunged down on the main deck to
haul up the sail. Men's heads bobbed up as the water
flung them irresistibly from side to side. Mr. Baker
grunted encouragingly in our midst, spluttering and
blowing amongst the tangled ropes like an energetic
porpoise. Favoured by an ominous and untrustworthy lull, the work was done without any one being
lost either off the deck or from the yard. For the
moment the gale seemed to take off, and the ship, as
if grateful for our efforts, plucked up heart and made
better weather of it.

At eight the men off duty, watching their chance,
ran forward over the flooded deck to get some rest.
The other half of the crew remained aft for their turn
of "seeing her through her trouble," as they expressed it.
The two mates urged the master to go below. Mr.
Baker grunted in his ear:—"Ough! surely now . . .
Ough! . . . confidence in us . . . nothing
more to do . . . she must lay it out or go.

Ough! Ough!" Tall young Mr. Creighton smiled down at him cheerfully:—". . . She's as right as a trivet! Take a spell, sir." He looked at them stonily with bloodshot, sleepless eyes. The rims of his eyelids were scarlet, and he moved his jaw unceasingly with a slow effort, as though he had been masticating a lump of india-rubber. He shook his head. He repeated:—"Never mind me. I must see it out—I must see it out," but he consented to sit down for a moment on the skylight, with his hard face turned unflinchingly to windward. The sea spat at it—and stoical, it streamed with water as though he had been weeping. On the weather side of the poop the watch, hanging on to the mizen rigging and to one another, tried to exchange encouraging words. Singleton, at the wheel, yelled out:—"Look out for yourselves!" His voice reached them in a warning whisper. They were startled.

A big, foaming sea came out of the mist; it made for the ship, roaring wildly, and in its rush it looked as mischievous and discomposing as a madman with an axe. One or two, shouting, scrambled up the rigging; most, with a convulsive catch of the breath, held on where they stood. Singleton dug his knees under the wheel-box, and carefully eased the helm to the headlong pitch of the ship, but without taking his eyes off the coming wave. It towered close-to and high, like a wall of green glass topped with snow. The ship rose to it as though she had soared on wings, and for a moment rested poised upon the foaming crest as if she had been a great sea-bird. Before we could draw breath a heavy gust struck her, another roller took her unfairly under the weather bow, she gave a toppling lurch, and filled her decks. Captain Allistoun leaped up, and fell; Archie rolled over him, screaming:—"She will rise!"

She gave another lurch to leeward; the lower deadeyes
dipped heavily; the men's feet flew from under them,
and they hung kicking above the slanting poop.   They
could see the ship putting her side in the water, and
shouted all together:—"She's going!"   Forward the
forecastle doors flew open, and the watch below were
seen leaping out one after another, throwing their
arms up; and, falling on hands and knees, scrambled
aft on all fours along the high side of the deck, sloping
more than the roof of a house.   From leeward the
seas rose, pursuing them; they looked wretched in a
hopeless struggle, like vermin fleeing before a flood;
they fought up the weather ladder of the poop one
after another, half naked and staring wildly; and as
soon as they got up they shot to leeward in clusters,
with closed eyes, till they brought up heavily with
their ribs against the iron stanchions of the rail; then,
groaning, they rolled in a confused mass.   The immense
volume of water thrown forward by the last scend of
the ship had burst the lee door of the forecastle.   They
could see their chests, pillows, blankets, clothing, come
out floating upon the sea.   While they struggled back
to windward they looked in dismay.   The straw beds
swam high, the blankets, spread out, undulated; while
the chests, waterlogged and with a heavy list, pitched
heavily like dismasted hulks, before they sank; Archie's
big coat passed with outspread arms, resembling a
drowned seaman floating with his head under water.
Men were slipping down while trying to dig their
fingers into the planks; others, jammed in corners,
rolled enormous eyes.   They all yelled unceasingly:—
"The masts!   Cut!   Cut! . . ."   A black squall
howled low over the ship, that lay on her side
with the weather yard-arms pointing to the clouds;
while the tall masts, inclined nearly to the horizon,

seemed to be of an immeasurable length. The carpenter let go his hold, rolled against the skylight, and began to crawl to the cabin entrance, where a big axe was kept ready for just such an emergency. At that moment the topsail sheet parted, the end of the heavy chain racketed aloft, and sparks of red fire streamed down through the flying sprays. The sail flapped once with a jerk that seemed to tear our hearts out through our teeth, and instantly changed into a bunch of fluttering narrow ribbons that tied themselves into knots and became quiet along the yard. Captain Allistoun struggled, managed to stand up with his face near the deck, upon which men swung on the ends of ropes, like nest robbers upon a cliff. One of his feet was on somebody's chest; his face was purple; his lips moved. He yelled also; he yelled, bending down:—"No! No!" Mr. Baker, one leg over the binnacle-stand, roared out: —"Did you say no? Not cut?" He shook his head madly. "No! No!" Between his legs the crawling carpenter heard, collapsed at once, and lay full length in the angle of the skylight. Voices took up the shout— "No! No!" Then all became still. They waited for the ship to turn over altogether, and shake them out into the sea; and upon the terrific noise of wind and sea not a murmur of remonstrance came out from those men, who each would have given ever so many years of life to see "them damned sticks go overboard!" They all believed it their only chance; but a little hard-faced man shook his grey head and shouted "No!" without giving them as much as a glance. They were silent, and gasped. They gripped rails, they had wound ropes'-ends under their arms; they clutched ringbolts, they crawled in heaps where there was foot-hold; they held on with both arms, hooked themselves to anything to windward with elbows, with chins, al-

most with their teeth: and some, unable to crawl away
from where they had been flung, felt the sea leap up,
striking against their backs as they struggled upwards.
Singleton had stuck to the wheel.   His hair flew out
in the wind; the gale seemed to take its life-long adversary by the beard and shake his old head.   He wouldn't
let go, and, with his knees forced between the spokes,
flew up and down like a man on a bough.   As Death
appeared unready, they began to look about.   Donkin, caught by one foot in a loop of some rope, hung,
head down, below us, and yelled, with his face to the
deck:—"Cut!   Cut!"   Two men lowered themselves
cautiously to him; others hauled on the rope.   They
caught him up, shoved him into a safer place, held
him.   He shouted curses at the master, shook his fist
at him with horrible blasphemies, called upon us in
filthy words to "Cut!   Don't mind that murdering
fool!   Cut, some of you!"   One of his rescuers struck
him a back-handed blow over the mouth; his head
banged on the deck, and he became suddenly very quiet,
with a white face, breathing hard, and with a few drops
of blood trickling from his cut lip.   On the lee side
another man could be seen stretched out as if stunned;
only the washboard prevented him from going over the
side.   It was the steward.   We had to sling him up
like a bale for he was paralysed with fright.   He had
rushed up out of the pantry when he felt the ship go
over, and had rolled down helplessly, clutching a china
mug.   It was not broken.   With difficulty we tore it
away from him, and when he saw it in our hands he was
amazed.   "Where did you get that thing?" he kept
on asking us in a trembling voice.   His shirt was blown
to shreds; the ripped sleeves flapped like wings.   Two
men made him fast, and, doubled over the rope that
held him, he resembled a bundle of wet rags.   Mr.

Baker crawled along the line of men, asking:—"Are you all there?" and looking them over. Some blinked vacantly, others shook convulsively; Wamibo's head hung over his breast; and in painful attitudes, cut by lashings, exhausted with clutching, screwed up in corners, they breathed heavily. Their lips twitched, and at every sickening heave of the overturned ship they opened them wide as if to shout. The cook, embracing a wooden stanchion, unconsciously repeated a prayer. In every short interval of the fiendish noises around he could be heard there, without cap or slippers, imploring in that storm the Master of our lives not to lead him into temptation. Soon he also became silent. In all that crowd of cold and hungry men, waiting wearily for a violent death, not a voice was heard; they were mute, and in sombre thoughtfulness listened to the horrible imprecations of the gale.

Hours passed. They were sheltered by the heavy inclination of the ship from the wind that rushed in one long unbroken moan above their heads, but cold rain showers fell at times into the uneasy calm of their refuge. Under the torment of that new infliction a pair of shoulders would writhe a little. Teeth chattered. The sky was clearing, and bright sunshine gleamed over the ship. After every burst of battering seas, vivid and fleeting rainbows arched over the drifting hull in the flick of sprays. The gale was ending in a clear blow, which gleamed and cut like a knife. Between two bearded shellbacks Charley, fastened with somebody's long muffler to a deck ring-bolt, wept quietly, with rare tears wrung out by bewilderment, cold, hunger, and general misery. One of his neighbours punched him in the ribs asking roughly:— "What's the matter with your cheek? In fine weather there's no holding you, youngster." Turning about with prudence he worked himself out of his coat and threw it over the boy. The other man closed up, muttering:—"'Twill make a bloomin' man of you, sonny." They flung their arms over and pressed against him. Charley drew his feet up and his eyelids dropped. Sighs were heard, as men, perceiving that they were not to be "drowned in a hurry," tried easier positions. Mr. Creighton, who had hurt his leg, lay amongst us with compressed lips. Some fellows belonging to his watch set about securing him better. Without a word or a glance he lifted his arms one after another to facilitate the operation, and not a muscle moved in his stern, young face. They asked him with solicitude:—"Easier now, sir?" He answered with a curt:—"That'll do." He was a hard young officer, but many of his watch used to say they liked him well enough because he had "such a gentlemanly way of damning us up and down the deck." Others unable to discern such fine shades of refinement, respected him for his smartness. For the first time since the ship had gone on her beam ends Captain Allistoun gave a short glance down at his men. He was almost upright—one foot against the side of the skylight, one knee on the deck; and with the end of the vang round his waist swung back and forth with his gaze fixed ahead, watchful, like a man looking out for a sign. Before his eyes the ship, with half her deck below water, rose and fell on heavy seas that rushed from under her flashing in the cold sunshine. We began to think she was wonderfully buoyant—considering. Confident voices were heard shouting:—"She'll do, boys!" Belfast exclaimed with fervour:—"I would giv' a month's pay for a draw at a pipe!" One or two, passing dry tongues on their salt lips, muttered something about a "drink of water." The cook, as if inspired, scrambled up with his breast against the poop water-cask and looked in. There was a little at the bottom. He yelled, waving his arms, and two men began to crawl backwards and forwards with the mug. We had a good mouthful all round. The master shook his head impatiently, refusing. When it came to Charley one of his neighbours shouted:—"That bloomin' boy's asleep." He slept as though he had been dosed with narcotics. They let him be. Singleton held to the wheel with one hand while he drank, bending down to shelter his lips from the wind. Wamibo had to be poked and yelled at before he saw the mug held before his eyes. Knowles said sagaciously:—"It's better'n a tot o' rum." Mr. Baker grunted:—"Thank ye." Mr. Creighton drank and nodded. Donkin gulped greedily, glaring over the rim. Belfast made us laugh when with grimacing mouth he shouted: —"Pass it this way. We're all taytottlers here." The master, presented with the mug again by a crouching man, who screamed up at him:—"We all had a drink, captain," groped for it without ceasing to look ahead, and handed it back stiffly as though he could not spare half a glance away from the ship. Faces brightened. We shouted to the cook:—"Well done, doctor!" He sat to leeward, propped by the water-cask and yelled back abundantly, but the seas were breaking in thunder just then, and we only caught snatches that sounded like: "Providence" and "born again." He was at his old game of preaching. We made friendly but derisive gestures at him, and from below he lifted one arm, holding on with the other, moved his lips; he beamed up to us, straining his voice —earnest, and ducking his head before the sprays.

Suddenly some one cried:—"Where's Jimmy?" and we were appalled once more. On the end of the row

the boatswain shouted hoarsely:—"Has any one seed
him come out?" Voices exclaimed dismally:—
"Drowned—is he? . . . No! In his cabin!
. . . Good Lord! . . . Caught like a
bloomin' rat in a trap. . . . Couldn't open his
door . . . Aye! She went over too quick and
the water jammed it . . . Poor beggar! . . .
No help for 'im. . . . Let's go and see . . ."
"Damn him, who could go?" screamed Donkin.—
"Nobody expects you to," growled the man next
to him: "you're only a thing."—"Is there half a
chance to get at 'im?" inquired two or three men together. Belfast untied himself with blind impetuosity,
and all at once shot down to leeward quicker than a
flash of lightning. We shouted all together with dismay; but with his legs overboard he held and yelled
for a rope. In our extremity nothing could be terrible;
so we judged him funny kicking there, and with his
scared face. Some one began to laugh, and, as if
hysterically infected with screaming merriment, all
those haggard men went off laughing, wild-eyed, like
a lot of maniacs tied up on a wall. Mr. Baker swung
off the binnacle-stand and tendered him one leg. He
scrambled up rather scared, and consigning us with
abominable words to the "divvle." "You are.
. . . Ough! You're a foul-mouthed beggar,
Craik," grunted Mr. Baker. He answered, stuttering
with indignation:—"Look at 'em, sorr. The bloomin'
dirty images! laughing at a chum going overboard.
Call themselves men, too." But from the break of
the poop the boatswain called out:—"Come along,"
and Belfast crawled away in a hurry to join him. The
five men, poised and gazing over the edge of the poop,
looked for the best way to get forward. They seemed
to hesitate. The others, twisting in their lashings,

turning painfully, stared with open lips. Captain
Allistoun saw nothing; he seemed with his eyes to hold
the ship up in a superhuman concentration of effort.
The wind screamed loud in sunshine; columns of spray
rose straight up; and in the glitter of rainbows bursting
over the trembling hull the men went over cautiously,
disappearing from sight with deliberate movements.

They went swinging from belaying pin to cleat above
the seas that beat the half-submerged deck. Their
toes scraped the planks. Lumps of green cold water
toppled over the bulwark and on their heads. They
hung for a moment on strained arms, with the breath
knocked out of them, and with closed eyes—then,
letting go with one hand, balanced with lolling heads,
trying to grab some rope or stanchion further forward.
The long-armed and athletic boatswain swung quickly,
gripping things with a fist hard as iron, and remembering suddenly snatches of the last letter from his "old
woman." Little Belfast scrambled in a rage spluttering "cursed nigger." Wamibo's tongue hung out
with excitement; and Archie, intrepid and calm,
watched his chance to move with intelligent coolness.

When above the side of the house, they let go one
after another, and falling heavily, sprawled, pressing
their palms to the smooth teak wood. Round them
the backwash of waves seethed white and hissing. All
the doors had become trap-doors, of course. The
first was the galley door. The galley extended from
side to side, and they could hear the sea splashing with
hollow noises in there. The next door was that of the
carpenter's shop. They lifted it, and looked down.
The room seemed to have been devastated by an
earthquake. Everything in it had tumbled on the
bulkhead facing the door, and on the other side of that
bulkhead there was Jimmy, dead or alive. The bench,

a half-finished meat-safe, saws, chisels, wire rods, axes, crowbars, lay in a heap besprinkled with loose nails. A sharp adze stuck up with a shining edge that gleamed dangerously down there like a wicked smile. The men clung to one another peering. A sickening, sly lurch of the ship nearly sent them overboard in a body. Belfast howled "Here goes!" and leaped down. Archie followed cannily, catching at shelves that gave way with him, and eased himself in a great crash of ripped wood. There was hardly room for three men to move. And in the sunshiny blue square of the door, the boatswain's face, bearded and dark, Wamibo's face, wild and pale, hung over—watching.

Together they shouted: "Jimmy! Jim!" From above the boatswain contributed a deep growl: "You . . . Wait!" In a pause, Belfast entreated: "Jimmy, darlin', are ye aloive?" The boatswain said: "Again! All together, boys!" All yelled excitedly. Wamibo made noises resembling loud barks. Belfast drummed on the side of the bulkhead with a piece of iron. All ceased suddenly. The sound of screaming and hammering went on thin and distinct—like a solo after a chorus. He was alive. He was screaming and knocking below us with the hurry of a man prematurely shut up in a coffin. We went to work. We attacked with desperation the abominable heap of things heavy, of things sharp, of things clumsy to handle. The boatswain crawled away to find somewhere a flying end of a rope; and Wamibo, held back by shouts:— "Don't jump! . . . Don't come in here, muddle-head!"—remained glaring above us—all shining eyes, gleaming fangs, tumbled hair; resembling an amazed and half-witted fiend gloating over the extraordinary agitation of the damned. The boatswain adjured us to "bear a hand," and a rope descended. We made things fast to it and they went up spinning, never to be seen by man again. A rage to fling things overboard possessed us. We worked fiercely cutting our hands, and speaking brutally to one another. Jimmy kept up a distracting row; he screamed piercingly, without drawing breath, like a tortured woman; he banged with hands and feet. The agony of his fear wrung our hearts so terribly that we longed to abandon him, to get out of that place deep as a well and swaying like a tree, to get out of his hearing, back on the poop where we could wait passively for death in incomparable repose. We shouted to him to "shut up, for God's sake." He redoubled his cries. He must have fancied we could not hear him. Probably he heard his own clamour but faintly. We could picture him crouching on the edge of the upper berth, letting out with both fists at the wood, in the dark, and with his mouth wide open for that unceasing cry. Those were loathsome moments. A cloud driving across the sun would darken the doorway menacingly. Every movement of the ship was pain. We scrambled about with no room to breathe, and felt frightfully sick. The boatswain yelled down at us:—"Bear a hand! Bear a hand! We two will be washed away from here directly if you ain't quick!" Three times a sea leaped over the high side and flung bucketfuls of water on our heads. Then Jimmy, startled by the shock, would stop his noise for a moment—waiting for the ship to sink, perhaps—and began again, distressingly loud, as if invigorated by the gust of fear. At the bottom the nails lay in a layer several inches thick. It was ghastly. Every nail in the world, not driven in firmly somewhere, seemed to have found its way into that carpenter's shop. There they were, of all kinds, the remnants of stores from seven voyages. Tin-tacks, copper tacks (sharp as

needles), pump nails, with big heads, like tiny iron
mushrooms; nails without any heads (horrible); French
nails polished and slim. They lay in a solid mass more
inabordable than a hedgehog. We hesitated, yearning
for a shovel, while Jimmy below us yelled as though
he had been flayed. Groaning, we dug our fingers in,
and very much hurt, shook our hands, scattering nails
and drops of blood. We passed up our hats full of
assorted nails to the boatswain, who, as if performing a
mysterious and appeasing rite, cast them wide upon a
raging sea.

We got to the bulkhead at last. Those were stout
planks. She was a ship, well finished in every detail—
the *Narcissus* was. They were the stoutest planks
ever put into a ship's bulkhead—we thought—and
then we perceived that, in our hurry, we had sent all
the tools overboard. Absurd little Belfast wanted to
break it down with his own weight, and with both feet
leaped straight up like a springbok, cursing the Clyde
shipwrights for not scamping their work. Incidentally
he reviled all North Britain, the rest of the earth, the
sea—and all his companions. He swore, as he alighted
heavily on his heels, that he would never, never any
more associate with any fool that "hadn't savee enough
to know his knee from his elbow." He managed by
his thumping to scare the last remnant of wits out of
Jimmy. We could hear the object of our exasperated
solicitude darting to and fro under the planks. He
had cracked his voice at last, and could only squeak
miserably. His back or else his head rubbed the
planks, now here, now there, in a puzzling manner.
He squeaked as he dodged the invisible blows. It was
more heartrending even than his yells. Suddenly
Archie produced a crowbar. He had kept it back; also
a small hatchet. We howled with satisfaction. He

struck a mighty blow and small chips flew at our eyes.
The boatswain above shouted:—"Look out! Look out
there. Don't kill the man. Easy does it!" Wamibo,
maddened with excitement, hung head down and insanely
urged us:—"Hoo! Strook 'im! Hoo! Hoo!" We were
afraid he would fall in and kill one of us and, hurriedly,
we entreated the boatswain to "shove the blamed Finn
overboard." Then, all together, we yelled down at the
planks:—"Stand from under! Get forward," and listened. We only heard the deep hum and moan of the
wind above us, the mingled roar and hiss of the seas.
The ship, as if overcome with despair, wallowed life-
lessly, and our heads swam with that unnatural motion.
Belfast clamoured:—"For the love of God, Jimmy,
where are ye? . . . Knock! Jimmy darlint! . . .
Knock! You bloody black beast! Knock!" He was
as quiet as a dead man inside a grave; and, like men
standing above a grave, we were on the verge of tears—
but with vexation, the strain, the fatigue; with the
great longing to be done with it, to get away, and lay
down to rest somewhere where we could see our danger
and breathe. Archie shouted:—"Gi'e me room!"
We crouched behind him, guarding our heads, and he
struck time after time in the joint of planks. They
cracked. Suddenly the crowbar went halfway in
through a splintered oblong hole. It must have missed
Jimmy's head by less than an inch. Archie withdrew
it quickly, and that infamous nigger rushed at the hole,
put his lips to it, and whispered "Help" in an almost
extinct voice; he pressed his head to it, trying madly
to get out through that opening one inch wide and
three inches long. In our disturbed state we were
absolutely paralysed by his incredible action. It
seemed impossible to drive him away. Even Archie
at last lost his composure. "If ye don't clear oot I'll

drive the crowbar thro' your head," he shouted in a
determined voice. He meant what he said, and his
earnestness seemed to make an impression on Jimmy.
He disappeared suddenly, and we set to prising and
tearing at the planks with the eagerness of men trying
to get at a mortal enemy, and spurred by the desire to
tear him limb from limb. The wood split, cracked,
gave way. Belfast plunged in head and shoulders
and groped viciously. "I've got 'im! Got 'im," he
shouted. "Oh! There! . . . He's gone; I've
got 'im! . . . Pull at my legs! . . .
Pull!" Wamibo hooted unceasingly. The boatswain
shouted directions:—"Catch hold of his hair, Belfast;
pull straight up, you two! . . . Pull fair!"
We pulled fair. We pulled Belfast out with a jerk,
and dropped him with disgust. In a sitting posture,
purple-faced, he sobbed despairingly:—"How can I
hold on to 'is blooming short wool?" Suddenly
Jimmy's head and shoulders appeared. He stuck halfway, and with rolling eyes foamed at our feet. We
flew at him with brutal impatience, we tore the shirt
off his back, we tugged at his ears, we panted over
him; and all at once he came away in our hands as
though somebody had let go his legs. With the same
movement, without a pause, we swung him up. His
breath whistled, he kicked our upturned faces, he
grasped two pairs of arms above his head, and he
squirmed up with such precipitation that he seemed
positively to escape from our hands like a bladder full
of gas. Streaming with perspiration, we swarmed up
the rope, and, coming into the blast of cold wind,
gasped like men plunged into icy water. With burning
faces we shivered to the very marrow of our bones.
Never before had the gale seemed to us more furious,
the sea more mad, the sunshine more merciless and

mocking, and the position of the ship more hopeless and appalling. Every movement of her was ominous of the end of her agony and of the beginning of ours. We staggered away from the door, and, alarmed by a sudden roll, fell down in a bunch. It appeared to us that the side of the house was more smooth than glass and more slippery than ice. There was nothing to hang on to but a long brass hook used sometimes to keep back an open door. Wamibo held on to it and we held on to Wamibo, clutching our Jimmy. He had completely collapsed now. He did not seem to have the strength to close his hand. We stuck to him blindly in our fear. We were not afraid of Wamibo letting go (we remembered that the brute was stronger than any three men in the ship), but we were afraid of the hook giving way, and we also believed that the ship had made up her mind to turn over at last. But she didn't. A sea swept over us. The boatswain spluttered:—"Up and away. There's a lull. Away aft with you, or we will all go to the devil here." We stood up surrounding Jimmy. We begged him to hold up, to hold on, at least. He glared with his bulging eyes, mute as a fish, and with all the stiffening knocked out of him. He wouldn't stand; he wouldn't even as much as clutch at our necks; he was only a cold black skin loosely stuffed with soft cotton wool; his arms and legs swung jointless and pliable; his head rolled about; the lower lip hung down, enormous and heavy. We pressed round him, bothered and dismayed; sheltering him we swung here and there in a body; and on the very brink of eternity we tottered all together with concealing and absurd gestures, like a lot of drunken men embarrassed with a stolen corpse.

Something had to be done. We had to get him aft. A rope was tied slack under his armpits, and, reaching

up at the risk of our lives, we hung him on the foresheet cleet. He emitted no sound; he looked as
ridiculously lamentable as a doll that had lost half its
sawdust, and we started on our perilous journey over
the main deck, dragging along with care that pitiful,
that limp, that hateful burden. He was not very
heavy, but had he weighed a ton he could not have
been more awkward to handle. We literally passed
him from hand to hand. Now and then we had to
hang him up on a handy belaying-pin, to draw a breath
and reform the line. Had the pin broken he would
have irretrievably gone into the Southern Ocean, but
he had to take his chance of that; and after a little
while, becoming apparently aware of it, he groaned
slightly, and with a great effort whispered a few words.
We listened eagerly. He was reproaching us with
our carelessness in letting him run such risks: "Now,
after I got myself out from there," he breathed out
weakly. "There" was his cabin. And he got himself
out. We had nothing to do with it apparently!
. . . No matter. . . . We went on and let
him take his chances, simply because we could not
help it; for though at that time we hated him more
than ever—more than anything under heaven—we
did not want to lose him. We had so far saved
him; and it had become a personal matter between us
and the sea. We meant to stick to him. Had we
(by an incredible hypothesis) undergone similar toil
and trouble for an empty cask, that cask would have
become as precious to us as Jimmy was. More precious, in fact, because we would have had no reason to
hate the cask. And we hated James Wait. We could
not get rid of the monstrous suspicion that this astounding black-man was shamming sick, had been malingering heartlessly in the face of our toil, of our scorn, of

our patience—and now was malingering in the face of
our devotion—in the face of death. Our vague and
imperfect morality rose with disgust at his unmanly lie.
But he stuck to it manfully—amazingly. No! It
couldn't be. He was at all extremity. His cantankerous
temper was only the result of the provoking invincible-
ness of that death he felt by his side. Any man may
be angry with such a masterful chum. But, then,
what kind of men were we—with our thoughts! Indignation and doubt grappled within us in a scuffle
that trampled upon the finest of our feelings. And
we hated him because of the suspicion; we detested him
because of the doubt. We could not scorn him safely—
neither could we pity him without risk to our dignity.
So we hated him, and passed him carefully from hand
to hand. We cried, "Got him?"—"Yes. All right.
Let go." And he swung from one enemy to another,
showing about as much life as an old bolster would do.
His eyes made two narrow white slits in the black face.
The air escaped through his lips with a noise like the
sound of bellows. We reached the poop ladder at
last, and it being a comparatively safe place, we lay
for a moment in an exhausted heap to rest a little.
He began to mutter. We were always incurably anxious to hear what he had to say. This time he mumbled
peevishly, "It took you some time to come. I began
to think the whole smart lot of you had been washed
overboard. What kept you back? Hey? Funk?"
We said nothing. With sighs we started again to drag
him up. The secret and ardent desire of our hearts
was the desire to beat him viciously with our fists about
the head; and we handled him as tenderly as though he
had been made of glass. . . .

The return on the poop was like the return of wan-
derers after many years amongst people marked by

the desolation of time. Eyes were turned slowly in
their sockets glancing at us. Faint murmurs were
heard, "Have you got 'im after all?" The well-
known faces looked strange and familiar; they seemed
faded and grimy; they had a mingled expression of
fatigue and eagerness. They seemed to have become
much thinner during our absence, as if all these men
had been starving for a long time in their abandoned
attitudes. The captain, with a round turn of a rope
on his wrist, and kneeling on one knee, swung with a
face cold and stiff; but with living eyes he was still
holding the ship up, heeding no one, as if lost in the
unearthly effort of that endeavour. We fastened up
James Wait in a safe place. Mr. Baker scrambled
along to lend a hand. Mr. Creighton, on his back,
and very pale, muttered, "Well done," and gave us,
Jimmy and the sky, a scornful glance, then closed his
eyes slowly. Here and there a man stirred a little, but
most of them remained apathetic, in cramped positions,
muttering between shivers. The sun was setting. A
sun enormous, unclouded and red, declining low as if
bending down to look into their faces. The wind
whistled across long sunbeams that, resplendent and
cold, struck full on the dilated pupils of staring eyes
without making them wink. The wisps of hair and
the tangled beards were grey with the salt of the sea.
The faces were earthy, and the dark patches under the
eyes extended to the ears, smudged into the hollows
of sunken cheeks. The lips were livid and thin, and
when they moved it was with difficulty, as though they
had been glued to the teeth. Some grinned sadly in
the sunlight, shaking with cold. Others were sad and
still. Charley, subdued by the sudden disclosure of
the insignificance of his youth, darted fearful glances.
The two smooth-faced Norwegians resembled decrepit

children, staring stupidly. To leeward, on the edge of the horizon, black seas leaped up towards the glowing sun. It sank slowly, round and blazing, and the crests of waves splashed on the edge of the luminous circle. One of the Norwegians appeared to catch sight of it, and, after giving a violent start, began to speak. His voice, startling the others, made them stir. They moved their heads stiffly, or turning with difficulty, looked at him with surprise, with fear, or in grave silence. He chattered at the setting sun, nodding his head, while the big seas began to roll across the crimson disc; and over miles of turbulent waters the shadows of high waves swept with a running darkness the faces of men. A crested roller broke with a loud hissing roar, and the sun, as if put out, disappeared. The chattering voice faltered, went out together with the light. There were sighs. In the sudden lull that follows the crash of a broken sea a man said wearily, "Here's that blooming Dutchman gone off his chump." A seaman, lashed by the middle, tapped the deck with his open hand with unceasing quick flaps. In the gathering greyness of twilight a bulky form was seen rising aft, and began marching on all fours with the movements of some big cautious beast. It was Mr. Baker passing along the line of men. He grunted encouragingly over every one, felt their fastenings. Some, with half-open eyes, puffed like men oppressed by heat; others mechanically and in dreamy voices answered him, "Aye! aye! sir!" He went from one to another grunting, "Ough! . . . See her through it yet;" and unexpectedly, with loud angry outbursts, blew up Knowles for cutting off a long piece from the fall of the relieving tackle. "Ough!——Ashamed of yourself——Relieving tackle——Don't you know better!——Ough!——Able seaman! Ough!" The

lame man was crushed. He muttered, "Get som'think
for a lashing for myself, sir."—"Ough! Lashing——
yourself. Are you a tinker or a sailor——What?
Ough!——May want that tackle directly——Ough!
——More use to the ship than your lame carcass.
Ough!——Keep it!——Keep it, now you've done it."
He crawled away slowly, muttering to himself about
some men being "worse than children." It had been
a comforting row. Low exclamations were heard:
"Hallo . . . Hallo." . . . Those who had
been painfully dozing asked with convulsive starts,
"What's up? . . . What is it?" The answers
came with unexpected cheerfulness: "The mate is
going bald-headed for lame Jack about something or
other." "No!" . . . . "What 'as he done?"
Some one even chuckled. It was like a whiff of hope,
like a reminder of safe days. Donkin, who had been
stupefied with fear, revived suddenly and began to
shout:—"'Ear 'im; that's the way they tawlk to us.
Vy donch 'ee 'it 'im—one ov yer? 'It 'im. 'It 'im!
Comin' the mate over us. We are as good men as 'ee!
We're all goin' to 'ell now. We 'ave been starved in
this rotten ship, an' now we're goin' to be drowned for
them black 'earted bullies! 'It 'im!" He shrieked
in the deepening gloom, he blubbered and sobbed,
screaming:—"'It 'im! 'It 'im!" The rage and fear
of his disregarded right to live tried the steadfastness
of hearts more than the menacing shadows of the night
that advanced through the unceasing clamour of the
gale. From aft Mr. Baker was heard:—"Is one of
you men going to stop him—must I come along?"
"Shut up!" . . . "Keep quiet!" cried various
voices, exasperated, trembling with cold.—"You'll
get one across the mug from me directly," said an
invisible seaman, in a weary tone, "I won't let the mate

have the trouble." He ceased and lay still with the silence of despair. On the black sky the stars, coming out, gleamed over an inky sea that, speckled with foam, flashed back at them the evanescent and pale light of a dazzling whiteness born from the black turmoil of the waves. Remote in the eternal calm they glittered hard and cold above the uproar of the earth; they surrounded the vanquished and tormented ship on all sides: more pitiless than the eyes of a triumphant mob, and as unapproachable as the hearts of men.

The icy south wind howled exultingly under the sombre splendour of the sky. The cold shook the men with a resistless violence as though it had tried to shake them to pieces. Short moans were swept unheard off the stiff lips. Some complained in mutters of "not feeling themselves below the waist;" while those who had closed their eyes, imagined they had a block of ice on their chests. Others, alarmed at not feeling any pain in their fingers, beat the deck feebly with their hands—obstinate and exhausted. Wamibo stared vacant and dreamy. The Scandinavians kept on a meaningless mutter through chattering teeth. The spare Scotchmen, with determined efforts, kept their lower jaws still. The West-country men lay big and stolid in an invulnerable surliness. A man yawned and swore in turns. Another breathed with a rattle in his throat. Two elderly hard-weather shellbacks, fast side by side, whispered dismally to one another about the landlady of a boarding-house in Sunderland, whom they both knew. They extolled her motherliness and her liberality; they tried to talk about the joint of beef and the big fire in the downstairs kitchen. The words dying faintly on their lips, ended in light sighs. A sudden voice cried into the cold night, "Oh Lord!" No one changed his position or took any notice of the cry. One or two passed, with a repeated and vague gesture, their hand over their faces, but most of them kept very still. In the benumbed immobility of their bodies they were excessively wearied by their thoughts, which rushed with the rapidity and vividness of dreams. Now and then, by an abrupt and startling exclamation, they answered the weird hail of some illusion; then, again, in silence contemplated the vision of known faces and familiar things. They recalled the aspect of forgotten shipmates and heard the voice of dead and gone skippers. They remembered the noise of gaslit streets, the steamy heat of tap-rooms or the scorching sunshine of calm days at sea.

Mr. Baker left his insecure place, and crawled, with stoppages, along the poop. In the dark and on all fours he resembled some carnivorous animal prowling amongst corpses. At the break, propped to windward of a stanchion, he looked down on the main deck. It seemed to him that the ship had a tendency to stand up a little more. The wind had eased a little, he thought, but the sea ran as high as ever. The waves foamed viciously, and the lee side of the deck disappeared under a hissing whiteness as of boiling milk, while the rigging sang steadily with a deep vibrating note, and, at every upward swing of the ship, the wind rushed with a long-drawn clamour amongst the spars. Mr. Baker watched very still. A man near him began to make a blabbing noise with his lips, all at once and very loud, as though the cold had broken brutally through him. He went on:—"Ba—ba—ba—brrr—brrr—ba—ba."—"Stop that!" cried Mr. Baker, groping in the dark. "Stop it!" He went on shaking the leg he found under his hand.—"What is it, sir?" called out Belfast, in the tone of a man awakened suddenly; "we are looking after that 'ere Jimmy."—"Are you? Ough! Don't make that row then. Who's that near you?"—"It's me—the boatswain, sir," growled the West-country man; "we are trying to keep life in that poor devil."—"Aye, aye!" said Mr. Baker. "Do it quietly, can't you."—"He wants us to hold him up above the rail," went on the boatswain, with irritation, "says he can't breathe here under our jackets."— "If we lift 'im, we drop 'im overboard," said another voice, "we can't feel our hands with cold."—"I don't care. I am choking!" exclaimed James Wait in a clear tone.—"Oh, no, my son," said the boatswain, desperately, "you don't go till we all go on this fine night."— "You will see yet many a worse," said Mr. Baker, cheerfully.—"It's no child's play, sir!" answered the boatswain. "Some of us further aft, here, are in a pretty bad way."—"If the blamed sticks had been cut out of her she would be running along on her bottom now like any decent ship, an' giv' us all a chance," said some one, with a sigh.—"The old man wouldn't have it . . . much he cares for us," whispered another.—"Care for you!" exclaimed Mr. Baker, angrily. "Why should he care for you? Are you a lot of women passengers to be taken care of? We are here to take care of the ship—and some of you ain't up to that. Ough! . . . What have you done so very smart to be taken care of? Ough! . . . Some of you can't stand a bit of a breeze without crying over it."—"Come, sorr. We ain't so bad," protested Belfast, in a voice shaken by shivers; "we ain't . . . brrr . . . "—"Again," shouted the mate, grabbing at the shadowy form; "again! . . . Why, you're in your shirt! What have you done?"—"I've put my oilskin and jacket over that half-dead nayggur—and he says he chokes," said Belfast, complainingly.—"You wouldn't call

me nigger if I wasn't half dead, you Irish beggar!"
boomed James Wait, vigorously.—"You . . . brrr
. . . You wouldn't be white if you were ever
so well . . . I will fight you . . . brrrr
. . . in fine weather . brrr . . . with
one hand tied behind my back . . . brrrrrr
. . ."—"I don't want your rags—I want air,"
gasped out the other faintly, as if suddenly exhausted.

The sprays swept over whistling and pattering.
Men disturbed in their peaceful torpor by the pain of
quarrelsome shouts, moaned, muttering curses. Mr.
Baker crawled off a little way to leeward where a water-
cask loomed up big, with something white against it.
"Is it you, Podmore?" asked Mr. Baker. He had to
repeat the question twice before the cook turned,
coughing feebly.—"Yes, sir. I've been praying in
my mind for a quick deliverance; for I am prepared
for any call. . . . I——"—"Look here, cook,"
interrupted Mr. Baker, "the men are perishing with
cold."—"Cold!" said the cook, mournfully; "they
will be warm enough before long."—"What?" asked
Mr. Baker, looking along the deck into the faint sheen
of frothing water.—"They are a wicked lot," continued the cook solemnly, but in an unsteady voice,
"about as wicked as any ship's company in this sinful
world! Now, I"—he trembled so that he could hardly
speak; his was an exposed place, and in a cotton shirt,
a thin pair of trousers, and with his knees under his
nose, he received, quaking, the flicks of stinging, salt
drops; his voice sounded exhausted—"now. I—any
time . . . My eldest youngster, Mr. Baker
. . . a clever boy . . . last Sunday on
shore before this voyage he wouldn't go to church, sir.
Says I, 'You go and clean yourself, or I'll know the

reason why!' What does he do? . . . Pond Mr.
Baker—fell into the pond in his best rig, sir! . . .
Accident? . . . 'Nothing will save you, fine
scholar though you are!' says I. . . . Accident!
. . . I whopped him, sir, till I couldn't lift my
arm. . . . " His voice faltered. "I whopped
'im!" he repeated, rattling his teeth; then, after a while,
let out a mournful sound that was half a groan, half
a snore. Mr. Baker shook him by the shoulders.
"Hey! Cook! Hold up, Podmore! Tell me—is
there any fresh water in the galley tank? The ship is
lying along less, I think; I would try to get forward.
A little water would do them good. Hallo! Look out!
Look out!" The cook struggled.—"Not you, sir—
not you!" He began to scramble to windward.
"Galley! . . . my business!" he shouted.—
"Cook's going crazy now," said several voices. He
yelled:—"Crazy, am I? I am more ready to die than
any of you, officers incloosive—there! As long as she
swims I will cook! I will get you coffee."—"Cook,
ye are a gentleman!" cried Belfast. But the cook was
already going over the weather-ladder. He stopped
for a moment to shout back on the poop:—"As long
as she swims I will cook!" and disappeared as though
he had gone overboard. The men who had heard sent
after him a cheer that sounded like a wail of sick children. An hour or more afterwards some one said
distinctly: "He's gone for good."—"Very likely,"
assented the boatswain; "even in fine weather he was
as smart about the deck as a milch-cow on her first
voyage. We ought to go and see." Nobody moved.
As the hours dragged slowly through the darkness Mr.
Baker crawled back and forth along the poop several
times. Some men fancied they had heard him exchange murmurs with the master, but at that time the

memories were incomparably more vivid than anything
actual, and they were not certain whether the murmurs
were heard now or many years ago. They did not
try to find out. A mutter more or less did not matter.
It was too cold for curiosity, and almost for hope.
They could not spare a moment or a thought from the
great mental occupation of wishing to live. And the
desire of life kept them alive, apathetic and enduring,
under the cruel persistence of wind and cold; while the
bestarred black dome of the sky revolved slowly above
the ship, that drifted, bearing their patience and their
suffering, through the stormy solitude of the sea.

Huddled close to one another, they fancied themselves utterly alone. They heard sustained loud noises,
and again bore the pain of existence through long hours
of profound silence. In the night they saw sunshine,
felt warmth, and suddenly, with a start, thought that
the sun would never rise upon a freezing world. Some
heard laughter, listened to songs; others, near the end
of the poop, could hear loud human shrieks, and opening their eyes, were surprised to hear them still, though
very faint, and far away. The boatswain said:—
"Why, it's the cook, hailing from forward, I think."
He hardly believed his own words or recognised his own
voice. It was a long time before the man next to him
gave a sign of life. He punched hard his other neighbour and said:—"The cook's shouting!" Many did
not understand, others did not care; the majority further aft did not believe. But the boatswain and another man had the pluck to crawl away forward to see.
They seemed to have been gone for hours, and were
very soon forgotten. Then suddenly men who had
been plunged in a hopeless resignation became as if
possessed with a desire to hurt. They belaboured one
another with fists. In the darkness they struck per-

sistently anything soft they could feel near, and, with a greater effort than for a shout, whispered excitedly:— "They've got some hot coffee. . . . Boss'en got it. . . ." "No! . . . Where?". . . . "It's coming! Cook made it." James Wait moaned. Donkin scrambled viciously, caring not where he kicked, and anxious that the officers should have none of it. It came in a pot, and they drank in turns. It was hot, and while it blistered the greedy palates, it seemed incredible. The men sighed out parting with the mug:—"How 'as he done it?" Some cried weakly:— "Bully for you, doctor!"

He had done it somehow. Afterwards Archie declared that the thing was "meeraculous." For many days we wondered, and it was the one ever-interesting subject of conversation to the end of the voyage. We asked the cook, in fine weather, how he felt when he saw his stove "reared up on end." We inquired, in the north-east trade and on serene evenings, whether he had to stand on his head to put things right somewhat. We suggested he had used his bread-board for a raft, and from there comfortably had stoked his grate; and we did our best to conceal our admiration under the wit of fine irony. He affirmed not to know anything about it, rebuked our levity, declared himself, with solemn animation, to have been the object of a special mercy for the saving of our unholy lives. Fundamentally he was right, no doubt; but he need not have been so offensively positive about it—he need not have hinted so often that it would have gone hard with us had he not been there, meritorious and pure, to receive the inspiration and the strength for the work of grace. Had we been saved by his recklessness or his agility, we could have at length become reconciled to the fact; but to admit our obligation to anybody's

virtue and holiness alone was as difficult for us as for
any other handful of mankind.   Like many benefactors
of humanity, the cook took himself too seriously, and
reaped the reward of irreverence.   We were not un-
ungrateful, however.   He remained heroic.   His saying—*the* saying of his life—became proverbial in the
mouth of men as are the sayings of conquerors or sages.
Later, whenever one of us was puzzled by a task and
advised to relinquish it, he would express his determination to persevere and to succeed by the words:—"As
long as she swims I will cook!"

The hot drink helped us through the bleak hours
that precede the dawn.   The sky low by the horizon
took on the delicate tints of pink and yellow like the
inside of a rare shell.   And higher, where it glowed
with a pearly sheen, a small black cloud appeared, like
a forgotten fragment of the night set in a border of
dazzling gold.   The beams of light skipped on the
crests of waves.   The eyes of men turned to the eastward.   The sunlight flooded their weary faces.   They
were giving themselves up to fatigue as though they
had done for ever with their work.   On Singleton's
black oilskin coat the dried salt glistened like hoar
frost.   He hung on by the wheel, with open and lifeless
eyes.   Captain Allistoun, unblinking, faced the rising
sun.   His lips stirred, opened for the first time in
twenty-four hours, and with a fresh firm voice he cried,
"Wear ship!"

The commanding sharp tones made all these torpid
men start like a sudden flick of a whip.   Then again,
motionless where they lay, the force of habit made some
of them repeat the order in hardly audible murmurs.
Captain Allistoun glanced down at his crew, and several, with fumbling fingers and hopeless movements,
tried to cast themselves adrift.   He repeated im-

patiently, "Wear ship. Now then, Mr. Baker, get the men along. What's the matter with them?" —"Wear ship. Do you hear there?—Wear ship!" thundered out the boatswain suddenly. His voice seemed to break through a deadly spell. Men began to stir and crawl.—"I want the fore-top-mast stay-sail run up smartly," said the master, very loudly; "if you can't manage it standing up you must do it lying down—that's all. Bear a hand!"—"Come along! Let's give the old girl a chance," urged the boatswain. —"Aye! aye! Wear ship!" exclaimed quavering voices. The forecastle men, with reluctant faces, prepared to go forward. Mr. Baker pushed ahead grunting on all fours to show the way, and they followed him over the break. The others lay still with a vile hope in their hearts of not being required to move till they got saved or drowned in peace.

After some time they could be seen forward appearing on the forecastle head, one by one in unsafe attitudes; hanging on to the rails, clambering over the anchors; embracing the cross-head of the windlass or hugging the fore-capstan. They were restless with strange exertions, waved their arms, knelt, lay flat down, staggered up, seemed to strive their hardest to go overboard. Suddenly a small white piece of canvas fluttered amongst them, grew larger, beating. Its narrow head rose in jerks—and at last it stood distended and triangular in the sunshine.—"They have done it!" cried the voices aft. Captain Allistoun let go the rope he had round his wrist and rolled to lee-ward headlong. He could be seen casting the lee main braces off the pins while the backwash of waves splashed over him.—"Square the main yard!" he shouted up to us—who stared at him in wonder. We hesitated to stir. "The main brace, men. Haul!

haul anyhow! Lay on your backs and haul!" he
screeched, half drowned down there. We did not believe we could move the main yard, but the strongest and the less discouraged tried to execute the
order. Others assisted half-heartedly. Singleton's eyes
blazed suddenly as he took a fresh grip of the spokes.
Captain Allistoun fought his way up to windward.—
"Haul men! Try to move it! Haul, and help the
ship." His hard face worked suffused and furious.
"Is she going off, Singleton?" he cried.—"Not a move
yet, sir," croaked the old seaman in a horribly hoarse
voice.—"Watch the helm, Singleton," spluttered the
master. "Haul men! Have you no more strength
than rats? Haul, and earn your salt." Mr. Creighton, on his back, with a swollen leg and a face as white
as a piece of paper, blinked his eyes; his bluish lips
twitched. In the wild scramble men grabbed at him,
crawled over his hurt leg, knelt on his chest. He kept
perfectly still, setting his teeth without a moan, without
a sigh. The master's ardour, the cries of that silent
man inspired us. We hauled and hung in bunches
on the rope. We heard him say with violence to
Donkin, who sprawled abjectly on his stomach,—"I
will brain you with this belaying pin if you don't catch
hold of the brace," and that victim of men's injustice,
cowardly and cheeky, whimpered:—"Are you goin'
to murder us now," while with sudden desperation
he gripped the rope. Men sighed, shouted, hissed
meaningless words, groaned. The yards moved, came
slowly square against the wind, that hummed loudly
on the yard-arms.—"Going off, sir," shouted Singleton,
"she's just started."—"Catch a turn with that brace.
Catch a turn!" clamoured the master. Mr. Creighton,
nearly suffocated and unable to move, made a mighty
effort, and with his left hand managed to nip the rope.

—"All fast!" cried some one. He closed his eyes as if going off into a swoon, while huddled together about the brace we watched with scared looks what the ship would do now.

She went off slowly as though she had been weary and disheartened like the men she carried. She paid off very gradually, making us hold our breath till we choked, and as soon as she had brought the wind abaft the beam she started to move, and fluttered our hearts. It was awful to see her, nearly overturned, begin to gather way and drag her submerged side through the water. The dead-eyes of the rigging churned the breaking seas. The lower half of the deck was full of mad whirlpools and eddies; and the long line of the lee rail could be seen showing black now and then in the swirls of a field of foam as dazzling and white as a field of snow. The wind sang shrilly amongst the spars; and at every slight lurch we expected her to slip to the bottom sideways from under our backs. When dead before it she made the first distinct attempt to stand up, and we encouraged her with a feeble and discordant howl. ~ A great sea came running up aft and hung for a moment over us with a curling top; then crashed down under the counter and spread out on both sides into a great sheet of bursting froth. Above its fierce hiss we heard Singleton's croak:—"She is steering!" He had both his feet now planted firmly on the grating, and the wheel spun fast as he eased the helm.—"Bring the wind on the port quarter and steady her!" called out the master, staggering to his feet, the first man up from amongst our prostrate heap. One or two screamed with excitement:—"She rises!" Far away forward, Mr. Baker and three others were seen erect and black on the clear sky, lifting their arms, and with open mouths as though they had been shouting all together. The ship trembled, trying to lift her side, lurched back, seemed to give up with a nerveless dip, and suddenly with an unexpected jerk swung violently to windward, as though she had torn herself out from a deadly grasp. The whole immense volume of water, lifted by her deck, was thrown bodily across to starboard. Loud cracks were heard. Iron ports breaking open thundered with ringing blows. The water topped over the starboard rail with the rush of a river falling over a dam. The sea on deck, and the seas on every side of her, mingled together in a deafening roar. She rolled violently. We got up and were helplessly run or flung about from side to side. Men, rolling over and over, yelled,—"The house will go!" —"She clears herself!" Lifted by a towering sea she ran along with it for a moment, spouting thick streams of water through every opening of her wounded sides. The lee braces having been carried away or washed off the pins, all the ponderous yards on the fore swung from side to side and with appalling rapidity at every roll. The men forward were seen crouching here and there with fearful glances upwards at the enormous spars that whirled about over their heads. The torn canvas and the ends of broken gear streamed in the wind like wisps of hair. Through the clear sunshine, over the flashing turmoil and uproar of the seas, the ship ran blindly, dishevelled and headlong, as if fleeing for her life; and on the poop we spun, we tottered about, distracted and noisy. We all spoke at once in a thin babble; we had the aspect of invalids and the gestures of maniacs. Eyes shone, large and haggard, in smiling, meagre faces that seemed to have been dusted over with powdered chalk. We stamped, clapped our hands, feeling ready to jump and do anything; but in reality hardly able to keep on our feet.

Captain Allistoun, hard and slim, gesticulated madly from the poop at Mr. Baker: "Steady these fore-yards! Steady them the best you can!" On the main deck, men excited by his cries, splashed, dashing aimlessly here and there with the foam swirling up to their waists. Apart, far aft, and alone by the helm, old Singleton had deliberately tucked his white beard under the top button of his glistening coat. Swaying upon the din and tumult of the seas, with the whole battered length of the ship launched forward in a rolling rush before his steady old eyes, he stood rigidly still, forgotten by all, and with an attentive face. In front of his erect figure only the two arms moved crosswise with a swift and sudden readiness, to check or urge again the rapid stir of circling spokes. He steered with care.

CHAPTER FOUR

ON MEN reprieved by its disdainful mercy, the immortal sea confers in its justice the full privilege of desired unrest. Through the perfect wisdom of its grace they are not permitted to meditate at ease upon the complicated and acrid savour of existence. They must without pause justify their life to the eternal pity that commands toil to be hard and unceasing, from sunrise to sunset, from sunset to sunrise; till the weary succession of nights and days tainted by the obstinate clamour of sages, demanding bliss and an empty heaven, is redeemed at last by the vast silence of pain and labour, by the dumb fear and the dumb courage of men obscure, forgetful, and enduring.

The master and Mr. Baker coming face to face stared for a moment, with the intense and amazed looks of men meeting unexpectedly after years of trouble. Their voices were gone, and they whispered desperately at one another.—"Any one missing?" asked Captain Allistoun.—"No. All there."—"Anybody hurt?"—"Only the second mate."—"I will look after him directly. We're lucky."—"Very," articulated Mr. Baker, faintly. He gripped the rail and rolled bloodshot eyes. The little grey man made an effort to raise his voice above a dull mutter, and fixed his chief mate with a cold gaze, piercing like a dart.—"Get sail on the ship," he said, speaking authoritatively and with an inflexible snap of his thin lips. "Get sail on her as soon as you can. This is a fair wind. At once, sir—Don't give the men time to feel themselves.

They will get done up and stiff, and we will never
. . . We must get her along now" . . . He
reeled to a long heavy roll; the rail dipped into the
glancing, hissing water. He caught a shroud, swung
helplessly against the mate . . . "now we
have a fair wind at last——Make——sail." His head
rolled from shoulder to shoulder. His eyelids began
to beat rapidly. "And the pumps——pumps, Mr.
Baker." He peered as though the face within a foot
of his eyes had been half a mile off. "Keep the men
on the move to——to get her along," he mumbled
in a drowsy tone, like a man going off into a doze. He
pulled himself together suddenly. "Mustn't stand.
Won't do," he said with a painful attempt at a smile.
He let go his hold, and, propelled by the dip of the
ship, ran aft unwillingly, with small steps, till he
brought up against the binnacle stand. Hanging on
there he looked up in an objectless manner at Singleton,
who, unheeding him, watched anxiously the end of
the jib-boom—"Steering gear works all right?" he
asked. There was a noise in the old seaman's throat,
as though the words had been rattling together before
they could come out.—"Steers . . . like a little boat," he said, at last, with hoarse tenderness,
without giving the master as much as half a glance—
then, watchfully, spun the wheel down, steadied, flung
it back again. Captain Allistoun tore himself away
from the delight of leaning against the binnacle, and
began to walk the poop, swaying and reeling to preserve
his balance. . . .

The pump-rods, clanking, stamped in short jumps
while the fly-wheels turned smoothly, with great speed,
at the foot of the mainmast, flinging back and forth
with a regular impetuosity two limp clusters of men
clinging to the handles. They abandoned themselves,

swaying from the hip with twitching faces and stony
eyes. The carpenter, sounding from time to time, exclaimed mechanically: "Shake her up! Keep her
going!" Mr. Baker could not speak, but found his
voice to shout; and under the goad of his objurgations,
men looked to the lashings, dragged out new sails; and
thinking themselves unable to move, carried heavy
blocks aloft—overhauled the gear. They went up
the rigging with faltering and desperate efforts. Their
heads swam as they shifted their hold, stepped blindly
on the yards like men in the dark; or trusted themselves
to the first rope at hand with the negligence of exhausted
strength. The narrow escapes from falls did not disturb the languid beat of their hearts; the roar of the
seas seething far below them sounded continuous and
faint like an indistinct noise from another world: the
wind filled their eyes with tears, and with heavy gusts
tried to push them off from where they swayed in insecure positions. With streaming faces and blowing
hair they flew up and down between sky and water,
bestriding the ends of yard-arms, crouching on foot-
ropes, embracing lifts to have their hands free, or standing up against chain ties. Their thoughts floated vaguely
between the desire of rest and the desire of life, while
their stiffened fingers cast off head-earrings, fumbled for
knives, or held with tenacious grip against the violent
shocks of beating canvas. They glared savagely at one
another, made frantic signs with one hand while they
held their life in the other, looked down on the
narrow strip of flooded deck, shouted along to leeward:" Light-to!" . . . "Haul out!" . . .
"Make fast!"ᐧ Their lips moved, their eyes started,
furious and eager with the desire to be understood,
but the wind tossed their words unheard upon the disturbed sea. In an unendurable and unending strain

they worked like men driven by a merciless dream to
toil in an atmosphere of ice or flame. They burnt and
shivered in turns. Their eyeballs smarted as if in the
smoke of a conflagration; their heads were ready to
burst with every shout. Hard fingers seemed to grip
their throats. At every roll they thought: Now I
must let go. It will shake us all off—and thrown
about aloft they cried wildly: "Look out there—catch
the end." . . . "Reeve clear" . . . "Turn
this block. . . . " They nodded desperately;
shook infuriated faces, "No! No! From down up."
They seemed to hate one another with a deadly hate.
The longing to be done with it all gnawed their breasts,
and the wish to do things well was a burning pain.
They cursed their fate, contemned their life, and wasted
their breath in deadly imprecations upon one another.
The sailmaker, with his bald head bared, worked feverishly, forgetting his intimacy with so many admirals.
The boatswain, climbing up with marlinspikes and
bunches of spunyarn rovings, or kneeling on the yard
and ready to take a turn with the midship-stop, had
acute and fleeting visions of his old woman and the
youngsters in a moorland village. Mr. Baker, feeling
very weak, tottered here and there, grunting and inflexible, like a man of iron. He waylaid those who,
coming from aloft, stood gasping for breath. He ordered, encouraged, scolded. "Now then—to the main
topsail now! Tally on to that gantline. Don't stand
about there!"—"Is there no rest for us?" muttered
voices. He spun round fiercely, with a sinking heart.
—"No! No rest till the work is done. Work till you
drop. That's what you're here for." A bowed seaman at his elbow gave a short laugh.—"Do or die," he
croaked bitterly, then spat into his broad palms, swung
up his long arms, and grasping the rope high above

his head sent out a mournful, wailing cry for a pull all
together. A sea boarded the quarter-deck and sent
the whole lot sprawling to leeward. Caps, handspikes
floated. Clenched hands, kicking legs, with here and
there a spluttering face, stuck out of the white hiss of
foaming water. Mr. Baker, knocked down with the
rest, screamed—"Don't let go that rope! Hold on to
it! Hold!" And sorely bruised by the brutal fling,
they held on to it, as though it had been the fortune of
their life. The ship ran, rolling heavily, and the topping crests glanced past port and starboard flashing
their white heads. Pumps were freed. Braces were
rove. The three topsails and foresail were set. She
spurted faster over the water, outpacing the swift rush
of waves. The menacing thunder of distanced seas
rose behind her—filled the air with the tremendous
vibrations of its voice. And devastated, battered,
and wounded she drove foaming to the northward, as
though inspired by the courage of a high endeavour. . . .

The forecastle was a place of damp desolation.
They looked at their dwelling with dismay. It was
slimy, dripping; it hummed hollow with the wind, and
was strewn with shapeless wreckage like a half-tide
cavern in a rocky and exposed coast. Many had lost
all they had in the world, but most of the starboard
watch had preserved their chests; thin streams of
water trickled out of them, however. The beds were
soaked; the blankets spread out and saved by some nail
squashed under foot. They dragged wet rags from
evil-smelling corners, and wringing the water out,
recognised their property. Some smiled stiffly. Others
looked round blank and mute. There were cries of
joy over old waistcoats, and groans of sorrow over
shapeless things found among the splinters of smashed

bed boards. One lamp was discovered jammed under
the bowsprit. Charley whimpered a little. Knowles
stumped here and there, sniffing, examining dark places
for salvage. He poured dirty water out of a boot, and
was concerned to find the owner. Those who, overwhelmed by their losses, sat on the forepeak hatch,
remained elbows on knees, and, with a fist against each
cheek, disdained to look up. He pushed it under their
noses. "Here's a good boot. Yours?" They snarled,
"No—get out." One snapped at him, "Take it to
hell out of this." He seemed surprised. "Why?
It's a good boot," but remembering suddenly that he
had lost every stitch of his clothing, he dropped his find
and began to swear. In the dim light cursing voices
clashed. A man came in and, dropping his arms,
stood still, repeating from the doorstep, "Here's a
bloomin' old go! Here's a bloomin' old go!" A few
rooted anxiously in flooded chests for tobacco. They
breathed hard, clamoured with heads down. "Look
at that Jack!" . . . "Here! Sam! Here's my
shore-going rig spoilt for ever." One blasphemed
tearfully holding up a pair of dripping trousers. No
one looked at him. The cat came out from somewhere.
He had an ovation. They snatched him from hand
to hand, caressed him in a murmur of pet names.
They wondered where he had "weathered it out;" disputed about it. A squabbling argument began. Two
men brought in a bucket of fresh water, and all crowded
round it; but Tom, lean and mewing, came up with
every hair astir and had the first drink. A couple of
hands went aft for oil and biscuits.

Then in the yellow light and in the intervals of mopping the deck they crunched hard bread, arranging to
"worry through somehow." Men chummed as to
beds. Turns were settled for wearing boots and having

the use of oilskin coats. They called one another "old man" and "sonny" in cheery voices. Friendly slaps resounded. Jokes were shouted. One or two stretched on the wet deck, slept with heads pillowed on their bent arms, and several, sitting on the hatch, smoked. Their weary faces appeared through a thin blue haze, pacified and with sparkling eyes. The boatswain put his head through the door. "Relieve the wheel, one of you"—he shouted inside—"it's six. Blamme if that old Singleton hasn't been there more'n thirty hours. You are a fine lot." He slammed the door again. "Mate's watch on deck," said some one. "Hey, Donkin, it's your relief!" shouted three or four together. He had crawled into an empty bunk and on wet planks lay still. "Donkin, your wheel." He made no sound. "Donkin's dead," guffawed some one. "Sell 'is bloomin' clothes," shouted another. "Donkin, if ye don't go to the bloomin' wheel they will sell your clothes—d'ye hear?" jeered a third. He groaned from his dark hole. He complained about pains in all his bones, he whimpered pitifully. "He won't go," exclaimed a contemptuous voice, "your turn, Davis." The young seaman rose painfully squaring his shoulders. Donkin stuck his head out, and it appeared in the yellow light, fragile and ghastly. "I will giv' yer a pound of tobaccer," he whined in a conciliating voice, "so soon as I draw it from aft. I will—s'elp me . . ." Davis swung his arm backhanded and the head vanished. "I'll go," he said, "but you will pay for it." He walked unsteady but resolute to the door. "So I will," yelped Donkin, popping out behind him. "So I will—s'elp me . . . a pound . . . three bob they chawrge." Davis flung the door open. "You will pay my price . . . in fine weather," he shouted over his shoulder. One of the men unbut-

toned his wet coat rapidly, threw it at his head.
"Here, Taffy—take that, you thief!" "Thank you!"
he cried from the darkness above the swish of rolling
water. He could be heard splashing; a sea came on
board with a thump. "He's got his bath already,"
remarked a grim shellback. "Aye, aye!" grunted
others. Then, after a long silence, Wamibo made
strange noises. "Hallo, what's up with you?" said
some one grumpily. "He says he would have gone for
Davy," explained Archie, who was the Finn's interpreter generally. "I believe him!" cried voices.
. . . "Never mind, Dutchy . . . You'll
do, muddle-head. . . . Your turn will come
soon enough . . . You don't know when ye're
well off." They ceased, and all together turned their
faces to the door. Singleton stepped in, made two
paces, and stood swaying slightly. The sea hissed,
flowed roaring past the bows, and the forecastle trembled, full of deep murmurs; the lamp flared, swinging
like a pendulum. He looked with a dreamy and puzzled
stare, as though he could not distinguish the still men
from their restless shadows. There were awestruck
exclamations:—"Hallo, hallo" . . . "How does
it look outside now, Singleton?" Those who sat
on the hatch lifted their eyes in silence, and the next
oldest seaman in the ship (those two understood one
another, though they hardly exchanged three words in a
day) gazed up at his friend attentively for a moment,
then taking a short clay pipe out of his mouth, offered
it without a word. Singleton put out his arm towards
it, missed, staggered, and suddenly fell forward, crashing down, stiff and headlong like an uprooted tree.
There was a swift rush. Men pushed, crying:—
"He's done!" . . . "Turn him over!" . . .
"Stand clear there!" Under a crowd of startled faces

bending over him he lay on his back, staring upwards in a continuous and intolerable manner. In the breathless silence of a general consternation, he said in a grating murmur:—"I am all right," and clutched with his hands. They helped him up, He mumbled despondently:—"I am getting old . . . old."—"Not you," cried Belfast, with ready tact. Supported on all sides, he hung his head.—"Are you better?" they asked. He glared at them from under his eyebrows with large black eyes, spreading over his chest the bushy whiteness of a beard long and thick.—"Old! old!" he repeated sternly. Helped along, he reached his bunk. There was in it a slimy soft heap of something that smelt, as does at dead low water a muddy foreshore. It was his soaked straw bed. With a convulsive effort he pitched himself on it, and in the darkness of the narrow place could be heard growling angrily, like an irritated and savage animal uneasy in its den:—"Bit of breeze . . . small thing . . . can't stand up . . . old!" He slept at last, high-booted, sou'wester on head, and his oilskin clothes rustled, when with a deep sighing groan he turned over. Men conversed about him in quiet, concerned whispers. "This will break 'im up" . . . "Strong as a horse" . . . "Aye. But he ain't what he used to be." . . . In sad murmurs they gave him up. Yet at midnight he turned out to duty as if nothing had been the matter, and answered to his name with a mournful "Here!" He brooded alone more than ever, in an impenetrable silence and with a saddened face. For many years he had heard himself called "Old Singleton," and had serenely accepted the qualification, taking it as a tribute of respect due to a man who through half a century had measured his strength against the favours and the rages of the

sea. He had never given a thought to his mortal self.
He lived unscathed, as though he had been indestructible, surrendering to all the temptations, weathering
many gales. He had panted in sunshine, shivered in
the cold; suffered hunger, thirst, debauch; passed
through many trials—known all the furies. Old! It
seemed to him he was broken at last. And like a
man bound treacherously while he sleeps, he woke up
fettered by the long chain of disregarded years. He
had to take up at once the burden of all his existence,
and found it almost too heavy for his strength. Old!
He moved his arms, shook his head, felt his limbs.
Getting old . . . and then? He looked upon
the immortal sea with the awakened and groping perception of its heartless might; he saw it unchanged,
black and foaming under the eternal scrutiny of the
stars; he heard its impatient voice calling for him out of
a pitiless vastness full of unrest, of turmoil, and of
terror. He looked afar upon it, and he saw an immensity tormented and blind, moaning and furious, that
claimed all the days of his tenacious life, and, when
life was over, would claim the worn-out body of its
slave. . . .

This was the last of the breeze. It veered quickly,
changed to a black south-easter, and blew itself out,
giving the ship a famous shove to the northward into
the joyous sunshine of the trade. Rapid and white she
ran homewards in a straight path, under a blue sky
and upon the plain of a blue sea. She carried Singleton's completed wisdom, Donkin's delicate susceptibilities, and the conceited folly of us all. The hours
of ineffective turmoil were forgotten; the fear and anguish of these dark moments were never mentioned
in the glowing peace of fine days. Yet from that time

our life seemed to start afresh as though we had died
and had been resuscitated. All the first part of the
voyage, the Indian Ocean on the other side of the Cape,
all that was lost in a haze, like an ineradicable suspicion
of some previous existence. It had ended—then there
were blank hours: a livid blurr—and again we lived!
Singleton was possessed of sinister truth; Mr. Creighton
of a damaged leg; the cook of fame—and shamefully
abused the opportunities of his distinction. Donkin
had an added grievance. He went about repeating
with insistence:—"'E said 'e would brain me—did yer
'ear? They are goin' to murder us now for the least
little thing." We began at last to think it was rather
awful. And we were conceited! We boasted of our
pluck, of our capacity for work, of our energy. We
remembered honourable episodes: our devotion, our
indomitable perseverance—and were proud of them as
though they had been the outcome of our unaided
impulses. We remembered our danger, our toil—and
conveniently forgot our horrible scare. We decried
our officers—who had done nothing—and listened to
the fascinating Donkin. His care for our rights, his
disinterested concern for our dignity, were not discouraged by the invariable contumely of our words, by
the disdain of our looks. Our contempt for him was
unbounded—and we could not but listen with interest
to that consummate artist. He told us we were good
men—a "bloomin' condemned lot of good men."
Who thanked us? Who took any notice of our wrongs?
Didn't we lead a "dorg's loife for two poun' ten a
month?" Did we. think that miserable pay enough
to compensate us for the risk to our lives and for the
loss of our clothes? "We've lost every rag!" he cried.
He made us forget that he, at any rate, had lost nothing
of his own. The younger men listened, thinking—

this 'ere Donkin's a long-headed chap, though no kind of man, anyhow. The Scandinavians were frightened at his audacities; Wamibo did not understand; and the older seamen thoughtfully nodded their heads making the thin gold earrings glitter in the fleshy lobes of hairy ears. Severe, sunburnt faces were propped meditatively on tattooed forearms. Veined, brown fists held in their knotted grip the dirty white clay of smouldering pipes. They listened, impenetrable, broad-backed, with bent shoulders, and in grim silence. He talked with ardour, despised and irrefutable. His picturesque and filthy loquacity flowed like a troubled stream from a poisoned source. His beady little eyes danced, glancing right and left, ever on the watch for the approach of an officer. Sometimes Mr. Baker going forward to take a look at the head sheets would roll with his uncouth gait through the sudden stillness of the men; or Mr. Creighton limped along, smooth-faced, youthful, and more stern than ever, piercing our short silence with a keen glance of his clear eyes. Behind his back Donkin would begin again darting stealthy, sidelong looks.—"'Ere's one of 'em. Some of yer 'as made 'im fast that day. Much thanks yer got for it. Ain't 'ee a-drivin' yer wusse'n ever? . . . Let 'im slip overboard. . . . Vy not? It would 'ave been less trouble. Vy not?" He advanced confidentially, backed away with great effect; he whispered, he screamed, waved his miserable arms no thicker than pipe-stems—stretched his lean neck—spluttered—squinted. In the pauses of his impassioned orations the wind sighed quietly aloft, the calm sea unheeded murmured in a warning whisper along the ship's side. We abominated the creature and could not deny the luminous truth of his contentions. It was all so obvious. We were indubitably good men; our deserts were great and our pay small. Through our exertions we had saved the ship and the skipper would get the credit of it. What had he done? we wanted to know. Donkin asked:—"What 'ee could do without hus?" and we could not answer. We were oppressed by the injustice of the world, surprised to perceive how long we had lived under its burden without realising our unfortunate state, annoyed by the uneasy suspicion of our undiscerning stupidity. Donkin assured us it was all our "good 'eartedness," but we would not be consoled by such shallow sophistry. We were men enough to courageously admit to ourselves our intellectual shortcomings; though from that time we refrained from kicking him, tweaking his nose, or from accidentally knocking him about, which last, after we had weathered the Cape, had been rather a popular amusement. Davis ceased to talk at him provokingly about black eyes and flattened noses. Charley, much subdued since the gale, did not jeer at him. Knowles deferentially and with a crafty air propounded questions such as:—"Could we all have the same grub as the mates? Could we all stop ashore till we got it? What would be the next thing to try for if we got that?" He answered readily with contemptuous certitude; he strutted with assurance in clothes that were much too big for him as though he had tried to disguise himself. These were Jimmy's clothes mostly—though he would accept anything from anybody; but nobody, except Jimmy, had anything to spare. His devotion to Jimmy was unbounded. He was for ever dodging in the little cabin, ministering to Jimmy's wants, humouring his whims, submitting to his exacting peevishness, often laughing with him. Nothing could keep him away from the pious work of visiting the sick, especially when there was some heavy hauling to be done on deck. Mr. Baker had on two occasions jerked him out from there by the scruff of the neck to our inexpressible scandal. Was a sick chap to be left without attendance? Were we to be ill-used for attending a shipmate?—"What?" growled Mr. Baker, turning menacingly at the mutter, and the whole half-circle like one man stepped back a pace. "Set the topmast stunsail. Away aloft, Donkin, overhaul the gear," ordered the mate inflexibly. "Fetch the sail along; bend the down-haul clear. Bear a hand." Then, the sail set, he would go slowly aft and stand looking at the compass for a long time, careworn, pensive, and breathing hard as if stifled by the taint of unaccountable ill-will that pervaded the ship. "What's up amongst them?" he thought. "Can't make out this hanging back and growling. A good crowd, too, as they go nowadays." On deck the men exchanged bitter words, suggested by a silly exasperation against something unjust and irremediable that would not be denied, and would whisper into their ears long after Donkin had ceased speaking. Our little world went on its curved and unswerving path carrying a discontented and aspiring population. They found comfort of a gloomy kind in an interminable and conscientious analysis of their unappreciated worth; and inspired by Donkin's hopeful doctrines they dreamed enthusiastically of the time when every lonely ship would travel over a serene sea, manned by a wealthy and well-fed crew of satisfied skippers.

It looked as if it would be a long passage. The south-east trades, light and unsteady, were left behind; and then, on the equator and under a low grey sky, the ship, in close heat, floated upon a smooth sea that resembled a sheet of ground glass. Thunder squalls hung on the horizon, circled round the ship, far off and growling angrily, like a troop of wild beasts afraid to charge home. The invisible sun, sweeping above the upright masts, made on the clouds a blurred stain of rayless light, and a similar patch of faded radiance kept pace with it from east to west over the unglittering level of the waters. At night, through the impenetrable darkness of earth and heaven, broad sheets of flame waved noiselessly; and for half a second the becalmed craft stood out with its masts and rigging, with every sail and every rope distinct and black in the centre of a fiery outburst, like a charred ship enclosed in a globe of fire. And, again, for long hours she remained lost in a vast universe of night and silence where gentle sighs wandering here and there like forlorn souls, made the still sails flutter as in sudden fear, and the ripple of a beshrouded ocean whisper its compassion afar—in a voice mournful, immense, and faint. . . .

When the lamp was put out, and through the door thrown wide open, Jimmy, turning on his pillow, could see vanishing beyond the straight line of top-gallant rail, the quick, repeated visions of a fabulous world made up of leaping fire and sleeping water. The lightning gleamed in his big sad eyes that seemed in a red flicker to burn themselves out in his black face, and then he would lie blinded and invisible in the midst of an intense darkness. He could hear on the quiet deck soft footfalls, the breathing of some man lounging on the doorstep; the low creak of swaying masts; or the calm voice of the watch-officer reverberating aloft, hard and loud, amongst the unstirring sails. He listened with avidity, taking a rest in the attentive perception of the slightest sound from the fatiguing wanderings of his sleeplessness. He was cheered by the rattling of blocks, reassured by the stir and murmur of the watch, soothed by the slow yawn of some sleepy and weary seaman settling himself deliberately for a snooze on the planks. Life seemed an indestructible thing. It went on in darkness, in sunshine, in sleep; tireless, it hovered affectionately round the imposture of his ready death. It was bright, like the twisted flare of lightning, and more full of surprises than the dark night. It made him safe, and the calm of its overpowering darkness was as precious as its restless and dangerous light.

But in the evening, in the dog-watches, and even far into the first night-watch, a knot of men could always be seen congregated before Jimmy's cabin. They leaned on each side of the door peacefully interested and with crossed legs; they stood astride the doorstep discoursing, or sat in silent couples on his sea-chest; while against the bulwark along the spare topmast, three or four in a row stared meditatively; with their simple faces lit up by the projected glare of Jimmy's lamp. The little place, repainted white, had, in the night, the brilliance of a silver shrine where a black idol, reclining stiffly under a blanket, blinked its weary eyes and received our homage. Donkin officiated. He had the air of a demonstrator showing a phenomenon, a manifestation bizarre, simple, and meritorious that, to the beholders, should be a profound and an everlasting lesson. "Just look at 'im, 'ee knows what's what—never fear!" he exclaimed now and then, flourishing a hand hard and fleshless like the claw of a snipe. Jimmy, on his back, smiled with reserve and without moving a limb. He affected the languor of extreme weakness, so as to make it manifest to us that our delay in hauling him out from his horrible confinement, and then that night spent on the poop among our selfish neglect of his needs, had "done for him." He rather liked to talk about it, and of course we were always interested. He spoke spasmodically, in fast rushes with long pauses between, as a tipsy man walks. . . . "Cook had just given me a pannikin of hot coffee. . . . Slapped it down there, on my chest— banged the door to. . . . I felt a heavy roll coming; tried to save my coffee, burnt my fingers . . . and fell out of my bunk. . . . She went over so quick. . . . Water came in through the ventilator. . . . I couldn't move the door . . . dark as a grave . . . tried to scramble up into the upper berth. . . . Rats . . . a rat bit my finger as I got up. . . . I could hear him swimming below me. . . . I thought you would never come. . . . I thought you were all gone overboard . . . of course . . . Could hear nothing but the wind. . . . Then you came . . . to look for the corpse, I suppose. A little more and . . ."

"Man! But ye made a rare lot of noise in here," observed Archie, thoughtfully.

"You chaps kicked up such a confounded row above. . . . Enough to scare any one. . . . I didn't know what you were up to. . . . Bash in the blamed planks . . . my head. . . . Just what a silly, scary gang of fools would do. . . . Not much good to me anyhow. . . . Just as well . . . drown. . . . Pah."

He groaned, snapped his big white teeth, and gazed with scorn. Belfast lifted a pair of dolorous eyes, with a broken-hearted smile, clenched his fists stealthily; blue-eyed Archie caressed his red whiskers with a hesitating hand; the boatswain at the door stared a moment, and brusquely went away with a loud guffaw. Wamibo dreamed. . . . Donkin felt all over

his sterile chin for the few rare hairs, and said, triumphantly, with a sidelong glance at Jimmy:—"Look
at 'im! Wish I was 'arf has 'ealthy as 'ee is—I do."
He jerked a short thumb over his shoulder towards
the after end of the ship. "That's the blooming way
to do 'em!" he yelped, with forced heartiness. Jimmy
said:—"Don't be a dam' fool," in a pleasant voice.
Knowles, rubbing his shoulder against the doorpost,
remarked shrewdly:—"We can't all go an' be took sick
—it would be mutiny."—"Mutiny—gawn!" jeered
Donkin, "there's no bloomin' law against bein' sick."—
"There's six weeks' hard for refoosing dooty," argued
Knowles, " I mind I once seed in Cardiff the crew of an
overloaded ship—leastways she weren't overloaded,
only a fatherly old gentleman with a white beard and
an umbreller came along the quay and talked to the
hands. Said as how it was crool hard to be drownded
in winter just for the sake of a few pounds more for
the owner—he said. Nearly cried over them—he did;
and he had a square mainsail coat, and a gaff-topsail
hat too—all proper. So they chaps they said they
wouldn't go to be drownded in winter—depending
upon that 'ere Plimsoll man to see 'em through the
court. They thought to have a bloomin' lark and
two or three days' spree. And the beak giv' 'em six
weeks—coss the ship warn't overloaded. Anyways
they made it out in court that she wasn't. There wasn't
one overloaded ship in Penarth Dock at all. 'Pears
that old coon he was only on pay and allowance from
some kind people, under orders to look for overloaded
ships, and he couldn't see no further than the length of
his umbreller. Some of us in the boarding-house,
where I live when I'm looking for a ship in Cardiff,
stood by to duck that old weeping spunger in the dock.
We kept a good look-out, too—but he topped his boom

directly he was outside the court. . . . Yes.
They got six weeks' hard. . . ."

They listened, full of curiosity, nodding in the pauses
their rough pensive faces. Donkin opened his mouth
once or twice, but restrained himself. Jimmy lay still
with open eyes and not at all interested. A seaman
emitted the opinion that after a verdict of atrocious
partiality "the bloomin' beaks go an' drink at the
skipper's expense." Others assented. It was clear,
of course. Donkin said:—"Well, six weeks ain't much
trouble. You sleep all night in, reg'lar, in chokey.
Do it on my 'ead." "You are used to it ainch'ee,
Donkin?" asked somebody. Jimmy condescended to
laugh. It cheered up every one wonderfully. Knowles,
with surprising mental agility, shifted his ground.
"If we all went sick what would become of the ship?
eh?" He posed the problem and grinned all round.
—"Let 'er go to 'ell," sneered Donkin. "Damn 'er.
She ain't yourn."—"What? Just let her drift?"
insisted Knowles in a tone of unbelief.—"Aye! Drift,
an' be blowed," affirmed Donkin with fine recklessness. The other did not see it—meditated.—"The
stores would run out," he muttered, "and . . .
never get anywhere . . . and what about pay-
day?" he added with greater assurance.—"Jack likes
a good pay-day," exclaimed a listener on the doorstep.
"Aye, because then the girls put one arm round his
neck an' t'other in his pocket, and call him ducky.
Don't they, Jack?"—"Jack, you're a terror with the
gals."—"He takes three of 'em in tow to once, like one
of 'em Watkinses two-funnel tugs waddling away with
three schooners behind."—"Jack, you're a lame
scamp."—"Jack, tell us about that one with a blue
eye and a black eye. Do."—"There's plenty of girls
with one black eye along the Highway by . . ."

—"No, that's a speshul one—come Jack." Donkin looked severe and disgusted; Jimmy very bored; a grey-haired sea-dog shook his head slightly, smiling at the bowl of his pipe, discreetly amused. Knowles turned about bewildered; stammered first at one, then at another.—"No! . . . I never! . . . can't talk sensible sense midst you. . . . Always on the kid." He retired bashfully—muttering and pleased. They laughed hooting in the crude light, around Jimmy's bed, where on a white pillow his hollowed black face moved to and fro restlessly. A puff of wind came, made the flame of the lamp leap, and outside, high up, the sails fluttered, while near by the block of the foresheet struck a ringing blow on the iron bulwark. A voice far off cried, "Helm up!" another, more faint, answered, "Hard-up, sir!" They became silent—waited expectantly. The grey-haired seaman knocked his pipe on the doorstep and stood up. The ship leaned over gently and the sea seemed to wake up, murmuring drowsily. "Here's a little wind comin'," said some one very low. Jimmy turned over slowly to face the breeze. The voice in the night cried loud and commanding:—"Haul the spanker out." The group before the door vanished out of the light. They could be heard tramping aft while they repeated with varied intonations:—"Spanker out!" . . . "Out spanker, sir!" Donkin remained alone with Jimmy. There was a silence. Jimmy opened and shut his lips several times as if swallowing draughts of fresher air; Donkin moved the toes of his bare feet and looked at them thoughtfully.

"Ain't you going to give them a hand with the sail?" asked Jimmy.

"No. If six ov 'em ain't 'nough beef to set that blamed, rotten spanker, they ain't fit to live," an-

swered Donkin in a bored, far-away voice, as though he
had been talking from the bottom of a hole. Jimmy
considered the conical, fowl-like profile with a queer
kind of interest; he was leaning out of his bunk with
the calculating, uncertain expression of a man who re-
flects how best to lay hold of some strange creature
that looks as though it could sting or bite. But he
said only:—"The mate will miss you—and there will
be ructions."

Donkin got up to go. "I will do for 'im some dark
night; see if I don't," he said over his shoulder.

Jimmy went on quickly:—"You're like a poll-parrot,
like a screechin' poll-parrot." Donkin stopped and
cocked his head attentively on one side. His big ears
stood out, transparent and veined, resembling the thin
wings of a bat.

"Yuss?" he said, with his back towards Jimmy.

"Yes! Chatter out all you know—like . . .
like a dirty white cockatoo."

Donkin waited. He could hear the other's breathing, long and slow; the breathing of a man with a hun-
dredweight or so on the breastbone. Then he asked
calmly:—"What do I know?"

"What? . . . What I tell you . . . not
much. What do you want . . . to talk about
my health so . . ."

"It's a blooming imposyshun. A bloomin', stinkin',
first-class imposyshun—but it don't tyke me in. Not
it."

Jimmy kept still. Donkin put his hands in his
pockets, and in one slouching stride came up to the
bunk.

"I talk—what's the odds. They ain't men 'ere—
sheep they are. A driven lot of sheep. I 'old you
up . . . Vy not? You're well orf."

"I am . . . I don't say anything about that. . . ."

"Well. Let 'em see it. Let 'em larn what a man can do. I am a man, I know all about yer. . . ." Jimmy threw himself further away on the pillow; the other stretched out his skinny neck, jerked his bird face down at him as though pecking at the eyes. "I am a man. I've seen the inside of every chokey in the Colonies rather'n give up my rights. . . ."

"You are a jail-prop," said Jimmy, weakly.

"I am . . . an' proud of it, too. You! You 'aven't the bloomin' nerve—so you inventyd this 'ere dodge. . . ." He paused; then with marked afterthought accentuated slowly:—"Yer ain't sick—are yer?"

"No," said Jimmy, firmly. "Been out of sorts now and again this year," he mumbled with a sudden drop in his voice.

Donkin closed one eye, amicable and confidential. He whispered:—"Ye 'ave done this afore 'aven't chee?" Jimmy smiled—then as if unable to hold back he let himself go:—"Last ship—yes. I was out of sorts on the passage. See? It was easy. They paid me off in Calcutta, and the skipper made no bones about it either. . . . I got my money all right. Laid up fifty-eight days! The fools! O Lord! The fools! Paid right off." He laughed spasmodically. Donkin chimed in giggling. Then Jimmy coughed violently. "I am as well as ever," he said, as soon as he could draw breath.

Donkin made a derisive gesture. "In course," he said, profoundly, "any one can see that."—"They don't," said Jimmy, gasping like a fish.—"They would swallow any yarn," affirmed Donkin.—"Don't you let on too much," admonished Jimmy in an exhausted voice.—"Your little gyme? Eh?" commented Donkin, jovially. Then with sudden disgust: "Yer all for yerself, s'long as ye're right. . . ."

So charged with egoism James Wait pulled the blanket up to his chin and lay still for awhile. His heavy lips protruded in an everlasting black pout. "Why are you so hot on making trouble?" he asked without much interest.

"'Cos it's a bloomin' shayme. We are put upon . . . bad food, bad pay . . . I want us to kick up a bloomin' row; a blamed 'owling row that would make 'em remember! Knocking people about . . . brain us . . . indeed! Ain't we men?" His altruistic indignation blazed. Then he said calmly:—"I've been airing yer clothes."— "All right," said Jimmy, languidly, "bring them in."— "Giv' us the key of your chest, I'll put 'em away for yer," said Donkin with friendly eagerness.—"Bring 'em in, I will put them away myself," answered James Wait with severity. Donkin looked down, muttering. . . . "What d'you say? What d'you say?" inquired Wait anxiously.—"Nothink. The night's dry, let 'em 'ang out till the morning," said Donkin, in a strangely trembling voice, as though restraining laughter or rage. Jimmy seemed satisfied.—"Give me a little water for the night in my mug—there," he said. Donkin took a stride over the doorstep.—"Git it yerself," he replied in a surly tone. "You can do it, unless you *are* sick."—"Of course I can do it," said Wait, "only . . . "—"Well, then, do it," said Donkin, viciously, "if yer can look after yer clothes, yer can look after yerself." He went on deck without a look back.

Jimmy reached out for the mug. Not a drop. He put it back gently with a faint sigh—and closed his

eyes. He thought:—That lunatic Belfast will bring
me some water if I ask. Fool. I am very thirsty.
. . . It was very hot in the cabin, and it seemed
to turn slowly round, detach itself from the ship, and
swing out smoothly into a luminous, arid space where
a black sun shone, spinning very fast. A place without
any water! No water! A policeman with the face
of Donkin drank a glass of beer by the side of an empty
well, and flew away flapping vigorously. A ship whose
mastheads protruded through the sky and could not
be seen, was discharging grain, and the wind whirled
the dry husks in spirals along the quay of a dock with
no water in it. He whirled along with the husks—very
tired and light. All his inside was gone. He felt
lighter than the husks—and more dry. He expanded
his hollow chest. The air streamed in carrying away
in its rush a lot of strange things that resembled houses,
trees, people, lamp-posts. . . . No more! There
was no more air—and he had not finished drawing his
long breath. But he was in jail! They were locking
him up. A door slammed. They turned the key
twice, flung a bucket of water over him—Phoo! What
for?

He opened his eyes, thinking the fall had been very
heavy for an empty man—empty—empty. He was
in his cabin. Ah! All right! His face was streaming
with perspiration, his arms heavier than lead. He saw
the cook standing in the doorway, a brass key in one
hand and a bright tin hook-pot in the other.

"I have locked up the galley for the night," said the
cook, beaming benevolently. "Eight-bells just gone.
I brought you a pot of cold tea for your night's drinking,
Jimmy. I sweetened it with some white cabin sugar,
too. Well—it won't break the ship."

He came in, hung the pot on the edge of the bunk,

asked perfunctorily, "How goes it?" and sat down on
the box.—"H'm," grunted Wait, inhospitably. The
cook wiped his face with a dirty cotton rag, which,
afterwards, he tied round his neck.—"That's how them
firemen do in steamboats," he said, serenely, and much
pleased with himself. "My work is as heavy as theirs
—I'm thinking—and longer hours. Did you ever see
them down the stokehold? Like fiends they look—
firing—firing—firing—down there."

He pointed his forefinger at the deck. Some gloomy
thought darkened his shining face, fleeting, like the
shadow of a travelling cloud over the light of a peaceful
sea. The relieved watch tramped noisily forward,
passing in a body across the sheen of the doorway.
Some one cried, "Good-night!" Belfast stopped for
a moment and looked at Jimmy, quivering and speechless with repressed emotion. He gave the cook a glance
charged with dismal foreboding, and vanished. The
cook cleared his throat. Jimmy stared upwards and
kept as still as a man in hiding.

The night was clear, with a gentle breeze. Above
the mastheads the resplendent curve of the Milky Way
spanned the sky like a triumphal arch of eternal light,
thrown over the dark pathway of the earth. On the
forecastle head a man whistled with loud precision a
lively jig, while another could be heard faintly, shuffling
and stamping in time. There came from forward a
confused murmur of voices, laughter—snatches of song.
The cook shook his head, glanced obliquely at Jimmy,
and began to mutter. "Aye. Dance and sing. That's
all they think of. I am surprised that Providence don't
get tired. . . . They forget the day that's sure
to come . . . but you. . . . "

Jimmy drank a gulp of tea, hurriedly, as though he
had stolen it, and shrank under his blanket, edging

away towards the bulkhead. The cook got up, closed the door, then sat down again and said distinctly:—

"Whenever I poke my galley fire I think of you chaps —swearing, stealing, lying, and worse—as if there was no such thing as another world. . . . Not bad fellows, either, in a way," he conceded, slowly; then, after a pause of regretful musing, he went on in a resigned tone:—"Well, well. They will have a hot time of it. Hot! Did I say? The furnaces of one of them White Star boats ain't nothing to it."

He kept very quiet for a while. There was a great stir in his brain; an addled vision of bright outlines; an exciting row of rousing songs and groans of pain. He suffered, enjoyed, admired, approved. He was delighted, frightened, exalted—as on that evening (the only time in his life—twenty-seven years ago; he loved to recall the number of years) when as a young man he had—through keeping bad company—become intoxicated in an East-end music-hall. A tide of sudden feeling swept him clean out of his body. He soared. He contemplated the secret of the hereafter. It commended itself to him. It was excellent; he loved it, himself, all hands, and Jimmy. His heart overflowed with tenderness, with comprehension, with the desire to meddle, with anxiety for the soul of that black man, with the pride of possessed eternity, with the feeling of might. Snatch him up in his arms and pitch him right into the middle of salvation. . . . The black soul—blacker—body—rot—Devil. No! Talk— strength—Samson. . . . There was a great din as of cymbals in his ears; he flashed through an ecstatic jumble of shining faces, lilies, prayer-books, unearthly joy, white shirts, gold harps, black coats, wings. He saw flowing garments, clean shaved faces, a sea of light—a lake of pitch. There were sweet scents, a smell of sulphur—red tongues of flame licking a white mist. An awesome voice thundered! . . . It lasted three seconds.

"Jimmy!" he cried in an inspired tone. Then he hesitated. A spark of human pity glimmered yet through the infernal fog of his supreme conceit.

"What?" said James Wait, unwillingly. There was a silence. He turned his head just the least bit, and stole a cautious glance. The cook's lips moved without a sound; his face was rapt, his eyes turned up. He seemed to be mentally imploring deck beams, the brass hook of the lamp, two cockroaches.

"Look here," said Wait, "I want to go to sleep. I I think I could."

"This is no time for sleep!" exclaimed the cook, very loud. He had prayerfully divested himself of the last vestige of his humanity. He was a voice—a fleshless and sublime thing, as on that memorable night —the night when he went walking over the sea to make coffee for perishing sinners. "This is no time for sleeping," he repeated with exaltation. "*I* can't sleep."

"Don't care damn," said Wait, with factitious energy. "I can. Go an' turn in."

"Swear . . . in the very jaws! . . . In the very jaws! Don't you see the everlasting fire . . . don't you feel it? Blind, chockfull of sin! Repent, repent! I can't bear to think of you. I hear the call to save you. Night and day. Jimmy, let me save you!" The words of entreaty and menace broke out of him in a roaring torrent. The cockroaches ran away. Jimmy perspired, wriggling stealthily under his blanket. The cook yelled. . . . "Your days are numbered! . . . "—"Get out of this," boomed Wait, courageously.—"Pray with me! . . . "—"I won't! . . . The little cabin was as hot as an oven. It contained an immensity of fear and pain; an atmosphere of shrieks and moans; prayers vociferated like blasphemies and whispered curses. Outside, the men called by Charley, who informed them in tones of delight that there was a holy row going on in Jimmy's place, crowded before the closed door, too startled to open it. All hands were there. The watch below had jumped out on deck in their shirts, as after a collision. Men running up, asked:—"What is it?" Others said:—"Listen!" The muffled screaming went on:—"On your knees! On your knees!"—"Shut up!"—"Never! You are delivered into my hands. . . . Your life has been saved. . . . Purpose. . . . Mercy. . . . Repent."—"You are a crazy fool! . . . "—"Account of you . . . you . . . Never sleep in this world, if I . . . "—"Leave off."—"No! . . . stokehold . . . only think! . . . " Then an impassioned screeching babble where words pattered like hail.—"No!" shouted Wait.—"Yes. You are! . . . No help. . . . Everybody says so."—"You lie!"—"I see you dying this minnyt . . . before my eyes . . . as good as dead already."—"Help!" shouted Jimmy, piercingly.—"Not in this valley. . . . look upwards," howled the other.—"Go away! Murder! Help!" clamoured Jimmy. His voice broke. There were moanings, low mutters, a few sobs.

"What's the matter now?" said a seldom-heard voice.—"Fall back, men! Fall back, there!" repeated Mr. Creighton, sternly, pushing through.—"Here's the old man," whispered some.—"The cook's in there, sir," exclaimed several, backing away. The door clattered open; a broad stream of light darted out on wondering faces; a warm whiff of vitiated air passed. The two

mates towered head and shoulders above the spare,
grey-haired man who stood revealed between them,
in shabby clothes, stiff and angular, like a small carved
figure, and with a thin, composed face. The cook got
up from his knees. Jimmy sat high in the bunk, clasping his drawn-up legs. The tassel of the blue night-cap
almost imperceptibly trembled over his knees. They
gazed astonished at his long, curved back, while the
white corner of one eye gleamed blindly at them. He
was afraid to turn his head, he shrank within himself;
and there was an aspect astounding and animal-like
in the perfection of his expectant immobility. A thing
of instinct—the unthinking stillness of a scared brute.
"What are you doing here?" asked Mr. Baker,
sharply.—"My duty," said the cook, with ardour.—
"Your . . . what?" began the mate. Captain
Allistoun touched his arm lightly.—"I know his caper,"
he said, in a low voice. "Come out of that, Podmore,"
he ordered, aloud.

The cook wrung his hands, shook his fists above his
head, and his arms dropped as if too heavy. For a
moment he stood distracted and speechless.—"Never,"
he stammered, "I . . . he . . . I."—
"What—do—you—say?" pronounced Captain Allistoun. "Come out at once—or . . . "—"I am
going," said the cook, with a hasty and sombre resignation. He strode over the doorstep firmly—hesitated
—made a few steps. They looked at him in silence.—
"I make you responsible!" he cried, desperately, turning half round. "That man is dying. I make you
. . . "—"You there yet?" called the master in a
threatening tone.—"No, sir," he exclaimed, hurriedly,
in a startled voice. The boatswain led him away by
the arm; some one laughed; Jimmy lifted his head for a
stealthy glance, and in one unexpected leap sprang out

of his bunk; Mr. Baker made a clever catch and felt him very limp in his arms; the group at the door grunted with surprise.—"He lies," gasped Wait, "he talked about black devils—he is a devil—a white devil—I am all right." He stiffened himself, and Mr. Baker, experimentally, let him go. He staggered a pace or two; Captain Allistoun watched him with a quiet and penetrating gaze; Belfast ran to his support. He did not appear to be aware of any one near him; he stood silent for a moment, battling single-handed with a legion of nameless terrors, amidst the eager looks of excited men who watched him far off, utterly alone in the impenetrable solitude of his fear. The sea gurgled through the scuppers as the ship heeled over to a short puff of wind.

"Keep him away from me," said James Wait at last in his fine baritone voice, and leaning with all his weight on Belfast's neck. "I've been better this last week . . . I am well . . . I was going back to duty . . . to-morrow—now if you like—Captain." Belfast hitched his shoulders to keep him upright.

"No," said the master, looking at him, fixedly.

Under Jimmy's armpit Belfast's red face moved uneasily. A row of eyes gleaming stared on the edge of light. They pushed one another with elbows, turned their heads, whispered. Wait let his chin fall on his breast and, with lowered eyelids, looked round in a suspicious manner.

"Why not?" cried a voice from the shadows, "the man's all right, sir."

"I am all right," said Wait, with eagerness. "Been sick . . . better . . . turn-to now." He sighed.—"Howly Mother!" exclaimed Belfast with a heave of the shoulders, "stand up, Jimmy."—

"Keep away from me then," said Wait, giving Belfast a petulant push, and reeling fetched against the door-post. His cheekbones glistened as though they had been varnished. He snatched off his night-cap, wiped his perspiring face with it, flung it on the deck. "I am coming out," he declared without stirring.

"No. You don't," said the master, curtly. Bare feet shuffled, disapproving voices murmured all round; he went on as if he had not heard:—"You have been skulking nearly all the passage and now you want to come out. You think you are near enough to the pay-table now. Smell the shore, hey?"

"I've been sick . . . now—better," mumbled Wait, glaring in the light.—"You have been shamming sick," retorted Captain Allistoun with severity; "Why . . ." he hesitated for less than half a second. "Why, anybody can see that. There's nothing the matter with you, but you choose to lie-up to please yourself—and now you shall lie-up to please me. Mr. Baker, my orders are that this man is not to be allowed on deck to the end of the passage."

There were exclamations of surprise, triumph, indignation. The dark group of men swung across the light. "What for?" "Told you so . . ." "Bloomin' shame . . ."—"We've got to say somethink about that," screeched Donkin from the rear.—"Never mind, Jim—we will see you righted," cried several together. An elderly seaman stepped to the front. "D'ye mean to say, sir," he asked, ominously, "that a sick chap ain't allowed to get well in this 'ere hooker?" Behind him Donkin whispered excitedly amongst a staring crowd where no one spared him a glance, but Captain Allistoun shook a forefinger at the angry bronzed face of the speaker.—"You— you hold your tongue," he said, warningly.—"This

isn't the way," clamoured two or three younger men.—
"Are we bloomin' masheens?" inquired Donkin in a
piercing tone, and dived under the elbows of the front
rank.—"Soon show 'im we ain't boys . . . "—
"The man's a man if he is black."—"We ain't goin'
to work this bloomin' ship shorthanded if Snowball's
all right . . . "—"He says he is."—"Well then,
strike, boys, strike!"—"That's the bloomin' ticket."
Captain Allistoun said sharply to the second mate:
"Keep quiet, Mr. Creighton," and stood composed in
the tumult, listening with profound attention to mixed
growls and screeches, to every exclamation and every
curse of the sudden outbreak. Somebody slammed the
cabin door to with a kick; the darkness full of menacing
mutters leaped with a short clatter over the streak of
light, and the men became gesticulating shadows that
growled, hissed, laughed excitedly. Mr. Baker whispered:—"Get away from them, sir." The big shape of
Mr. Creighton hovered silently about the slight figure
of the master.—"We have been hymposed upon all this
voyage," said a gruff voice, "but this 'ere fancy takes
the cake."—"That man is a shipmate."—"Are we
bloomin' kids?"—"The port watch will refuse duty."
Charley carried away by his feeling whistled shrilly,
then yelped:—"Giv' us our Jimmy!" This seemed to
cause a variation in the disturbance. There was a
fresh burst of squabbling uproar. A lot of quarrels
were set going at once.—"Yes."—"No."—"Never been
sick."—"Go for them to once."—"Shut yer mouth,
youngster—this is men's work."—"Is it?" muttered
Captain Allistoun, bitterly. Mr. Baker grunted:
"Ough! They're gone silly. They've been simmering
for the last month."—"I did notice," said the master.
—"They have started a row amongst themselves now,"
said Mr. Creighton with disdain, "better get aft, sir.

We will soothe them.—"Keep your temper, Creighton," said the master. And the three men began to
move slowly towards the cabin door.

In the shadows of the fore rigging a dark mass
stamped, eddied, advanced, retreated. There were
words of reproach, encouragement, unbelief, execration.
The elder seamen, bewildered and angry, growled their
determination to go through with something or other;
but the younger school of advanced thought exposed
their and Jimmy's wrongs with confused shouts,
arguing amongst themselves. They clustered round
that moribund carcass, the fit emblem of their aspirations, and encouraging one another they swayed, they
tramped on one spot, shouting that they would not be
"put upon." Inside the cabin, Belfast, helping Jimmy
into his bunk, twitched all over in his desire not to miss
all the row, and with difficulty restrained the tears of
his facile emotion. James Wait, flat on his back under
the blanket, gasped complaints.—"We will back you
up, never fear," assured Belfast, busy about his feet.—
"I'll come out to-morrow morning——take my chance
——you fellows must——" mumbled Wait, "I come out
to-morrow——skipper or no skipper." He lifted one arm
with great difficulty, passed the hand over his face;
"Don't you let that cook . . . " he breathed out.
—"No, no," said Belfast, turning his back on the bunk,
"I will put a head on him if he comes near you."—"I
will smash his mug!" exclaimed faintly Wait, enraged
and weak; "I don't want to kill a man, but . . ."
He panted fast like a dog after a run in sunshine. Some
one just outside the door shouted, "He's as fit as any
ov us!" Belfast put his hand on the door-handle.—
"Here!" called James Wait, hurriedly, and in such a clear
voice that the other spun round with a start. James
Wait, stretched out black and deathlike in the dazzling

light, turned his head on the pillow. His eyes stared at Belfast, appealing and impudent. "I am rather weak from lying-up so long," he said, distinctly. Belfast nodded. "Getting quite well now," insisted Wait.— "Yes. I noticed you getting better this . . . last month," said Belfast, looking down. "Hallo! What's this?" he shouted and ran out.

He was flattened directly against the side of the house by two men who lurched against him. A lot of disputes seemed to be going on all round. He got clear and saw three indistinct figures standing alone in the fainter darkness under the arched foot of the mainsail, that rose above their heads like a convex wall of a high edifice. Donkin hissed:—"Go for them . . . it's dark!" The crowd took a short run aft in a body— then there was a check. Donkin, agile and thin, flitted past with his right arm going like a windmill—and then stood still suddenly with his arm pointing rigidly above his head. The hurtling flight of some heavy object was heard; it passed between the heads of the two mates, bounded heavily along the deck, struck the after hatch with a ponderous and deadened blow. The bulky shape of Mr. Baker grew distinct. "Come to your senses, men!" he cried, advancing at the arrested crowd. "Come back, Mr. Baker!" called the master's quiet voice. He obeyed unwillingly. There was a minute of silence, then a deafening hubbub arose. Above it Archie was heard energetically:—"If ye do oot ageen I wull tell!" There were shouts. "Don't!" "Drop it!"—"We ain't that kind!" The black cluster of human forms reeled against the bulwark, back again towards the house. Ringbolts rang under stumbling feet.—"Drop it!" "Let me!"—"No!"—"Curse you . . . hah!" Then sounds as of some one's face being slapped; a piece of iron fell on the deck; a short scuffle, and some one's shadowy body scuttled rapidly across the main hatch before the shadow of a kick. A raging voice sobbed out a torrent of filthy language . . . —"Throwing things—good God!" grunted Mr. Baker in dismay.—"That was meant for me," said the master, quietly; "I felt the wind of that thing; what was it—an iron belaying-pin?"—"By Jove!" muttered Mr. Creighton. The confused voices of men talking amidships mingled with the wash of the sea, ascended between the silent and distended sails— seemed to flow away into the night, further than the horizon, higher than the sky. The stars burned steadily over the inclined mastheads. Trails of light lay on the water, broke before the advancing hull, and, after she had passed, trembled for a long time as if in awe of the murmuring sea.

Meantime the helmsman, anxious to know what the row was about, had let go the wheel, and, bent double, ran with long, stealthy footsteps to the break of the poop. The *Narcissus*, left to herself, came up gently to the wind without any one being aware of it. She gave a slight roll, and the sleeping sails woke suddenly, coming all together with a mighty flap against the masts, then filled again one after another in a quick succession of loud reports that ran down the lofty spars, till the collapsed mainsail flew out last with a violent jerk. The ship trembled from trucks to keel; the sails kept on rattling like a discharge of musketry; the chain sheets and loose shackles jingled aloft in a thin peal; the gin blocks groaned. It was as if an invisible hand had given the ship an angry shake to recall the men that peopled her decks to the sense of reality, vigilance, and duty.—"Helm up!" cried the master, sharply. "Run aft, Mr. Creighton, and see what that fool there is up to."—"Flatten in the head sheets. Stand by the

weather fore-braces," growled Mr. Baker. Startled
men ran swiftly repeating the orders. The watch below, abandoned all at once by the watch on deck,
drifted towards the forecastle in twos and threes,
arguing noisily as they went—"We shall see to-morrow!" cried a loud voice, as if to cover with a menacing
hint an inglorious retreat. And then only orders were
heard, the falling of heavy coils of rope, the rattling of
blocks. Singleton's white head flitted here and there
in the night, high above the deck, like the ghost of a
bird.—"Going off, sir!" shouted Mr. Creighton from
aft.—"Full again."—"All right . . . "—"Ease
off the head sheets. That will do the braces. Coil
the ropes up," grunted Mr. Baker, bustling about.

Gradually the tramping noises, the confused sound of
voices, died out, and the officers, coming together on the
poop, discussed the events. Mr. Baker was bewildered
and grunted; Mr. Creighton was calmly furious; but
Captain Allistoun was composed and thoughtful. He
listened to Mr. Baker's growling argumentation, to
Creighton's interjected and severe remarks, while looking down on the deck he weighed in his hand the iron
belaying-pin—that a moment ago had just missed his
head—as if it had been the only tangible fact of the
whole transaction. He was one of those commanders
who speak little, seem to hear nothing, look at no one—
and know everything, hear every whisper, see every
fleeting shadow of their ship's life. His two big officers
towered above his lean, short figure; they talked over
his head; they were dismayed, surprised, and angry,
while between them the little quiet man seemed to have
found his taciturn serenity in the profound depths of a
larger experience. Lights were burning in the forecastle; now and then a loud gust of babbling chatter
came from forward, swept over the decks, and became

faint, as if the unconscious ship, gliding gently through
the great peace of the sea, had left behind and for ever
the foolish noise of turbulent mankind. But it was renewed again and again. Gesticulating arms, profiles
of heads with open mouths appeared for a moment in
the illuminated squares of doorways; black fists darted
—withdrew . . . "Yes. It was most damn-
able to have such an unprovoked row sprung on one,"
assented the master. . . . A tumult of yells rose
in the light, abruptly ceased. . . . He didn't
think there would be any further trouble just then.
. . . A bell was struck aft, another, forward, answered in a deeper tone, and the clamour of ringing
metal spread round the ship in a circle of wide vibrations that ebbed away into the immeasurable night of an
empty sea. . . . Didn't he know them! Didn't
he! In past years. Better men, too. Real men to
stand by one in a tight place. Worse than devils too
sometimes—downright, horned devils. Pah! This—
nothing. A miss as good as a mile. . . . The
wheel was being relieved in the usual way.—"Full
and by," said, very loud, the man going off.—"Full
and by," repeated the other, catching hold of the spokes.
—"This head wind is my trouble," exclaimed the
master, stamping his foot in sudden anger; "head
wind! all the rest is nothing." He was calm again in a
moment. "Keep them on the move to-night, gentlemen; just to let them feel we've got hold all the time—
quietly, you know. Mind you keep your hands off
them, Creighton. To-morrow I will talk to them like a
Dutch Uncle. A crazy crowd of tinkers! Yes, tinkers!
I could count the real sailors amongst them on the
fingers of one hand. Nothing will do but a row—if—
you—please." He paused. "Did you think I had
gone wrong there, Mr. Baker?" He tapped his fore-

head, laughed short. "When I saw him standing there, three parts dead and so scared—black amongst that gaping lot—no grit to face what's coming to us all—the notion came to me all at once, before I could think. Sorry for him—like you would be for a sick brute. If ever creature was in a mortal funk to die! . . . I thought I would let him go out in his own way. Kind of impulse. It never came into my head, those fools. . . . H'm! Stand to it now—of course." He stuck the belaying-pin in his pocket, seemed ashamed of himself, then sharply:—"If you see Podmore at his tricks again tell him I will have him put under the pump. Had to do it once before. The fellow breaks out like that now and then. Good cook tho'." He walked away quickly, came back to the companion. The two mates followed him through the starlight with amazed eyes. He went down three steps, and changing his tone, spoke with his head near the deck:—"I shan't turn in to-night, in case of anything; just call out if . . . Did you see the eyes of that sick nigger, Mr. Baker? I fancied he begged me for something. What? Past all help. One lone black beggar amongst the lot of us, and he seemed to look through me into the very hell. Fancy, this wretched Podmore! Well, let him die in peace. I am master here after all. Let him be. He might have been half a man once . . . Keep a good look-out." He disappeared down below, leaving his mates facing one another, and more impressed than if they had seen a stone image shed a miraculous tear of compassion over the incertitudes of life and death. . . .

In the blue mist spreading from twisted threads that stood upright in the bowls of pipes, the forecastle appeared as vast as a hall. Between the beams a heavy cloud stagnated; and the lamps surrounded by halos

burned each at the core of a purple glow in two lifeless flames without rays. Wreaths drifted in denser
wisps. Men sprawled about on the deck, sat in negligent poses, or, bending a knee, drooped with one
shoulder against a bulkhead. Lips moved, eyes
flashed, waving arms made sudden eddies in the smoke.
The murmur of voices seemed to pile itself higher and
higher as if unable to run out quick enough through the
narrow doors. The watch below in their shirts, and
striding on long white legs, resembled raving somnam-
bulists; while now and then one of the watch on deck
would rush in, looking strangely over-dressed, listen a
moment, fling a rapid sentence into the noise and run
out again; but a few remained near the door, fascinated,
and with one ear turned to the deck. "Stick together,
boys," roared Davis. Belfast tried to make himself
heard. Knowles grinned in a slow, dazed way. A
short fellow with a thick clipped beard kept on yelling
periodically:—"Who's afeard? Who's afeard?" Another one jumped up, excited, with blazing eyes, sent
out a string of unattached curses and sat down quietly.
Two men discussed familiarly, striking one another's
breast in turn, to clinch arguments. Three others,
with their heads in a bunch, spoke all together with a
confidential air, and at the top of their voices. It was
a stormy chaos of speech where intelligible fragments
tossing, struck the ear. One could hear:—"In the last
ship"—"Who cares? Try it on any one of us if——."
"Knock under"—"Not a hand's turn"—"He says he
is all right"—"I always thought"—"Never mind.
. . ." Donkin, crouching all in a heap against the
bowsprit, hunched his shoulderblades as high as his ears,
and hanging a peaked nose, resembled a sick vulture
with ruffled plumes. Belfast, straddling his legs, had a
face red with yelling, and with arms thrown up, figured

a Maltese cross. The two Scandinavians, in a corner, had the dumbfounded and distracted aspect of men gazing at a cataclysm. And, beyond the light, Singleton stood in the smoke, monumental, indistinct, with his head touching the beam; like a statue of heroic size in the gloom of a crypt.

He stepped forward, impassive and big. The noise subsided like a broken wave: but Belfast cried once more with uplifted arms:—"The man is dying I tell ye!" then sat down suddenly on the hatch and took his head between his hands. All looked at Singleton, gazing upwards from the deck, staring out of dark corners, or turning their heads with curious glances. They were expectant and appeased as if that old man, who looked at no one, had possessed the secret of their uneasy indignations and desires, a sharper vision, a clearer knowledge. And indeed standing there amongst them, he had the uninterested appearance of one who had seen multitudes of ships, had listened many times to voices such as theirs, had already seen all that could happen on the wide seas. They heard his voice rumble in his broad chest as though the words had been rolling towards them out of a rugged past. "What do you want to do?" he asked. No one answered. Only Knowles muttered—"Aye, aye," and somebody said low:—"It's a bloomin' shame." He waited, made a contemptuous gesture.—"I have seen rows aboard ship before some of you were born," he said, slowly, "for something or nothing; but never for such a thing." —"The man is dying, I tell ye," repeated Belfast, woefully, sitting at Singleton's feet.—"And a black fellow, too," went on the old seaman, "I have seen them die like flies." He stopped, thoughtful, as if trying to recollect gruesome things, details of horrors, hecatombs of niggers. They looked at him fascinated. He was old enough to remember slavers, bloody mutinies, pirates perhaps; who could tell through what violences and terrors he had lived! What would he say? He said:—"You can't help him; die he must." He made another pause. His moustache and beard stirred. He chewed words, mumbled behind tangled white hairs; incomprehensible and exciting, like an oracle behind a veil. . . .—"Stop ashore——sick.——Instead—— bringing all this head wind. Afraid. The sea will have her own.——Die in sight of land. Always so. They know it ——long passage——more days, more dollars.——You keep quiet.——What do you want? Can't help him." He seemed to wake up from a dream. "You can't help yourselves," he said, austerely, "Skipper's no fool. He has something in his mind. Look out—I say! I know 'em!" With eyes fixed in front he turned his head from right to left, from left to right, as if inspecting a long row of astute skippers.—"'Ee said 'ee would brain me!" cried Donkin in a heartrending tone. Singleton peered downwards with puzzled attention, as though he couldn't find him.—"Damn you!" he said, vaguely, giving it up. He radiated unspeakable wisdom, hard unconcern, the chilling air of resignation. Round him all the listeners felt themselves somehow completely enlightened by their disappointment, and mute, they lolled about with the careless ease of men who can discern perfectly the irremediable aspect of their existence. He, profound and unconscious, waved his arm once, and strode out on deck without another word.

Belfast was lost in a round-eyed meditation. One or two vaulted heavily into upper berths, and, once there, sighed; others dived head first inside lower bunks —swift, and turning round instantly upon themselves, like animals going into lairs. The grating of a knife

scraping burnt clay was heard. Knowles grinned no
more. Davies said, in a tone of ardent conviction:—
"Then our skipper's looney." Archie muttered:—
"My faith! we haven't heard the last of it yet!"
Four bells were struck.—"Half our watch below
gone!" cried Knowles in alarm, then reflected. "Well,
two hours' sleep is something towards a rest," he
observed, consolingly. Some already pretended to
slumber; and Charley, sound asleep, suddenly said a
few slurred words in an arbitrary, blank voice.—
"This blamed boy has worrums!" commented Knowles
from under a blanket, in a learned manner. Belfast
got up and approached Archie's berth.—"We pulled
him out," he whispered, sadly.—"What?" said the
other, with sleepy discontent.—"And now we will have
to chuck him overboard," went on Belfast, whose lower
lip trembled.—"Chuck what?" asked Archie.—
"Poor Jimmy," breathed out Belfast.—"He be
blowed!" said Archie with untruthful brutality, and
sat up in his bunk; "It's all through him. If it hadn't
been for me, there would have been murder on board
this ship!"—"'Tain't his fault, is it?" argued Belfast,
in a murmur; "I've put him to bed . . . an' he
ain't no heavier than an empty beef-cask," he added,
with tears in his eyes. Archie looked at him steadily,
then turned his nose to the ship's side with determination. Belfast wandered about as though he had lost
his way in the dim forecastle, and nearly fell over
Donkin. He contemplated him from on high for a
while. "Ain't ye going to turn in?" he asked. Donkin looked up hopelessly.—"That black 'earted Scotch
son of a thief kicked me!" he whispered from the floor,
in a tone of utter desolation.—"And a good job, too!"
said Belfast, still very depressed; "You were as near
hanging as damn-it to-night, sonny. Don't you play

any of your murthering games around my Jimmy!
You haven't pulled him out. You just mind! 'Cos if
I start to kick you"—he brightened up a bit—"if I
start to kick you, it will be Yankee fashion—to break
something!" He tapped lightly with his knuckles the
top of the bowed head. "You moind that, my bhoy!"
he concluded, cheerily. Donkin let it pass.—"Will
they split on me?" he asked, with pained anxiety.—
"Who—split?" hissed Belfast, coming back a step.
"I would split your nose this minyt if I hadn't Jimmy
to look after! Who d'ye think we are?" Donkin
rose and watched Belfast's back lurch through the doorway. On all sides invisible men slept, breathing
calmly. He seemed to draw courage and fury from the
peace around him. Venomous and thin-faced, he
glared from the ample misfit of borrowed clothes as if
looking for something he could smash. His heart
leaped wildly in his narrow chest. They slept! He
wanted to wring necks, gouge eyes, spit on faces. He
shook a dirty pair of meagre fists at the smoking
lights. "Ye're no men!" he cried, in a deadened tone.
No one moved. "Yer 'aven't the pluck of a mouse!"
His voice rose to a husky screech. Wamibo darted
out a dishevelled head, and looked at him wildly.
"Ye're sweepings ov ships! I 'ope you will all rot
before you die!" Wamibo blinked, uncomprehending
but interested. Donkin sat down heavily; he blew with
force through quivering nostrils, he ground and snapped his teeth, and, with the chin pressed hard against
the breast, he seemed busy gnawing his way through it,
as if to get at the heart within. . . .

In the morning the ship, beginning another day of
her wandering life, had an aspect of sumptuous freshness, like the spring-time of the earth. The washed

decks glistened in a long clear stretch; the oblique sun-light struck the yellow brasses in dazzling splashes, darted over the polished rods in lines of gold, and the single drops of salt water forgotten here and there along the rail were as limpid as drops of dew, and sparkled more than scattered diamonds. The sails slept, hushed by a gentle breeze. The sun, rising lonely and splendid in the blue sky, saw a solitary ship gliding close-hauled on the blue sea.

The men pressed three deep abreast of the mainmast and opposite the cabin-door. They shuffled, pushed, had an irresolute mien and stolid faces. At every slight movement Knowles lurched heavily on his short leg. Donkin glided behind backs, restless and anxious, like a man looking for an ambush. Captain Allistoun came out on the quarter-deck suddenly. He walked to and fro before the front. He was grey, slight, alert, shabby in the sunshine, and as hard as adamant. He had his right hand in the side-pocket of his jacket, and also something heavy in there that made folds all down that side. One of the seamen cleared his throat ominously.—"I haven't till now found fault with you men," said the master, stopping short. He faced them with his worn, steely gaze, that by an universal illu-sion looked straight into every individual pair of the twenty pairs of eyes before his face. At his back Mr. Baker, gloomy and bull-necked, grunted low; Mr. Creighton, fresh as paint, had rosy cheeks and a ready, resolute bearing. "And I don't now," continued the master; "but I am here to drive this ship and keep every man-jack aboard of her up to the mark. If you knew your work as well as I do mine, there would be no trouble. You've been braying in the dark about 'See to-morrow morning!' Well, you see me now. What do you want?" He waited, stepping quickly to and fro, giving them searching glances. What did they want? They shifted from foot to foot, they balanced their bodies; some, pushing back their caps, scratched their heads. What did they want? Jimmy was forgotten; no one thought of him, alone forward in his cabin, fighting great shadows, clinging to brazen lies, chuckling painfully over his transparent deceptions. No, not Jimmy; he was more forgotten than if he had been dead. They wanted great things. And suddenly all the simple words they knew seemed to be lost for ever in the immensity of their vague and burning desire. They knew what they wanted, but they could not find anything worth saying. They stirred on one spot, swinging, at the end of muscular arms, big tarry hands with crooked fingers. A murmur died out.— "What is it—food?" asked the master, "you know the stores have been spoiled off the Cape."—"We know that, sir," said a bearded shell-back in the front rank.— "Work too hard—eh? Too much for your strength?" he asked again. There was an offended silence.— "We don't want to go shorthanded, sir," began at last Davies in a wavering voice, "and this 'ere black— . . ."—"Enough!" cried the master. He stood scanning them for a moment, then walking a few steps this way and that began to storm at them coldly, in gusts violent and cutting like the gales of those icy seas that had known his youth.—"Tell you what's the matter? Too big for your boots. Think yourselves damn good men. Know half your work. Do half your duty. Think it too much. If you did ten times as much it wouldn't be enough."—"We did our best by her, sir," cried some one with shaky exasperation.—"Your best," stormed on the master; "You hear a lot on shore, don't you? They don't tell you there your best isn't much to boast of. I tell you—your best is no better than bad.

You can do no more? No, I know, and say nothing. But you stop your caper or I will stop it for you. I am ready for you! Stop it!" He shook a finger at the crowd. "As to that man," he raised his voice very much; "as to that man, if he puts his nose out on deck without my leave I will clap him in irons. There!" The cook heard him forward, ran out of the galley lifting his arms, horrified, unbelieving, amazed, and ran in again. There was a moment of profound silence during which a bow-legged seaman, stepping aside, expectorated decorously into the scupper. "There is another thing," said the master, calmly. He made a quick stride and with a swing took an iron belaying-pin out of his pocket. "This!" His movement was so unexpected and sudden that the crowd stepped back. He gazed fixedly at their faces, and some at once put on a surprised air as though they had never seen a belaying-pin before. He held it up. "This is my affair. I don't ask you any questions, but you all know it; it has got to go where it came from." His eyes became angry. The crowd stirred uneasily. They looked away from the piece of iron, they appeared shy, they were embarrassed and shocked as though it had been something horrid, scandalous, or indelicate, that in common decency should not have been flourished like this in broad daylight. The master watched them attentively. "Donkin," he called out in a short, sharp tone.

Donkin dodged behind one, then behind another, but they looked over their shoulders and moved aside. The ranks kept on opening before him, closing behind, till at last he appeared alone before the master as though he had come up through the deck. Captain Allistoun moved close to him. They were much of a size, and at short range the master exchanged a deadly glance with the beady eyes. They wavered.—"You know this," asked the master.—"No, I don't," answered the other with cheeky trepidation.—"You are a cur. Take it," ordered the master. Donkin's arms seemed glued to his thighs; he stood, eyes front, as if drawn on parade. "Take it," repeated the master, and stepped closer; they breathed on one another. "Take it," said Captain Allistoun again, making a menacing gesture. Donkin tore away one arm from his side.—"Vy are yer down on me?" he mumbled with effort and as if his mouth had been full of dough.—"If you don't . . ." began the master. Donkin snatched at the pin as though his intention had been to run away with it, and remained stock still holding it like a candle. "Put it back where you took it from," said Captain Allistoun, looking at him fiercely. Donkin stepped back opening wide eyes. "Go, you blackguard, or I will make you," cried the master, driving him slowly backwards by a menacing advance. He dodged, and with the dangerous iron tried to guard his head from a threatening fist. Mr. Baker ceased grunting for a moment.—"Good! By Jove," murmured appreciatively Mr. Creighton in the tone of a connoisseur.—"Don't tech me," snarled Donkin, backing away.—"Then go. Go faster."— "Don't yer 'it me. . . . I will pull yer up afore the magistryt. . . . I'll show yer up." Captain Allistoun made a long stride, and Donkin, turning his back fairly, ran off a little, then stopped and over his shoulder showed yellow teeth.—"Further on, fore-rigging," urged the master, pointing with his arm.—"Are yer goin' to stand by and see me bullied," screamed Donkin at the silent crowd that watched him. Captain Allistoun walked at him smartly. He started off again with a leap, dashed at the fore-rigging, rammed the pin into its hole violently. "I'll be even with yer yet," he screamed at the ship at large and vanished beyond the foremast. Captain Allistoun spun round and walked back aft with a composed face, as though he had already forgotten the scene. Men moved out of his way. He looked at no one.—"That will do, Mr. Baker. Send the watch below," he said, quietly. "And you men try to walk straight for the future," he added in a calm voice. He looked pensively for a while at the backs of the impressed and retreating crowd. "Breakfast, steward," he called in a tone of relief through the cabin door.—"I didn't like to see you— Ough!—give that pin to that chap, sir," observed Mr. Baker; "he could have bust—Ough!—bust your head like an eggshell with it.—"O! he!" muttered the master, absently. "Queer lot," he went on in a low voice. "I suppose it's all right now. Can never tell tho', nowadays, with such a . . . Years ago; I was a young master then—one China voyage I had a mutiny; real mutiny, Baker. Different men tho'. I knew what they wanted: they wanted to broach the cargo and get at the liquor. Very simple. . . . We knocked them about for two days, and when they had enough—gentle as lambs. Good crew. And a smart trip I made." He glanced aloft at the yards braced sharp up. "Head wind day after day," he exclaimed, bitterly. "Shall we never get a decent slant this passage?"—"Ready, sir," said the steward, appearing before them as if by magic and with a stained napkin in his hand.—"Ah! All right. Come along, Mr. Baker —it's late—with all this nonsense."

CHAPTER FIVE

A HEAVY atmosphere of oppressive quietude pervaded the ship. In the afternoon men went about washing clothes and hanging them out to dry in the unprosperous breeze with the meditative languor of disenchanted philosophers. Very little was said. The problem of life seemed too voluminous for the narrow limits of human speech, and by common consent it was abandoned to the great sea that had from the beginning enfolded it in its immense grip; to the sea that knew all, and would in time infallibly unveil to each the wisdom hidden in all the errors, the certitude that lurks in doubts, the realm of safety and peace beyond the frontiers of sorrow and fear. And in the confused current of impotent thoughts that set unceasingly this way and that through bodies of men, Jimmy bobbed up upon the surface, compelling attention, like a black buoy chained to the bottom of a muddy stream. Falsehood triumphed. It triumphed through doubt, through stupidity, through pity, through sentimentalism. We set ourselves to bolster it up, from compassion, from recklessness, from a sense of fun. Jimmy's steadfastness to his untruthful attitude in the face of the inevitable truth had the proportions of a colossal enigma—of a manifestation grand and incomprehensible that at times inspired a wondering awe; and there was also, to many, something exquisitely droll in fooling him thus to the top of his bent. The latent egoism of tenderness to suffering appeared in the developing anxiety not to see him die. His obstinate non-recognition of the only certitude whose approach we could watch from day to day was as disquieting as the failure of some law of nature. He was so utterly wrong about himself that one could not but suspect him of having access to some source of supernatural knowledge. He was absurd to the point of inspiration. He was unique, and as fascinating as only something inhuman could be; he seemed to shout his denials already from beyond the awful border. He was becoming immaterial like an apparition; his cheekbones rose, the forehead slanted more; the face was all hollows, patches of shade; and the fleshless head resembled a disinterred black skull, fitted with two restless globes of silver in the sockets of eyes. He was demoralising. Through him we were becoming highly humanised, tender, complex, excessively decadent: we understood the subtlety of his fear, sympathised with all his repulsions, shrinkings, evasions, delusions—as though we had been over-civilised, and rotten, and without any knowledge of the meaning of life. We had the air of being initiated in some infamous mysteries; we had the profound grimaces of conspirators, exchanged meaning glances, significant short words. We were inexpressibly vile and very much pleased with ourselves. We lied to him with gravity, with emotion, with unction, as if performing some moral trick with a view to an eternal reward. We made a chorus of affirmation to his wildest assertions, as though he had been a millionaire, a politician, or a reformer—and we a crowd of ambitious lubbers. When we ventured to question his statements we did it after the manner of obsequious sycophants, to the end that his glory should be augmented by the flattery of our dissent. He influenced the moral tone of our world as though he had it in his power to distribute honours, treasures, or pain; and he could give us nothing but his contempt. It was immense; it seemed to grow gradually larger, as his body day by day shrank a little more, while we looked. It was the only thing about him—of him—that gave the impression of durability and vigour. It lived within him with an unquenchable life. It spoke through the eternal pout of his black lips; it looked at us through the impertinent mournfulness of his languid and enormous stare. We watched him intently. He seemed unwilling to move, as if distrustful of his own solidity. The slightest gesture must have disclosed to him (it could not surely be otherwise) his bodily weakness, and caused a pang of mental suffering. He was chary of movements. He lay stretched out, chin on blanket, in a kind of sly, cautious immobility. Only his eyes roamed over faces: his eyes disdainful, penetrating and sad.

It was at that time that Belfast's devotion—and also his pugnacity—secured universal respect. He spent every moment of his spare time in Jimmy's cabin. He tended him, talked to him; was as gentle as a woman, as tenderly gay as an old philanthropist, as sentimentally careful of his nigger as a model slave-owner. But outside he was irritable, explosive as gunpowder, sombre, suspicious, and never more brutal than when most sorrowful. With him it was a tear and a blow: a tear for Jimmy, a blow for any one who did not seem to take a scrupulously orthodox view of Jimmy's case. We talked about nothing else. The two Scandinavians, even, discussed the situation—but it was impossible to know in what spirit, because they quarrelled in their own language. Belfast suspected one of them of irreverence, and in this incertitude thought that there was no option but to fight them both. They became very much terrified by his truculence, and henceforth lived amongst us, dejected, like a pair of mutes. Wamibo never spoke intelligibly, but he was as smileless as an animal—seemed to know much less about it all than the cat—and consequently was safe. Moreover, he had belonged to the chosen band of Jimmy's rescuers, and was above suspicion. Archie was silent generally, but often spent an hour or so talking to Jimmy quietly with an air of proprietorship. At any time of the day and often through the night some man could be seen sitting on Jimmy's box. In the evening, between six and eight, the cabin was crowded, and there was an interested group at the door. Every one stared at the nigger.

He basked in the warmth of our interest. His eyes gleamed ironically, and in a weak voice he reproached us with our cowardice. He would say, "If you fellows had stuck out for me I would be now on deck." We hung our heads. "Yes, but if you think I am going to let them put me in irons just to show you sport. . . . Well, no. . . . It ruins my health, this lying-up, it does. You don't care." We were as abashed as if it had been true. His superb impudence carried all before it. We would not have dared to revolt. We didn't want to, really. We wanted to keep him alive till home—to the end of the voyage.

Singleton as usual held aloof, appearing to scorn the insignificant events of an ended life. Once only he came along, and unexpectedly stopped in the doorway. He peered at Jimmy in profound silence, as if desirous to add that black image to the crowd of Shades that peopled his old memory. We kept very quiet, and for a long time Singleton stood there as though he had come by appointment to call for some one, or to see some important event. James Wait lay perfectly still, and apparently not aware of the gaze scrutinising him with a steadiness full of expectation. There was a sense of a contest in the air. We felt the inward strain of men watching a wrestling bout. At last Jimmy with perceptible apprehension turned his head on the pillow.— "Good evening," he said in a conciliating tone.— "H'm," answered the old seaman, grumpily. For a moment longer he looked at Jimmy with severe fixity, then suddenly went away. It was a long time before any one spoke in the little cabin, though we all breathed more freely as men do after an escape from some dangerous situation. We all knew the old man's ideas about Jimmy, and nobody dared to combat them. They were unsettling, they caused pain; and, what was worse, they might have been true for all we knew. Only once did he condescend to explain them fully, but the impression was lasting. He said that Jimmy was the cause of head winds. Mortally sick men—he maintained—linger till the first sight of land, and then die; and Jimmy knew that the very first land would draw his life from him. It is so in every ship. Didn't we know it? He asked us with austere contempt: what did we know? What would we doubt next? Jimmy's desire encouraged by us and aided by Wamibo's (he was a Finn—wasn't he? Very well!) by Wamibo's spells delayed the ship in the open sea. Only lubberly fools couldn't see it. Whoever heard of such a run of calms and head winds? It wasn't natural. . . . We could not deny that it was strange. We felt uneasy. The common saying, "More days, more dollars," did not give the usual comfort because the stores were running short. Much had been spoiled off the Cape, and we were on half allowance of biscuit. Peas, sugar and tea had been finished long ago. Salt meat was giving out. We had plenty of coffee but very little water to make it with. We took up another hole in our belts and went on scraping, polishing, painting the ship from morning to night. And soon she looked as though she had come out of a band-box; but hunger lived on board of her. Not dead starvation, but steady, living hunger that stalked about the decks, slept in the forecastle; the tormentor of waking moments, the disturber of dreams. We looked to windward for signs of change. Every few hours of night and day we put her round with the hope that she would come up on that tack at last! She didn't. She seemed to have forgotten the way home; she rushed to and fro, heading northwest, heading east; she ran backwards and forwards, distracted, like a timid creature at the foot of a wall. Sometimes, as if tired to death, she would wallow languidly for a day in the smooth swell of an unruffled sea. All up the swinging masts the sails trashed furiously through the hot stillness of the calm. We were weary, hungry, thirsty; we commenced to believe Singleton, but with unshaken fidelity dissembled to Jimmy. We spoke to him with jocose allusiveness, like cheerful accomplices in a clever plot; but we looked to the westward over the rail with longing eyes for a sign of hope, for a sign of fair wind; even if its first breath should bring death to our reluctant Jimmy. In vain! The universe conspired with James Wait. Light airs from the northward sprang up again; the sky remained clear; and round our weariness the glittering sea, touched by the breeze, basked voluptuously in the great sunshine, as though it had forgotten our life and trouble.

Donkin looked out for a fair wind along with the rest. No one knew the venom of his thoughts now. He was silent, and appeared thinner, as if consumed slowly by an inward rage at the injustice of men and of fate. He was ignored by all and spoke to no one, but his hate for every man dwelt in his furtive eyes. He talked with the cook only, having somehow persuaded the good man that he—Donkin—was a much calumniated and persecuted person. Together they bewailed the immorality of the ship's company. There could be no greater criminals than we, who by our lies conspired to send the unprepared soul of a poor ignorant black man to everlasting perdition. Podmore cooked what there was to cook, remorsefully, and felt all the time that by preparing the food of such sinners he imperilled his own salvation. As to the Captain—he had sailed with him for seven years, now, he said, and would not have believed it possible that such a man . . . "Well. Well . . . There it was . . . Can't get out of it. Judgment capsized all in a minute . . . Struck in all his pride . . . More like a sudden visitation than anything else." Donkin, perched sullenly on the coal-locker, swung his legs and concurred. He paid in the coin of spurious assent for the privilege to sit in the galley; he was disheartened and scandalised; he agreed with the cook; could find no words severe enough to criticise our conduct; and when in the heat of reprobation he swore at us, Podmore, who would have liked to swear also if it hadn't been for his principles, pretended not to hear. So Donkin, unrebuked, cursed enough for two, cadged for matches, borrowed tobacco, loafed for hours and very much at home before the stove. From there he could hear us on the other side of the bulkhead, talking to Jimmy. The cook knocked the saucepans about, slammed the oven door, muttered prophesies of damnation for all the ship's company; and Donkin, who did not admit of any hereafter (except for purposes of blasphemy) listened, concentrated and angry, gloating fiercely over a called-up image of infinite torment—as men gloat over the accursed images of cruelty and revenge, of greed, and of power. . . .

On clear evenings the silent ship, under the cold sheen of the dead moon, took on a false aspect of passionless repose resembling the winter of the earth. Under her a long band of gold barred the black disc of the sea. Footsteps echoed on her quiet decks. The moonlight clung to her like a frosted mist, and the white sails stood out in dazzling cones as of stainless snow. In the magnificence of the phantom rays the ship appeared pure like a vision of ideal beauty, illusive like a tender dream of serene peace. And nothing in her was real, nothing was distinct and solid but the heavy shadows that filled her decks with their unceasing and noiseless stir: the shadows darker than the night and more restless than the thoughts of men.

Donkin prowled spiteful and alone amongst the shadows, thinking that Jimmy too long delayed to die. That evening land had been reported from aloft, and the master, while adjusting the tubes of the long glass, had observed with quiet bitterness to Mr. Baker that, after fighting our way inch by inch to the Western Islands, there was nothing to expect now but a spell of calm. The sky was clear and the barometer high. The light breeze dropped with the sun, and an enormous stillness, forerunner of a night without wind, descended upon the heated waters of the ocean. As long as daylight lasted, the hands collected on the forecastle-head watched on the eastern sky the island of Flores, that rose above the level expanse of the sea with irregular and broken outlines like a sombre ruin upon a vast and deserted plain. It was the first land seen for nearly four months. Charley was excited, and in the midst of general indulgence took liberties with his betters. Men strangely elated without knowing why, talked in groups, and pointed with bared arms. For the first time that voyage Jimmy's sham existence seemed for a moment

forgotten in the face of a solid reality. We had got so
far anyhow. Belfast discoursed, quoting imaginary
examples of short homeward runs from the Islands.
"Them smart fruit schooners do it in five days," he
affirmed. "What do you want?—only a good little
breeze." Archie maintained that seven days was the
record passage, and they disputed amicably with insulting words. Knowles declared he could already
smell home from there, and with a heavy list on his
short leg laughed fit to split his sides. A group of
grizzled sea-dogs looked out for a time in silence and
with grim absorbed faces. One said suddenly—
" 'Tain't far to London now."—"My first night ashore,
blamme if I haven't steak and onions for supper
. . . and a pint of bitter," said another.—"A
barrel ye mean," shouted someone.—"Ham an' eggs
three times a day. That's the way I live!" cried an
excited voice. There was a stir, appreciative murmurs;
eyes began to shine; jaws champed; short, nervous
laughs were heard. Archie smiled with reserve all to
himself. Singleton came up, gave a careless glance,
and went down again without saying a word, indifferent, like a man who had seen Flores an incalculable
number of times. The night travelling from the East
blotted out of the limpid sky the purple stain of the
high land. "Dead calm," said somebody quietly.
The murmur of lively talk suddenly wavered, died
out; the clusters broke up; men began to drift away one
by one, descending the ladders slowly and with serious
faces as if sobered by that reminder of their dependence
upon the invisible. And when the big yellow moon
ascended gently above the sharp rim of the clear horizon
it found the ship wrapped up in a breathless silence; a
fearless ship that seemed to sleep profoundly, dream-
lessly on the bosom of the sleeping and terrible sea.

Donkin chafed at the peace—at the ship—at the sea that stretching away on all sides merged into the illimitable silence of all creation. He felt himself pulled up sharp by unrecognised grievances. He had been physically cowed, but his injured dignity remained indomitable, and nothing could heal his lacerated feelings. Here was land already—home very soon—a bad pay-day—no clothes—more hard work. How offensive all this was. Land. The land that draws away life from sick sailors. That nigger there had money—clothes—easy times; and would not die. Land draws life away. . . . He felt tempted to go and see whether it did. Perhaps already . . . It would be a bit of luck. There was money in the beggar's chest. He stepped briskly out of the shadows into the moonlight, and, instantly, his craving, hungry face from sallow became livid. He opened the door of the cabin and had a shock. Sure enough, Jimmy was dead! He moved no more than a recumbent figure with clasped hands, carved on the lid of a stone coffin. Donkin glared with avidity. Then Jimmy, without stirring, blinked his eyelids, and Donkin had another shock. Those eyes were rather startling. He shut the door behind his back with gentle care, looking intently the while at James Wait as though he had come in there at a great risk to tell some secret of startling importance. Jimmy did not move but glanced languidly out of the corners of his eyes.—"Calm?" he asked.—"Yuss," said Donkin, very disappointed, and sat down on the box.

Jimmy was used to such visits at all times of night or day. Men succeeded one another. They spoke in clear voices, pronounced cheerful words, repeated old jokes, listened to him; and each, going out, seemed to leave behind a little of his own vitality, surrender some of his own strength, renew the assurance of life—the indestructible thing! He did not like to be alone in his cabin, because, when he was alone, it seemed to him as if he hadn't been there at all. There was nothing. No pain. Not now. 'Perfectly right—but he couldn't enjoy his healthful repose unless some one was by to see it. This man would do as well as anybody. Donkin watched him stealthily:—"Soon home now," observed Wait.—"Vy d'yer whisper?" asked Donkin with interest, "can't yer speak up?" Jimmy looked annoyed and said nothing for a while; then in a lifeless, unringing voice:—"Why should I shout? You ain't deaf that I know."—"Oh! I can 'ear right enough," answered Donkin in a low tone, and looked down. He was thinking sadly of going out when Jimmy spoke again.— "Time we did get home . . . to get something decent to eat . . . I am always hungry." Donkin felt angry all of a sudden.—"What about me," he hissed, "I am 'ungry too an' got ter work. You, 'ungry!"—"Your work won't kill you," commented Wait, feebly; "there's a couple of biscuits in the lower bunk there—you may have one. I can't eat them." Donkin dived in, groped in the corner and when he came up again his mouth was full. He munched with ardour. Jimmy seemed to doze with open eyes. Donkin finished his hard bread and got up.—"You're not going?" asked Jimmy, staring at the ceiling.— "No," said Donkin, impulsively, and instead of going out leaned his back against the closed door. He looked at James Wait, and saw him long, lean, dried up, as though all his flesh had shrivelled on his bones in the heat of a white furnace; the meagre fingers of one hand moved lightly upon the edge of the bunk playing an endless tune. To look at him was irritating and fatiguing; he could last like this for days; he was out-

rageous—belonging wholly neither to death nor life,
and perfectly invulnerable in his apparent ignorance
of both. Donkin felt tempted to enlighten him.—
"What are yer thinkin' of?" he asked, surlily. James
Wait had a grimacing smile that passed over the deathlike impassiveness of his bony face, incredible and
frightful as would, in a dream, have been the sudden
smile of a corpse.

"There is a girl," whispered Wait. . . . "Canton Street girl.——She chucked a third engineer of a
Rennie boat——for me. Cooks oysters just as I like
. . . She says——she would chuck——any toff——
for a coloured gentleman. . . . That's me. I am
kind to wimmen," he added, a shade louder.

Donkin could hardly believe his ears. He was
scandalised —"Would she? Yer wouldn't be any
good to 'er," he said with unrestrained disgust. Wait
was not there to hear him. He was swaggering up the
East India Dock Road; saying kindly, " Come along
for a treat," pushing glass swing-doors, posing with
superb assurance in the gaslight above a mahogany
counter.—"D'yer think yer will ever get ashore?"
asked Donkin, angrily. Wait came back with a start.
—"Ten days," he said, promptly, and returned at
once to the regions of memory that know nothing of
time. He felt untired, calm, and safely withdrawn
within himself beyond the reach of every grave incertitude. There was something of the immutable quality
of eternity in the slow moments of his complete restfulness. He was very quiet and easy amongst his vivid
reminiscences which he mistook joyfully for images of an
undoubted future. He cared for no one. Donkin
felt this vaguely like a blind man feeling in his darkness
the fatal antagonism of all the surrounding existences,
that to him shall for ever remain irrealisable, unseen

and enviable. He had a desire to assert his importance, to break, to crush; to be even with everybody for everything; to tear the veil, unmask, expose, leave no refuge—a perfidious desire of truthfulness! He laughed in a mocking splutter and said:

"Ten days. Strike me blind if I ever! . . . You will be dead by this time to-morrow p'r'aps. Ten days!" He waited for a while. "D'ye 'ear me? Blamme if yer don't look dead already."

Wait must have been collecting his strength for he said almost aloud—"You're a stinking, cadging liar. Every one knows you." And sitting up, against all probability, startled his visitor horribly. But very soon Donkin recovered himself. He blustered,

"What? What? Who's a liar? You are—the crowd are—the skipper—everybody. I ain't! Putting on airs! Who's yer?" He nearly choked himself with indignation. "Who's yer to put on airs," he repeated, trembling. "''Ave one—'ave one, says 'ee—an' cawn't eat 'em 'isself. Now I'll 'ave both. By Gawd—I will! Yer nobody!"

He plunged into the lower bunk, rooted in there and brought to light another dusty biscuit. He held it up before Jimmy—then took a bite defiantly.

"What now?" he asked with feverish impudence. "Yer may take one—says yer. Why not giv' me both? No. I'm a mangy dorg. One fur a mangy dorg. I'll tyke both. Can yer stop me? Try. Come on. Try."

Jimmy was clasping his legs and hiding his face on the knees. His shirt clung to him. Every rib was visible. His emaciated back was shaken in repeated jerks by the panting catches of his breath.

"Yer won't? Yer can't! What did I say?" went on Donkin, fiercely. He swallowed another dry mouthful with a hasty effort. The other's silent helplessness, his weakness, his shrinking attitude exasperated him. "Ye're done!" he cried. "Who's yer to be lied to; to be waited on 'and an' foot like a bloomin' ymperor. Yer nobody. Yer no one at all!" he spluttered with such a strength of unerring conviction that it shook him from head to foot in coming out, and left him vibrating like a released string.

James Wait rallied again. He lifted his head and turned bravely at Donkin, who saw a strange face, an unknown face, a fantastic and grimacing mask of despair and fury. Its lips moved rapidly; and hollow, moaning, whistling sounds filled the cabin with a vague mutter full of menace, complaint and desolation, like the far-off murmur of a rising wind. Wait shook his head; rolled his eyes; he denied, cursed, threatened— and not a word had the strength to pass beyond the sorrowful pout of those black lips. It was incomprehensible and disturbing; a gibberish of emotions, a frantic dumb show of speech pleading for impossible things, promising a shadowy vengeance. It sobered Donkin into a scrutinising watchfulness.

"Yer can't oller. See? What did I tell yer?" he said, slowly, after a moment of attentive examination. The other kept on headlong and unheard, nodding passionately, grinning with grotesque and appalling flashes of big white teeth. Donkin, as if fascinated by the dumb eloquence and anger of that black phantom, approached, stretching his neck out with distrustful curiosity; and it seemed to him suddenly that he was looking only at the shadow of a man crouching high in the bunk on the level with his eyes.—"What? What?" he said. He seemed to catch the shape of some words in the continuous panting hiss. "Yer will tell Belfast! Will yer? Are yer a bloomin' kid?" He trembled with alarm and rage, "Tell yer gran'mother! Yer afeard! Who's yer ter be afeard more'n any one?" His passionate sense of his own importance ran away with a last remnant of caution. "Tell an' be damned! Tell, if yer can!" he cried. "I've been treated worser'n a dorg by your blooming back-lickers. They 'as set me on, only to turn aginst me. I am the only man 'ere. They clouted me, kicked me—an' yer laffed—yer black, rotten incumbrance, you! You will pay fur it. They giv' yer their grub, their water—yer will pay fur it to me, by Gawd! Who axed me ter 'ave a drink of water? They put their bloomin' rags on yer that night, an' what did they giv' ter me—a clout on the bloomin' mouth—blast their . . . S'elp me! . . . Yer will pay fur it with yer money. I'm goin' ter 'ave it in a minyte; as soon has ye're dead, yer bloomin' useless fraud. That's the man I am. An' ye're a thing—a bloody thing. Yah—you corpse!"

He flung at Jimmy's head the biscuit he had been all the time clutching hard, but it only grazed, and striking with a loud crack the bulkhead beyond burst like a hand-grenade into flying pieces. James Wait, as if wounded mortally, fell back on the pillow. His lips ceased to move and the rolling eyes became quiet and stared upwards with an intense and steady persistence. Donkin was surprised; he sat suddenly on the chest, and looked down, exhausted and gloomy. After a moment, he began to mutter to himself, "Die, you beggar—die. Somebody'll come in . . . I wish I was drunk . . . Ten days . . . oysters . . ." He looked up and spoke louder. "No . . . No more for yer . . . no more bloomin' gals that cook oysters . . . Who's yer? It's my turn now . . . I wish I was drunk; I would soon giv' you a leg up. That's where yer bound to go.

Feet fust, through a port . . . Splash! Never see yer any more. Overboard! Good 'nuff fur yer."

Jimmy's head moved slightly and he turned his eyes to Donkin's face; a gaze unbelieving, desolated and appealing, of a child frightened by the menace of being shut up alone in the dark. Donkin observed him from the chest with hopeful eyes; then, without rising, tried the lid. Locked. "I wish I was drunk," he muttered and getting up listened anxiously to the distant sound of footsteps on the deck. They approached—ceased. Some one yawned interminably just outside the door, and the footsteps went away shuffling lazily. Donkin's fluttering heart eased its pace, and when he looked towards the bunk again Jimmy was staring as before at the white beam.—"'Ow d'yer feel now?" he asked.—"Bad," breathed out Jimmy.

Donkin sat down patient and purposeful. Every half-hour the bells spoke to one another ringing along the whole length of the ship. Jimmy's respiration was so rapid that it couldn't be counted, so faint that it couldn't be heard. His eyes were terrified as though he had been looking at unspeakable horrors; and by his face one could see that he was thinking of abominable things. Suddenly with an incredibly strong and heart-breaking voice he sobbed out:

"Overboard! . . . I! . . . My God!"

Donkin writhed a little on the box. He looked unwillingly. James Wait was mute. His two long bony hands smoothed the blanket upwards, as though he had wished to gather it all up under his chin. A tear, a big solitary tear, escaped from the corner of his eye and, without touching the hollow cheek, fell on the pillow. His throat rattled faintly.

And Donkin, watching the end of that hateful nigger, felt the anguishing grasp of a great sorrow on his heart at the thought that he himself, some day, would have to go through it all—just like this—perhaps! His eyes became moist. "Poor beggar," he murmured. The night seemed to go by in a flash; it seemed to him he could hear the irremediable rush of precious minutes. How long would this blooming affair last? Too long surely. No luck. He could not restrain himself. He got up and approached the bunk. Wait did not stir. Only his eyes appeared alive and his hands continued their smoothing movement with a horrible and tireless industry. Donkin bent over.

"Jimmy," he called low. There was no answer, but the rattle stopped. "D'yer see me?" he asked, trembling. Jimmy's chest heaved. Donkin, looking away, bent his ear to Jimmy's lips, and heard a sound like the rustle of a single dry leaf driven along the smooth sand of a beach. It shaped itself.

"Light . . . the lamp . . . and . . . go," breathed out Wait.

Donkin, instinctively, glanced over his shoulder at the brilliant flame; then, still looking away, felt under the pillow for a key. He got it at once and for the next few minutes remained on his knees shakily but swiftly busy inside the box. When he got up, his face —for the first time in his life—had a pink flush—perhaps of triumph.

He slipped the key under the pillow again, avoiding to glance at Jimmy, who had not moved. He turned his back squarely from the bunk, and started to the door as though he were going to walk a mile. At his second stride he had his nose against it. He clutched the handle cautiously, but at that moment he received the irresistible impression of something happening behind his back. He spun round as though he had been tapped on the shoulder. He was just in time to see Wait's eyes

blaze up and go out at once, like two lamps overturned
together by a sweeping blow.   Something resembling a
scarlet thread hung down his chin out of the corner of
his lips—and he had ceased to breathe.

Donkin closed the door behind him gently but firmly.
Sleeping men, huddled under jackets, made on the
lighted deck shapeless dark mounds that had the appearance of neglected graves.   Nothing had been done
all through the night and he hadn't been missed.   He
stood motionless and perfectly astounded to find the
world outside as he had left it; there was the sea, the
ship—sleeping men; and he wondered absurdly at it, as
though he had expected to find the men dead, familiar
things gone for ever: as though, like a wanderer returning after many years, he had expected to see bewildering
changes.   He shuddered a little in the penetrating
freshness of the air, and hugged himself forlornly.
The declining moon drooped sadly in the western board
as if withered by the cold touch of a pale dawn.   The
ship slept.   And the immortal sea stretched away,
immense and hazy, like the image of life, with a glittering surface and lightless depths.   Donkin gave it a
defiant glance and slunk off noiselessly as if judged
and cast out by the august silence of its might.

Jimmy's death, after all, came as a tremendous surprise.   We did not know till then how much faith we
had put in his delusions.   We had taken his chances of
life so much at his own valuation that his death,
like the death of an old belief, shook the foundations of
our society.   A common bond was gone; the strong,
effective and respectable bond of a sentimental lie.
All that day we mooned at our work, with suspicious
looks and a disabused air.   In our hearts we thought
that in the matter of his departure Jimmy had acted in

a perverse and unfriendly manner. He didn't back us
up, as a shipmate should. In going he took away with
himself the gloomy and solemn shadow in which our
folly had posed, with humane satisfaction, as a tender
arbiter of fate. And now we saw it was no such thing.
It was just common foolishness; a silly and ineffectual
meddling with issues of majestic import—that is, if
Podmore was right. Perhaps he was? Doubt survived
Jimmy; and, like a community of banded criminals
disintegrated by a touch of grace, we were profoundly
scandalised with each other. Men spoke unkindly to
their best chums. Others refused to speak at all.
Singleton only was not surprised. "Dead—is he?
Of course," he said, pointing at the island right abeam:
for the calm still held the ship spell-bound within
sight of Flores. Dead—of course. *He* wasn't surprised. Here was the land, and there, on the fore-
hatch and waiting for the sailmaker—there was that
corpse. Cause and effect. And for the first time that
voyage, the old seaman became quite cheery and garru-
lous, explaining and illustrating from the stores of experience how, in sickness, the sight of an island (even
a very small one) is generally more fatal than the view of
a continent. But he couldn't explain why.

Jimmy was to be buried at five, and it was a long day
till then—a day of mental disquiet and even of physical
disturbance. We took no interest in our work and,
very properly, were rebuked for it. This, in our constant state of hungry irritation, was exasperating.
Donkin worked with his brow bound in a dirty rag, and
looked so ghastly that Mr. Baker was touched with
compassion at the sight of this plucky suffering.—
"Ough! You, Donkin! Put down your work and go
lay-up this watch. You look ill."—"I am bad, sir—
in my 'ead," he said in a subdued voice, and vanished

speedily. This annoyed many, and they thought the
mate "bloomin' soft to-day." Captain Allistoun
could be seen on the poop watching the sky to the
southwest, and it soon got to be known about the decks
that the barometer had begun to fall in the night, and
that a breeze might be expected before long. This,-
by a subtle association of ideas, led to violent quarrelling as to the exact moment of Jimmy's death. Was
it before or after "that 'ere glass started down?"
It was impossible to know, and it caused much contemptuous growling at one another. All of a sudden
there was a great tumult forward. Pacific Knowles and
good-tempered Davies had come to blows over it. The
watch below interfered with spirit, and for ten minutes
there was a noisy scrimmage round the hatch, where,
in the balancing shade of the sails, Jimmy's body, wrapped up in a white blanket, was watched over by the
sorrowful Belfast, who, in his desolation, disdained the
fray. When the noise had ceased, and the passions had
calmed into surly silence, he stood up at the head of the
swathed body, lifting both arms on high, cried with
pained indignation:—"You ought to be ashamed of
yourselves! . . ." We were.

Belfast took his bereavement very hard. He gave
proofs of unextinguishable devotion. It was he, and no
other man, who would help the sailmaker to prepare
what was left of Jimmy for a solemn surrender to the
insatiable sea. He arranged the weights carefully at
the feet: two holystones, an old anchor-shackle without
its pin, some broken links of a worn-out stream cable.
He arranged them this way, then that. "Bless my
soul! you aren't afraid he will chafe his heel?" said
the sailmaker, who hated the job. He pushed the
needle, puffing furiously, with his head in a cloud of
tobacco smoke; he turned the flaps over, pulled at the

stitches, stretched at the canvas.—"Lift his shoulders. . . . Pull to you a bit. . . . So—o—o. Steady." Belfast obeyed, pulled, lifted, overcome with sorrow, dropping tears on the tarred twine.— "Don't you drag the canvas too taut over his poor face, Sails," he entreated, tearfully.—"What are you fashing yourself for? He will be comfortable enough," assured the sailmaker, cutting the thread after the last stitch, which came about the middle of Jimmy's forehead. He rolled up the remaining canvas, put away the needles. "What makes you take on so?" he asked. Belfast looked down at the long package of grey sailcloth.—"I pulled him out," he whispered, "and he did not want to go. If I had sat up with him last night he would have kept alive for me . . . but something made me tired." The sailmaker took vigorous draws at his pipe and mumbled:—"When I . . . West India Station . . . In the *Blanche* frigate . . . Yellow Jack . . . sewed in twenty men a week . . . Portsmouth-Devonport men—townies—knew their fathers, mothers, sisters—the whole boiling of 'em. Thought nothing of it. And these niggers like this one—you don't know where it comes from. Got nobody. No use to nobody. Who will miss him?"—"I do—I pulled him out," mourned Belfast dismally.

On two planks nailed together and apparently resigned and still under the folds of the Union Jack with a white border, James Wait, carried aft by four men, was deposited slowly, with his feet pointing at an open port. A swell had set in from the westward, and following on the roll of the ship, the red ensign, at half-mast, darted out and collapsed again on the grey sky, like a tongue of flickering fire; Charley tolled the bell; and at every swing to starboard the whole vast semicircle of steely waters visible on that side seemed to come up with a rush to the edge of the port, as if impatient to get at our Jimmy. Every one was there but Donkin, who was too ill to come; the Captain and Mr. Creighton stood bareheaded on the break of the poop; Mr. Baker, directed by the master, who had said to him gravely:—"You know more about the prayer book than I do," came out of the cabin door quickly and a little embarrassed. All the caps went off. He began to read in a low tone, and with his usual harmlessly menacing utterance, as though he had been for the last time reproving confidentially that dead seaman at his feet. The men listened in scattered groups; they leaned on the fife rail, gazing on the deck; they held their chins in their hands thoughtfully, or, with crossed arms and one knee slightly bent, hung their heads in an attitude of upright meditation. Wamibo dreamed. Mr. Baker read on, grunting reverently at the turn of every page. The words, missing the unsteady hearts of men, rolled out to wander without a home upon the heartless sea; and James Wait, silenced for ever, lay uncritical and passive under the hoarse murmur of despair and hopes.

Two men made ready and waited for those words that send so many of our brothers to their last plunge. Mr. Baker began the passage. "Stand by," muttered the boatswain. Mr. Baker read out: "To the deep," and paused. The men lifted the inboard end of the planks, the boatswain snatched off the Union Jack, and James Wait did not move.—"Higher," muttered the boatswain angrily. All the heads were raised; every man stirred uneasily, but James Wait gave no sign of going. In death and swathed up for all eternity, he yet seemed to cling to the ship with the grip of an undying fear. "Higher! Lift!" whispered the boatswain, fiercely.—"He won't go," stammered one of the men, shakily, and both appeared ready to drop everything. Mr. Baker waited, burying his face in the book, and shuffling his feet nervously. All the men looked profoundly disturbed; from their midst a faint humming noise spread out—growing louder. . . . "Jimmy!" cried Belfast in a wailing tone, and there was a second of shuddering dismay.

"Jimmy, be a man!" he shrieked, passionately. Every mouth was wide open, not an eyelid winked. He stared wildly, twitching all over; he bent his body forward like a man peering at an horror. "Go!" he shouted, and sprang out of the crowd with his arm extended. "Go, Jimmy!—Jimmy, go! Go!" His fingers touched the head of the body, and the grey package started reluctantly to whizz off the lifted planks all at once, with the suddenness of a flash of lightning. The crowd stepped forward like one man; a deep Ah—h—h! came out vibrating from the broad chests. The ship rolled as if relieved of an unfair burden; the sails flapped. Belfast, supported by Archie, gasped hysterically; and Charley, who anxious to see Jimmy's last dive, leaped headlong on the rail, was too late to see anything but the faint circle of a vanishing ripple.

Mr. Baker, perspiring abundantly, read out the last prayer in a deep rumour of excited men and fluttering sails. "Amen!" he said in an unsteady growl, and closed the book.

"Square the yards!" thundered a voice above his head. All hands gave a jump; one or two dropped their caps; Mr. Baker looked up surprised. The master, standing on the break of the poop, pointed to the westward. "Breeze coming," he said, "Man the weather braces." Mr. Baker crammed the book hurriedly into his pocket.—"Forward, there—let go the foretack!" he hailed joyfully, bareheaded and brisk; "Square the foreyard, you port-watch!"—"Fair wind —fair wind," muttered the men going to the braces.— "What did I tell you?" mumbled old Singleton, flinging down coil after coil with hasty energy; "I knowed it —he's gone, and here it comes."

It came with the sound of a lofty and powerful sigh. The sails filled, the ship gathered way, and the waking sea began to murmur sleepily of home to the ears of men.

That night, while the ship rushed foaming to the Northward before a freshening gale, the boatswain unbosomed himself to the petty officers' berth:—"The chap was nothing but trouble," he said, "from the moment he came aboard—d'ye remember—that night in Bombay? Been bullying all that softy crowd—cheeked the old man—we had to go fooling all over a half-drowned ship to save him. Dam' nigh a mutiny all for him—and now the mate abused me like a pickpocket for forgetting to dab a lump of grease on them planks. So I did, but you ought to have known better, too, than to leave a nail sticking up—hey, Chips?"

"And you ought to have known better than to chuck all my tools overboard for 'im, like a skeary greenhorn," retorted the morose carpenter. "Well—he's gone after 'em now," he added in an unforgiving tone. —"On the China Station, I remember once, the Admiral he says to me . . ." began the sailmaker.

A week afterwards the *Narcissus* entered the chops of the Channel.

Under white wings she skimmed low over the blue sea like a great tired bird speeding to its nest. The clouds raced with her mastheads; they rose astern enormous and white, soared to the zenith, flew past, and, falling

down the wide curve of the sky, seemed to dash headlong into the sea—the clouds swifter than the ship, more
free, but without a home. The coast to welcome her
stepped out of space into the sunshine. The lofty
headlands trod masterfully into the sea; the wide bays
smiled in the light; the shadows of homeless clouds ran
along the sunny plains, leaped over valleys, without a
check darted up the hills, rolled down the slopes; and the
sunshine pursued them with patches of running bright-
ness. On the brows of dark cliffs white lighthouses
shone in pillars of light. The Channel glittered like
a blue mantle shot with gold and starred by the silver
of the capping seas. The *Narcissus* rushed past the
headlands and the bays. Outward-bound vessels
crossed her track, lying over, and with their masts
stripped for a slogging fight with the hard sou'wester.
And, inshore, a string of smoking steamboats waddled,
hugging the coast, like migrating and amphibious mon-
sters, distrustful of the restless waves.

At night the headlands retreated, the bays advanced
into one unbroken line of gloom. The lights of the
earth mingled with the lights of heaven; and above the
tossing lanterns of a trawling fleet a great lighthouse
shone steadily, like an enormous riding light burning above a vessel of fabulous dimensions. Below its
steady glow, the coast, stretching away straight and
black, resembled the high side of an indestructible craft
riding motionless upon the immortal and unresting sea.
The dark land lay alone in the midst of waters, like
a mighty ship bestarred with vigilant lights—a ship
carrying the burden of millions of lives—a ship freighted
with dross and with jewels, with gold and with steel.
She towered up immense and strong, guarding priceless
traditions and untold suffering, sheltering glorious
memories and base forgetfulness, ignoble virtues and

splendid transgressions. A great ship! For ages had the ocean battered in vain her enduring sides; she was there when the world was vaster and darker, when the sea was great and mysterious, and ready to surrender the prize of fame to audacious men. A ship mother of fleets and nations! The great flagship of the race; stronger than the storms! and anchored in the open sea.

The *Narcissus*, heeling over to off-shore gusts, rounded the South Foreland, passed through the Downs, and, in tow, entered the river. Shorn of the glory of her white wings, she wound obediently after the tug through the maze of invisible channels. As she passed them the red-painted light-vessels, swung at their moorings, seemed for an instant to sail with great speed in the rush of tide, and the next moment were left hopelessly behind. The big buoys on the tails of banks slipped past her sides very low, and, dropping in her wake, tugged at their chains like fierce watch-dogs. The reach narrowed; from both sides the land approached the ship. She went steadily up the river. On the riverside slopes the houses appeared in groups—seemed to stream down the declivities at a run to see her pass, and, checked by the mud of the foreshore, crowded on the banks. Further on, the tall factory chimneys appeared in insolent bands and watched her go by, like a straggling crowd of slim giants, swaggering and upright under the black plummets of smoke, cavalierly aslant. She swept round the bends; an impure breeze shrieked a welcome between her stripped spars; and the land, closing in, stepped between the ship and the sea.

A low cloud hung before her—a great opalescent and tremulous cloud, that seemed to rise from the steaming brows of millions of men. Long drifts of smoky vapours soiled it with livid trails; it throbbed to the beat of millions of hearts, and from it came an immense and lamentable murmur—the murmur of millions of lips praying, cursing, sighing, jeering—the undying murmur of folly, regret, and hope exhaled by the crowds of the anxious earth. The *Narcissus* entered the cloud; the shadows deepened; on all sides there was the clang of iron, the sound of mighty blows, shrieks, yells. Black barges drifted stealthily on the murky stream. A mad jumble of begrimed walls loomed up vaguely in the smoke, bewildering and mournful, like a vision of disaster. The tugs backed and filled in the stream, to hold the ship steady at the dock-gates; from her bows two lines went through the air whistling, and struck at the land viciously, like a pair of snakes. A bridge broke in two before her, as if by enchantment; big hydraulic capstans began to turn all by themselves, as though animated by a mysterious and unholy spell. She moved through a narrow lane of water between two low walls of granite, and men with check-ropes in their hands kept pace with her, walking on the broad flagstones. A group waited impatiently on each side of the vanished bridge: rough heavy men in caps; sallow-faced men in high hats; two bareheaded women; ragged children, fascinated, and with wide eyes. A cart coming at a jerky trot pulled up sharply. One of the women screamed at the silent ship—"Hallo, Jack!" without looking at any one in particular, and all hands looked at her from the forecastle head.—"Stand clear! Stand clear of that rope!" cried the dockmen, bending over stone posts. The crowd murmured, stamped where they stood.—"Let go your quarter-checks! Let go!" sang out a ruddy-faced old man on the quay. The ropes splashed heavily falling in the water, and the *Narcissus* entered the dock.

The stony shores ran away right and left in straight lines, enclosing a sombre and rectangular pool. Brick

walls rose high above the water—soulless walls, staring
through hundreds of windows as troubled and dull as the
eyes of over-fed brutes. At their base monstrous iron
cranes crouched, with chains hanging from their long
necks, balancing cruel-looking hooks over the decks of
lifeless ships. A noise of wheels rolling over stones,
the thump of heavy things falling, the racket of feverish
winches, the grinding of strained chains, floated on the
air. Between high buildings the dust of all the continents soared in short flights; and a penetrating smell of
perfumes and dirt, of spices and hides, of things costly
and of things filthy, pervaded the space, made for it an
atmosphere precious and disgusting. The *Narcissus*
came gently into her berth; the shadows of soulless
walls fell upon her, the dust of all the continents leaped
upon her deck, and a swarm of strange men, clambering
up her sides, took possession of her in the name of the
sordid earth. She had ceased to live.

A toff in a black coat and high hat scrambled with
agility, came up to the second mate, shook hands, and
said:—"Hallo, Herbert." It was his brother. A lady
appeared suddenly. A real lady, in a black dress and
with a parasol. She looked extremely elegant in the
midst of us, and as strange as if she had fallen there from
the sky. Mr. Baker touched his cap to her. It was
the master's wife. And very soon the Captain, dressed
very smartly and in a white shirt, went with her over
the side. We didn't recognise him at all till, turning
on the quay, he called to Mr. Baker:—"Don't forget to
wind up the chronometers to-morrow morning."
An underhand lot of seedy-looking chaps with shifty
eyes wandered in and out of the forecastle looking for a
job—they said.—"More likely for something to steal,"
commented Knowles, cheerfully. Poor beggars. Who
cared? Weren't we home! But Mr. Baker went for

one of them who had given him some cheek, and we were delighted. Everything was delightful.—"I've finished aft, sir," called out Mr. Creighton.—"No water in the well, sir," reported for the last time the carpenter, sounding-rod in hand. Mr. Baker glanced along the decks at the expectant group of sailors, glanced aloft at the yards.—"Ough! That will do, men," he grunted. The group broke up. The voyage was ended.

Rolled-up beds went flying over the rail; lashed chests went sliding down the gangway—mighty few of both at that. "The rest is having a cruise off the Cape," explained Knowles enigmatically to a dock-loafer with whom he had struck a sudden friendship. Men ran, calling to one another, hailing utter strangers to "lend a hand with the dunnage," then with sudden decorum approached the mate to shake hands before going ashore.—"Good-bye, sir," they repeated in various tones. Mr. Baker grasped hard palms, grunted in a friendly manner at every one, his eyes twinkled.— "Take care of your money, Knowles. Ough! Soon get a nice wife if you do." The lame man was delighted.—"Good-bye, sir," said Belfast, with emotion, wringing the mate's hand, and looked up with swimming eyes. "I thought I would take 'im ashore with me," he went on, plaintively. Mr. Baker did not understand, but said kindly:—"Take care of yourself, Craik," and the bereaved Belfast went over the rail mourning and alone.

Mr. Baker, in the sudden peace of the ship, moved about solitary and grunting, trying door-handles, peering into dark places, never done—a model chief mate! No one waited for him ashore. Mother dead; father and two brothers, Yarmouth fishermen, drowned together on the Dogger Bank; sister married and unfriendly. Quite a lady. Married to the leading tailor of a little town, and its leading politician, who did not think his sailor brother-in-law quite respectable enough for him. Quite a lady, quite a lady, he thought, sitting down for a moment's rest on the quarter-hatch. Time enough to go ashore and get a bite and sup, and a bed somewhere. He didn't like to part with a ship. No one to think about then. The darkness of a misty evening fell, cold and damp, upon the deserted deck; and Mr. Baker sat smoking, thinking of all the successive ships to whom through many long years he had given the best of a seaman's care. And never a command in sight. Not once!—"I haven't somehow the cut of a skipper about me," he meditated, placidly, while the shipkeeper (who had taken possession of the galley), a wizened old man with bleared eyes, cursed him in whispers for "hanging about so."—"Now, Creighton," he pursued the unenvious train of thought, "quite a gentleman . . . swell friends . . . will get on. Fine young fellow . . . a little more experience." He got up and shook himself. "I'll be back first thing to-morrow morning for the hatches. Don't you let them touch anything before I come, shipkeeper," he called out. Then, at last, he also went ashore—a model chief mate!

The men scattered by the dissolving contact of the land came together once more in the shipping office.— "The *Narcissus* pays off," shouted outside a glazed door a brass-bound old fellow with a crown and the capitals B. T. on his cap. A lot trooped in at once but many were late. The room was large, white-washed, and bare; a counter surmounted by a brass-wire grating fenced off a third of the dusty space, and behind the grating a pasty-faced clerk, with his hair parted in the middle, had the quick, glittering eyes and the vivacious, jerky movements of a caged bird. Poor Captain

Allistoun also in there, and sitting before a little table with piles of gold and notes on it, appeared subdued by his captivity. Another Board of Trade bird was perching on a high stool near the door: an old bird that did not mind the chaff of elated sailors. The crew of the *Narcissus*, broken up into knots, pushed in the corners. They had new shore togs, smart jackets that looked as if they had been shaped with an axe, glossy trousers that seemed made of crumpled sheet-iron, collarless flannel shirts, shiny new boots. They tapped on shoulders, button-holed one another, asked:— "Where did you sleep last night?" whispered gaily, slapped their thighs with bursts of subdued laughter. Most had clean, radiant faces; only one or two turned up dishevelled and sad; the two young Norwegians looked tidy, meek, and altogether of a promising material for the kind ladies who patronise the Scandinavian Home. Wamibo, still in his working clothes, dreamed, upright and burly in the middle of the room, and, when Archie came in, woke up for a smile. But the wide-awake clerk called out a name, and the paying-off business began.

One by one they came up to the pay-table to get the wages of their glorious and obscure toil. They swept the money with care into broad palms, rammed it trustfully into trousers' pockets, or, turning their backs on the table, reckoned with difficulty in the hollow of their stiff hands.—"Money right? Sign the release. There —there," repeated the clerk, impatiently. "How stupid those sailors are!" he thought. Singleton came up, venerable—and uncertain as to daylight; brown drops of tobacco juice hung in his white beard; his hands, that never hesitated in the great light of the open sea, could hardly find the small pile of gold in the profound darkness of the shore. "Can't write?" said the

clerk, shocked. "Make a mark, then." Singleton
painfully sketched in a heavy cross, blotted the page.
"What a disgusting old brute," muttered the clerk.
Somebody opened the door for him, and the patriarchal
seaman passed through unsteadily, without as much as
a glance at any of us.

Archie displayed a pocket-book. He was chaffed.
Belfast, who looked wild, as though he had already
luffed up through a public-house or two, gave signs of
emotion and wanted to speak to the Captain privately.
The master was surprised. They spoke through the
wires, and we could hear the Captain saying:—"I've
given it up to the Board of Trade." "I should 've liked
to get something of his," mumbled Belfast. "But
you can't, my man. It's given up, locked and sealed,
to the Marine Office," expostulated the master; and
Belfast stood back, with drooping mouth and troubled
eyes. In a pause of the business we heard the master
and the clerk talking. We caught: "James Wait—
deceased—found no papers of any kind—no relations
—no trace—the Office must hold his wages then."
Donkin entered. He seemed out of breath, was grave,
full of business. He went straight to the desk, talked
with animation to the clerk, who thought him an intelligent man. They discussed the account, dropping
h's against one another as if for a wager—very friendly.
Captain Allistoun paid. "I give you a bad discharge,"
he said, quietly. Donkin raised his voice:—"I don't
want your bloomin' discharge—keep it. I'm goin' ter
'ave a job ashore." He turned to us. "No more
bloomin' sea fur me," he said, aloud. All looked at
him. He had better clothes, had an easy air, appeared
more at home than any of us; he stared with assurance,
enjoying the effect of his declaration. "Yuss. I'ave
friends well off. That's more'n you got. But I am

a man. Yer shipmates for all that. Who's comin fur a drink?"

No one moved. There was a silence; a silence of blank faces and stony looks. He waited a moment, smiled bitterly, and went to the door. There he faced round once more. "You won't? You bloomin' lot of yrpocrits. No? What 'ave I done to yer? Did I bully yer? Did I 'urt yer? Did I? . . . You won't drink? . . . No! . . . Then may ye die of thirst, every mother's son of yer! Not one of yer 'as the sperrit of a bug. Ye're the scum of the world. Work and starve!"

He went out, and slammed the door with such violence that the old Board of Trade bird nearly fell off his perch.

"He's mad," declared Archie. "No! No! He's drunk," insisted Belfast, lurching about, and in a maudlin tone. Captain Allistoun sat smiling thoughtfully at the cleared pay-table.

Outside, on Tower Hill, they blinked, hesitated clumsily, as if blinded by the strange quality of the hazy light, as if discomposed by the view of so many men; and they who could hear one another in the howl of gales seemed deafened and distracted by the dull roar of the busy earth.—"To the Black Horse! To the Black Horse!" cried some. "Let us have a drink together before we part." They crossed the road, clinging to one another. Only Charley and Belfast wandered off alone. As I came up I saw a red-faced, blowsy woman, in a grey shawl, and with dusty, fluffy hair, fall on Charley's neck. It was his mother. She slobbered over him:—"O, my boy! My boy!"— "Leggo of me," said Charley, "Leggo, mother!" I was passing him at the time, and over the untidy head of the blubbering woman he gave me a humorous smile and a glance ironic, courageous, and profound, that seemed to put all my knowledge of life to shame. I nodded and passed on, but heard him say again, good-naturedly:—"If you leggo of me this minyt—ye shall 'ave a bob for a drink out of my pay." In the next few steps I came upon Belfast. He caught my arm with tremulous enthusiasm.—"I couldn't go wi' 'em," he stammered, indicating by a nod our noisy crowd, that drifted slowly along the other sidewalk. "When I think of Jimmy . . . Poor Jim! When I think of him I have no heart for drink. You were his chum, too . . . but I pulled him out . . . didn't I? Short wool he had. . . . Yes. And I stole the blooming pie. . . . He wouldn't go. . . . He wouldn't go for nobody." He burst into tears. "I never touched him—never—never!" he sobbed. "He went for me like . . . like . . . a lamb."

I disengaged myself gently. Belfast's crying fits generally ended in a fight with some one, and I wasn't anxious to stand the brunt of his inconsolable sorrow. Moreover, two bulky policemen stood near by, looking at us with a disapproving and incorruptible gaze.—"So long!" I said, and went on my way.

But at the corner I stopped to take my last look at the crew of the *Narcissus*. They were swaying irresolute and noisy on the broad flagstones before the Mint. They were bound for the Black Horse, where men, in fur caps with brutal faces and in shirt sleeves, dispense out of varnished barrels the illusions of strength, mirth, happiness; the illusion of splendour and poetry of life, to the paid-off crews of southern-going ships. From afar I saw them discoursing, with jovial eyes and clumsy gestures, while the sea of life thundered into their ears ceaseless and unheeded. And swaying

about there on the white stones, surrounded by the
hurry and clamour of men, they appeared to be creatures
of another kind—lost, alone, forgetful, and doomed;
they were like castaways, like reckless and joyous castaways, like mad castaways making merry in the storm
and upon an insecure ledge of a treacherous rock. The
roar of the town resembled the roar of topping breakers,
merciless and strong, with a loud voice and cruel purpose; but overhead the clouds broke; a flood of sunshine
streamed down the walls of grimy houses. The dark
knot of seamen drifted in sunshine. To the left of them
the trees in Tower Gardens sighed, the stones of the
Tower gleaming, seemed to stir in the play of light, as if
remembering suddenly all the great joys and sorrows of
the past, the fighting prototypes of these men; press-
gangs; mutinous cries; the wailing of women by the
riverside, and the shouts of men welcoming victories.
The sunshine of heaven fell like a gift of grace on the
mud of the earth, on the remembering and mute stones,
on greed, selfishness; on the anxious faces of forgetful
men. And to the right of the dark group the stained
front of the Mint, cleansed by the flood of light, stood
out for a moment dazzling and white like a marble
palace in a fairy tale. The crew of the *Narcissus*
drifted out of sight.

I never saw them again. The sea took some, the
steamers took others, the graveyards of the earth will
account for the rest. Singleton has no doubt taken with
him the long record of his faithful work into the peaceful
depths of an hospitable sea. And Donkin, who never
did a decent day's work in his life, no doubt earns his
living by discoursing with filthy eloquence upon the
right of labour to live. So be it! Let the earth and
the sea each have its own.

A gone shipmate, like any other man, is gone for ever;

and I never met one of them again. But at times the spring-flood of memory sets with force up the dark River of the Nine Bends. Then on the waters of the forlorn stream drifts a ship—a shadowy ship manned by a crew of Shades. They pass and make a sign, in a shadowy hail. Haven't we, together and upon the immortal sea, wrung out a meaning from our sinful lives? Good-bye, brothers! You were a good crowd. As good a crowd as ever fisted with wild cries the beating canvas of a heavy foresail; or tossing aloft, invisible in the night, gave back yell for yell to a westerly gale.

THE END

TYPHOON
AND OTHER STORIES

To
R. B. Cunninghame Graham

AUTHOR'S NOTE

THE main characteristic of this volume consists in this, that all the stories composing it belong not only to the same period but have been written one after another in the order in which they appear in the book.

The period is that which follows on my connection with *Blackwood's Magazine*. I had just finished writing "The End of the Tether" and was casting about for some subject which could be developed in a shorter form than the tales in the volume of "Youth" when the instance of a steamship full of returning coolies from Singapore to some port in northern China occurred to my recollection. Years before I had heard it being talked about in the East as a recent occurrence. It was for us merely one subject of conversation amongst many others of the kind. Men earning their bread in any very specialized occupation will talk shop, not only because it is the most vital interest of their lives but also because they have not much knowledge of other subjects. They have never had the time to get acquainted with them. Life, for most of us, is not so much a hard as an exacting taskmaster.

I never met anybody personally concerned in this affair, the interest of which for us was, of course, not the bad weather but the extraordinary complication brought into the ship's life at a moment of exceptional stress by the human element below her deck. Neither was the story itself ever enlarged upon in my hearing. In that company each of us could imagine easily what the whole thing was like. The financial difficulty of it, presenting also a human problem, was solved by a mind much too simple to be perplexed by anything in the world except men's idle talk for which it was not adapted.

From the first the mere anecdote, the mere statement I might say, that such a thing had happened on the high seas, appeared to me a sufficient subject for meditation. Yet it was but a bit of a sea yarn after all. I felt that to bring out its deeper significance which was quite apparent to me, something other, something more was required; a leading motive that would harmonize all these violent noises, and a point of view that would put all that elemental fury into its proper place.

What was needed of course was Captain MacWhirr. Directly I perceived him I could see that he was the man for the situation. I don't mean to say that I ever saw Captain MacWhirr in the flesh, or had ever come in contact with his literal mind and his dauntless temperament. MacWhirr is not an acquaintance of a few hours, or a few weeks, or a few months. He is the product of twenty years of life. My own life. Conscious invention had little to do with him. If it is true that Captain MacWhirr never walked and breathed on this earth (which I find for my part extremely difficult to believe) I can also assure my readers that he is perfectly authentic. I may venture to assert the same of every aspect of the story, while I confess that the particular typhoon of the tale was not a typhoon of my actual experience.

At its first appearance "Typhoon," the story, was classed by some critics as a deliberately intended storm-piece. Others picked out MacWhirr, in whom they perceived a definite symbolic intention. Neither was exclusively my intention. Both the typhoon and Captain MacWhirr presented themselves to me as the necessities of the deep conviction with which I approached the subject of the story. It was their opportunity. It was also my opportunity; and it would be vain to discourse about what I made of it in a handful of pages, since the pages themselves are here, between the covers of this volume, to speak for themselves.

This is a belated reflection. If it had occurred to me before it would have perhaps done away with the existence of this Author's Note; for, indeed, the same remark applies to every story in this volume. None of them are stories of experience in the absolute sense of the word. Experience in them is but the canvas of the attempted picture. Each of them has its more than one intention. With each the question is what the writer has done with his opportunity; and each answers the question for itself in words which, if I may say so without undue solemnity, were written with a conscientious regard for the truth of my own sensations. And each of those stories, to mean something, must justify itself in its own way to the conscience of each successive reader.

"Falk"—the second story in the volume—offended the delicacy of one critic at least by certain peculiarities of its subject. But what is the subject of "Falk"? I personally do not feel so very certain about it. He who reads must find out for himself. My intention in writing "Falk" was not to shock anybody. As in most of my writings I insist not on the events but on their effect upon the persons in the tale. But in everything I have written there is always one invariable intention, and that is to capture the reader's attention, by securing his interest and enlisting his sympathies for the matter in hand, whatever it may be, within the limits of the visible world and within the boundaries of human emotions.

I may safely say that Falk is absolutely true to my experience of certain straightforward characters combining a perfectly natural ruthlessness with a certain amount of moral delicacy. Falk obeys the law of self-preservation without the slightest misgivings as to his right, but at a crucial turn of that ruthlessly preserved life he will not condescend to dodge the truth. As he is presented as sensitive enough to be affected permanently by a certain unusual experience, that experience had to be set by me before the reader vividly; but it is not the subject of the tale. If we go by mere facts then the subject is Falk's attempt to get married; in which the narrator of the tale finds himself unexpectedly involved both on its ruthless and its delicate side.

Falk shares with one other of my stories ("The Return" in the "Tales of Unrest" volume) the distinction of never having been serialized. I think the copy was shown to the editor of some magazine who rejected it indignantly on the sole ground that "the girl never says anything." This is perfectly true. From first to last Hermann's niece utters no word in the tale—and it is not because she is dumb, but for the simple reason that whenever she happens to come under the observation of the narrator she has either no occasion or is too profoundly moved to speak. The editor, who obviously had read the story, might have perceived that for himself. Apparently he did not, and I refrained from pointing out the impossibility to him because, since he did not venture to say that "the girl" did not live, I felt no concern at his indignation.

All the other stories were serialized. The "Typhoon" appeared in the early numbers of the *Pall Mall Magazine*, then under the direction of the late Mr.

Halkett. It was on that occasion, too, that I saw for the first time my conceptions rendered by an artist in another medium. Mr. Maurice Greiffenhagen knew how to combine in his illustrations the effect of his own most distinguished personal vision with an absolute fidelity to the inspiration of the writer. "Amy Foster" was published in *The Illustrated London News* with a fine drawing of Amy on her day out giving tea to the children at her home, in a hat with a big feather. "To-morrow" appeared first in the *Pall Mall Magazine.* Of that story I will only say that it struck many people by its adaptability to the stage and that I was induced to dramatize it under the title of "One Day More"; up to the present my only effort in that direction. I may also add that each of the four stories on their appearance in book form was picked out on various grounds as the "best of the lot" by different critics, who reviewed the volume with a warmth of appreciation and understanding, a sympathetic insight and a friendliness of expression for which I cannot be sufficiently grateful.

1919. J. C.

CONTENTS

TYPHOON

TYPHOON

I

CAPTAIN MACWHIRR, of the steamer *Nan-Shan*, had a physiognomy that, in the order of material appearances, was the exact counterpart of his mind: it presented no marked characteristics of firmness or stupidity; it had no pronounced characteristics whatever; it was simply ordinary, irresponsive, and unruffled.

The only thing his aspect might have been said to suggest, at times, was bashfulness; because he would sit, in business offices ashore, sunburnt and smiling faintly, with downcast eyes. When he raised them, they were perceived to be direct in their glance and of blue colour. His hair was fair and extremely fine, clasping from temple to temple the bald dome of his skull in a clamp as of fluffy silk. The hair of his face, on the contrary, carroty and flaming, resembled a growth of copper wire clipped short to the line of the lip; while, no matter how close he shaved, fiery metallic gleams passed, when he moved his head, over the surface of his cheeks. He was rather below the medium height, a bit round-shouldered, and so sturdy of limb that his clothes always looked a shade too tight for his arms and legs. As if unable to grasp what is due to the difference of latitudes, he wore a brown bowler hat, a complete suit of a brownish hue, and clumsy black boots. These harbour togs gave to his thick figure an air of stiff and uncouth smartness. A thin silver watch-

3

chain looped his waistcoat, and he never left his ship for the shore without clutching in his powerful, hairy fist an elegant umbrella of the very best quality, but generally unrolled. Young Jukes, the chief mate, attending his commander to the gangway, would sometimes venture to say, with the greatest gentleness, "Allow me, sir"—and possessing himself of the umbrella deferentially, would elevate the ferule, shake the folds, twirl a neat furl in a jiffy, and hand it back; going through the performance with a face of such portentous gravity, that Mr. Solomon Rout, the chief engineer, smoking his morning cigar over the skylight, would turn away his head in order to hide a smile. "Oh! aye! The blessed gamp. . . . Thank 'ee, Jukes, thank 'ee," would mutter Captain MacWhirr, heartily, without looking up.

Having just enough imagination to carry him through each successive day, and no more, he was tranquilly sure of himself; and from the very same cause he was not in the least conceited. It is your imaginative superior who is touchy, overbearing, and difficult to please; but every ship Captain MacWhirr commanded was the floating abode of harmony and peace. It was, in truth, as impossible for him to take a flight of fancy as it would be for a watchmaker to put together a chronometer with nothing except a two-pound hammer and a whip-saw in the way of tools. Yet the uninteresting lives of men so entirely given to the actuality of the bare existence have their mysterious side. It was impossible in Captain MacWhirr's case, for instance, to understand what under heaven could have induced that perfectly satisfactory son of a petty grocer in Belfast to run away to sea. And yet he had done that very thing at the age of fifteen. It was enough, when you thought it over, to give you the idea of an

immense, potent, and invisible hand thrust into the
ant-heap of the earth, laying hold of shoulders, knocking heads together, and setting the unconscious faces
of the multitude towards inconceivable goals and
in undreamt-of directions.

His father never really forgave him for this undutiful
stupidity. "We could have got on without him," he
used to say later on, "but there's the business. And
he an only son, too!" His mother wept very much
after his disappearance. As it had never occurred to
him to leave word behind, he was mourned over for
dead till, after eight months, his first letter arrived
from Talcahuano. It was short, and contained the
statement: "We had very fine weather on our passage
out." But evidently, in the writer's mind, the only
important intelligence was to the effect that his captain
had, on the very day of writing, entered him regularly
on the ship's articles as Ordinary Seaman. "Because
I can do the work," he explained. The mother again
wept copiously, while the remark, "Tom's an ass,"
expressed the emotions of the father. He was a
corpulent man, with a gift for sly chaffing, which to
the end of his life he exercised in his intercourse with
his son, a little pityingly, as if upon a half-witted
person.

MacWhirr's visits to his home were necessarily rare,
and in the course of years he despatched other letters
to his parents, informing them of his successive promo-
tions and of his movements upon the vast earth. In
these missives could be found sentences like this: "The
heat here is very great." Or: "On Christmas day at
4 P. M. we fell in with some icebergs." The old people
ultimately became acquainted with a good many names
of ships, and with the names of the skippers who
commanded them—with the names of Scots and

English shipowners—with the names of seas, oceans, straits, promontories—with outlandish names of lumber-ports, of rice-ports, of cotton-ports—with the names of islands—with the name of their son's young woman. She was called Lucy. It did not suggest itself to him to mention whether he thought the name pretty. And then they died.

The great day of MacWhirr's marriage came in due course, following shortly upon the great day when he got his first command.

All these events had taken place many years before the morning when, in the chart-room of the steamer *Nan-Shan*, he stood confronted by the fall of a barometer he had no reason to distrust. The fall—taking into account the excellence of the instrument, the time of the year, and the ship's position on the terrestrial globe—was of a nature ominously prophetic; but the red face of the man betrayed no sort of inward disturbance. Omens were as nothing to him, and he was unable to discover the message of a prophecy till the fulfilment had brought it home to his very door. "That's a fall, and no mistake," he thought. "There must be some uncommonly dirty weather knocking about."

The *Nan-Shan* was on her way from the southward to the treaty port of Fu-chau, with some cargo in her lower holds, and two hundred Chinese coolies returning to their village homes in the province of Fo-kien, after a few years of work in various tropical colonies. The morning was fine, the oily sea heaved without a sparkle, and there was a queer white misty patch in the sky like a halo of the sun. The fore-deck, packed with Chinamen, was full of sombre clothing, yellow faces, and pigtails, sprinkled over with a good many naked shoulders, for there was no wind, and the heat was close. The coolies lounged, talked, smoked, or stared over the rail; some, drawing water over the side, sluiced each other; a few slept on hatches, while several small parties of six sat on their heels surrounding iron trays with plates of rice and tiny teacups; and every single Celestial of them was carrying with him all he had in the world—a wooden chest with a ringing lock and brass on the corners, containing the savings of his labours: some clothes of ceremony, sticks of incense, a little opium maybe, bits of nameless rubbish of conventional value, and a small hoard of silver dollars, toiled for in coal lighters, won in gambling-houses or in petty trading, grubbed out of earth, sweated out in mines, on railway lines, in deadly jungle, under heavy burdens—amassed patiently, guarded with care, cherished fiercely.

A cross swell had set in from the direction of Formosa Channel about ten o'clock, without disturbing these passengers much, because the *Nan-Shan*, with her flat bottom, rolling chocks on bilges, and great breadth of beam, had the reputation of an exceptionally steady ship in a sea-way. Mr. Jukes, in moments of expansion on shore, would proclaim loudly that the "old girl was as good as she was pretty." It would never have occurred to Captain MacWhirr to express his favourable opinion so loud or in terms so fanciful.

She was a good ship, undoubtedly, and not old either. She had been built in Dumbarton less than three years before, to the order of a firm of merchants in Siam— Messrs. Sigg and Son. When she lay afloat, finished in every detail and ready to take up the work of her life, the builders contemplated her with pride.

"Sigg has asked us for a reliable skipper to take her out," remarked one of the partners; and the other, after reflecting for a while, said: "I think MacWhirr is ashore just at present." "Is he? Then wire him at once. He's the very man," declared the senior, without a moment's hesitation.

Next morning MacWhirr stood before them unperturbed, having travelled from London by the midnight express after a sudden but undemonstrative parting with his wife. She was the daughter of a superior couple who had seen better days.

"We had better be going together over the ship, Captain," said the senior partner; and the three men started to view the perfections of the *Nan-Shan* from stem to stern, and from her keelson to the trucks of her two stumpy pole-masts.

Captain MacWhirr had begun by taking off his coat, which he hung on the end of a steam windlass embodying all the latest improvements.

"My uncle wrote of you favourably by yesterday's mail to our good friends—Messrs. Sigg, you know—and doubtless they'll continue you out there in command," said the junior partner. "You'll be able to boast of being in charge of the handiest boat of her size on the coast of China, Captain," he added.

"Have you? Thank 'ee," mumbled vaguely Mac-Whirr, to whom the view of a distant eventuality could appeal no more than the beauty of a wide landscape to a purblind tourist; and his eyes happening at the moment to be at rest upon the lock of the cabin door, he walked up to it, full of purpose, and began to rattle the handle vigorously, while he observed, in his low, earnest voice, "You can't trust the workmen nowadays. A brand-new lock, and it won't act at all. Stuck fast. See? See?"

As soon as they found themselves alone in their office across the yard: "You praised that fellow up to Sigg. What is it you see in him?" asked the nephew, with faint contempt.

"I admit he has nothing of your fancy skipper about him, if that's what you mean," said the elder man, curtly. "Is the foreman of the joiners on the *Nan-Shan* outside? . . . Come in, Bates. How is it that you let Tait's people put us off with a defective lock on the cabin door? The Captain could see directly he set eye on it. Have it replaced at once. The little straws, Bates . . . the little straws. . . ."

The lock was replaced accordingly, and a few days afterwards the *Nan-Shan* steamed out to the East, without MacWhirr having offered any further remark as to her fittings, or having been heard to utter a single word hinting at pride in his ship, gratitude for his appointment, or satisfaction at his prospects.

With a temperament neither loquacious nor taciturn he found very little occasion to talk. There were matters of duty, of course—directions, orders, and so on; but the past being to his mind done with, and the future not there yet, the more general actualities of the day required no comment—because facts can speak for themselves with overwhelming precision.

Old Mr. Sigg liked a man of few words, and one that "you could be sure would not try to improve upon his instructions." MacWhirr satisfying these requirements, was continued in command of the *Nan-Shan*, and applied himself to the careful navigation of his ship in the China seas. She had come out on a British register, but after some time Messrs. Sigg judged it expedient to transfer her to the Siamese flag.

At the news of the contemplated transfer Jukes grew restless, as if under a sense of personal affront. He went about grumbling to himself, and uttering short scornful laughs. "Fancy having a ridiculous Noah's Ark elephant in the ensign of one's ship," he said once at the engine-room door. "Dash me if I can stand it:

I'll throw up the billet. Don't it make *you* sick, Mr. Rout?" The chief engineer only cleared his throat with the air of a man who knows the value of a good billet.

The first morning the new flag floated over the stern of the *Nan-Shan* Jukes stood looking at it bitterly from the bridge. He struggled with his feelings for a while, and then remarked, "Queer flag for a man to sail under, sir."

"What's the matter with the flag?" inquired Captain MacWhirr. "Seems all right to me." And he walked across to the end of the bridge to have a good look.

"Well, it looks queer to me," burst out Jukes, greatly exasperated, and flung off the bridge.

Captain MacWhirr was amazed at these manners. After a while he stepped quietly into the chart-room, and opened his International Signal Code-book at the plate where the flags of all the nations are correctly figured in gaudy rows. He ran his finger over them, and when he came to Siam he contemplated with great attention the red field and the white elephant. Nothing could be more simple; but to make sure he brought the book out on the bridge for the purpose of comparing the coloured drawing with the real thing at the flag-staff astern. When next Jukes, who was carrying on the duty that day with a sort of suppressed fierceness, happened on the bridge, his commander observed:

"There's nothing amiss with that flag."

"Isn't there?" mumbled Jukes, falling on his knees before a deck-locker and jerking therefrom viciously a spare lead-line.

"No. I looked up the book. Length twice the breadth and the elephant exactly in the middle. I thought the people ashore would know how to make the local flag. Stands to reason. You were wrong, Jukes. . . ."

"Well, sir," began Jukes, getting up excitedly, "all I can say——" He fumbled for the end of the coil of line with trembling hands.

"That's all right." Captain MacWhirr soothed him, sitting heavily on a little canvas folding-stool he greatly affected. "All you have to do is to take care they don't hoist the elephant upside-down before they get quite used to it."

Jukes flung the new lead-line over on the fore-deck with a loud "Here you are, bo'ss'en—don't forget to wet it thoroughly," and turned with immense resolution towards his commander; but Captain MacWhirr spread his elbows on the bridge-rail comfortably.

"Because it would be, I suppose, understood as a signal of distress," he went on. "What do you think? That elephant there, I take it, stands for something in the nature of the Union Jack in the flag. . . ."

"Does it!" yelled Jukes, so that every head on the *Nan-Shan's* decks looked towards the bridge. Then he sighed, and with sudden resignation: "It would certainly be a dam' distressful sight," he said, meekly.

Later in the day he accosted the chief engineer with a confidential, "Here, let me tell you the old man's latest."

Mr. Solomon Rout (frequently alluded to as Long Sol, Old Sol, or Father Rout), from finding himself almost invariably the tallest man on board every ship he joined, had acquired the habit of a stooping, leisurely condescension. His hair was scant and sandy, his flat cheeks were pale, his bony wrists and long scholarly hands were pale, too, as though he had lived all his life in the shade.

He smiled from on high at Jukes, and went on smoking and glancing about quietly, in the manner of a kind uncle lending an ear to the tale of an excited schoolboy. Then, greatly amused but impassive, he asked:

"And did you throw up the billet?"

"No," cried Jukes, raising a weary, discouraged voice above the harsh buzz of the *Nan-Shan's* friction winches. All of them were hard at work, snatching slings of cargo, high up, to the end of long derricks, only, as it seemed, to let them rip down recklessly by the run. The cargo chains groaned in the gins, clinked on coamings, rattled over the side; and the whole ship quivered, with her long gray flanks smoking in wreaths of steam. "No," cried Jukes, "I didn't. What's the good? I might just as well fling my resignation at this bulkhead. I don't believe you can make a man like that understand anything. He simply knocks me over."

At that moment Captain MacWhirr, back from the shore, crossed the deck, umbrella in hand, escorted by a mournful, self-possessed Chinaman, walking behind in paper-soled silk shoes, and who also carried an umbrella.

The master of the *Nan-Shan*, speaking just audibly and gazing at his boots as his manner was, remarked that it would be necessary to call at Fu-chau this trip, and desired Mr. Rout to have steam up to-morrow afternoon at one o'clock sharp. He pushed back his hat to wipe his forehead, observing at the same time that he hated going ashore anyhow; while overtopping him Mr. Rout, without deigning a word, smoked austerely, nursing his right elbow in the palm of his left hand. Then Jukes was directed in the same subdued voice to keep the forward 'tween-deck clear of cargo. Two hundred coolies were going to be put down there. The Bun Hin Company were sending that lot home. Twenty-five bags of rice would be coming off in a sampan directly, for stores. All seven-years'-men they were, said Captain MacWhirr, with a camphor-wood chest to every man. The carpenter should be set to work nailing three-inch battens along the deck below, fore and aft, to keep these boxes from shifting in a sea-way. Jukes had better look to it at once. "D'ye hear, Jukes?" This Chinaman here was coming with the ship as far as Fu-chau—a sort of interpreter he would be. Bun Hin's clerk he was, and wanted to have a look at the space. Jukes had better take him forward. "D'ye hear, Jukes?"

Jukes took care to punctuate these instructions in proper places with the obligatory "Yes, sir," ejaculated without enthusiasm. His brusque "Come along, John; make look see" set the Chinaman in motion at his heels.

"Wanchee look see, all same look see can do," said Jukes, who having no talent for foreign languages mangled the very pidgin-English cruelly. He pointed at the open hatch. "Catchee number one piecie place to sleep in. Eh?"

He was gruff, as became his racial superiority, but not unfriendly. The Chinaman, gazing sad and speechless into the darkness of the hatchway, seemed to stand at the head of a yawning grave.

"No catchee rain down there—savee?" pointed out Jukes. "Suppose all'ee same fine weather, one piecie coolie-man come topside," he pursued, warming up imaginatively. "Make so—Phooooo!" He expanded his chest and blew out his cheeks. "Savee, John? Breathe—fresh air. Good. Eh? Washee him piecie pants, chow-chow top-side—see, John?"

With his mouth and hands he made exuberant motions of eating rice and washing clothes; and the Chinaman, who concealed his distrust of this pantomime under a collected demeanour tinged by a gentle and refined melancholy, glanced out of his almond eyes from Jukes to the hatch and back again. "Velly good," he murmured, in a disconsolate undertone, and hastened smoothly along the decks, dodging obstacles in his course. He disappeared, ducking low under a sling of ten dirty gunny-bags full of some costly merchandise and exhaling a repulsive smell.

Captain MacWhirr meantime had gone on the bridge, and into the chart-room, where a letter, commenced two days before, awaited termination. These long letters began with the words, "My darling wife," and the steward, between the scrubbing of the floors and the dusting of chronometer-boxes, snatched at every opportunity to read them. They interested him much more than they possibly could the woman for whose eye they were intended; and this for the reason that they related in minute detail each successive trip of the *Nan-Shan*.

Her master, faithful to facts, which alone his consciousness reflected, would set them down with painstaking care upon many pages. The house in a northern suburb to which these pages were addressed had a bit of garden before the bow-windows, a deep porch of good appearance, coloured glass with imitation lead frame in the front door. He paid five-and-forty pounds a year for it, and did not think the rent too high, because Mrs. MacWhirr (a pretentious person with a scraggy neck and a disdainful manner) was admittedly ladylike, and in the neighbourhood considered as "quite superior." The only secret of her life was her abject terror of the time when her husband would come home to stay for good. Under the same roof there dwelt also a daughter called Lydia and a son, Tom. These two were but slightly acquainted with their father. Mainly, they knew him as a rare but privileged visitor, who of an evening smoked his pipe in the dining-room and slept in the house. The lanky girl, upon the whole, was rather ashamed of him; the boy was frankly and utterly indifferent in a straightforward, delightful, unaffected way manly boys have.

And Captain MacWhirr wrote home from the coast of China twelve times every year, desiring quaintly to be "remembered to the children," and subscribing himself "your loving husband," as calmly as if the words so long used by so many men were, apart from their shape, worn-out things, and of a faded meaning.

The China seas north and south are narrow seas. They are seas full of every-day, eloquent facts, such as islands, sand-banks, reefs, swift and changeable currents—tangled facts that nevertheless speak to a seaman in clear and definite language. Their speech appealed to Captain MacWhirr's sense of realities so forcibly that he had given up his state-room below and practically lived all his days on the bridge of his ship, often having his meals sent up, and sleeping at night in the chart-room. And he indited there his home letters. Each of them, without exception, contained the phrase, "The weather has been very fine this trip," or some other form of a statement to that effect. And this statement, too, in its wonderful persistence, was of the same perfect accuracy as all the others they contained.

Mr. Rout likewise wrote letters; only no one on board knew how chatty he could be pen in hand, because the chief engineer had enough imagination to keep his desk locked. His wife relished his style greatly. They were a childless couple, and Mrs. Rout, a big, high-bosomed, jolly woman of forty, shared with Mr. Rout's toothless and venerable mother a little cottage near Teddington. She would run over her correspondence, at breakfast, with lively eyes, and scream out interesting passages in a joyous voice at the deaf old lady, prefacing each extract by the warning shout,

"Solomon says!" She had the trick of firing off Solomon's utterances also upon strangers, astonishing them easily by the unfamiliar text and the unexpectedly jocular vein of these quotations. On the day the new curate called for the first time at the cottage, she found occasion to remark, "As Solomon says: 'the engineers that go down to the sea in ships behold the wonders of sailor nature';" when a change in the visitor's countenance made her stop and stare.

"Solomon. . . . Oh! . . . Mrs. Rout," stuttered the young man, very red in the face, "I must say . . . I don't. . . ."

"He's my husband," she announced in a great shout, throwing herself back in the chair. Perceiving the joke, she laughed immoderately with a handkerchief to her eyes, while he sat wearing a forced smile, and, from his inexperience of jolly women, fully persuaded that she must be deplorably insane. They were excellent friends afterwards; for, absolving her from irreverent intention, he came to think she was a very worthy person indeed; and he learned in time to receive without flinching other scraps of Solomon's wisdom.

"For my part," Solomon was reported by his wife to have said once, "give me the dullest ass for a skipper before a rogue. There is a way to take a fool; but a rogue is smart and slippery." This was an airy generalization drawn from the particular case of Captain MacWhirr's honesty, which, in itself, had the heavy obviousness of a lump of clay. On the other hand, Mr. Jukes, unable to generalize, unmarried, and unengaged, was in the habit of opening his heart after another fashion to an old chum and former shipmate, actually serving as second officer on board an Atlantic liner.

First of all he would insist upon the advantages of the Eastern trade, hinting at its superiority to the

Western ocean service. He extolled the sky, the seas,
the ships, and the easy life of the Far East. The *Nan-
Shan*, he affirmed, was second to none as a sea-boat.

"We have no brass-bound uniforms, but then we are
like brothers here," he wrote. "We all mess together
and live like fighting-cocks. . . . All the chaps of
the black-squad are as decent as they make that kind,
and old Sol, the Chief, is a dry stick. We are good
friends. As to our old man, you could not find a quieter
skipper. Sometimes you would think he hadn't sense
enough to see anything wrong. And yet it isn't that.
Can't be. He has been in command for a good few
years now. He doesn't do anything actually foolish,
and gets his ship along all right without worrying anybody. I believe he hasn't brains enough to enjoy kicking up a row. I don't take advantage of him. I would
scorn it. Outside the routine of duty he doesn't seem to
understand more than half of what you tell him. We
get a laugh out of this at times; but it is dull, too, to
be with a man like this—in the long-run. Old Sol says
he hasn't much conversation. Conversation! O Lord!
He never talks. The other day I had been yarning
under the bridge with one of the engineers, and he
must have heard us. When I came up to take my
watch, he steps out of the chart-room and has a good
look all round, peeps over at the sidelights, glances at
the compass, squints upwards at the stars. That's his
regular performance. By-and-by he says: 'Was that
you talking just now in the port alleyway?' 'Yes, sir.'
'With the third engineer?' 'Yes, sir.' He walks off to
starboard, and sits under the dodger on a little camp-
stool of his, and for half an hour perhaps he makes no
sound, except that I heard him sneeze once. Then after
a while I hear him getting up over there, and he strolls
across to port, where I was. 'I can't understand what

you can find to talk about,' says he. 'Two solid hours.
I am not blaming you. I see people ashore at it all day
long, and then in the evening they sit down and keep
at it over the drinks. Must be saying the same things
over and over again. I can't understand.'

"Did you ever hear anything like that? And he
was so patient about it. It made me quite sorry for him.
But he is exasperating, too, sometimes. Of course one
would not do anything to vex him even if it were worth
while. But it isn't. He's so jolly innocent that if you
were to put your thumb to your nose and wave your
fingers at him he would only wonder gravely to himself
what got into you. He told me once quite simply that
he found it very difficult to make out what made people
always act so queerly. He's too dense to trouble about,
and that's the truth."

Thus wrote Mr. Jukes to his chum in the Western
ocean trade, out of the fulness of his heart and the
liveliness of his fancy.

He had expressed his honest opinion. It was not
worth while trying to impress a man of that sort. If
the world had been full of such men, life would have
probably appeared to Jukes an unentertaining and un-
profitable business. He was not alone in his opinion.
The sea itself, as if sharing Mr. Jukes' good-natured
forbearance, had never put itself out to startle the silent
man, who seldom looked up, and wandered innocently
over the waters with the only visible purpose of getting
food, raiment, and house-room for three people ashore.
Dirty weather he had known, of course. He had been
made wet, uncomfortable, tired in the usual way, felt
at the time and presently forgotten. So that upon the
whole he had been justified in reporting fine weather
at home. But he had never been given a glimpse of immeasurable strength and of immoderate wrath, the

wrath that passes exhausted but never appeased—the wrath and fury of the passionate sea. He knew it existed, as we know that crime and abominations exist; he had heard of it as a peaceable citizen in a town hears of battles, famines, and floods, and yet knows nothing of what these things mean—though, indeed, he may have been mixed up in a street row, have gone without his dinner once, or been soaked to the skin in a shower. Captain MacWhirr had sailed over the surface of the oceans as some men go skimming over the years of existence to sink gently into a placid grave, ignorant of life to the last, without ever having been made to see all it may contain of perfidy, of violence, and of terror. There are on sea and land such men thus fortunate—or thus disdained by destiny or by the sea.

II

OBSERVING the steady fall of the barometer, Captain MacWhirr thought, "There's some dirty weather knocking about." This is precisely what he thought. He had had an experience of moderately dirty weather —the term dirty as applied to the weather implying only moderate discomfort to the seaman. Had he been informed by an indisputable authority that the end of the world was to be finally accomplished by a catastrophic disturbance of the atmosphere, he would have assimilated the information under the simple idea of dirty weather, and no other, because he had no experience of cataclysms, and belief does not necessarily imply comprehension. The wisdom of his county had pronounced by means of an Act of Parliament that before he could be considered as fit to take charge of a ship he should be able to answer certain simple questions on the subject of circular storms such as hurricanes, cyclones, typhoons; and apparently he had answered them, since he was now in command of the *Nan-Shan* in the China seas during the season of typhoons. But if he had answered he remembered nothing of it. He was, however, conscious of being made uncomfortable by the clammy heat. He came out on the bridge, and found no relief to this oppression. The air seemed thick. He gasped like a fish, and began to believe himself greatly out of sorts.

The *Nan-Shan* was ploughing a vanishing furrow upon the circle of the sea that had the surface and the shimmer of an undulating piece of gray silk. The sun, pale and without rays, poured down leaden heat in a strangely indecisive light, and the Chinamen were lying prostrate about the decks. Their bloodless, pinched, yellow faces were like the faces of bilious invalids. Captain MacWhirr noticed two of them especially, stretched out on their backs below the bridge. As soon as they had closed their eyes they seemed dead. Three others, however, were quarrelling barbarously away forward; and one big fellow, half naked, with herculean shoulders, was hanging limply over a winch; another, sitting on the deck, his knees up and his head drooping sideways in a girlish attitude, was plaiting his pigtail with infinite languor depicted in his whole person and in the very movement of his fingers. The smoke struggled with difficulty out of the funnel, and instead of streaming away spread itself out like an infernal sort of cloud, smelling of sulphur and raining soot all over the decks.

"What the devil are you doing there, Mr. Jukes?" asked Captain MacWhirr.

This unusual form of address, though mumbled rather than spoken, caused the body of Mr. Jukes to start as though it had been prodded under the fifth rib. He had had a low bench brought on the bridge, and sitting on it, with a length of rope curled about his feet and a piece of canvas stretched over his knees, was pushing a sail-needle vigorously. He looked up, and his surprise gave to his eyes an expression of innocence and candour.

"I am only roping some of that new set of bags we made last trip for whipping up coals," he remonstrated, gently. "We shall want them for the next coaling, sir."

"What became of the others?"

"Why, worn out of course, sir."

Captain MacWhirr, after glaring down irresolutely at his chief mate, disclosed the gloomy and cynical conviction that more than half of them had been lost overboard, "if only the truth was known," and retired to the other end of the bridge. Jukes, exasperated by this unprovoked attack, broke the needle at the second stitch, and dropping his work got up and cursed the heat in a violent undertone.

The propeller thumped, the three Chinamen forward had given up squabbling very suddenly, and the one who had been plaiting his tail clasped his legs and stared dejectedly over his knees. The lurid sunshine cast faint and sickly shadows. The swell ran higher and swifter every moment, and the ship lurched heavily in the smooth, deep hollows of the sea.

"I wonder where that beastly swell comes from," said Jukes aloud, recovering himself after a stagger.

"North-east," grunted the literal MacWhirr, from his side of the bridge. "There's some dirty weather knocking about. Go and look at the glass."

When Jukes came out of the chart-room, the cast of his countenance had changed to thoughtfulness and concern. He caught hold of the bridge-rail and stared ahead.

The temperature in the engine-room had gone up to a hundred and seventeen degrees. Irritated voices were ascending through the skylight and through the fiddle of the stokehold in a harsh and resonant uproar, mingled with angry clangs and scrapes of metal, as if men with limbs of iron and throats of bronze had been quarrelling down there. The second engineer was falling foul of the stokers for letting the steam go down. He was a man with arms like a blacksmith, and generally feared; but that afternoon the stokers were answering him back recklessly, and slammed the furnace doors with the fury of despair. Then the noise ceased suddenly, and the second engineer appeared, emerging out of the stokehold streaked with grime and soaking wet like a chimney-sweep coming out of a well. As soon as his head was clear of the fiddle he began to scold Jukes for not trimming properly the stokehold ventilators; and in answer Jukes made with his hands deprecatory soothing signs meaning: No wind—can't be helped—you can see for yourself. But the other wouldn't hear reason. His teeth flashed angrily in his dirty face. He didn't mind, he said, the trouble of punching their blanked heads down there, blank his soul, but did the condemned sailors think you could keep steam up in the God-forsaken boilers simply by knocking the blanked stokers about? No, by George! You had to get some draught, too—may he be everlastingly blanked for a swab-headed deck-hand if you didn't! And the chief, too, rampaging before the steam-gauge and carrying on like a lunatic up and down the engine-room ever since noon. What did Jukes think he was stuck up there for, if he couldn't get one of his decayed, good-for-nothing deck-cripples to turn the ventilators to the wind?

The relations of the "engine-room" and the "deck" of the *Nan-Shan* were, as is known, of a brotherly nature; therefore Jukes leaned over and begged the other in a restrained tone not to make a disgusting ass of himself; the skipper was on the other side of the bridge. But the second declared mutinously that he didn't care a rap who was on the other side of the bridge, and Jukes, passing in a flash from lofty disapproval into a state of exaltation, invited him in unflattering terms to come up and twist the beastly things to please himself, and catch such wind as a donkey of his sort could find. The second rushed up to the fray. He flung himself at the port ventilator as though he meant to tear it out bodily and toss it overboard. All he did was to move the cowl round a few inches, with an enormous expenditure of force, and seemed spent in the effort. He leaned against the back of the wheelhouse, and Jukes walked up to him.

"Oh, Heavens!" ejaculated the engineer in a feeble voice. He lifted his eyes to the sky, and then let his glassy stare descend to meet the horizon that, tilting up to an angle of forty degrees, seemed to hang on a slant for a while and settled down slowly. "Heavens! Phew! What's up, anyhow?"

Jukes, straddling his long legs like a pair of compasses, put on an air of superiority. "We're going to catch it this time," he said. "The barometer is tumbling down like anything, Harry. And you trying to kick up that silly row. . . ."

The word "barometer" seemed to revive the second engineer's mad animosity. Collecting afresh all his energies, he directed Jukes in a low and brutal tone to shove the unmentionable instrument down his gory throat. Who cared for his crimson barometer? It was the steam—the steam—that was going down; and what between the firemen going faint and the chief going silly, it was worse than a dog's life for him; he didn't care a tinker's curse how soon the whole show was blown out of the water. He seemed on the point of having a cry, but after regaining his breath he muttered darkly, "I'll faint them," and dashed off. He stopped upon the fiddle long enough to shake his fist at the unnatural daylight, and dropped into the dark hole with a whoop.

When Jukes turned, his eyes fell upon the rounded back and the big red ears of Captain MacWhirr, who had come across. He did not look at his chief officer, but said at once, "That's a very violent man, that second engineer."

"Jolly good second, anyhow," grunted Jukes. "They can't keep up steam," he added, rapidly, and made a grab at the rail against the coming lurch.

Captain MacWhirr, unprepared, took a run and brought himself up with a jerk by an awning stanchion.

"A profane man," he said, obstinately. "If this goes on, I'll have to get rid of him the first chance."

"It's the heat," said Jukes. "The weather's awful. It would make a saint swear. Even up here I feel exactly as if I had my head tied up in a woollen blanket."

Captain MacWhirr looked up. "D'ye mean to say, Mr. Jukes, you ever had your head tied up in a blanket? What was that for?"

"It's a manner of speaking, sir," said Jukes, stolidly.

"Some of you fellows do go on! What's that about saints swearing? I wish you wouldn't talk so wild. What sort of saint would that be that would swear? No more saint than yourself, I expect. And what's a blanket got to do with it—or the weather either. . . . The heat does not make me swear—does it? It's filthy bad temper. That's what it is. And what's the good of your talking like this?"

Thus Captain MacWhirr expostulated against the use of images in speech, and at the end electrified Jukes by a contemptuous snort, followed by words of passion and resentment: "Damme! I'll fire him out of the ship if he don't look out."

And Jukes, incorrigible, thought: "Goodness me! Somebody's put a new inside to my old man. Here's temper, if you like. Of course it's the weather; what else? It would make an angel quarrelsome—let alone a saint."

All the Chinamen on deck appeared at their last gasp.

At its setting the sun had a diminished diameter and an expiring brown, rayless glow, as if millions of centuries elapsing since the morning had brought it near its end. A dense bank of cloud became visible to the northward; it had a sinister dark olive tint, and lay low and motionless upon the sea, resembling a solid obstacle in the path of the ship. She went floundering towards it like an exhausted creature driven to its death. The coppery twilight retired slowly, and the darkness brought out overhead a swarm of unsteady, big stars, that, as if blown upon, flickered exceedingly and seemed to hang very near the earth. At eight o'clock Jukes went into the chart-room to write up the ship's log.

He copied neatly out of the rough-book the number of miles, the course of the ship, and in the column for "wind" scrawled the word "calm" from top to bottom of the eight hours since noon. He was exasperated by the continuous, monotonous rolling of the ship. The heavy inkstand would slide away in a manner that suggested perverse intelligence in dodging the pen. Having written in the large space under the head of "Remarks" "Heat very oppressive," he stuck the end of the penholder in his teeth, pipe fashion, and mopped his face carefully.

"Ship rolling heavily in a high cross swell," he began again, and commented to himself, "Heavily is no word for it." Then he wrote: "Sunset threatening, with a low bank of clouds to N. and E. Sky clear overhead."

Sprawling over the table with arrested pen, he glanced out of the door, and in that frame of his vision he saw all the stars flying upwards between the teakwood jambs on a black sky. The whole lot took flight together and disappeared, leaving only a blackness flecked with white flashes, for the sea was as black as the sky and speckled with foam afar. The stars that had

flown to the roll came back on the return swing of the
ship, rushing downwards in their glittering multitude,
not of fiery points, but enlarged to tiny discs brilliant
with a clear wet sheen.

Jukes watched the flying big stars for a moment, and
then wrote: "8 P.M. Swell increasing. Ship labouring
and taking water on her decks. Battened down the
coolies for the night. Barometer still falling." He
paused, and thought to himself, "Perhaps nothing
whatever'll come of it." And then he closed resolutely
his entries: "Every appearance of a typhoon coming
on."

On going out he had to stand aside, and Captain Mac-
Whirr strode over the doorstep without saying a word or
making a sign.

"Shut the door, Mr. Jukes, will you?" he cried from
within.

Jukes turned back to do so, muttering ironically:
"Afraid to catch cold, I suppose." It was his watch
below, but he yearned for communion with his kind;
and he remarked cheerily to the second mate: "Doesn't
look so bad, after all—does it?"

The second mate was marching to and fro on the
bridge, tripping down with small steps one moment,
and the next climbing with difficulty the shifting slope
of the deck. At the sound of Jukes' voice he stood still,
facing forward, but made no reply.

"Hallo! That's a heavy one," said Jukes, swaying
to meet the long roll till his lowered hand touched the
planks. This time the second mate made in his throat
a noise of an unfriendly nature.

He was an oldish, shabby little fellow, with bad teeth
and no hair on his face. He had been shipped in a
hurry in Shanghai, that trip when the second officer
brought from home had delayed the ship three hours

in port by contriving (in some manner Captain Mac-
Whirr could never understand) to fall overboard into
an empty coal-lighter lying alongside, and had to be
sent ashore to the hospital with concussion of the brain
and a broken limb or two.

Jukes was not discouraged by the unsympathetic
sound. "The Chinamen must be having a lovely time
of it down there," he said. "It's lucky for them the
old girl has the easiest roll of any ship I've ever been
in. There now! This one wasn't so bad."

"You wait," snarled the second mate.

With his sharp nose, red at the tip, and his thin
pinched lips, he always looked as though he were raging
inwardly; and he was concise in his speech to the point
of rudeness. All his time off duty he spent in his cabin
with the door shut, keeping so still in there that he was
supposed to fall asleep as soon as he had disappeared;
but the man who came in to wake him for his watch on
deck would invariably find him with his eyes wide open,
flat on his back in the bunk, and glaring irritably from a
soiled pillow. He never wrote any letters, did not
seem to hope for news from anywhere; and though he
had been heard once to mention West Hartlepool, it
was with extreme bitterness, and only in connection
with the extortionate charges of a boarding-house.
He was one of those men who are picked up at need in
the ports of the world. They are competent enough,
appear hopelessly hard up, show no evidence of any
sort of vice, and carry about them all the signs of manifest failure. They come aboard on an emergency, care
for no ship afloat, live in their own atmosphere of casual
connection amongst their shipmates who know nothing
of them, and make up their minds to leave at inconvenient times. They clear out with no words of leave-
taking in some God-forsaken port other men would fear

to be stranded in, and go ashore in company of a shabby sea-chest, corded like a treasure-box, and with an air of shaking the ship's dust off their feet.

"You wait," he repeated, balanced in great swings with his back to Jukes, motionless and implacable.

"Do you mean to say we are going to catch it hot?" asked Jukes with boyish interest.

"Say? . . . I say nothing. You don't catch me," snapped the little second mate, with a mixture of pride, scorn, and cunning, as if Jukes' question had been a trap cleverly detected. "Oh, no! None of you here shall make a fool of me if I know it," he mumbled to himself.

Jukes reflected rapidly that this second mate was a mean little beast, and in his heart he wished poor Jack Allen had never smashed himself up in the coal-lighter. The far-off blackness ahead of the ship was like another night seen through the starry night of the earth—the starless night of the immensities beyond the created universe, revealed in its appalling stillness through a low fissure in the glittering sphere of which the earth is the kernel.

"Whatever there might be about," said Jukes, "we are steaming straight into it."

"*You've* said it," caught up the second mate, always with his back to Jukes. "You've said it, mind—not I."

"Oh, go to Jericho!" said Jukes, frankly; and the other emitted a triumphant little chuckle.

"You've said it," he repeated.

"And what of that?"

"I've known some real good men get into trouble with their skippers for saying a dam' sight less," answered the second mate feverishly. "Oh, no! You don't catch me."

"You seem deucedly anxious not to give yourself away," said Jukes, completely soured by such absurdity. "I wouldn't be afraid to say what I think."

"Aye, to me   That's no great trick.   I am nobody, and well I know it."

The ship, after a pause of comparative steadiness, started upon a series of rolls, one worse than the other, and for a time Jukes, preserving his equilibrium, was too busy to open his mouth.   As soon as the violent swinging had quieted down somewhat, he said: "This is a bit too much of a good thing.   Whether anything is coming or not I think she ought to be put head on to that swell.   The old man is just gone in to lie down. Hang me if I don't speak to him."

But when he opened the door of the chart-room he saw his captain reading a book.   Captain MacWhirr was not lying down: he was standing up with one hand grasping the edge of the bookshelf and the other holding open before his face a thick volume.   The lamp wriggled in the gimbals, the loosened books toppled from side to side on the shelf, the long barometer swung in jerky circles, the table altered its slant every moment.   In the midst of all this stir and movement Captain MacWhirr, holding on, showed his eyes above the upper edge, and asked, "What's the matter?"

"Swell getting worse, sir."

"Noticed that in here," muttered Captain MacWhirr. "Anything wrong?"

Jukes, inwardly disconcerted by the seriousness of the eyes looking at him over the top of the book, produced an embarrassed grin.

"Rolling like old boots," he said, sheepishly.

"Aye! Very heavy—very heavy. What do you want?"

At this Jukes lost his footing and began to flounder.

"I was thinking of our passengers," he said, in the manner of a man clutching at a straw.

"Passengers?" wondered the Captain, gravely. "What passengers?"

"Why, the Chinamen, sir," explained Jukes, very sick of this conversation.

"The Chinamen! Why don't you speak plainly? Couldn't tell what you meant. Never heard a lot of coolies spoken of as passengers before. Passengers, indeed! What's come to you?"

Captain MacWhirr, closing the book on his forefinger, lowered his arm and looked completely mystified. "Why are you thinking of the Chinamen, Mr. Jukes?" he inquired.

Jukes took a plunge, like a man driven to it. "She's rolling her decks full of water, sir. Thought you might put her head on perhaps—for a while. Till this goes down a bit—very soon, I dare say. Head to the eastward. I never knew a ship roll like this."

He held on in the doorway, and Captain MacWhirr, feeling his grip on the shelf inadequate, made up his mind to let go in a hurry, and fell heavily on the couch.

"Head to the eastward?" he said, struggling to sit up. "That's more than four points off her course."

"Yes, sir. Fifty degrees. . . . Would just bring her head far enough round to meet this. . . ."

Captain MacWhirr was now sitting up. He had not dropped the book, and he had not lost his place.

"To the eastward?" he repeated, with dawning astonishment. "To the . . . Where do you think we are bound to? You want me to haul a full-powered steamship four points off her course to make the Chinamen comfortable! Now, I've heard more than enough of mad things done in the world—but this. . . . If I didn't know you, Jukes, I would think you were in liquor. Steer four points off. . . . And what afterwards? Steer four points over the other way, I suppose, to make the course good. What put it into your head that I would start to tack a steamer as if she were a sailing-ship?"

"Jolly good thing she isn't," threw in Jukes, with bitter readiness. "She would have rolled every blessed stick out of her this afternoon."

"Aye! And you just would have had to stand and see them go," said Captain MacWhirr, showing a certain animation. "It's a dead calm, isn't it?"

"It is, sir. But there's something out of the common coming, for sure."

"Maybe. I suppose you have a notion I should be getting out of the way of that dirt," said Captain Mac-Whirr, speaking with the utmost simplicity of manner and tone, and fixing the oilcloth on the floor with a heavy stare. Thus he noticed neither Jukes' discomfiture nor the mixture of vexation and astonished respect on his face.

"Now, here's this book," he continued with deliberation, slapping his thigh with the closed volume. "I've been reading the chapter on the storms there."

This was true. He had been reading the chapter on the storms. When he had entered the chart-room, it was with no intention of taking the book down. Some influence in the air—the same influence, probably, that caused the steward to bring without orders the Captain's sea-boots and oilskin coat up to the chart-room—had as it were guided his hand to the shelf; and without taking the time to sit down he had waded with a conscious effort into the terminology of the subject. He lost himself amongst advancing semi-circles, left- and right-hand quadrants, the curves of the tracks, the probable bearing of the centre, the shifts of wind and the readings of barometer. He tried to bring all these things into a definite relation to himself, and ended by becoming contemptuously angry with such a lot of words and with so much advice, all head-work and supposition, without a glimmer of certitude.

"It's the damnedest thing, Jukes," he said. "If a fellow was to believe all that's in there, he would be running most of his time all over the sea trying to get behind the weather."

Again he slapped his leg with the book; and Jukes opened his mouth, but said nothing.

"Running to get behind the weather! Do you understand that, Mr. Jukes? It's the maddest thing!" ejaculated Captain MacWhirr, with pauses, gazing at the floor profoundly. "You would think an old woman had been writing this. It passes me. If that thing means anything useful, then it means that I should at once alter the course away, away to the devil somewhere, and come booming down on Fu-chau from the northward at the tail of this dirty weather that's supposed to be knocking about in our way. From the north! Do you understand, Mr. Jukes? Three hundred extra miles to the distance, and a pretty coal bill to show. I couldn't bring myself to do that if every word in there was gospel truth, Mr. Jukes. Don't you expect me. . . ."

And Jukes, silent, marvelled at this display of feeling and loquacity.

"But the truth is that you don't know if the fellow is right, anyhow. How can you tell what a gale is made of till you get it? He isn't aboard here, is he? Very well. Here he says that the centre of them things bears eight points off the wind; but we haven't got any wind, for all the barometer falling. Where's his centre now?"

"We will get the wind presently," mumbled Jukes.

"Let it come, then," said Captain MacWhirr, with dignified indignation. "It's only to let you see, Mr. Jukes, that you don't find everything in books. All these rules for dodging breezes and circumventing the winds of heaven, Mr. Jukes, seem to me the maddest thing, when you come to look at it sensibly."

He raised his eyes, saw Jukes gazing at him dubiously, and tried to illustrate his meaning.

"About as queer as your extraordinary notion of dodging the ship head to sea, for I don't know how long, to make the Chinamen comfortable; whereas all we've got to do is to take them to Fu-chau, being timed to get there before noon on Friday. If the weather delays me—very well. There's your log-book to talk straight about the weather. But suppose I went swinging off my course and came in two days late, and they asked me: 'Where have you been all that time, Captain?' What could I say to that? 'Went around to dodge the bad weather,' I would say. 'It must've been dam' bad,' they would say. 'Don't know,' I would have to say; 'I've dodged clear of it.' See that, Jukes? I have been thinking it all out this afternoon."

He looked up again in his unseeing, unimaginative way. No one had ever heard him say so much at one time. Jukes, with his arms open in the doorway, was like a man invited to behold a miracle. Unbounded wonder was the intellectual meaning of his eye, while incredulity was seated in his whole countenance.

"A gale is a gale, Mr. Jukes," resumed the Captain, "and a full-powered steam-ship has got to face it. There's just so much dirty weather knocking about the world, and the proper thing is to go through it with none of what old Captain Wilson of the *Melita* calls 'storm strategy.' The other day ashore I heard him hold forth about it to a lot of shipmasters who came in and sat at a table next to mine. It seemed to me the greatest nonsense. He was telling them how he out-manœuvred, I think he said, a terrific gale, so that it never came nearer than fifty miles to him. A neat piece of head-work he called it. How he knew there was a terrific gale fifty miles off beats me altogether. It was like listening to a crazy man. I would have thought Captain Wilson was old enough to know better."

Captain MacWhirr ceased for a moment, then said, "It's your watch below, Mr. Jukes?"

Jukes came to himself with a start. "Yes, sir."

"Leave orders to call me at the slightest change," said the Captain. He reached up to put the book away, and tucked his legs upon the couch. "Shut the door so that it don't fly open, will you? I can't stand a door banging. They've put a lot of rubbishy locks into this ship, I must say."

Captain MacWhirr closed his eyes.

He did so to rest himself. He was tired, and he experienced that state of mental vacuity which comes at the end of an exhaustive discussion that had liberated some belief matured in the course of meditative years. He had indeed been making his confession of faith, had he only known it; and its effect was to make Jukes, on the other side of the door, stand scratching his head for a good while.

Captain MacWhirr opened his eyes.

He thought he must have been asleep. What was that loud noise? Wind? Why had he not been called? The lamp wriggled in its gimbals, the barometer swung in circles, the table altered its slant every moment; a pair of limp sea-boots with collapsed tops went sliding past the couch. He put out his hand instantly, and captured one.

Jukes' face appeared in a crack of the door: only his face, very red, with staring eyes. The flame of the lamp leaped, a piece of paper flew up, a rush of air enveloped Captain MacWhirr. Beginning to draw on the boot, he directed an expectant gaze at Jukes' swollen, excited features.

"Came on like this," shouted Jukes, "five minutes ago . . . all of a sudden."

The head disappeared with a bang, and a heavy splash and patter of drops swept past the closed door as if a pailful of melted lead had been flung against the house. A whistling could be heard now upon the deep vibrating noise outside. The stuffy chart-room seemed as full of draughts as a shed. Captain MacWhirr collared the other sea-boot on its violent passage along the floor. He was not flustered, but he could not find at once the opening for inserting his foot. The shoes he had flung off were scurrying from end to end of the cabin, gambolling playfully over each other like puppies. As soon as he stood up he kicked at them viciously, but without effect.

He threw himself into the attitude of a lunging fencer, to reach after his oilskin coat; and afterwards he staggered all over the confined space while he jerked himself into it. Very grave, straddling his legs far apart, and stretching his neck, he started to tie deliberately the strings of his sou'-wester under his chin, with thick fingers that trembled slightly. He went through all the movements of a woman putting on her bonnet before a glass, with a strained, listening attention, as though he had expected every moment to hear the shout of his name in the confused clamour that had suddenly beset his ship. Its increase filled his ears while he was getting ready to go out and confront whatever it might mean. It was tumultuous and very loud—made up of the rush of the wind, the crashes of the sea, with that prolonged deep vibration of the air, like the roll of an immense and remote drum beating the charge of the gale.

He stood for a moment in the light of the lamp, thick, clumsy, shapeless in his panoply of combat, vigilant and red-faced.

"There's a lot of weight in this," he muttered.

As soon as he attempted to open the door the wind caught it. Clinging to the handle, he was dragged out over the doorstep, and at once found himself engaged with the wind in a sort of personal scuffle whose object was the shutting of that door. At the last moment a tongue of air scurried in and licked out the flame of the lamp.

Ahead of the ship he perceived a great darkness lying upon a multitude of white flashes; on the starboard beam a few amazing stars drooped, dim and fitful, above an immense waste of broken seas, as if seen through a mad drift of smoke.

On the bridge a knot of men, indistinct and toiling, were making great efforts in the light of the wheelhouse windows that shone mistily on their heads and backs. Suddenly darkness closed upon one pane, then on another. The voices of the lost group reached him after the manner of men's voices in a gale, in shreds and fragments of forlorn shouting snatched past the ear. All at once Jukes appeared at his side, yelling, with his head down.

"Watch—put in—wheelhouse shutters—glass—afraid—blow in."

Jukes heard his commander upbraiding.

"This—come—anything—warning—call me."

He tried to explain, with the uproar pressing on his lips.

"Light air—remained—bridge—sudden—north-east—could turn—thought—you—sure—hear."

They had gained the shelter of the weather-cloth, and could converse with raised voices, as people quarrel.

"I got the hands along to cover up all the ventilators. Good job I had remained on deck. I didn't think you would be asleep, and so . . . What did you say, sir? What?"

"Nothing," cried Captain MacWhirr. "I said—all right."

"By all the powers! We've got it this time," observed Jukes in a howl.

"You haven't altered her course?" inquired Captain MacWhirr, straining his voice.

"No, sir. Certainly not. Wind came out right ahead. And here comes the head sea."

A plunge of the ship ended in a shock as if she had landed her forefoot upon something solid. After a moment of stillness a lofty flight of sprays drove hard with the wind upon their faces.

"Keep her at it as long as we can," shouted Captain MacWhirr.

Before Jukes had squeezed the salt water out of his eyes all the stars had disappeared.

III

JUKES was as ready a man as any half-dozen young mates that may be caught by casting a net upon the waters; and though he had been somewhat taken aback by the startling viciousness of the first squall, he had pulled himself together on the instant, had called out the hands and had rushed them along to secure such openings about the deck as had not been already battened down earlier in the evening. Shouting in his fresh, stentorian voice, "Jump, boys, and bear a hand!" he led in the work, telling himself the while that he had "just expected this."

But at the same time he was growing aware that this was rather more than he had expected. From the first stir of the air felt on his cheek the gale seemed to take upon itself the accumulated impetus of an avalanche. Heavy sprays enveloped the *Nan-Shan* from stem to stern, and instantly in the midst of her regular rolling she began to jerk and plunge as though she had gone mad with fright.

Jukes thought, "This is no joke." While he was exchanging explanatory yells with his captain, a sudden lowering of the darkness came upon the night, falling before their vision like something palpable. It was as if the masked lights of the world had been turned down. Jukes was uncritically glad to have his captain at hand. It relieved him as though that man had, by simply coming on deck, taken most of the gale's weight upon his shoulders. Such is the prestige, the privilege, and the burden of command.

Captain MacWhirr could expect no relief of that sort from any one on earth. Such is the loneliness of command. He was trying to see, with that watchful manner of a seaman who stares into the wind's eye as if into the eye of an adversary, to penetrate the hidden intention and guess the aim and force of the thrust. The strong wind swept at him out of a vast obscurity; he felt under his feet the uneasiness of his ship, and he could not even discern the shadow of her shape. He wished it were not so; and very still he waited, feeling stricken by a blind man's helplessness.

To be silent was natural to him, dark or shine. Jukes, at his elbow, made himself heard yelling cheerily in the gusts, "We must have got the worst of it at once, sir." A faint burst of lightning quivered all round, as if flashed into a cavern—into a black and secret chamber of the sea, with a floor of foaming crests.

It unveiled for a sinister, fluttering moment a ragged mass of clouds hanging low, the lurch of the long outlines of the ship, the black figures of men caught on the bridge, heads forward, as if petrified in the act of butting. The darkness palpitated down upon all this, and then the real thing came at last.

It was something formidable and swift, like the sudden smashing of a vial of wrath. It seemed to explode all round the ship with an overpowering concussion and a rush of great waters, as if an immense dam had been blown up to windward. In an instant the men lost touch of each other. This is the disintegrating power of a great wind: it isolates one from one's kind. An earthquake, a landslip, an avalanche, overtake a man incidentally, as it were—without passion. A furious gale attacks him like a personal enemy, tries to grasp his limbs, fastens upon his mind, seeks to rout his very spirit out of him.

Jukes was driven away from his commander. He fancied himself whirled a great distance through the air. Everything disappeared—even, for a moment, his power of thinking; but his hand had found one of the rail-stanchions. His distress was by no means alleviated by an inclination to disbelieve the reality of this experience. Though young, he had seen some bad weather, and had never doubted his ability to imagine the worst; but this was so much beyond his powers of fancy that it appeared incompatible with the existence of any ship whatever. He would have been incredulous about himself in the same way, perhaps, had he not been so harassed by the necessity of exerting a wrestling effort against a force trying to tear him away from his hold. Moreover, the conviction of not being utterly destroyed returned to him through the sensations of being half-drowned, bestially shaken, and partly choked.

It seemed to him he remained there precariously alone with the stanchion for a long, long time. The rain poured on him, flowed, drove in sheets. He breathed in gasps; and sometimes the water he swallowed was fresh and sometimes it was salt. For the most part he kept his eyes shut tight, as if suspecting his sight might be destroyed in the immense flurry of the elements. When he ventured to blink hastily, he derived some moral support from the green gleam on the starboard light shining feebly upon the flight of rain and sprays. He was actually looking at it when its ray fell upon the uprearing sea which put it out. He saw the head of the wave topple over, adding the mite of its crash to the tremendous uproar raging around him, and almost at the same instant the stanchion was wrenched away from his embracing arms. After a crushing thump on his back he found himself suddenly afloat and borne upwards. His first irresistible notion

was that the whole China Sea had climbed on the
bridge. Then, more sanely, he concluded himself gone
overboard. All the time he was being tossed, flung,
and rolled in great volumes of water, he kept on repeating mentally, with the utmost precipitation, the words:
"My God! My God! My God! My God!"

All at once, in a revolt of misery and despair, he
formed the crazy resolution to get out of that. And he
began to thresh about with his arms and legs. But
as soon as he commenced his wretched struggles he
discovered that he had become somehow mixed up
with a face, an oilskin coat, somebody's boots. He
clawed ferociously all these things in turn, lost them,
found them again, lost them once more, and finally was
himself caught in the firm clasp of a pair of stout arms.
He returned the embrace closely round a thick solid
body. He had found his captain.

They tumbled over and over, tightening their hug.
Suddenly the water let them down with a brutal bang;
and, stranded against the side of the wheelhouse, out of
breath and bruised, they were left to stagger up in the
wind and hold on where they could.

Jukes came out of it rather horrified, as though he
had escaped some unparalleled outrage directed at his
feelings. It weakened his faith in himself. He started
shouting aimlessly to the man he could feel near him
in that fiendish blackness, "Is it you, sir? Is it you,
sir?" till his temples seemed ready to burst. And he
heard in answer a voice, as if crying far away, as if
screaming to him fretfully from a very great distance,
the one word "Yes!" Other seas swept again over the
bridge. He received them defencelessly right over his
bare head, with both his hands engaged in holding.

The motion of the ship was extravagant. Her lurches
had an appalling helplessness: she pitched as if taking

a header into a void, and seemed to find a wall to hit
every time. When she rolled she fell on her side headlong, and she would be righted back by such a demol-
ishing blow that Jukes felt her reeling as a clubbed man
reels before he collapses. The gale howled and scuffled
about gigantically in the darkness, as though the entire
world were one black gully. At certain moments the
air streamed against the ship as if sucked through a
tunnel with a concentrated solid force of impact that
seemed to lift her clean out of the water and keep her
up for an instant with only a quiver running through
her from end to end. And then she would begin her
tumbling again as if dropped back into a boiling cauldron. Jukes tried hard to compose his mind and judge
things coolly.

The sea, flattened down in the heavier gusts, would
uprise and overwhelm both ends of the *Nan-Shan* in
snowy rushes of foam, expanding wide, beyond both
rails, into the night. And on this dazzling sheet, spread
under the blackness of the clouds and emitting a bluish
glow, Captain MacWhirr could catch a desolate glimpse
of a few tiny specks black as ebony, the tops of the
hatches, the battened companions, the heads of the
covered winches, the foot of a mast. This was all he
could see of his ship. Her middle structure, covered
by the bridge which bore him, his mate, the closed
wheelhouse where a man was steering shut up with the
fear of being swept overboard together with the whole
thing in one great crash—her middle structure was like
a half-tide rock awash upon a coast. It was like an
outlying rock with the water boiling up, streaming over,
pouring off, beating round—like a rock in the surf to
which shipwrecked people cling before they let go—
only it rose, it sank, it rolled continuously, without
respite and rest, like a rock that should have miracu-

lously struck adrift from a coast and gone wallowing upon the sea.

The *Nan-Shan* was being looted by the storm with a senseless, destructive fury: trysails torn out of the extra gaskets, double-lashed awnings blown away, bridge swept clean, weather-cloths burst, rails twisted, light-screens smashed—and two of the boats had gone already. They had gone unheard and unseen, melting, as it were, in the shock and smother of the wave. It was only later, when upon the white flash of another high sea hurling itself amidships, Jukes had a vision of two pairs of davits leaping black and empty out of the solid blackness, with one overhauled fall flying and an iron-bound block capering in the air, that he became aware of what had happened within about three yards of his back.

He poked his head forward, groping for the ear of his commander. His lips touched it—big, fleshy, very wet. He cried in an agitated tone, "Our boats are going now, sir."

And again he heard that voice, forced and ringing feebly, but with a penetrating effect of quietness in the enormous discord of noises, as if sent out from some remote spot of peace beyond the black wastes of the gale; again he heard a man's voice—the frail and indomitable sound that can be made to carry an infinity of thought, resolution and purpose, that shall be pronouncing confident words on the last day, when heavens fall, and justice is done—again he heard it, and it was crying to him, as if from very, very far—"All right."

He thought he had not managed to make himself understood. "Our boats—I say boats—the boats, sir! Two gone!"

The same voice, within a foot of him and yet so remote, yelled sensibly, "Can't be helped."

Captain MacWhirr had never turned his face, but
Jukes caught some more words on the wind.

"What can—expect—when hammering through—
such—— Bound to leave—something behind—stands
to reason."

Watchfully Jukes listened for more. No more came.
This was all Captain MacWhirr had to say; and Jukes
could picture to himself rather than see the broad
squat back before him. An impenetrable obscurity
pressed down upon the ghostly glimmers of the sea.
A dull conviction seized upon Jukes that there was
nothing to be done.

If the steering-gear did not give way, if the immense
volumes of water did not burst the deck in or smash
one of the hatches, if the engines did not give up, if
way could be kept on the ship against this terrific
wind, and she did not bury herself in one of these
awful seas, of whose white crests alone, topping high
above her bows, he could now and then get a sickening
glimpse—then there was a chance of her coming out
of it. Something within him seemed to turn over,
bringing uppermost the feeling that the *Nan-Shan*
was lost.

"She's done for," he said to himself, with a surprising
mental agitation, as though he had discovered an unexpected meaning in this thought. One of these things
was bound to happen. Nothing could be prevented
now, and nothing could be remedied. The men on
board did not count, and the ship could not last. This
weather was too impossible.

Jukes felt an arm thrown heavily over his shoulders;
and to this overture he responded with great intelligence
by catching hold of his captain round the waist.

They stood clasped thus in the blind night, bracing
each other against the wind, cheek to cheek and lip to

ear, in the manner of two hulks lashed stem to stern together.

And Jukes heard the voice of his commander hardly any louder than before, but nearer, as though, starting to march athwart the prodigious rush of the hurricane, it had approached him, bearing that strange effect of quietness like the serene glow of a halo.

"D'ye know where the hands got to?" it asked, vigorous and evanescent at the same time, overcoming the strength of the wind, and swept away from Jukes instantly.

Jukes didn't know. They were all on the bridge when the real force of the hurricane struck the ship. He had no idea where they had crawled to. Under the circumstances they were nowhere, for all the use that could be made of them. Somehow the Captain's wish to know distressed Jukes.

"Want the hands, sir?" he cried, apprehensively.

"Ought to know," asserted Captain MacWhirr. "Hold hard."

They held hard. An outburst of unchained fury, a vicious rush of the wind absolutely steadied the ship; she rocked only, quick and light like a child's cradle, for a terrific moment of suspense, while the whole atmosphere, as it seemed, streamed furiously past her, roaring away from the tenebrous earth.

It suffocated them, and with eyes shut they tightened their grasp. What from the magnitude of the shock might have been a column of water running upright in the dark, butted against the ship, broke short, and fell on her bridge, crushingly, from on high, with a dead burying weight.

A flying fragment of that collapse, a mere splash, enveloped them in one swirl from their feet ever their heads, filling violently their ears, mouths and nostrils

with salt water. It knocked out their legs, wrenched
in haste at their arms, seethed away swiftly under their
chins; and opening their eyes, they saw the piled-up
masses of foam dashing to and fro amongst what looked
like the fragments of a ship. She had given way as if
driven straight in. Their panting hearts yielded, too,
before the tremendous blow; and all at once she sprang
up again to her desperate plunging, as if trying to
scramble out from under the ruins.

The seas in the dark seemed to rush from all sides
to keep her back where she might perish. There was
hate in the way she was handled, and a ferocity in the
blows that fell. She was like a living creature thrown
to the rage of a mob: hustled terribly, struck at, borne
up, flung down, leaped upon. Captain MacWhirr and
Jukes kept hold of each other, deafened by the noise,
gagged by the wind; and the great physical tumult
beating about their bodies, brought, like an unbridled
display of passion, a profound trouble to their souls.
One of these wild and appalling shrieks that are heard
at times passing mysteriously overhead in the steady
roar of a hurricane, swooped, as if borne on wings,
upon the ship, and Jukes tried to outscream it.

"Will she live through this?"

The cry was wrenched out of his breast. It was as
unintentional as the birth of a thought in the head, and
he heard nothing of it himself. It all became extinct
at once—thought, intention, effort—and of his cry the
inaudible vibration added to the tempest waves of the
air.

He expected nothing from it. Nothing at all. For
indeed what answer could be made? But after a while
he heard with amazement the frail and resisting voice
in his ear, the dwarf sound, unconquered in the giant
tumult.

"She may!"

It was a dull yell, more difficult to seize than a whisper. And presently the voice returned again, half submerged in the vast crashes, like a ship battling against the waves of an ocean.

"Let's hope so!" it cried—small, lonely and unmoved, a stranger to the visions of hope or fear; and it flickered into disconnected words: "Ship. . . . . This. . . . Never—Anyhow . . . for the best." Jukes gave it up.

Then, as if it had come suddenly upon the one thing fit to withstand the power of a storm, it seemed to gain force and firmness for the last broken shouts:

"Keep on hammering . . . builders . . . good men. . . . . And chance it . . . engines. . . . Rout . . . good man."

Captain MacWhirr removed his arm from Jukes' shoulders, and thereby ceased to exist for his mate, so dark it was; Jukes, after a tense stiffening of every muscle, would let himself go limp all over. The gnawing of profound discomfort existed side by side with an incredible disposition to somnolence, as though he had been buffeted and worried into drowsiness. The wind would get hold of his head and try to shake it off his shoulders; his clothes, full of water, were as heavy as lead, cold and dripping like an armour of melting ice: he shivered—it lasted a long time; and with his hands closed hard on his hold, he was letting himself sink slowly into the depths of bodily misery. His mind became concentrated upon himself in an aimless, idle way, and when something pushed lightly at the back of his knees he nearly, as the saying is, jumped out of his skin.

In the start forward he bumped the back of Captain MacWhirr, who didn't move; and then a hand gripped

his thigh. A lull had come, a menacing lull of the wind, the holding of a stormy breath—and he felt himself pawed all over. It was the boatswain. Jukes recognized these hands, so thick and enormous that they seemed to belong to some new species of man.

The boatswain had arrived on the bridge, crawling on all fours against the wind, and had found the chief mate's legs with the top of his head. Immediately he crouched and began to explore Jukes' person upwards with prudent, apologetic touches, as became an inferior.

He was an ill-favoured, undersized, gruff sailor of fifty, coarsely hairy, short-legged, long-armed, resembling an elderly ape. His strength was immense; and in his great lumpy paws, bulging like brown boxing-gloves on the end of furry forearms, the heaviest objects were handled like playthings. Apart from the grizzled pelt on his chest, the menacing demeanour and the hoarse voice, he had none of the classical attributes of his rating. His good nature almost amounted to imbecility: the men did what they liked with him, and he had not an ounce of initiative in his character, which was easy-going and talkative. For these reasons Jukes disliked him; but Captain MacWhirr, to Jukes' scornful disgust, seemed to regard him as a first-rate petty officer.

He pulled himself up by Jukes' coat, taking that liberty with the greatest moderation, and only so far as it was forced upon him by the hurricane. "What is it, boss'n, what is it?" yelled Jukes, impatiently. What could that fraud of a boss'n want on the bridge? The typhoon had got on Jukes' nerves. The husky bellowings of the other, though unintelligible, seemed to suggest a state of lively satisfaction.

There could be no mistake.   The old fool was pleased
with something.

The boatswain's other hand had found some other
body, for in a changed tone he began to inquire: "Is
it you, sir?   Is it you, sir?"   The wind strangled his
howls.

"Yes!" cried Captain MacWhirr.

IV

ALL that the boatswain, out of a superabundance of yells, could make clear to Captain MacWhirr was the bizarre intelligence that "All them Chinamen in the fore 'tween deck have fetched away, sir."

Jukes to leeward could hear these two shouting within six inches of his face, as you may hear on a still night half a mile away two men conversing across a field. He heard Captain MacWhirr's exasperated "What? What?" and the strained pitch of the other's hoarseness. "In a lump . . . seen them myself. . . . Awful sight, sir . . . thought . . . tell you."

Jukes remained indifferent, as if rendered irresponsible by the force of the hurricane, which made the very thought of action utterly vain. Besides, being very young, he had found the occupation of keeping his heart completely steeled against the worst so engrossing that he had come to feel an overpowering dislike towards any other form of activity whatever. He was not scared; he knew this because, firmly believing he would never see another sunrise, he remained calm in that belief.

These are the moments of do-nothing heroics to which even good men surrender at times. Many officers of ships can no doubt recall a case in their experience when just such a trance of confounded stoicism would come all at once over a whole ship's company. Jukes, however, had no wide experience of men or storms. He conceived himself to be calm—inexorably calm; but as a matter of fact he was daunted; not abjectly, but only so far as a decent man may, without becoming loathsome to himself.

It was rather like a forced-on numbness of spirit. The long, long stress of a gale does it; the suspense of the interminably culminating catastrophe; and there is a bodily fatigue in the mere holding on to existence within the excessive tumult; a searching and insidious fatigue that penetrates deep into a man's breast to cast down and sadden his heart, which is incorrigible, and of all the gifts of the earth—even before life itself—aspires to peace.

Jukes was benumbed much more than he supposed. He held on—very wet, very cold, stiff in every limb; and in a momentary hallucination of swift visions (it is said that a drowning man thus reviews all his life) he beheld all sorts of memories altogether unconnected with his present situation. He remembered his father, for instance: a worthy business man, who at an unfortunate crisis in his affairs went quietly to bed and died forthwith in a state of resignation. Jukes did not recall these circumstances, of course, but remaining otherwise unconcerned he seemed to see distinctly the poor man's face; a certain game of nap played when quite a boy in Table Bay on board a ship, since lost with all hands; the thick eyebrows of his first skipper; and without any emotion, as he might years ago have walked listlessly into her room and found her sitting there with a book, he remembered his mother—dead, too, now—the resolute woman, left badly off, who had been very firm in his bringing up.

It could not have lasted more than a second, perhaps not so much. A heavy arm had fallen about his shoulders; Captain MacWhirr's voice was speaking his name into his ear.

"Jukes! Jukes!"

He detected the tone of deep concern. The wind had thrown its weight on the ship, trying to pin her down amongst the seas. They made a clean breach over her, as over a deep-swimming log; and the gathered weight of crashes menaced monstrously from afar. The breakers flung out of the night with a ghostly light on their crests—the light of sea-foam that in a ferocious, boiling-up pale flash showed upon the slender body of the ship the toppling rush, the downfall, and the seething mad scurry of each wave. Never for a moment could she shake herself clear of the water; Jukes, rigid, perceived in her motion the ominous sign of haphazard floundering. She was no longer struggling intelligently. It was the beginning of the end; and the note of busy concern in Captain MacWhirr's voice sickened him like an exhibition of blind and pernicious folly.

The spell of the storm had fallen upon Jukes. He was penetrated by it, absorbed by it; he was rooted in it with a rigour of dumb attention. Captain Mac-Whirr persisted in his cries, but the wind got between them like a solid wedge. He hung round Jukes' neck as heavy as a millstone, and suddenly the sides of their heads knocked together.

"Jukes! Mr. Jukes, I say!"

He had to answer that voice that would not be silenced. He answered in the customary manner: ". . . Yes, sir."

And directly, his heart, corrupted by the storm that breeds a craving for peace, rebelled against the tyranny of training and command.

Captain MacWhirr had his mate's head fixed firm in the crook of his elbow, and pressed it to his yelling lips mysteriously. Sometimes Jukes would break in, admonishing hastily: "Look out, sir!" or Captain Mac-Whirr would bawl an earnest exhortation to "Hold hard, there!" and the whole black universe seemed to reel together with the ship. They paused. She floated yet. And Captain MacWhirr would resume his shouts. ". . . . Says . . . whole lot . . . fetched away. . . . Ought to see . . . what's the matter."

Directly the full force of the hurricane had struck the ship, every part of her deck became untenable; and the sailors, dazed and dismayed, took shelter in the port alleyway under the bridge. It had a door aft, which they shut; it was very black, cold, and dismal. At each heavy fling of the ship they would groan all together in the dark, and tons of water could be heard scuttling about as if trying to get at them from above. The boatswain had been keeping up a gruff talk, but a more unreasonable lot of men, he said afterwards, he had never been with. They were snug enough there, out of harm's way, and not wanted to do anything, either; and yet they did nothing but grumble and complain peevishly like so many sick kids. Finally, one of them said that if there had been at least some light to see each other's noses by, it wouldn't be so bad. It was making him crazy, he declared, to lie there in the dark waiting for the blamed hooker to sink.

"Why don't you step outside, then, and be done with it at once?" the boatswain turned on him.

This called up a shout of execration. The boatswain found himself overwhelmed with reproaches of all sorts. They seemed to take it ill that a lamp was not instantly created for them out of nothing. They would whine after a light to get drowned by—anyhow! And though the unreason of their revilings was patent—since no one could hope to reach the lamp-room, which was forward—he became greatly distressed. He did not think it was decent of them to be nagging at him like

this. He told them so, and was met by general contumely. He sought refuge, therefore, in an embittered
silence. At the same time their grumbling and sighing
and muttering worried him greatly, but by-and-by it
occurred to him that there were six globe lamps hung
in the 'tween-deck, and that there could be no harm in
depriving the coolies of one of them.

The *Nan-Shan* had an athwartship coal-bunker,
which, being at times used as cargo space, communi-
cated by an iron door with the fore 'tween-deck. It was
empty then, and its manhole was the foremost one in
the alleyway. The boatswain could get in, therefore,
without coming out on deck at all; but to his great
surprise he found he could induce no one to help him
in taking off the manhole cover. He groped for it all
the same, but one of the crew lying in his way refused
to budge.

"Why, I only want to get you that blamed light you
are crying for," he expostulated, almost pitifully.

Somebody told him to go and put his head in a bag.
He regretted he could not recognize the voice, and that
it was too dark to see, otherwise, as he said, he would
have put a head on *that* son of a sea-cook, anyway, sink
or swim. Nevertheless, he had made up his mind to
show them he could get a light, if he were to die for it.

Through the violence of the ship's rolling, every
movement was dangerous. To be lying down seemed
labour enough. He nearly broke his neck dropping
into the bunker. He fell on his back, and was sent
shooting helplessly from side to side in the dangerous
company of a heavy iron bar—a coal-trimmer's slice
probably—left down there by somebody. This thing
made him as nervous as though it had been a wild beast.
He could not see it, the inside of the bunker coated with
coal-dust being perfectly and impenetrably black; but

he heard it sliding and clattering, and striking here and there, always in the neighbourhood of his head. It seemed to make an extraordinary noise, too—to give heavy thumps as though it had been as big as a bridge girder. This was remarkable enough for him to notice while he was flung from port to starboard and back again, and clawing desperately the smooth sides of the bunker in the endeavour to stop himself. The door into the 'tween-deck not fitting quite true, he saw a thread of dim light at the bottom.

Being a sailor, and a still active man, he did not want much of a chance to regain his feet; and as luck would have it, in scrambling up he put his hand on the iron slice, picking it up as he rose. Otherwise he would have been afraid of the thing breaking his legs, or at least knocking him down again. At first he stood still. He felt unsafe in this darkness that seemed to make the ship's motion unfamiliar, unforeseen, and difficult to counteract. He felt so much shaken for a moment that he dared not move for fear of "taking charge again." He had no mind to get battered to pieces in that bunker.

He had struck his head twice; he was dazed a little. He seemed to hear yet so plainly the clatter and bangs of the iron slice flying about his ears that he tightened his grip to prove to himself he had it there safely in his hand. He was vaguely amazed at the plainness with which down there he could hear the gale raging. Its howls and shrieks seemed to take on, in the emptiness of the bunker, something of the human character, of human rage and pain—being not vast but infinitely poignant. And there were, with every roll, thumps, too—profound, ponderous thumps, as if a bulk object of five-ton weight or so had got play in the hold. But there was no such thing in the cargo. Something on deck? Impossible. Or alongside? Couldn't be.

He thought all this quickly, clearly, competently, like a seaman, and in the end remained puzzled. This noise, though, came deadened from outside, together with the washing and pouring of water on deck above his head. Was it the wind? Must be. It made down there a row like the shouting of a big lot of crazed men. And he discovered in himself a desire for a light, too—if only to get drowned by—and a nervous anxiety to get out of that bunker as quickly as possible.

He pulled back the bolt: the heavy iron plate turned on its hinges; and it was though he had opened the door to the sounds of the tempest. A gust of hoarse yelling met him: the air was still; and the rushing of water overhead was covered by a tumult of strangled, throaty shrieks that produced an effect of desperate confusion. He straddled his legs the whole width of the doorway and stretched his neck. And at first he perceived only what he had come to seek: six small yellow flames swinging violently on the great body of the dusk.

It was stayed like the gallery of a mine, with a row of stanchions in the middle, and cross-beams overhead, penetrating into the gloom ahead—indefinitely. And to port there loomed, like the caving in of one of the sides, a bulky mass with a slanting outline. The whole place, with the shadows and the shapes, moved all the time. The boatswain glared: the ship lurched to starboard, and a great howl came from that mass that had the slant of fallen earth.

Pieces of wood whizzed past. Planks, he thought, inexpressibly startled, and flinging back his head. At his feet a man went sliding over, open-eyed, on his back, straining with uplifted arms for nothing: and another came bounding like a detached stone with his head between his legs and his hands clenched. His

pigtail whipped in the air; he made a grab at the boatswain's legs, and from his opened hand a bright white
disc rolled against the boatswain's foot. He recognized a silver dollar, and yelled at it with astonishment. With a precipitated sound of trampling and
shuffling of bare feet, and with guttural cries, the
mound of writhing bodies piled up to port detached
itself from the ship's side and sliding, inert and struggling, shifted to starboard, with a dull, brutal thump.
The cries ceased. The boatswain heard a long moan
through the roar and whistling of the wind; he saw an
inextricable confusion of heads and shoulders, naked
soles kicking upwards, fists raised, tumbling backs, legs,
pigtails, faces.

"Good Lord!" he cried, horrified, and banged-to the
iron door upon this vision.

This was what he had come on the bridge to tell. He
could not keep it to himself; and on board ship there is
only one man to whom it is worth while to unburden
yourself. On his passage back the hands in the alleyway swore at him for a fool. Why didn't he bring that
lamp? What the devil did the coolies matter to anybody? And when he came out, the extremity of the
ship made what went on inside of her appear of little
moment.

At first he thought he had left the alleyway in the
very moment of her sinking. The bridge ladders had
been washed away, but an enormous sea filling the
after-deck floated him up. After that he had to lie on
his stomach for some time, holding to a ring-bolt, getting
his breath now and then, and swallowing salt water.
He struggled farther on his hands and knees, too
frightened and distracted to turn back. In this way
he reached the after-part of the wheelhouse. In that
comparatively sheltered spot he found the second mate.

The boatswain was pleasantly surprised—his impression being that everybody on deck must have been washed away a long time ago. He asked eagerly where the captain was.

The second mate was lying low, like a malignant little animal under a hedge.

"Captain? Gone overboard, after getting us into this mess." The mate, too, for all he knew or cared. Another fool. Didn't matter. Everybody was going by-and-by.

The boatswain crawled out again into the strength of the wind; not because he much expected to find anybody, he said, but just to get away from "that man." He crawled out as outcasts go to face an inclement world. Hence his great joy at finding Jukes and the Captain. But what was going on in the 'tween-deck was to him a minor matter by that time. Besides, it was difficult to make yourself heard. But he managed to convey the idea that the Chinaman had broken adrift together with their boxes, and that he had come up on purpose to report this. As to the hands, they were all right. Then, appeased, he subsided on the deck in a sitting posture, hugging with his arms and legs the stand of the engine-room telegraph—an iron casting as thick as a post. When that went, why, he expected he would go, too. He gave no more thought to the coolies.

Captain MacWhirr had made Jukes understand that he wanted him to go down below—to see.

"What am I to do then, sir?" And the trembling of his whole wet body caused Jukes' voice to sound like bleating.

"See first . . . Boss'n . . . says . . . adrift."

"That boss'n is a confounded fool," howled Jukes, shakily.

The absurdity of the demand made upon him revolted Jukes. He was as unwilling to go as if the moment he had left the deck the ship were sure to sink.

"I must know . . . can't leave. . . ."

"They'll settle, sir."

"Fight . . . boss'n says they fight. . . . Why? Can't have . . . fighting . . . board ship. . . . Much rather keep you here . . . case . . . . I should . . . washed overboard myself. . . . Stop it . . . some way. You see and tell me . . . through engine-room tube. Don't want you . . . come up here . . . too often. Dangerous . . . moving about . . . deck."

Jukes, held with his head in chancery, had to listen to what seemed horrible suggestions.

"Don't want . . . you get lost . . . so long . . . ship isn't. . . . Rout . . . Good man . . . Ship . . . may . . . through this . . . all right yet."

All at once Jukes understood he would have to go.

"Do you think she may?" he screamed.

But the wind devoured the reply, out of which Jukes heard only the one word, pronounced with great energy ". . . . Always. . . ."

Captain MacWhirr released Jukes, and bending over the boatswain, yelled "Get back with the mate." Jukes only knew that the arm was gone off his shoulders. He was dismissed with his orders—to do what? He was exasperated into letting go his hold carelessly, and on the instant was blown away. It seemed to him that nothing could stop him from being blown right over the stern. He flung himself down hastily, and the boatswain, who was following, fell on him.

"Don't you get up yet, sir," cried the boatswain. "No hurry!"

A sea swept over. Jukes understood the boatswain to splutter that the bridge ladders were gone. "I'll lower you down, sir, by your hands," he screamed. He shouted also something about the smoke-stack being as likely to go overboard as not. Jukes thought it very possible, and imagined the fires out, the ship helpless. . . . The boatswain by his side kept on yelling. "What? What is it?" Jukes cried distressfully; and the other repeated, "What would my old woman say if she saw me now?"

In the alleyway, where a lot of water had got in and splashed in the dark, the men were still as death, till Jukes stumbled against one of them and cursed him savagely for being in the way. Two or three voices then asked, eager and weak, "Any chance for us, sir?"

"What's the matter with you fools?" he said, brutally. He felt as though he could throw himself down amongst them and never move any more. But they seemed cheered; and in the midst of obsequious warnings, "Look out! Mind that manhole lid, sir," they lowered him into the bunker. The boatswain tumbled down after him, and as soon as he had picked himself up he remarked, "She would say, 'Serve you right, you old fool, for going to sea.'"

The boatswain had some means, and made a point of alluding to them frequently. His wife—a fat woman —and two grown-up daughters kept a greengrocer's shop in the East-end of London.

In the dark, Jukes, unsteady on his legs, listened to a faint thunderous patter. A deadened screaming went on steadily at his elbow, as it were; and from above the louder tumult of the storm descended upon these near sounds. His head swam. To him, too, in that bunker, the motion of the ship seemed novel and menacing, sapping his resolution as though he had never been afloat before.

He had half a mind to scramble out again; but the remembrance of Captain MacWhirr's voice made this impossible. His orders were to go and see. What was the good of it, he wanted to know. Enraged, he told himself he would see—of course. But the boatswain, staggering clumsily, warned him to be careful how he opened that door; there was a blamed fight going on. And Jukes, as if in great bodily pain, desired irritably to know what the devil they were fighting for.

"Dollars! Dollars, sir. All their rotten chests got burst open. Blamed money skipping all over the place, and they are tumbling after it head over heels—tearing and biting like anything. A regular little hell in there."

Jukes convulsively opened the door. The short boatswain peered under his arm.

One of the lamps had gone out, broken perhaps. Rancorous, guttural cries burst out loudly on their ears, and a strange panting sound, the working of all these straining breasts. A hard blow hit the side of the ship: water fell above with a stunning shock, and in the forefront of the gloom, where the air was reddish and thick, Jukes saw a head bang the deck violently, two thick calves waving on high, muscular arms twined round a naked body, a yellow-face, open-mouthed and with a set wild stare, look up and slide away. An empty chest clattered turning over; a man fell head first with a jump, as if lifted by a kick; and farther off, indistinct, others streamed like a mass of rolling stones down a bank, thumping the deck with their feet and flourishing their arms wildly. The hatchway ladder was loaded with coolies swarming on it like bees on a branch. They hung on the steps in a crawling, stirring

cluster, beating madly with their fists the underside of
the battened hatch, and the headlong rush of the water
above was heard in the intervals of their yelling. The
ship heeled over more, and they began to drop off:
first one, then two, then all the rest went away together,
falling straight off with a great cry.

Jukes was confounded. The boatswain, with gruff
anxiety, begged him, "Don't you go in there, sir."

The whole place seemed to twist upon itself, jumping
incessantly the while; and when the ship rose to a sea
Jukes fancied that all these men would be shot upon
him in a body. He backed out, swung the door to,
and with trembling hands pushed at the bolt. . . .

As soon as his mate had gone Captain MacWhirr,
left alone on the bridge, sidled and staggered as far as
the wheelhouse. Its door being hinged forward, he
had to fight the gale for admittance, and when at last he
managed to enter, it was with an instantaneous clatter
and a bang, as though he had been fired through the
wood. He stood within, holding on to the handle.

The steering-gear leaked steam, and in the confined
space the glass of the binnacle made a shiny oval of
light in a thin white fog. The wind howled, hummed,
whistled, with sudden booming gusts that rattled the
doors and shutters in the vicious patter of sprays.
Two coils of lead-line and a small canvas bag hung on
a long lanyard, swung wide off, and came back clinging
to the bulkheads. The gratings underfoot were nearly
afloat; with every sweeping blow of a sea, water squirted
violently through the cracks all round the door, and the
man at the helm had flung down his cap, his coat, and
stood propped against the gear-casing in a striped cotton
shirt open on his breast. The little brass wheel in his
hands had the appearance of a bright and fragile toy.
The cords of his neck stood hard and lean, a dark patch

lay in the hollow of his throat, and his face was still and sunken as in death.

Captain MacWhirr wiped his eyes. The sea 'that had nearly taken him overboard had, to his great annoyance, washed his sou'-wester hat off his bald head. The fluffy, fair hair, soaked and darkened, resembled a mean skein of cotton threads festooned round his bare skull. His face, glistening with sea-water, had been made crimson with the wind, with the sting of sprays. He looked as though he had come off sweating from before a furnace.

"You here?" he muttered, heavily.

The second mate had found his way into the wheel-house some time before. He had fixed himself in a corner with his knees up, a fist pressed against each temple; and this attitude suggested rage, sorrow, resignation, surrender, with a sort of concentrated unforgiveness. He said mournfully and defiantly, "Well, it's my watch below now: ain't it?"

The steam gear clattered, stopped, clattered again; and the helmsman's eyeballs seemed to project out of a hungry face as if the compass card behind the binnacle glass had been meat. God knows how long he had been left there to steer, as if forgotten by all his shipmates. The bells had not been struck; there had been no reliefs; the ship's routine had gone down wind; but he was trying to keep her head north-north-east. The rudder might have been gone for all he knew, the fires out, the engines broken down, the ship ready to roll over like a corpse. He was anxious not to get muddled and lose control of her head, because the compass-card swung far both ways, wriggling on the pivot, and sometimes seemed to whirl right round. He suffered from mental stress. He was horribly afraid, also, of the wheelhouse going. Mountains of water kept on tumbling against it. When the ship took one of her desperate dives the corners of his lips twitched.

Captain MacWhirr looked up at the wheelhouse clock. Screwed to the bulk-head, it had a white face on which the black hands appeared to stand quite still. It was half-past one in the morning.

"Another day," he muttered to himself.

The second mate heard him, and lifting his head as one grieving amongst ruins, "You won't see it break," he exclaimed. His wrists and his knees could be seen to shake violently. "No, by God! You won't. . . ."

He took his face again between his fists.

The body of the helmsman had moved slightly, but his head didn't budge on his neck,—like a stone head fixed to look one way from a column. During a roll that all but took his booted legs from under him, and in the very stagger to save himself, Captain Mac-Whirr said austerely, "Don't you pay any attention to what that man says." And then, with an indefinable change of tone, very grave, he added, "He isn't on duty."

The sailor said nothing.

The hurricane boomed, shaking the little place, which seemed air-tight; and the light of the binnacle flickered all the time.

"You haven't been relieved," Captain MacWhirr went on, looking down. "I want you to stick to the helm, though, as long as you can. You've got the hang of her. Another man coming here might make a mess of it. Wouldn't do. No child's play. And the hands are probably busy with a job down below. . . . Think you can?"

The steering-gear leaped into an abrupt short clatter, stopped smouldering like an ember; and the still man, with a motionless gaze, burst out, as if all the passion

in him had gone into his lips: "By Heavens, sir! I
can steer for ever if nobody talks to me."

"Oh! aye! All right. . . ." The Captain lifted
his eyes for the first time to the man, ". . . Hackett."

And he seemed to dismiss this matter from his mind.
He stooped to the engine-room speaking-tube, blew in,
and bent his head. Mr. Rout below answered, and at
once Captain MacWhirr put his lips to the mouthpiece.

With the uproar of the gale around him he applied
alternately his lips and his ear, and the engineer's voice
mounted to him, harsh and as if out of the heat of an
engagement. One of the stokers was disabled, the others
had given in, the second engineer and the donkey-man
were firing-up. The third engineer was standing by
the steam-valve. The engines were being tended by
hand. How was it above?

"Bad enough. It mostly rests with you," said Captain MacWhirr. Was the mate down there yet? No?
Well, he would be presently. Would Mr. Rout let him
talk through the speaking-tube?—through the deck
speaking-tube, because he—the Captain—was going
out again on the bridge directly. There was some
trouble amongst the Chinamen. They were fighting,
it seemed. Couldn't allow fighting anyhow. . . .

Mr. Rout had gone away, and Captain MacWhirr
could feel against his ear the pulsation of the engines,
like the beat of the ship's heart. Mr. Rout's voice
down there shouted something distantly. The ship
pitched headlong, the pulsation leaped with a hissing
tumult, and stopped dead. Captain MacWhirr's face
was impassive, and his eyes were fixed aimlessly on
the crouching shape of the second mate. Again Mr.
Rout's voice cried out in the depths, and the pulsating
beats recommenced, with slow strokes—growing swifter.

Mr. Rout had returned to the tube. "It don't matter much what they do," he said, hastily; and then, with irritation, "She takes these dives as if she never meant to come up again."

"Awful sea," said the Captain's voice from above.

"Don't let me drive her under," barked Solomon Rout up the pipe.

"Dark and rain. Can't see what's coming," uttered the voice. "Must—keep—her—moving—enough to steer—and chance it," it went on to state distinctly.

"I am doing as much as I dare."

"We are—getting—smashed up—a good deal up here," proceeded the voice mildly. "Doing—fairly well—though. Of course, if the wheelhouse should go. . . ."

Mr. Rout, bending an attentive ear, muttered peevishly something under his breath.

But the deliberate voice up there became animated to ask: "Jukes turned up yet?" Then, after a short wait, "I wish he would bear a hand. I want him to be done and come up here in case of anything. To look after the ship. I am all alone. The second mate's lost. . . ."

"What?" shouted Mr. Rout into the engine-room, taking his head away. Then up the tube he cried, "Gone overboard?" and clapped his ear to.

"Lost his nerve," the voice from above continued in a matter-of-fact tone. "Damned awkward circumstance."

Mr. Rout, listening with bowed neck, opened his eyes wide at this. However, he heard something like the sounds of a scuffle and broken exclamations coming down to him. He strained his hearing; and all the time Beale, the third engineer, with his arms uplifted, held between the palms of his hands the rim of a little black wheel projecting at the side of a big copper pipe.

He seemed to be poising it above his head, as though it were a correct attitude in some sort of game.

To steady himself, he pressed his shoulder against the white bulkhead, one knee bent, and a sweat-rag tucked in his belt hanging on his hip. His smooth cheek was begrimed and flushed, and the coal dust on his eyelids, like the black pencilling of a make-up, enhanced the liquid brilliance of the whites, giving to his youthful face something of a feminine, exotic and fascinating aspect. When the ship pitched he would with hasty movements of his hands screw hard at the little wheel.

"Gone crazy," began the Captain's voice suddenly in the tube. "Rushed at me. . . . Just now. Had to knock him down. . . . This minute. You heard, Mr. Rout?"

"The devil!" muttered Mr. Rout. "Look out, Beale!"

His shout rang out like the blast of a warning trumpet, between the iron walls of the engine-room. Painted white, they rose high into the dusk of the skylight, sloping like a roof; and the whole lofty space resembled the interior of a monument, divided by floors of iron grating, with lights flickering at different levels, and a mass of gloom lingering in the middle, within the columnar stir of machinery under the motionless swelling of the cylinders. A loud and wild resonance, made up of all the noises of the hurricane, dwelt in the still warmth of the air. There was in it the smell of hot metal, of oil, and a slight mist of steam. The blows of the sea seemed to traverse it in an unringing, stunning shock, from side to side.

Gleams, like pale long flames, trembled upon the polish of metal; from the flooring below the enormous crank-heads emerged in their turns with a flash of brass and steel—going over; while the connecting-rods, big-jointed, like skeleton limbs, seemed to thrust them down and pull them up again with an irresistible precision. And deep in the half-light other rods dodged deliberately to and fro, crossheads nodded, discs of metal rubbed smoothly against each other, slow and gentle, in a commingling of shadows and gleams.

Sometimes all those powerful and unerring movements would slow down simultaneously, as if they had been the functions of a living organism, stricken suddenly by the blight of languor; and Mr. Rout's eyes would blaze darker in his long sallow face. He was fighting this fight in a pair of carpet slippers. A short shiny jacket barely covered his loins, and his white wrists protruded far out of the tight sleeves, as though the emergency had added to his stature, had lengthened his limbs, augmented his pallor, hollowed his eyes.

He moved, climbing high up, disappearing low down, with a restless, purposeful industry, and when he stood still, holding the guard-rail in front of the starting-gear, he would keep glancing to the right at the steam-gauge, at the water-gauge, fixed upon the white wall in the light of a swaying lamp. The mouths of two speaking-tubes gaped stupidly at his elbow, and the dial of the engine-room telegraph resembled a clock of large diameter, bearing on its face curt words instead of figures. The grouped letters stood out heavily black, around the pivot-head of the indicator, emphatically symbolic of loud exclamations: AHEAD, ASTERN, SLOW, HALF, STAND BY; and the fat black hand pointed downwards to the word FULL, which, thus singled out, captured the eye as a sharp cry secures attention.

The wood-encased bulk of the low-pressure cylinder, frowning portly from above, emitted a faint wheeze at every thrust, and except for that low hiss the engines worked their steel limbs headlong or slow with a silent, determined smoothness. And all this, the white walls, the moving steel, the floor plates under Solomon Rout's feet, the floors of iron grating above his head, the dusk and the gleams, uprose and sank continuously, with one accord, upon the harsh wash of the waves against the ship's side. The whole loftiness of the place, booming hollow to the great voice of the wind, swayed at the top like a tree, would go over bodily, as if borne down this way and that by the tremendous blasts.

"You've got to hurry up," shouted Mr. Rout, as soon as he saw Jukes appear in the stokehold doorway.

Jukes' glance was wandering and tipsy; his red face was puffy, as though he had overslept himself. He had had an arduous road, and had travelled over it with immense vivacity, the agitation of his mind corresponding to the exertions of his body. He had rushed up out of the bunker, stumbling in the dark alleyway amongst a lot of bewildered men who, trod upon, asked "What's up, sir?" in awed mutters all round him;—down the stokehold ladder, missing many iron rungs in his hurry, down into a place deep as a well, black as Tophet, tipping over back and forth like a see-saw. The water in the bilges thundered at each roll, and lumps of coal skipped to and fro, from end to end, rattling like an avalanche of pebbles on a slope of iron.

Somebody in there moaned with pain, and somebody else could be seen crouching over what seemed the prone body of a dead man; a lusty voice blasphemed; and the glow under each fire-door was like a pool of flaming blood radiating quietly in a velvety blackness.

A gust of wind struck upon the nape of Jukes' neck and next moment he felt it streaming about his wet ankles. The stokehold ventilators hummed: in front of the six fire-doors two wild figures, stripped to the waist, staggered and stooped, wrestling with two shovels.

"Hallo! Plenty of draught now," yelled the second engineer at once, as though he had been all the time looking out for Jukes. The donkeyman, a dapper little chap with a dazzling fair skin and a tiny, gingery moustache, worked in a sort of mute transport. They were keeping a full head of steam, and a profound rumbling, as of an empty furniture van trotting over a bridge, made a sustained bass to all the other noises of the place.

"Blowing off all the time," went on yelling the second. With a sound as of a hundred scoured saucepans, the orifice of a ventilator spat upon his shoulder a sudden gush of salt water, and he volleyed a stream of curses upon all things on earth including his own soul, ripping and raving, and all the time attending to his business. With a sharp clash of metal the ardent pale glare of the fire opened upon his bullet head, showing his spluttering lips, his insolent face, and with another clang closed like the white-hot wink of an iron eye.

"Where's the blooming ship? Can you tell me? blast my eyes! Under water—or what? It's coming down here in tons. Are the condemned cowls gone to Hades? Hey? Don't you know anything—you jolly sailor-man you . . . ?"

Jukes, after a bewildered moment, had been helped by a roll to dart through; and as soon as his eyes took in the comparative vastness, peace and brilliance of the engine-room, the ship, setting her stern heavily in the water, sent him charging head down upon Mr. Rout.

The chief's arm, long like a tentacle, and straightening as if worked by a spring, went out to meet him, and

deflected his rush into a spin towards the speaking-tubes. At the same time Mr. Rout repeated earnestly:
"You've got to hurry up, whatever it is."

Jukes yelled "Are you there, sir?" and listened. Nothing. Suddenly the roar of the wind fell straight into his ear, but presently a small voice shoved aside the shouting hurricane quietly.

"You, Jukes?—Well?"

Jukes was ready to talk: it was only time that seemed to be wanting. It was easy enough to account for everything. He could perfectly imagine the coolies battened down in the reeking 'tween-deck, lying sick and scared between the rows of chests. Then one of these chests—or perhaps several at once—breaking loose in a roll, knocking out others, sides splitting, lids flying open, and all these clumsy Chinamen rising up in a body to save their property. Afterwards every fling of the ship would hurl that tramping, yelling mob here and there, from side to side, in a whirl of smashed wood, torn clothing, rolling dollars. A struggle once started, they would be unable to stop themselves. Nothing could stop them now except main force. It was a disaster. He had seen it, and that was all he could say. Some of them must be dead, he believed. The rest would go on fighting. . . .

He sent up his words, tripping over each other, crowding the narrow tube. They mounted as if into a silence of an enlightened comprehension dwelling alone up there with a storm. And Jukes wanted to be dismissed from the face of that odious trouble intruding on the great need of the ship.

V

He waited. Before his eyes the engines turned with slow labour, that in the moment of going off into a mad fling would stop dead at Mr. Rout's shout, "Look out, Beale!" They paused in an intelligent immobility, stilled in mid-stroke, a heavy crank arrested on the cant, as if conscious of danger and the passage of time. Then, with a "Now, then!" from the chief, and the sound of a breath expelled through clenched teeth, they would accomplish the interrupted revolution and begin another.

There was the prudent sagacity of wisdom and the deliberation of enormous strength in their movements. This was their work—this patient coaxing of a distracted ship over the fury of the waves and into the very eye of the wind. At times Mr. Rout's chin would sink on his breast, and he watched them with knitted eyebrows as if lost in thought.

The voice that kept the hurricane out of Jukes' ear began: "Take the hands with you . . . ," and left off unexpectedly.

"What could I do with them, sir?"

A harsh, abrupt, imperious clang exploded suddenly. The three pairs of eyes flew up to the telegraph dial to see the hand jump from Full to Stop, as if snatched by a devil. And then these three men in the engine-room had the intimate sensation of a check upon the ship, of a strange shrinking, as if she had gathered herself for a desperate leap.

"Stop her!" bellowed Mr. Rout.

Nobody—not even Captain MacWhirr, who alone on deck had caught sight of a white line of foam coming on at such a height that he couldn't believe his eyes—nobody was to know the steepness of that sea and the awful depth of the hollow the hurricane had scooped out behind the running wall of water. ⌣

It raced to meet the ship, and, with a pause, as of girding the loins, the *Nan-Shan* lifted her bows and leaped. The flames in all the lamps sank, darkening the engine-room. One went out. With a tearing crash and a swirling, raving tumult, tons of water fell upon the deck, as though the ship had darted under the foot of a cataract.

Down there they looked at each other, stunned.

"Swept from end to end, by God!" bawled Jukes.

She dipped into the hollow straight down, as if going over the edge of the world. The engine-room toppled forward menacingly, like the inside of a tower nodding in an earthquake. An awful racket, of iron things falling, came from the stokehold. She hung on this appalling slant long enough for Beale to drop on his hands and knees and begin to crawl as if he meant to fly on all fours out of the engine-room, and for Mr. Rout to turn his head slowly, rigid, cavernous, with the lower jaw dropping. Jukes had shut his eyes, and his face in a moment became hopelessly blank and gentle, like the face of a blind man.

At last she rose slowly, staggering, as if she had to lift a mountain with her bows.

Mr. Rout shut his mouth; Jukes blinked; and little Beale stood up hastily.

"Another one like this, and that's the last of her," cried the chief.

He and Jukes looked at each other, and the same thought came into their heads. The Captain! Everything must have been swept away. Steering-gear gone —ship like a log. All over directly.

"Rush!" ejaculated Mr. Rout thickly, glaring with enlarged, doubtful eyes at Jukes, who answered him by an irresolute glance.

The clang of the telegraph gong soothed them instantly. The black hand dropped in a flash from STOP to FULL.

"Now then, Beale!" cried Mr. Rout.

The steam hissed low. The piston-rods slid in and out. Jukes put his ear to the tube. The voice was ready for him. It said: "Pick up all the money. Bear a hand now. I'll want you up here." And that was all.

"Sir?" called up Jukes. There was no answer.

He staggered away like a defeated man from the field of battle. He had got, in some way or other, a cut above his left eyebrow—a cut to the bone. He was not aware of it in the least: quantities of the China Sea, large enough to break his neck for him, had gone over his head, had cleaned, washed, and salted that wound. It did not bleed, but only gaped red; and this gash over the eye, his dishevelled hair, the disorder of his clothes, gave him the aspect of a man worsted in a fight with fists.

"Got to pick up the dollars." He appealed to Mr. Rout, smiling pitifully at random.

"What's that?" asked Mr. Rout, wildly. "Pick up . . . ? I don't care. . . ." Then, quivering in every muscle, but with an exaggeration of paternal tone, "Go away now, for God's sake. You deck people'll drive me silly. There's that second mate been going for the old man. Don't you know? You fellows are going wrong for want of something to do. . . ."

At these words Jukes discovered in himself the

beginnings of anger. Want of something to do—indeed. . . . Full of hot scorn against the chief, he turned to go the way he had come. In the stokehold the plump donkeyman toiled with his shovel mutely, as if his tongue had been cut out; but the second was carrying on like a noisy, undaunted maniac, who had preserved his skill in the art of stoking under a marine boiler.

"Hallo, you wandering officer! Hey! Can't you get some of your slush-slingers to wind up a few of them ashes? I am getting choked with them there. Curse it! Hallo! Hey! Remember the articles: *Sailors and firemen to assist each other.* Hey! D'ye hear?"

Jukes was climbing out frantically, and the other, lifting up his face after him, howled, "Can't you speak? What are you poking about here for? What's your game, anyhow?"

A frenzy possessed Jukes. By the time he was back amongst the men in the darkness of the alleyway, he felt ready to wring all their necks at the slightest sign of hanging back. The very thought of it exasperated him. *He* couldn't hang back. They shouldn't.

The impetuosity with which he came amongst them carried them along. They had already been excited and startled at all his comings and goings—by the fierceness and rapidity of his movements; and more felt than seen in his rushes, he appeared formidable—busied with matters of life and death that brooked no delay. At his first word he heard them drop into the bunker one after another obediently, with heavy thumps.

They were not clear as to what would have to be done. "What is it? What is it?" they were asking each other. The boatswain tried to explain; the sounds of a great scuffle surprised them: and the mighty shocks, reverberating awfully in the black bunker, kept them in mind of their danger. When the boatswain threw open the door it seemed that an eddy of the hurricane, stealing through the iron sides of the ship, had set all these bodies whirling like dust: there came to them a confused uproar, a tempestuous tumult, a fierce mutter, gusts of screams dying away, and the tramping of feet mingling with the blows of the sea.

For a moment they glared amazed, blocking the doorway. Jukes pushed through them brutally. He said nothing, and simply darted in. Another lot of coolies on the ladder, struggling suicidally to break through the battened hatch to a swamped deck, fell off as before, and he disappeared under them like a man overtaken by a landslide.

The boatswain yelled excitedly: "Come along. Get the mate out. He'll be trampled to death. Come on."

They charged in, stamping on breasts, on fingers, on faces, catching their feet in heaps of clothing, kicking broken wood; but before they could get hold of him Jukes emerged waist deep in a multitude of clawing hands. In the instant he had been lost to view, all the buttons of his jacket had gone, its back had got split up to the collar, his waistcoat had been torn open. The central struggling mass of Chinamen went over to the roll, dark, indistinct, helpless, with a wild gleam of many eyes in the dim light of the lamps.

"Leave me alone—damn you. I am all right," screeched Jukes. "Drive them forward. Watch your chance when she pitches. Forward with 'em. Drive them against the bulkhead. Jam 'em up."

The rush of the sailors into the seething 'tween-deck was like a splash of cold water into a boiling cauldron. The commotion sank for a moment.

The bulk of Chinamen were locked in such a compact

scrimmage that, linking their arms and aided by an appalling dive of the ship, the seamen sent it forward in one great shove, like a solid block. Behind their backs small clusters and loose bodies tumbled from side to side.

The boatswain performed prodigious feats of strength. With his long arms open, and each great paw clutching at a stanchion, he stopped the rush of seven entwined Chinamen rolling like a boulder. His joints cracked; he said, "Ha!" and they flew apart. But the carpenter showed the greater intelligence. Without saying a word to anybody he went back into the alley-way, to fetch several coils of cargo gear he had seen there—chain and rope. With these life-lines were rigged.

There was really no resistance. The struggle, how-ever it began, had turned into a scramble of blind panic. If the coolies had started up after their scattered dollars they were by that time fighting only for their footing. They took each other by the throat merely to save themselves from being hurled about. Whoever got a hold anywhere would kick at the others who caught at his legs and hung on, till a roll sent them flying together across the deck.

The coming of the white devils was a terror. Had they come to kill? The individuals torn out of the ruck became very limp in the seamen's hands: some, dragged aside by the heels, were passive, like dead bodies, with open, fixed eyes. Here and there a coolie would fall on his knees as if begging for mercy; several, whom the excess of fear made unruly, were hit with hard fists between the eyes, and cowered; while those who were hurt submitted to rough handling, blinking rapidly without a plaint. Faces streamed with blood; there were raw places on the shaven heads, scratches, bruises, torn wounds, gashes. The broken porcelain out of the chests was mostly responsible for the latter. Here and there a Chinaman, wild-eyed, with his tail unplaited, nursed a bleeding sole.

They had been ranged closely, after having been shaken into submission, cuffed a little to allay excitement, addressed in gruff words of encouragement that sounded like promises of evil. They sat on the deck in ghastly, drooping rows, and at the end the carpenter, with two hands to help him, moved busily from place to place, setting taut and hitching the life-lines. The boatswain, with one leg and one arm embracing a stanchion, struggled with a lamp pressed to his breast, trying to get a light, and growling all the time like an industrious gorilla. The figures of seamen stooped repeatedly, with the movements of gleaners, and everything was being flung into the bunker: clothing, smashed wood, broken china, and the dollars, too, gathered up in men's jackets. Now and then a sailor would stagger towards the doorway with his arms full of rubbish; and dolorous, slanting eyes followed his movements.

With every roll of the ship the long rows of sitting Celestials would sway forward brokenly, and her headlong dives knocked together the line of shaven polls from end to end. When the wash of water rolling on the deck died away for a moment, it seemed to Jukes, yet quivering from his exertions, that in his mad struggle down there he had overcome the wind somehow: that a silence had fallen upon the ship, a silence in which the sea struck thunderously at her sides.

Everything had been cleared out of the 'tween-deck —all the wreckage, as the men said. They stood erect and tottering above the level of heads and drooping shoulders. Here and there a coolie sobbed for his

breath. Where the high light fell, Jukes could see the
salient ribs of one, the yellow, wistful face of another;
bowed necks; or would meet a dull stare directed at his
face. He was amazed that there had been no corpses;
but the lot of them seemed at their last gasp, and they
appeared to him more pitiful than if they had been all
dead.

Suddenly one of the coolies began to speak. The
light came and went on his lean, straining face; he threw
his head up like a baying hound. From the bunker
came the sounds of knocking and the tinkle of some
dollars rolling loose; he stretched out his arm, his
mouth yawned black, and the incomprehensible
guttural hooting sounds, that did not seem to belong to
a human language, penetrated Jukes with a strange
emotion as if a brute had tried to be eloquent.

Two more started mouthing what seemed to Jukes
fierce denunciations; the others stirred with grunts and
growls. Jukes ordered the hands out of the 'tween-
decks hurriedly. He left last himself, backing through
the door, while the grunts rose to a loud murmur and
hands were extended after him as after a malefactor.
The boatswain shot the bolt, and remarked uneasily,
"Seems as if the wind had dropped, sir."

The seamen were glad to get back into the alleyway.
Secretly each of them thought that at the last moment
he could rush out on deck—and that was a comfort.
There is something horribly repugnant in the idea of
being drowned under a deck. Now they had done with
the Chinamen, they again became conscious of the
ship's position.

Jukes on coming out of the alleyway found himself
up to the neck in the noisy water. He gained the
bridge, and discovered he could detect obscure shapes
as if his sight had become preternaturally acute. He

saw faint outlines. They recalled not the familiar aspect of the *Nan-Shan,* but something remembered— an old dismantled steamer he had seen years ago rotting on a mudbank. She recalled that wreck.

There was no wind, not a breath, except the faint currents created by the lurches of the ship. The smoke tossed out of the funnel was settling down upon her deck. He breathed it as he passed forward. He felt the deliberate throb of the engines, and heard small sounds that seemed to have survived the great uproar: the knocking of broken fittings, the rapid tumbling of some piece of wreckage on the bridge. He perceived dimly the squat shape of his captain holding on to a twisted bridge-rail, motionless and swaying as if rooted to the planks. The unexpected stillness of the air oppressed Jukes.

"We have done it, sir," he gasped.

"Thought you would," said Captain MacWhirr.

"Did you?" murmured Jukes to himself.

"Wind fell all at once," went on the Captain.

Jukes burst out: "If you think it was an easy job——"

But his captain, clinging to the rail, paid no attention. "According to the books the worst is not over yet."

"If most of them hadn't been half dead with sea-sickness and fright, not one of us would have come out of that 'tween-deck alive," said Jukes.

'Had to do what's fair by them," mumbled MacWhirr, stolidly. "You don't find everything in books."

"Why, I believe they would have risen on us if I hadn't ordered the hands out of that pretty quick," continued Jukes with warmth.

After the whisper of their shouts, their ordinary

tones, so distinct, rang out very loud to their ears in the amazing stillness of the air. It seemed to them they were talking in a dark and echoing vault.

Through a jagged aperture in the dome of clouds the light of a few stars fell upon the black sea, rising and falling confusedly. Sometimes the head of a watery cone would topple on board and mingle with the rolling flurry of foam on the swamped deck; and the *Nan-Shan* wallowed heavily at the bottom of a circular cistern of clouds. This ring of dense vapours, gyrating madly round the calm of the centre, encompassed the ship like a motionless and unbroken wall of an aspect inconceivably sinister. Within, the sea, as if agitated by an internal commotion, leaped in peaked mounds that jostled each other, slapping heavily against her sides; and a low moaning sound, the infinite plaint of the storm's fury, came from beyond the limits of the menacing calm. Captain MacWhirr remained silent, and Jukes' ready ear caught suddenly the faint, long-drawn roar of some immense wave rushing unseen under that thick blackness, which made the appalling boundary of his vision.

"Of course," he started resentfully, "they thought we had caught at the chance to plunder them. Of course! You said—pick up the money. Easier said than done. They couldn't tell what was in our heads. We came in, smash—right into the middle of them. Had to do it by a rush."

"As long as it's done . . . ," mumbled the Captain, without attempting to look at Jukes. "Had to do what's fair."

"We shall find yet there's the devil to pay when this is over," said Jukes, feeling very sore. "Let them only recover a bit, and you'll see. They will fly at our throats, sir. Don't forget, sir, she isn't a British ship now. These brutes know it well, too. The damned Siamese flag."

"We are on board, all the same," remarked Captain MacWhirr.

"The trouble's not over yet," insisted Jukes, pro-phetically, reeling and catching on. "She's a wreck," he added, faintly.

"The trouble's not over yet," assented Captain MacWhirr, half aloud. . . . "Look out for her a minute."

"Are you going off the deck, sir?" asked Jukes, hurriedly, as if the storm were sure to pounce upon him as soon as he had been left alone with the ship.

He watched her, battered and solitary, labouring heavily in a wild scene of mountainous black waters lit by the gleams of distant worlds. She moved slowly, breathing into the still core of the hurricane the excess of her strength in a white cloud of steam—and the deep-toned vibration of the escape was like the defiant trumpeting of a living creature of the sea impatient for the renewal of the contest. It ceased suddenly. The still air moaned. Above Jukes' head a few stars shone into a pit of black vapours. The inky edge of the cloud-disc frowned upon the ship under the patch of glittering sky. The stars, too, seemed to look at her intently, as if for the last time, and the cluster of their splendour sat like a diadem on a lowering brow.

Captain MacWhirr had gone into the chart-room. There was no light there; but he could feel the disorder of that place where he used to live tidily. His armchair was upset. The books had tumbled out on the floor: he scrunched a piece of glass under his boot. He groped for the matches, and found a box on a shelf with a deep ledge. He struck one, and puckering the corners of his eyes, held out the little flame towards the barometer whose glittering top of glass and metals nodded at him continuously.

It stood very low—incredibly low, so low that Captain MacWhirr grunted. The match went out, and hurriedly he extracted another, with thick, stiff fingers.

Again a little flame flared up before the nodding glass and metal of the top. His eyes looked at it narrowed with attention, as if expecting an imperceptible sign. With his grave face he resembled a booted and misshapen pagan burning incense before the oracle of a Joss. There was no mistake. It was the lowest reading he had ever seen in his life.

Captain MacWhirr emitted a low whistle. He forgot himself till the flame diminished to a blue spark, burnt his fingers and vanished. Perhaps something had gone wrong with the thing!

There was an aneroid glass screwed above the couch. He turned that way, struck another match, and discovered the white face of the other instrument looking at him from the bulkhead, meaningly, not to be gainsaid, as though the wisdom of men were made unerring by the indifference of matter. There was no room for doubt now. Captain MacWhirr pshawed at it, and threw the match down.

The worst was to come, then—and if the books were right this worst would be very bad. The experience of the last six hours had enlarged his conception of what heavy weather could be like. "It'll be terrific," he pronounced, mentally. He had not consciously looked at anything by the light of the matches except at the barometer; and yet somehow he had seen that his water-bottle and the two tumblers had been flung out of their stand. It seemed to give him a more intimate knowledge of the tossing the ship had gone through. "I wouldn't have believed it," he thought. And his table had been cleared, too; his rulers, his pencils, the inkstand—all the things that had their safe appointed places—they were gone, as if a mischievous hand had plucked them out one by one and flung them on the wet floor. The hurricane had broken in upon the orderly arrangements of his privacy. This had never happened before, and the feeling of dismay reached the very seat of his composure. And the worst was to come yet! He was glad the trouble in the 'tween-deck had been discovered in time. If the ship had to go after all, then, at least, she wouldn't be going to the bottom with a lot of people in her fighting teeth and claw. That would have been odious. And in that feeling there was a humane intention and a vague sense of the fitness of things.

These instantaneous thoughts were yet in their essence heavy and slow, partaking of the nature of the man. He extended his hand to put back the matchbox in its corner of the shelf. There were always matches there—by his order. The steward had his instructions impressed upon him long before. "A box . . . just there, see? Not so very full . . . where I can put my hand on it, steward. Might want a light in a hurry. Can't tell on board ship *what* you might want in a hurry. Mind, now."

And of course on his side he would be careful to put it back in its place scrupulously. He did so now, but before he removed his hand it occurred to him that perhaps he would never have occasion to use that box any more. The vividness of the thought checked him and for an infinitesimal fraction of a second his fingers closed again on the small object as though it had been the symbol of all these little habits that chain us to the weary round of life. He released it at last, and letting himself fall on the settee, listened for the first sounds of returning wind.

Not yet. He heard only the wash of water, the heavy splashes, the dull shocks of the confused seas boarding his ship from all sides. She would never have a chance to clear her decks.

But the quietude of the air was startlingly tense and unsafe, like a slender hair holding a sword suspended over his head. By this awful pause the storm penetrated the defences of the man and unsealed his lips. He spoke out in the solitude and the pitch darkness of the cabin, as if addressing another being awakened within his breast.

"I shouldn't like to lose her," he said half aloud.

He sat unseen, apart from the sea, from his ship, isolated, as if withdrawn from the very current of his own existence, where such freaks as talking to himself surely had no place. His palms reposed on his knees, he bowed his short neck and puffed heavily, surrendering to a strange sensation of weariness he was not enlightened enough to recognize for the fatigue of mental stress.

From where he sat he could reach the door of a washstand locker. There should have been a towel there. There was. Good. . . . He took it out, wiped his face, and afterwards went on rubbing his wet head. He towelled himself with energy in the dark, and then remained motionless with the towel on his knees. A moment passed, of a stillness so profound that no one could have guessed there was a man sitting in that cabin. Then a murmur arose.

"She may come out of it yet."

When Captain MacWhirr came out on deck, which he did brusquely, as though he had suddenly become conscious of having stayed away too long, the calm had lasted already more than fifteen minutes—long enough to make itself intolerable even to his imagination. Jukes, motionless on the forepart of the bridge, began to speak at once. His voice, blank and forced as though he were talking through hard-set teeth, seemed to flow away on all sides into the darkness, deepening again upon the sea.

"I had the wheel relieved. Hackett began to sing out that he was done. He's lying in there alongside the steering-gear with a face like death. At first I couldn't get anybody to crawl out and relieve the poor devil. That boss'en's worse than no good, I always said. Thought I would have had to go myself and haul out one of them by the neck."

"Ah, well," muttered the Captain. He stood watchful by Jukes' side.

"The second mate's in there, too, holding his head. Is he hurt, sir?"

"No—crazy," said Captain MacWhirr, curtly.

"Looks as if he had a tumble, though."

"I had to give him a push," explained the Captain.

Jukes gave an impatient sigh.

"It will come very sudden," said Captain MacWhirr, "and from over there, I fancy. God only knows though. These books are only good to muddle your head and make you jumpy. It will be bad, and there's an end. If we only can steam her round in time to meet it. . . ."

A minute passed. Some of the stars winked rapidly and vanished.

"You left them pretty safe?" began the Captain abruptly, as though the silence were unbearable.

"Are you thinking of the coolies, sir? I rigged life-lines all ways across that 'tween-deck."

"Did you? Good idea, Mr. Jukes."

"I didn't . . . think you cared to . . . know," said Jukes—the lurching of the ship cut his speech as though somebody had been jerking him around while he talked—"how I got on with . . . that infernal job. We did it. And it may not matter in the end."

"Had to do what's fair, for all—they are only Chinamen. Give them the same chance with ourselves—hang it all. She isn't lost yet. Bad enough to be shut up below in a gale——"

"That's what I thought when you gave me the job, sir," interjected Jukes, moodily.

"——without being battered to pieces," pursued Captain MacWhirr with rising vehemence. "Couldn't let that go on in my ship, if I knew she hadn't five minutes to live. Couldn't bear it, Mr. Jukes."

A hollow echoing noise, like that of a shout rolling in a rocky chasm, approached the ship and went away again. The last star, blurred, enlarged, as if returning to the fiery mist of its beginning, struggled with the colossal depth of blackness hanging over the ship—and went out.

"Now for it!" muttered Captain MacWhirr. "Mr. Jukes."

"Here, sir."

The two men were growing indistinct to each other.

"We must trust her to go through it and come out on the other side. That's plain and straight. There's no room for Captain Wilson's storm-strategy here."

"No, sir."

"She will be smothered and swept again for hours," mumbled the Captain. "There's not much left by this time above deck for the sea to take away—unless you or me."

"Both, sir," whispered Jukes, breathlessly.

"You are always meeting trouble half way, Jukes," Captain MacWhirr remonstrated quaintly. "Though

it's a fact that the second mate is no good. D'ye hear,
Mr. Jukes? You would be left alone if. . . ."

Captain MacWhirr interrupted himself, and Jukes,
glancing on all sides, remained silent.

"Don't you be put out by anything," the Captain
continued, mumbling rather fast. "Keep her facing it.
They may say what they like, but the heaviest seas run
with the wind. Facing it—always facing it—that's the
way to get through. You are a young sailor. Face it.
That's enough for any man. Keep a cool head."

"Yes, sir," said Jukes, with a flutter of the heart.

In the next few seconds the Captain spoke to the engine-room and got an answer.

For some reason Jukes experienced an access of confidence, a sensation that came from outside like a warm
breath, and made him feel equal to every demand. The
distant muttering of the darkness stole into his ears.
He noted it unmoved, out of that sudden belief in
himself, as a man safe in a shirt of mail would watch
a point.

The ship laboured without intermission amongst the
black hills of water, paying with this hard tumbling the
price of her life. She rumbled in her depths, shaking
a white plummet of steam into the night, and Jukes'
thought skimmed like a bird through the engine-room,
where Mr. Rout—good man—was ready. When the
rumbling ceased it seemed to him that there was a
pause of every sound, a dead pause in which Captain
MacWhirr's voice rang out startlingly.

"What's that? A puff of wind?"—it spoke much
louder than Jukes had ever heard it before—"On the
bow. That's right. She may come out of it yet."

The mutter of the winds drew near apace. In the
forefront could be distinguished a drowsy waking
plaint passing on, and far off the growth of a multiple

clamour, marching and expanding. There was the throb as of many drums in it, a vicious rushing note, and like the chant of a tramping multitude.

Jukes could no longer see his captain distinctly. The darkness was absolutely piling itself upon the ship. At most he made out movements, a hint of elbows spread out, of a head thrown up.

Captain MacWhirr was trying to do up the top button of his oilskin coat with unwonted haste. The hurricane, with its power to madden the seas, to sink ships, to uproot trees, to overturn strong walls and dash the very birds of the air to the ground, had found this taciturn man in its path, and, doing its utmost, had managed to wring out a few words. Before the renewed wrath of winds swooped on his ship, Captain MacWhirr was moved to declare, in a tone of vexation, as it were: "I wouldn't like to lose her."

He was spared that annoyance.

VI

On a bright sunshiny day, with the breeze chasing her smoke far ahead, the *Nan-Shan* came into Fu-chau. Her arrival was at once noticed on shore, and the seamen in harbour said: "Look! Look at that steamer. What's that? Siamese—isn't she? Just look at her!"

She seemed, indeed, to have been used as a running target for the secondary batteries of a cruiser. A hail of minor shells could not have given her upper works a more broken, torn, and devastated aspect: and she had about her the worn, weary air of ships coming from the far ends of the world—and indeed with truth, for in her short passage she had been very far; sighting, verily, even the coast of the Great Beyond, whence no ship ever returns to give up her crew to the dust of the earth. She was incrusted and gray with salt to the trucks of her masts and to the top of her funnel; as though (as some facetious seaman said) "the crowd on board had fished her out somewhere from the bottom of the sea and brought her in here for salvage." And further, excited by the felicity of his own wit, he offered to give five pounds for her—"as she stands."

Before she had been quite an hour at rest, a meagre little man, with a red-tipped nose and a face cast in an angry mould, landed from a sampan on the quay of the Foreign Concession, and incontinently turned to shake his fist at her.

A tall individual, with legs much too thin for a rotund stomach, and with watery eyes, strolled up and remarked, "Just left her—eh? Quick work."

He wore a soiled suit of blue flannel with a pair of dirty cricketing shoes; a dingy gray moustache drooped from his lip, and daylight could be seen in two places between the rim and the crown of his hat.

"Hallo! what are you doing here?" asked the ex-second-mate of the *Nan-Shan*, shaking hands hurriedly.

"Standing by for a job—chance worth taking—got a quiet hint," explained the man with the broken hat, in jerky, apathetic wheezes.

The second shook his fist again at the *Nan-Shan*. "There's a fellow there that ain't fit to have the command of a scow," he declared, quivering with passion, while the other looked about listlessly.

"Is there?"

But he caught sight on the quay of a heavy seaman's chest, painted brown under a fringed sailcloth cover, and lashed with new manila line. He eyed it with awakened interest.

"I would talk and raise trouble if it wasn't for that damned Siamese flag. Nobody to go to—or I would make it hot for him. The fraud! Told his chief engineer—that's another fraud for you—I had lost my nerve. The greatest lot of ignorant fools that ever sailed the seas. No! You can't think . . ."

"Got your money all right?" inquired his seedy acquaintance suddenly.

"Yes. Paid me off on board," raged the second mate. "'Get your breakfast on shore,' says he."

"Mean skunk!" commented the tall man, vaguely, and passed his tongue on his lips. "What about having a drink of some sort?"

"He struck me," hissed the second mate.

"No! Struck! You don't say?" The man in blue began to bustle about sympathetically. "Can't possibly talk here. I want to know all about it.

Struck—eh? Let's get a fellow to carry your chest. I know a quiet place where they have some bottled beer. . . ."

Mr. Jukes, who had been scanning the shore through a pair of glasses, informed the chief engineer afterwards that "our late second mate hasn't been long in finding a friend. A chap looking uncommonly like a bummer. I saw them walk away together from the quay."

The hammering and banging of the needful repairs did not disturb Captain MacWhirr. The steward found in the letter he wrote, in a tidy chart-room, passages of such absorbing interest that twice he was nearly caught in the act. But Mrs. MacWhirr, in the drawing-room of the forty-pound house, stifled a yawn—perhaps out of self-respect—for she was alone.

She reclined in a plush-bottomed and gilt hammock-chair near a tiled fireplace, with Japanese fans on the mantel and a glow of coals in the grate. Lifting her hands, she glanced wearily here and there into the many pages. It was not her fault they were so prosy, so completely uninteresting—from "My darling wife" at the beginning, to "Your loving husband" at the end. She couldn't be really expected to understand all these ship affairs. She was glad, of course, to hear from him, but she had never asked herself why, precisely.

". . . They are called typhoons . . . The mate did not seem to like it . . . Not in books . . . Couldn't think of letting it go on. . . ."

The paper rustled sharply. ". . . . A calm that lasted more than twenty minutes," she read perfunctorily; and the next words her thoughtless eyes caught, on the top of another page, were: "see you and the children again. . . ." She had a movement of impatience. He was always thinking of coming home. He had never had such a good salary before. What was the matter now?

It did not occur to her to turn back overleaf to look. She would have found it recorded there that between 4 and 6 A. M. on December 25th, Captain MacWhirr did actually think that his ship could not possibly live another hour in such a sea, and that he would never see his wife and children again. Nobody was to know this (his letters got mislaid so quickly)—nobody whatever but the steward, who had been greatly impressed by that disclosure. So much so, that he tried to give the cook some idea of the "narrow squeak we all had" by saying solemnly, "The old man himself had a dam' poor opinion of our chance."

"How do you know?" asked, contemptuously, the cook, an old soldier. "He hasn't told you, maybe?"

"Well, he did give me a hint to that effect," the steward brazened it out.

"Get along with you! He will be coming to tell *me* next," jeered the old cook, over his shoulder.

Mrs. MacWhirr glanced farther, on the alert. ". . . Do what's fair. . . . Miserable objects . . . . Only three, with a broken leg each, and one . . . Thought had better keep the matter quiet . . . hope to have done the fair thing. . . ."

She let fall her hands. No: there was nothing more about coming home. Must have been merely expressing a pious wish. Mrs. MacWhirr's mind was set at ease, and a black marble clock, priced by the local jeweller at £3 18s. 6d., had a discreet stealthy tick.

The door flew open, and a girl in the long-legged, short-frocked period of existence, flung into the room.

A lot of colourless, rather lanky hair was scattered over
her shoulders. Seeing her mother, she stood still,
and directed her pale prying eyes upon the letter.

"From father," murmured Mrs. MacWhirr. "What
have you done with your ribbon?"

The girl put her hands up to her head and pouted.

"He's well," continued Mrs. MacWhirr, languidly.
"At least I think so. He never says." She had a little
laugh. The girl's face expressed a wandering indifference, and Mrs. MacWhirr surveyed her with fond
pride.

"Go and get your hat," she said after a while. "I
am going out to do some shopping. There is a sale at
Linom's."

"Oh, how jolly!" uttered the child, impressively, in
unexpectedly grave vibrating tones, and bounded out
of the room.

It was a fine afternoon, with a gray sky and dry
sidewalks. Outside the draper's Mrs. MacWhirr smiled
upon a woman in a black mantle of generous proportions
armoured in jet and crowned with flowers blooming falsely above a bilious matronly countenance.
They broke into a swift little babble of greetings and
exclamations both together, very hurried, as if the
street were ready to yawn open and swallow all that
pleasure before it could be expressed.

Behind them the high glass doors were kept on the
swing. People couldn't pass, men stood aside waiting
patiently, and Lydia was absorbed in poking the end
of her parasol between the stone flags. Mrs. MacWhirr
talked rapidly.

"Thank you very much. He's not coming home yet.
Of course it's very sad to have him away, but it's such
a comfort to know he keeps so well." Mrs. MacWhirr
drew breath. "The climate there agrees with him,"

she added, beamingly, as if poor MacWhirr had been away touring in China for the sake of his health.

Neither was the chief engineer coming home yet. Mr. Rout knew too well the value of a good billet.

"Solomon says wonders will never cease," cried Mrs. Rout joyously at the old lady in her armchair by the fire. Mr. Rout's mother moved slightly, her withered hands lying in black half-mittens on her lap.

The eyes of the engineer's wife fairly danced on the paper. "That captain of the ship he is in—a rather simple man, you remember, mother?—has done something rather clever, Solomon says."

"Yes, my dear," said the old woman meekly, sitting with bowed silvery head, and that air of inward stillness characteristic of very old people who seem lost in watching the last flickers of life. "I think I remember."

Solomon Rout, Old Sol, Father Sol, the Chief, "Rout, good man"—Mr. Rout, the condescending and paternal friend of youth, had been the baby of her many children—all dead by this time. And she remembered him best as a boy of ten—long before he went away to serve his apprenticeship in some great engineering works in the North. She had seen so little of him since, she had gone through so many years, that she had now to retrace her steps very far back to recognize him plainly in the mist of time. Sometimes it seemed that her daughter-in-law was talking of some strange man.

Mrs. Rout junior was disappointed. "H'm. H'm." She turned the page. "How provoking! He doesn't say what it is. Says I couldn't understand how much there was in it. Fancy! What could it be so very clever? What a wretched man not to tell us!"

She read on without further remark soberly, and at last sat looking into the fire. The chief wrote just a word or two of the typhoon; but something had moved

him to express an increased longing for the companionship of the jolly woman. "If it hadn't been that
mother must be looked after, I would send you your
passage-money to-day. You could set up a small
house out here. I would have a chance to see you sometimes then. We are not growing younger. . . ."

"He's well, mother," sighed Mrs. Rout, rousing herself.

"He always was a strong healthy boy," said the old
woman, placidly.

But Mr. Jukes' account was really animated and very
full. His friend in the Western Ocean trade imparted
it freely to the other officers of his liner. "A chap I
know writes to me about an extraordinary affair that
happened on board his ship in that typhoon—you
know—that we read of in the papers two months ago.
It's the funniest thing! Just see for yourself what he
says. I'll show you his letter."

There were phrases in it calculated to give the impression of light-hearted, indomitable resolution. Jukes
had written them in good faith, for he felt thus when he
wrote. He described with lurid effect the scenes in
the 'tween-deck. ". . . It struck me in a flash that
those confounded Chinamen couldn't tell we weren't a
desperate kind of robbers. 'Tisn't good to part the
Chinaman from his money if he is the stronger party.
We need have been desperate indeed to go thieving in
such weather, but what could these beggars know of us?
So, without thinking of it twice, I got the hands away
in a jiffy. Our work was done—that the old man had
set his heart on. We cleared out without staying to
inquire how they felt. I am convinced that if they had
not been so unmercifully shaken, and afraid—each individual one of them—to stand up, we would have been
torn to pieces. Oh! It was pretty complete, I can

tell you; and you may run to and fro across the Pond to the end of time before you find yourself with such a job on your hands."

After this he alluded professionally to the damage done to the ship, and went on thus:

"It was when the weather quieted down that the situation became confoundedly delicate. It wasn't made any better by us having been lately transferred to the Siamese flag; though the skipper can't see that it makes any difference—'as long as *we* are on board'— he says. There are feelings that this man simply hasn't got—and there's an end of it. You might just as well try to make a bedpost understand. But apart from this it is an infernally lonely state for a ship to be going about the China seas with no proper consuls, not even a gunboat of her own anywhere, nor a body to go to in case of some trouble.

"My notion was to keep these Johnnies under hatches for another fifteen hours or so; as we weren't much farther than that from Fu-chau. We would find there, most likely, some sort of a man-of-war, and once under her guns we were safe enough; for surely any skipper of a man-of-war—English, French or Dutch— would see white men through as far as row on board goes. We could get rid of them and their money after-wards by delivering them to their Mandarin or Taotai, or whatever they call these chaps in goggles you see being carried about in sedan-chairs through their stink-ing streets.

"The old man wouldn't see it somehow. He wanted to keep the matter quiet. He got that notion into his head, and a steam windlass couldn't drag it out of him. He wanted as little fuss made as possible, for the sake of the ship's name and for the sake of the owners—'for the sake of all concerned,' says he, looking at me very hard.

It made me angry hot. Of course you couldn't keep a thing like that quiet; but the chests had been secured in the usual manner and were safe enough for any earthly gale, while this had been an altogether fiendish business I couldn't give you even an idea of.

"Meantime, I could hardly keep on my feet. None of us had a spell of any sort for nearly thirty hours, and there the old man sat rubbing his chin, rubbing the top of his head, and so bothered he didn't even think of pulling his long boots off.

"'I hope, sir,' says I, 'you won't be letting them out on deck before we make ready for them in some shape or other.' Not, mind you, that I felt very sanguine about controlling these beggars if they meant to take charge. A trouble with a cargo of Chinamen is no child's play. I was dam' tired, too. 'I wish,' said I, 'you would let us throw the whole lot of these dollars down to them and leave them to fight it out amongst themselves, while we get a rest.'

"'Now you talk wild, Jukes,' says he, looking up in his slow way that makes you ache all over, somehow. 'We must plan out something that would be fair to all parties.'

"I had no end of work on hand, as you may imagine, so I set the hands going, and then I thought I would turn in a bit. I hadn't been asleep in my bunk ten minutes when in rushes the steward and begins to pull at my leg.

"'For God's sake, Mr. Jukes, come out! Come on deck quick, sir. Oh, do come out!'

"The fellow scared all the sense out of me. I didn't know what had happened: another hurricane—or what. Could hear no wind.

"'The Captain's letting them out. Oh, he is letting them out! Jump on deck, sir, and save us. The chief engineer has just run below for his revolver.'

"That's what I understood the fool to say. However, Father Rout swears he went in there only to get a clean pocket-handkerchief. Anyhow, I made one jump into my trousers and flew on deck aft. There was certainly a good deal of noise going on forward of the bridge. Four of the hands with the boss'en were at work abaft. I passed up to them some of the rifles all the ships on the China coast carry in the cabin, and led them on the bridge. On the way I ran against Old Sol, looking startled and sucking at an unlighted cigar.

"'Come along,' I shouted to him.

"We charged, the seven of us, up to the chart-room. All was over. There stood the old man with his sea-boots still drawn up to the hips and in shirt-sleeves—got warm thinking it out, I suppose. Bun-hin's dandy clerk at his elbow, as dirty as a sweep, was still green in the face. I could see directly I was in for something.

"'What the devil are these monkey tricks, Mr Jukes?' asks the old man, as angry as ever he could be. I tell you frankly it made me lose my tongue. 'For God's sake, Mr. Jukes,' says he, 'do take away these rifles from the men. Somebody's sure to get hurt before long if you don't. Damme, if this ship isn't worse than Bedlam! Look sharp now. I want you up here to help me and Bun-hin's Chinaman to count that money. You wouldn't mind lending a hand, too, Mr. Rout, now you are here. The more of us the better.'

"He had settled it all in his mind while I was having a snooze. Had we been an English ship, or only going to land our cargo of coolies in an English port, like Hong-Kong, for instance, there would have been no end of inquiries and bother, claims for damages and so on. But these Chinamen know their officials better than we do.

"The hatches had been taken off already, and they were all on deck after a night and a day down below. It made you feel queer to see so many gaunt, wild faces together. The beggars stared about at the sky, at the sea, at the ship, as though they had expected the whole thing to have been blown to pieces. And no wonder! They had had a doing that would have shaken the soul out of a white man. But then they say a Chinaman has no soul. He has, though, something about him that is deuced tough. There was a fellow (amongst others of the badly hurt) who had had his eye all but knocked out. It stood out of his head the size of half a hen's egg. This would have laid out a white man on his back for a month: and yet there was that chap elbowing here and there in the crowd and talking to the others as if nothing had been the matter. They made a great hubbub amongst themselves, and whenever the old man showed his bald head on the foreside of the bridge, they would all leave off jawing and look at him from below.

"It seems that after he had done his thinking he made that Bun-hin's fellow go down and explain to them the only way they could get their money back. He told me afterwards that, all the coolies having worked in the same place and for the same length of time, he reckoned he would be doing the fair thing by them as near as possible if he shared all the cash we had picked up equally among the lot. You couldn't tell one man's dollars from another's, he said, and if you asked each man how much money he brought on board he was afraid they would lie, and he would find himself a long way short. I think he was right there. As to giving up the money to any Chinese official he could scare up in Fu-chau, he said he might just as well put the lot in his own pocket at once for all the good it would be to them. I suppose they thought so, too.

"We finished the distribution before dark. It was rather a sight: the sea running high, the ship a wreck to look at, these Chinamen staggering up on the bridge one by one for their share, and the old man still booted, and in his shirt-sleeves, busy paying out at the chart-room door, perspiring like anything, and now and then coming down sharp on myself or Father Rout about one thing or another not quite to his mind. He took the share of those who were disabled himself to them on the No. 2 hatch. There were three dollars left over, and these went to the three most damaged coolies, one to each. We turned-to afterwards, and shovelled out on deck heaps of wet rags, all sorts of fragments of things without shape, and that you couldn't give a name to, and let them settle the ownership themselves.

"This certainly is coming as near as can be to keeping the thing quiet for the benefit of all concerned. What's your opinion, you pampered mail-boat swell? The old chief says that this was plainly the only thing that could be done. The skipper remarked to me the other day, 'There are things you find nothing about in books. I think that he got out of it very well for such a stupid man.'"

AMY FOSTER

AMY FOSTER

KENNEDY is a country doctor, and lives in Colebrook, on the shores of Eastbay. The high ground rising abruptly behind the red roofs of the little town crowds the quaint High Street against the wall which defends it from the sea. Beyond the sea-wall there curves for miles in a vast and regular sweep the barren beach of shingle, with the village of Brenzett standing out darkly across the water, a spire in a clump of trees; and still further out the perpendicular column of a lighthouse, looking in the distance no bigger than a lead-pencil, marks the vanishing-point of the land. The country at the back of Brenzett is low and flat; but the bay is fairly well sheltered from the seas, and occasionally a big ship, windbound or through stress of weather, makes use of the anchoring ground a mile and a half due north from you as you stand at the back door of the "Ship Inn" in Brenzett. A dilapidated windmill near by, lifting its shattered arms from a mound no loftier than a rubbish-heap, and a Martello tower squatting at the water's edge half a mile to the south of the Coastguard cottages, are familiar to the skippers of small craft. These are the official seamarks for the patch of trustworthy bottom represented on the Admiralty charts by an irregular oval of dots enclosing several figures six, with a tiny anchor engraved among them, and the legend "mud and shells" over all.

The brow of the upland overtops the square tower of the Colebrook Church. The slope is green and looped by a white road. Ascending along this road, you open

a valley broad and shallow, a wide green trough of
pastures and hedges merging inland into a vista of
purple tints and flowing lines closing the view.

In this valley down to Brenzett and Colebrook and
up to Darnford, the market town fourteen miles away,
lies the practice of my friend Kennedy. He had begun
life as surgeon in the Navy, and afterwards had been
the companion of a famous traveller, in the days when
there were continents with unexplored interiors. His
papers on the fauna and flora made him known to
scientific societies. And now he had come to a country
practice—from choice. The penetrating power of his
mind, acting like a corrosive fluid, had destroyed his
ambition, I fancy. His intelligence is of a scientific
order, of an investigating habit, and of that unappeasable curiosity which believes that there is a particle of
a general truth in every mystery.

A good many years ago now, on my return from
abroad, he invited me to stay with him. I came
readily enough, and as he could not neglect his patients
to keep me company, he took me on his rounds—thirty
miles or so of an afternoon, sometimes. I waited for
him on the roads; the horse reached after the leafy
twigs, and, sitting high in the dogcart, I could hear
Kennedy's laugh through the half-open door of some
cottage. He had a big, hearty laugh that would have
fitted a man twice his size, a brisk manner, a bronzed
face, and a pair of gray, profoundly attentive eyes.
He had the talent of making people talk to him freely,
and an inexhaustible patience in listening to their tales.

One day, as we trotted out of a large village into
a shady bit of road, I saw on our left hand a low,
black cottage, with diamond panes in the windows, a
creeper on the end wall, a roof of shingle, and some
roses climbing on the rickety trellis-work of the tiny

porch. Kennedy pulled up to a walk. A woman, in full sunlight, was throwing a dripping blanket over a line stretched between two old apple-trees. And as the bobtailed, long-necked chestnut, trying to get his head, jerked the left hand, covered by a thick dogskin glove, the doctor raised his voice over the hedge: "How's your child, Amy?"

I had the time to see her dull face, red, not with a mantling blush, but as if her flat cheeks had been vigorously slapped, and to take in the squat figure, the scanty, dusty brown hair drawn into a tight knot at the back of the head. She looked quite young. With a distinct catch in her breath, her voice sounded low and timid.

"He's well, thank you."

We trotted again. "A young patient of yours," I said; and the doctor, flicking the chestnut absently, muttered, "Her husband used to be."

"She seems a dull creature," I remarked, listlessly.

"Precisely," said Kennedy. "She is very passive. It's enough to look at the red hands hanging at the end of those short arms, at those slow, prominent brown eyes, to know the inertness of her mind—an inertness that one would think made it everlastingly safe from all the surprises of imagination. And yet which of us is safe? At any rate, such as you see her, she had enough imagination to fall in love. She's the daughter of one Isaac Foster, who from a small farmer has sunk into a shepherd; the beginning of his misfortunes dating from his runaway marriage with the cook of his widowed father—a well-to-do, apoplectic grazier, who passionately struck his name off his will, and had been heard to utter threats against his life. But this old affair, scandalous enough to serve as a motive for a Greek tragedy, arose from the similarity of their characters. There are other tragedies, less scandalous and of a subtler poignancy, arising from irreconcilable differences and from that fear of the Incomprehensible that hangs over all our heads—over all our heads. . . ."

The tired chestnut dropped into a walk; and the rim of the sun, all red in a speckless sky, touched familiarly the smooth top of a ploughed rise near the road as I had seen it times innumerable touch the distant horizon of the sea. The uniform brownness of the harrowed field glowed with a rose tinge, as though the powdered clods had sweated out in minute pearls of blood the toil of uncounted ploughmen. From the edge of a copse a waggon with two horses was rolling gently along the ridge. Raised above our heads upon the sky-line, it loomed up against the red sun, triumphantly big, enormous, like a chariot of giants drawn by two slow-stepping steeds of legendary proportions. And the clumsy figure of the man plodding at the head of the leading horse projected itself on the background of the Infinite with a heroic uncouthness. The end of his carter's whip quivered high up in the blue. Kennedy discoursed.

"She's the eldest of a large family. At the age of fifteen they put her out to service at the New Barns Farm. I attended Mrs. Smith, the tenant's wife, and saw that girl there for the first time. Mrs. Smith, a genteel person with a sharp nose, made her put on a black dress every afternoon. I don't know what induced me to notice her at all. There are faces that call your attention by a curious want of definiteness in their whole aspect, as, walking in a mist, you peer attentively at a vague shape which, after all, may be nothing more curious or strange than a signpost. The only peculiarity I perceived in her was a slight hesitation in her utterance, a sort of preliminary stammer which passes away with the first word. When sharply spoken to, she was apt to lose her head at once; but her heart was of the kindest. She had never been heard to express a dislike for a single human being, and she was tender to every living creature. She was devoted to Mrs. Smith, to Mr. Smith, to their dogs, cats, canaries; and as to Mrs. Smith's gray parrot, its peculiarities exercised upon her a positive fascination. Nevertheless, when that outlandish bird, attacked by the cat, shrieked for help in human accents, she ran out into the yard stopping her ears, and did not prevent the crime. For Mrs. Smith this was another evidence of her stupidity; on the other hand, her want of charm, in view of Smith's well-known frivolousness, was a great recommendation. Her short-sighted eyes would swim with pity for a poor mouse in a trap, and she had been seen once by some boys on her knees in the wet grass helping a toad in difficulties. If it's true, as some German fellow has said, that without phosphorus there is no thought, it is still more true that there is no kindness of heart without a certain amount of imagination. She had some. She had even more than is necessary to understand suffering and to be moved by pity. She fell in love under circumstances that leave no room for doubt in the matter; for you need imagination to form a notion of beauty at all, and still more to discover your ideal in an unfamiliar shape.

"How this aptitude came to her, what it did feed upon, is an inscrutable mystery. She was born in the village, and had never been further away from it than Colebrook or perhaps Darnford. She lived for four years with the Smiths. New Barns is an isolated farmhouse a mile away from the road, and she was content to look day after day at the same fields, hollows, rises; at the trees and the hedgerows; at the faces of the four men about the farm, always the same—day after day,

month after month, year after year. She never showed
a desire for conversation, and, as it seemed to me, she
did not know how to smile. Sometimes of a fine
Sunday afternoon she would put on her best dress, a
pair of stout boots, a large gray hat trimmed with a
black feather (I've seen her in that finery), seize an
absurdly slender parasol, climb over two stiles, tramp
over three fields and along two hundred yards of road—
never further. There stood Foster's cottage. She
would help her mother to give their tea to the younger
children, wash up the crockery, kiss the little ones, and
go back to the farm. That was all. All the rest, all the
change, all the relaxation. She never seemed to wish
for anything more. And then she fell in love. She fell
in love silently, obstinately—perhaps helplessly. It
came slowly, but when it came it worked like a powerful
spell; it was love as the Ancients understood it: an irresistible and fateful impulse—a possession! Yes, it
was in her to become haunted and possessed by a face,
by a presence, fatally, as though she had been a pagan
worshipper of form under a joyous sky—and to be
awakened at last from that mysterious forgetfulness of
self, from that enchantment, from that transport, by a
fear resembling the unaccountable terror of a
brute. . . ."

With the sun hanging low on its western limit, the
expanse of the grass-lands framed in the counter-scarps
of the rising ground took on a gorgeous and sombre
aspect. A sense of penetrating sadness, like that
inspired by a grave strain of music, disengaged itself
from the silence of the fields. The men we met walked
past, slow, unsmiling, with downcast eyes, as if the
melancholy of an over-burdened earth had weighted
their feet, bowed their shoulders, borne down their
glances.

"Yes," said the doctor to my remark, "one would think the earth is under a curse, since of all her children these that cling to her the closest are uncouth in body and as leaden of gait as if their very hearts were loaded with chains. But here on this same road you might have seen amongst these heavy men a being lithe, supple and long-limbed, straight like a pine, with something striving upwards in his appearance as though the heart within him had been buoyant. Perhaps it was only the force of the contrast, but when he was passing one of these villagers here, the soles of his feet did not seem to me to touch the dust of the road. He vaulted over the stiles, paced these slopes with a long elastic stride that made him noticeable at a great distance, and had lustrous black eyes. He was so different from the mankind around that, with his freedom of movement, his soft—a little startled, glance, his olive complexion and graceful bearing, his humanity suggested to me the nature of a woodland creature. He came from there."

The doctor pointed with his whip, and from the summit of the descent seen over the rolling tops of the trees in a park by the side of the road, appeared the level sea far below us, like the floor of an immense edifice inlaid with bands of dark ripple, with still trails of glitter, ending in a belt of glassy water at the foot of the sky. The light blur of smoke, from an invisible steamer, faded on the great clearness of the horizon like the mist of a breath on a mirror; and, inshore, the white sails of a coaster, with the appearance of disentangling themselves slowly from under the branches, floated clear of the foliage of the trees.

"Shipwrecked in the bay?" I said.

"Yes; he was a castaway. A poor emigrant from Central Europe bound to America and washed ashore here in a storm. And for him, who knew nothing of the earth, England was an undiscovered country. It was some time before he learned its name; and for all I know he might have expected to find wild beasts or wild men here, when, crawling in the dark over the sea-wall, he rolled down the other side into a dyke, where it was another miracle he didn't get drowned. But he struggled instinctively like an animal under a net, and this blind struggle threw him out into a field. He must have been, indeed, of a tougher fibre than he looked to withstand without expiring such buffetings, the violence of his exertions, and so much fear. Later on, in his broken English that resembled curiously the speech of a young child, he told me himself that he put his trust in God, believing he was no longer in this world. And truly—he would add—how was he to know? He fought his way against the rain and the gale on all fours, and crawled at last among some sheep huddled close under the lee of a hedge. They ran off in all directions, bleating in the darkness, and he welcomed the first familiar sound he heard on these shores. It must have been two in the morning then. And this is all we know of the manner of his landing, though he did not arrive unattended by any means. Only his grisly company did not begin to come ashore till much later in the day. . . ."

The doctor gathered the reins, clicked his tongue; we trotted down the hill. Then turning, almost directly, a sharp corner into High Street, we rattled over the stones and were home.

Late in the evening Kennedy, breaking a spell of moodiness that had come over him, returned to the story. Smoking his pipe, he paced the long room from end to end. A reading-lamp concentrated all its light upon the papers on his desk; and, sitting by the open window, I saw, after the windless, scorching day, the frigid splendour of a hazy sea lying motionless under the moon. Not a whisper, not a splash, not a stir of the shingle, not a footstep, not a sigh came up from the earth below—never a sign of life but the scent of climbing jasmine: and Kennedy's voice, speaking behind me, passed through the wide casement, to vanish outside in a chill and sumptuous stillness.

". . . . The relations of shipwrecks in the olden time tell us of much suffering. Often the castaways were only saved from drowning to die miserably from starvation on a barren coast; others suffered violent death or else slavery, passing through years of precarious existence with people to whom their strangeness was an object of suspicion, dislike or fear. We read about these things, and they are very pitiful. It is indeed hard upon a man to find himself a lost stranger, helpless, incomprehensible, and of a mysterious origin, in some obscure corner of the earth. Yet amongst all the adventurers shipwrecked in all the wild parts of the world, there is not one, it seems to me, that ever had to suffer a fate so simply tragic as the man I am speaking of, the most innocent of adventurers cast out, by the sea in the bight of this bay, almost within sight from this very window.

"He did not know the name of his ship. Indeed, in the course of time we discovered he did not even know that ships had names—'like Christian people'; and when, one day, from the top of Talfourd Hill, he beheld the sea lying open to his view, his eyes roamed afar, lost in an air of wild surprise, as though he had never seen such a sight before. And probably he had not. As far as I could make out, he had been hustled together with many others on board an emigrant ship at the mouth of the Elbe, too bewildered to take note of his surroundings, too weary to see anything, too anxious to care. They were driven below into the 'tween-deck and battened down from the very start. It was a low timber dwelling—he would say—with wooden beams overhead, like the houses in his country, but you went into it down a ladder. It was very large, very cold, damp and sombre, with places in the manner of wooden boxes where people had to sleep one above another, and it kept on rocking all ways at once all the time. He crept into one of these boxes and lay down there in the clothes in which he had left his home many days before, keeping his bundle and his stick by his side. People groaned, children cried, water dripped, the lights went out, the walls of the place creaked, and everything was being shaken so that in one's little box one dared not lift one's head. He had lost touch with his only companion (a young man from the same valley, he said), and all the time a great noise of wind went on outside and heavy blows fell—boom! boom! An awful sickness overcame him, even to the point of making him neglect his prayers. Besides, one could not tell whether it was morning or evening. It seemed always to be night in that place.

"Before that he had been travelling a long, long time on the iron track. He looked out of the window, which had a wonderfully clear glass in it, and the trees, the houses, the fields, and the long roads seemed to fly round and round about him till his head swam. He gave me to understand that he had on his passage beheld uncounted multitudes of people—whole nations—all dressed in such clothes as the rich wear. Once he was made to get out of the carriage, and slept through a night on a bench in a house of bricks with his bundle under his head; and once for many hours he had to sit on a floor of flat stones dozing, with his knees up and with his bundle between his feet. There was a roof over him, which seemed made of glass, and was so high that the tallest mountain-pine he had ever seen would have had room to grow under it. Steam-machines rolled in at one end and out at the other. People swarmed more than you can see on a feast-day round the miraculous Holy Image in the yard of the Carmelite Convent down in the plains where, before he left his home, he drove his mother in a wooden cart:—a pious old woman who wanted to offer prayers and make a vow for his safety. He could not give me an idea of how large and lofty and full of noise and smoke and gloom, and clang of iron, the place was, but someone had told him it was called Berlin. Then they rang a bell, and another steam-machine came in, and again he was taken on and on through a land that wearied his eyes by its flatness without a single bit of a hill to be seen anywhere. One more night he spent shut up in a building like a good stable with a litter of straw on the floor, guarding his bundle amongst a lot of men, of whom not one could understand a single word he said. In the morning they were all led down to the stony shores of an extremely broad muddy river, flowing not between hills but between houses that seemed immense. There was a steam-machine that went on the water, and they all stood upon it packed tight, only now there were with them many women and children who made much noise. A cold rain fell, the wind blew in his face; he was wet through, and his teeth chattered. He and the young man from the same valley took each other by the hand.

"They thought they were being taken to America straight away, but suddenly the steam-machine bumped against the side of a thing like a great house on the water. The walls were smooth and black, and there uprose, growing from the roof as it were, bare trees in the shape of crosses, extremely high. That's how it

appeared to him then, for he had never seen a ship before. This was the ship that was going to swim all the
way to America. Voices shouted, everything swayed;
there was a ladder dipping up and down. He went up
on his hands and knees in mortal fear of falling into the
water below, which made a great splashing. He got
separated from his companion, and when he descended
into the bottom of that ship his heart seemed to melt
suddenly within him.

"It was then also, as he told me, that he lost contact
for good and all with one of those three men who the
summer before had been going about through all the
little town in the foothills of his country. They would
arrive on market-days driving in a peasant's cart, and
would set up an office in an inn or some other Jew's
house. There were three of them, of whom one with a
long beard looked venerable; and they had red cloth
collars round their necks and gold lace on their sleeves
like Government officials. They sat proudly behind a
long table; and in the next room, so that the common
people shouldn't hear, they kept a cunning telegraph
machine, through which they could talk to the Emperor
of America. The fathers hung about the door, but the
young men of the mountains would crowd up to the
table asking many questions, for there was work to be
got all the year round at three dollars a day in America,
and no military service to do.

"But the American Kaiser would not take everybody.
Oh, no! He himself had a great difficulty in getting
accepted, and the venerable man in uniform had to
go out of the room several times to work the telegraph
on his behalf. The American Kaiser engaged him at
last at three dollars, he being young and strong. However, many able young men backed out, afraid of the
great distance; besides, those only who had some

money could be taken. There were some who sold
their huts and their land because it cost a lot of money
to get to America; but then, once there, you had three
dollars a day, and if you were clever you could find
places where true gold could be picked up on the
ground. His father's house was getting over full.
Two of his brothers were married and had children.
He promised to send money home from America by
post twice a year. His father sold an old cow, a pair of
piebald mountain ponies of his own raising, and a cleared
plot of fair pasture land on the sunny slope of a pine-
clad pass to a Jew inn-keeper, in order to pay the people
of the ship that took men to America to get rich in a
short time.

"He must have been a real adventurer at heart, for
how many of the greatest enterprises in the conquest
of the earth had for their beginning just such a bargain-
ing away of the paternal cow for the mirage or true
gold far away! I have been telling you more or less in
my own words what I learned fragmentarily in the
course of two or three years, during which I seldom
missed an opportunity of a friendly chat with him. He
told me this story of his adventure with many flashes
of white teeth and lively glances of black eyes, at first
in a sort of anxious baby-talk, then, as he acquired the
language, with great fluency, but always with that
singing, soft, and at the same time vibrating intonation
that instilled a strangely penetrating power into the
sound of the most familiar English words, as if they had
been the words of an unearthly language. And he always would come to an end, with many emphatic
shakes of his head, upon that awful sensation of his
heart melting within him directly he set foot on board
that ship. Afterwards there seemed to come for him a
period of blank ignorance, at any rate as to facts. No

doubt he must have been abominably seasick and abominably unhappy—this soft and passionate adventurer, taken thus out of his knowledge, and feeling bitterly as he lay in his emigrant bunk his utter loneliness; for his was a highly sensitive nature. The next thing we know of him for certain is that he had been hiding in Hammond's pig-pound by the side of the road to Norton, six miles, as the crow flies, from the sea. Of these experiences he was unwilling to speak: they seemed to have seared into his soul a sombre sort of wonder and indignation. Through the rumours of the country-side, which lasted for a good many days after his arrival, we know that the fishermen of West Colebrook had been disturbed and startled by heavy knocks against the walls of weatherboard cottages, and by a voice crying piercingly strange words in the night. Several of them turned out even, but, no doubt, he had fled in sudden alarm at their rough angry tones hailing each other in the darkness. A sort of frenzy must have helped him up the steep Norton hill. It was he, no doubt, who early the following morning had been seen lying (in a swoon, I should say) on the roadside grass by the Brenzett carrier, who actually got down to have a nearer look, but drew back, intimidated by the perfect immobility, and by something queer in the aspect of that tramp, sleeping so still under the showers. As the day advanced, some children came dashing into school at Norton in such a fright that the schoolmistress went out and spoke indignantly to a 'horrid-looking man' on the road. He edged away, hanging his head, for a few steps, and then suddenly ran off with extraordinary fleetness. The driver of Mr. Bradley's milk-cart made no secret of it that he had lashed with his whip at a hairy sort of gipsy fellow who, jumping up at a turn of the road by the Vents, made a snatch at the pony's bridle. And he caught him a good one, too, right over the face, he said, that made him drop down in the mud a jolly sight quicker than he had jumped up; but it was a good half a mile before he could stop the pony. Maybe that in his desperate endeavours to get help, and in his need to get in touch with someone, the poor devil had tried to stop the cart. Also three boys confessed afterwards to throwing stones at a funny tramp, knocking about all wet and muddy, and, it seemed, very drunk, in the narrow deep lane by the limekilns. All this was the talk of three villages for days; but we have Mrs. Finn's (the wife of Smith's waggoner) unimpeachable testimony that she saw him get over the low wall of Hammond's pig-pound and lurch straight at her, babbling aloud in a voice that was enough to make one die of fright. Having the baby with her in a perambulator, Mrs. Finn called out to him to go away, and as he persisted in coming nearer, she hit him courageously with her umbrella over the head, and, without once looking back, ran like the wind with the perambulator as far as the first house in the village. She stopped then, out of breath, and spoke to old Lewis, hammering there at a heap of stones; and the old chap, taking off his immense black wire goggles, got up on his shaky legs to look where she pointed. Together they followed with their eyes the figure of the man running over a field; they saw him fall down, pick himself up, and run on again, staggering and waving his long arms above his head, in the direction of the New Barns Farm. From that moment he is plainly in the toils of his obscure and touching destiny. There is no doubt after this of what happened to him. All is certain now: Mrs. Smith's intense terror; Amy Foster's stolid conviction held against the other's nervous attack, that the man 'meant no harm'; Smith's exasperation (on his return from Darnford Market) at finding the dog barking himself into a fit, the back-door locked, his wife in hysterics; and all for an unfortunate dirty tramp, supposed to be even then lurking in his stackyard, Was he? He would teach him to frighten women.

"Smith is notoriously hot-tempered, but the sight of some nondescript and miry creature sitting cross-legged amongst a lot of loose straw, and swinging itself to and fro like a bear in a cage, made him pause. Then this tramp stood up silently before him, one mass of mud and filth from head to foot. Smith, alone amongst his stacks with this apparition, in the stormy twilight ringing with the infuriated barking of the dog, felt the dread of an inexplicable strangeness. But when that being, parting with his black hands the long matted locks that hung before his face, as you part the two halves of a curtain, looked out at him with glistening, wild, black-and-white eyes, the weirdness of this silent encounter fairly staggered him. He has admitted since (for the story has been a legitimate subject of conversation about here for years) that he made more than one step backwards. Then a sudden burst of rapid, senseless speech persuaded him at once that he had to do with an escaped lunatic. In fact, that impression never wore off completely. Smith has not in his heart given up his secret conviction of the man's essential insanity to this very day.

"As the creature approached him, jabbering in a most discomposing manner, Smith (unaware that he was being addressed as 'gracious lord,' and adjured in God's name to afford food and shelter) kept on speaking firmly but gently to it, and retreating all the time into the other yard. At last, watching his chance, by a sudden charge he bundled him headlong into the wood-lodge, and instantly shot the bolt. Thereupon he

wiped his brow, though the day was cold. He had done
his duty to the community by shutting up a wandering
and probably dangerous maniac. Smith isn't a hard
man at all, but he had room in his brain only for that
one idea of lunacy. He was not imaginative enough to
ask himself whether the man might not be perishing
with cold and hunger. Meantime, at first, the maniac
made a great deal of noise in the lodge. Mrs. Smith
was screaming upstairs, where she had locked herself in
her bedroom; but Amy Foster sobbed piteously at
the kitchen-door, wringing her hands and muttering,
'Don't! don't!' I daresay Smith had a rough time of it
that evening with one noise and another, and this insane, disturbing voice crying obstinately through the
door only added to his irritation. He couldn't possibly
have connected this troublesome lunatic with the sinking of a ship in Eastbay, of which there had been a
rumour in the Darnford market place. And I daresay
the man inside had been very near to insanity on that
night. Before his excitement collapsed and he became
unconscious he was throwing himself violently about
in the dark, rolling on some dirty sacks, and biting his
fists with rage, cold, hunger, amazement, and despair.

"He was a mountaineer of the eastern range of the
Carpathians, and the vessel sunk the night before in
Eastbay was the Hamburg emigrant-ship *Herzogin
Sophia-Dorothea*, of appalling memory.

"A few months later we could read in the papers the
accounts of the bogus 'Emigration Agencies' among the
Sclavonian peasantry in the more remote provinces
of Austria. The object of these scoundrels was to get
hold of the poor ignorant people's homesteads, and they
were in league with the local usurers. They exported
their victims through Hamburg mostly. As to the ship,
I had watched her out of this very window, reaching

close-hauled under short canvas into the bay on a dark, threatening afternoon. She came to an anchor, correctly by the chart, off the Brenzett Coastguard station. I remember before the night fell looking out again at the outlines of her spars and rigging that stood out dark and pointed on a background of ragged, slaty clouds like another and a slighter spire to the left of the Brenzett church-tower. In the evening the wind rose. At midnight I could hear in my bed the terrific gusts and the sounds of a driving deluge.

"About that time the Coastguardmen thought they saw the lights of a steamer over the anchoring-ground. In a moment they vanished; but it is clear that another vessel of some sort had tried for shelter in the bay on that awful, blind night, had rammed the German ship amidships (a breach—as one of the divers told me afterwards—'that you could sail a Thames barge through'), and then had gone out either scathless or damaged, who shall say; but had gone out, unknown, unseen, and fatal, to perish mysteriously at sea. Of her nothing ever came to light, and yet the hue and cry that was raised all over the world would have found her out if she had been in existence anywhere on the face of the waters.

"A completeness without a clue, and a stealthy silence as of a neatly executed crime, characterize this murderous disaster, which, as you may remember, had its gruesome celebrity. The wind would have prevented the loudest outcries from reaching the shore; there had been evidently no time for signals of distress. It was death without any sort of fuss. The Hamburg ship, filling all at once, capsized as she sank, and at daylight there was not even the end of a spar to be seen above water. She was missed, of course, and at first the Coastguardmen surmised that she had either dragged her anchor or parted her cable some time during the night, and had been blown out to sea. Then, after the tide turned, the wreck must have shifted a little and released some of the bodies, because a child—a little fair-haired child in a red frock—came ashore abreast of the Martello tower. By the afternoon you could see along three miles of beach dark figures with bare legs dashing in and out of the tumbling foam, and rough-looking men, women with hard faces, children, mostly fair-haired, were being carried, stiff and dripping, on stretchers, on wattles, on ladders, in a long procession past the door of the "Ship Inn," to be laid out in a row under the north wall of the Brenzett Church.

"Officially, the body of the little girl in the red frock is the first thing that came ashore from that ship. But I have patients amongst the seafaring population of West Colebrook, and, unofficially, I am informed that very early that morning two brothers, who went down to look after their cobble hauled up on the beach, found a good way from Brenzett, an ordinary ship's hencoop, lying high and dry on the shore, with eleven drowned ducks inside. Their families ate the birds, and the hencoop was split into firewood with a hatchet. It is possible that a man (supposing he happened to be on deck at the time of the accident) might have floated ashore on that hencoop. He might. I admit it is improbable, but there was the man—and for days, nay, for weeks— it didn't enter our heads that we had amongst us the only living soul that had escaped from that disaster. The man himself, even when he learned to speak intelligibly, could tell us very little. He remembered he had felt better (after the ship had anchored, I suppose), and that the darkness, the wind, and the rain took his breath away. This looks as if he had been on deck some time during that night. But we mustn't forget he had been

taken out of his knowledge, that he had been sea-sick
and battened down below for four days, that he had no
general notion f a ship or of the sea, and therefore
could have no definite idea of what was happening to
him. The rain, the wind, the darkness he knew; he
understood the bleating of the sheep, and he remembered the pain of his wretchedness and misery, his
heartbroken astonishment that it was neither seen nor
understood, his dismay at finding all the men angry and
all the women fierce. He had approached them as a
beggar, it is true, he said; but in his country, even if
they gave nothing, they spoke gently to beggars. The
children in his country were not taught to throw stones
at those who asked for compassion. Smith's strategy
overcame him completely. The wood-lodge presented the horrible aspect of a dungeon. What would
be done to him next? . . . No wonder that Amy
Foster appeared to his eyes with the aureole of an angel
of light. The girl had not been able to sleep for thinking of the poor man, and in the morning, before the
Smiths were up, she slipped out across the back yard.
Holding the door of the wood-lodge ajar, she looked in
and extended to him half a loaf of white bread—
'such bread as the rich eat in my country,' he used
to say.

"At this he got up slowly from amongst all sorts of
rubbish, stiff, hungry, trembling, miserable, and doubtful. 'Can you eat this?' she asked in her soft and
timid voice. He must have taken her for a 'gracious
lady.' He devoured ferociously, and tears were falling
on the crust. Suddenly he dropped the bread, seized
her wrist, and imprinted a kiss on her hand. She was
not frightened. Through his forlorn condition she had
observed that he was good-looking. She shut the door
and walked back slowly to the kitchen. Much later on,

she told Mrs. Smith, who shuddered at the bare idea of being touched by that creature.

"Through this act of impulsive pity he was brought back again within the pale of human relations with his new surroundings. He never forgot it—never.

"That very same morning old Mr. Swaffer (Smith's nearest neighbour) came over to give his advice, and ended by carrying him off. He stood, unsteady on his legs, meek, and caked over in half-dried mud, while the two men talked around him in an incomprehensible tongue. Mrs. Smith had refused to come downstairs till the madman was off the premises; Amy Foster, far from within the dark kitchen, watched through the open back-door; and he obeyed the signs that were made to him to the best of his ability. But Smith was full of mistrust. 'Mind, sir! It may be all his cunning,' he cried repeatedly in a tone of warning. When Mr. Swaffer started the mare, the deplorable being sitting humbly by his side, through weakness, nearly fell out over the back of the high two-wheeled cart. Swaffer took him straight home. And it is then that I come upon the scene.

"I was called in by the simple process of the old man beckoning to me with his forefinger over the gate of his house as I happened to be driving past. I got down, of course.

"'I've got something here,' he mumbled, leading the way to an outhouse at a little distance from his other farm-buildings.

"It was there that I saw him first, in a long, low room taken upon the space of that sort of coach-house. It was bare and whitewashed, with a small square aperture glazed with one cracked, dusty pane at its further end. He was lying on his back upon a straw pallet; they had given him a couple of horse-blankets, and he seemed to have spent the remainder of his strength in the exertion of cleaning himself. He was almost speechless; his quick breathing under the blankets pulled up to his chin, his glittering, restless black eyes reminded me of a wild bird caught in a snare. While I was examining him, old Swaffer stood silently by the door, passing the tips of his fingers along his shaven upper lip. I gave some directions, promised to send a bottle of medicine, and naturally made some inquiries.

"'Smith caught him in the stackyard at New Barns,' said the old chap in his deliberate, unmoved manner, and as if the other had been indeed a sort of wild animal. 'That's how I came by him. Quite a curiosity, isn't he? Now tell me, doctor—you've been all over the world—don't you think that's a bit of a Hindoo we've got hold of here?'

"I was greatly surprised. His long black hair scattered over the straw bolster contrasted with the olive pallor of his face. It occurred to me he might be a Basque. It didn't necessarily follow that he should understand Spanish; but I tried him with the few words I know, and also with some French. The whispered sounds I caught by bending my ear to his lips puzzled me utterly. That afternoon the young ladies from the Rectory (one of them read Goethe with a dictionary, and the other had struggled with Dante for years), coming to see Miss Swaffer, tried their German and Italian on him from the doorway. They retreated, just the least bit scared by the flood of passionate speech which, turning on his pallet, he let out at them. They admitted that the sound was pleasant, soft, musical— but, in conjunction with his looks perhaps, it was start- ling—so excitable, so utterly unlike anything one had ever heard. The village boys climbed up the bank to have a peep through the little square aperture. Everybody was wondering what Mr. Swaffer would do with him.

"He simply kept him.

"Swaffer would be called eccentric were he not so much respected. They will tell you that Mr. Swaffer sits up as late as ten o'clock at night to read books, and they will tell you also that he can write a cheque for two hundred pounds without thinking twice about it. He himself would tell you that the Swaffers had owned land between this and Darnford for these three hundred years. He must be eighty-five to-day, but he does not look a bit older than when I first came here. He is a great breeder of sheep, and deals extensively in cattle. He attends market days for miles around in every sort of weather, and drives sitting bowed low over the reins, his lank gray hair curling over the collar of his warm coat, and with a green plaid rug round his legs. The calmness of advanced age gives a solemnity to his manner. He is clean-shaved; his lips are thin and sensitive; something rigid and monachal in the set of his features lends a certain elevation to the character of his face. He has been known to drive miles in the rain to see a new kind of rose in somebody's garden, or a monstrous cabbage grown by a cottager. He loves to hear tell of or to be shown something what he calls 'outlandish.' Perhaps it was just that outlandishness of the man which influenced old Swaffer. Perhaps it was only an inexplicable caprice. All I know is that at the end of three weeks I caught sight of Smith's lunatic digging in Swaffer's kitchen garden. They had found out he could use a spade. He dug barefooted.

"His black hair flowed over his shoulders. I suppose it was Swaffer who had given him the striped old cotton shirt; but he wore still the national brown cloth trousers (in which he had been washed ashore) fitting to the

leg almost like tights; was belted with a broad leathern
belt studded with little brass discs; and had never yet
ventured into the village. The land he looked upon
seemed to him kept neatly, like the grounds round a
landowner's house; the size of the cart-horses struck
him with astonishment; the roads resembled garden
walks, and the aspect of the people, especially on Sundays, spoke of opulence. He wondered what made
them so hardhearted and their children so bold. He
got his food at the back-door, carried it in both hands,
carefully, to his outhouse, and, sitting alone on his
pallet, would make the sign of the cross before he began.
Beside the same pallet, kneeling in the early darkness of
the short days, he recited aloud the Lord's Prayer before he slept. Whenever he saw old Swaffer he would
bow with veneration from the waist, and stand erect
while the old man, with his fingers over his upper lip,
surveyed him silently. He bowed also to Miss Swaffer,
who kept house frugally for her father—a broad-
shouldered, big-boned woman of forty-five, with the
pocket of her dress full of keys, and a gray, steady eye.
She was Church—as people said (while her father was
one of the trustees of the Baptist Chapel)—and wore a
little steel cross at her waist. She dressed severely in
black, in memory of one of the innumerable Bradleys
of the neighbourhood, to whom she had been engaged
some twenty-five years ago—a young farmer who
broke his neck out hunting on the eve of the wedding-
day. She had the unmoved countenance of the deaf,
spoke very seldom, and her lips, thin like her father's,
astonished one sometimes by a mysteriously ironic
curl.

  "These were the people to whom he owed allegiance,
and an overwhelming loneliness seemed to fall from the
leaden sky of that winter without sunshine. All the

faces were sad. He could talk to no one, and had no hope of ever understanding anybody. It was as if these had been the faces of people from the other world —dead people—he used to tell me years afterwards. Upon my word, I wonder he did not go mad. He didn't know where he was. Somewhere very far from his mountains—somewhere over the water. Was this America, he wondered?

"If it hadn't been for the steel cross at Miss Swaffer's belt he would not, he confessed, have known whether he was in a Christian country at all. He used to cast stealthy glances at it, and feel comforted. There was nothing here the same as in his country! The earth and the water were different; there were no images of the Redeemer by the roadside. The very grass was different, and the trees. All the trees but the three old Norway pines on the bit of lawn before Swaffer's house, and these reminded him of his country. He had been detected once, after dusk, with his forehead against the trunk of one of them, sobbing, and talking to himself. They had been like brothers to him at that time, he affirmed. Everything else was strange. Conceive you the kind of an existence over-shadowed, oppressed, by the everyday material appearances, as if by the visions of a nightmare. At night, when he could not sleep, he kept on thinking of the girl who gave him the first piece of bread he had eaten in this foreign land. She had been neither fierce nor angry, nor frightened. Her face he remembered as the only comprehensible face amongst all these faces that were as closed, as mysterious, and as mute as the faces of the dead who are possessed of a knowledge beyond the comprehension of the living. I wonder whether the memory of her compassion prevented him from cutting his throat. But there! I suppose I am an old sentimentalist, and forget the instinctive love of life which it takes all the strength of the uncommon despair to overcome.

"He did the work which was given him with an intelligence which surprised old Swaffer. By-and-by it was discovered that he could help at the ploughing, could milk the cows, feed the bullocks in the cattle-yard, and was of some use with the sheep. He began to pick up words, too, very fast; and suddenly, one fine morning in spring, he rescued from an untimely death a grand-child of old Swaffer.

"Swaffer's younger daughter is married to Willcox, a solicitor and the Town Clerk of Colebrook. Regularly twice a year they come to stay with the old man for a few days. Their only child, a little girl not three years old at the time, ran out of the house alone in her little white pinafore, and, toddling across the grass of a terraced garden, pitched herself over a low wall head first into the horsepond in the yard below.

"Our man was out with the waggoner and the plough in the field nearest to the house, and as he was leading the team round to begin a fresh furrow, he saw, through the gap of a gate, what for anybody else would have been a mere flutter of something white. But he had straight-glancing, quick, far-reaching eyes, that only seemed to flinch and lose their amazing power before the immensity of the sea. He was barefooted, and looking as outlandish as the heart of Swaffer could desire. Leaving the horses on the turn, to the inexpressible disgust of the waggoner he bounded off, going over the ploughed ground in long leaps, and suddenly appeared before the mother, thrust the child into her arms, and strode away.

"The pond was not very deep; but still, if he had not had such good eyes, the child would have perished—miserably suffocated in the foot or so of sticky mud at the bottom. Old Swaffer walked out slowly into the field, waited till the plough came over to his side, had a good look at him, and without saying a word went back to the house. But from that time they laid out his meals on the kitchen table; and at first, Miss Swaffer, all in black and with an inscrutable face, would come and stand in the doorway of the living-room to see him make a big sign of the cross before he fell to. I believe that from that day, too, Swaffer began to pay him regular wages.

"I can't follow step by step his development. He cut his hair short, was seen in the village and along the road going to and fro to his work like any other man. Children ceased to shout after him. He became aware of social differences, but remained for a long time surprised at the bare poverty of the churches among so much wealth. He couldn't understand either why they were kept shut up on week-days. There was nothing to steal in them. Was it to keep people from praying too often? The rectory took much notice of him about that time, and I believe the young ladies attempted to prepare the ground for his conversion. They could not, however, break him of his habit of crossing himself, but he went so far as to take off the string with a couple of brass medals the size of a sixpence, a tiny metal cross, and a square sort of scapulary which he wore round his neck. He hung them on the wall by the side of his bed, and he was still to be heard every evening reciting the Lord's Prayer, in incomprehensible words and in a slow, fervent tone, as he had heard his old father do at the head of all the kneeling family, big and little, on every evening of his life. And though he wore corduroys at work, and a slop-made pepper-and-salt suit on Sundays, strangers would turn round to look after him on the road. His foreignness had a peculiar and indelible stamp. At last people became used to see him. But they never became used to him. His rapid, skimming walk; his swarthy complexion; his hat cocked on the left ear; his habit, on warm evenings, of wearing his coat over one shoulder, like a hussar's dolman; his manner of leaping over the stiles, not as a feat of agility, but in the ordinary course of progression—all these peculiarities were, as one may say, so many causes of scorn and offence to the inhabitants of the village. *They* wouldn't in their dinner hour lie flat on their backs on the grass to stare at the sky. Neither did they go about the fields screaming dismal tunes. Many times have I heard his high-pitched voice from behind the ridge of some sloping sheep-walk, a voice light and soaring, like a lark's, but with a melancholy human note, over our fields that hear only the song of birds. And I would be startled myself. Ah! He was different; innocent of heart, and full of good will, which nobody wanted, this castaway, that, like a man transplanted into another planet, was separated by an immense space from his past and by an immense ignorance from his future. His quick, fervent utterance positively shocked everybody. 'An excitable devil,' they called him. One evening, in the tap-room of the Coach and Horses, (having drunk some whisky), he upset them all by singing a love-song of his country. They hooted him down, and he was pained; but Preble, the lame wheelwright, and Vincent, the fat blacksmith, and the other notables, too, wanted to drink their evening beer in peace. On another occasion he tried to show them how to dance. The dust rose in clouds from the sanded floor; he leaped straight up amongst the deal tables, struck his heels together, squatted on one heel in front of old Preble, shooting out the other leg, uttered wild and exulting cries, jumped up to whirl on one foot, snapping his fingers above his head—and a strange carter who was having a drink in there began to swear, and cleared out with his half-pint in his hand into the bar. But when suddenly he sprang upon a table and continued to dance among the glasses, the landlord interfered. He didn't want any 'acrobat tricks in the tap-room.' They laid their hands on him. Having had a glass or two, Mr. Swaffer's foreigner tried to expostulate: was ejected forcibly: got a black eye.

"I believe he felt the hostility of his human surroundings. But he was tough—tough in spirit, too, as well as in body. Only the memory of the sea frightened him, with that vague terror that is left by a bad dream. His home was far away; and he did not want now to go to America. I had often explained to him that there is no place on earth where true gold can be found lying ready and to be got for the trouble of the picking up. How, then, he asked, could he ever return home with empty hands when there had been sold a cow, two ponies, and a bit of land to pay for his going? His eyes would fill with tears, and, averting them from the immense shimmer of the sea, he would throw himself face down on the grass. But sometimes, cocking his hat with a little conquering air, he would defy my wisdom. He had found his bit of true gold. That was Amy Foster's heart; which was 'a golden heart, and soft to people's misery,' he would say in the accents of overwhelming conviction.

"He was called Yanko. He had explained that this meant Little John; but as he would also repeat very often that he was a mountaineer (some word sounding in the dialect of his country like Goorall) he got it for his surname. And this is the only trace of him that the succeeding ages may find in the marriage register of the parish. There it stands—Yanko Goorall—in the rector's handwriting. The crooked cross made by the castaway, a cross whose tracing no doubt seemed to him the most solemn part of the whole ceremony, is all that remains now to perpetuate the memory of his name.

"His courtship had lasted some time—ever since he got his precarious footing in the community. It began by his buying for Amy Foster a green satin ribbon in Darnford. This was what you did in his country. You bought a ribbon at a Jew's stall on a fair-day. I don't suppose the girl knew what to do with it, but he seemed to think that his honourable intentions could not be mistaken.

"It was only when he declared his purpose to get married that I fully understood how, for a hundred futile and inappreciable reasons, how—shall I say odious?—he was to all the countryside. Every old woman in the village was up in arms. Smith, coming upon him near the farm, promised to break his head for him if he found him about again. But he twisted his little black moustache with such a bellicose air and rolled such big, black fierce eyes at Smith that this promise came to nothing. Smith, however, told the girl that she must be mad to take up with a man who was surely wrong in his head. All the same, when she heard him in the gloaming whistle from beyond the orchard a couple of bars of a weird and mournful tune, she would drop whatever she had in her hand—she would leave Mrs. Smith in the middle of a sentence—and she would run out to his call. Mrs. Smith called her a shameless hussy. She answered nothing. She said nothing at all to anybody, and went on her way as if she had been deaf. She and I alone in all the land, I fancy, could see his very real beauty. He was very good-looking, and most graceful in his bearing, with that something wild as of a woodland creature in his aspect.

Her mother moaned over her dismally whenever the girl came to see her on her day out. The father was surly, but pretended not to know; and Mrs. Finn once told her plainly that 'this man, my dear, will do you some harm some day yet.' And so it went on. They could be seen on the roads, she tramping stolidly in her finery—gray dress, black feather, stout boots, prominent white cotton gloves that caught your eye a hundred yards away; and he, his coat slung picturesquely over one shoulder, pacing by her side, gallant of bearing and casting tender glances upon the girl with the golden heart. I wonder whether he saw how plain she was. Perhaps among types so different from what he had ever seen, he had not the power to judge; or perhaps he was seduced by the divine quality of her pity.

"Yanko was in great trouble meantime. In his country you get an old man for an ambassador in marriage affairs. He did not know how to proceed. However, one day in the midst of sheep in a field (he was now Swaffer's under-shepherd with Foster) he took off his hat to the father and declared himself humbly. 'I daresay she's fool enough to marry you,' was all Foster said. 'And then,' he used to relate, 'he puts his hat on his head, looks black at me as if he wanted to cut my throat, whistles the dog, and off he goes, leaving me to do the work.' The Fosters, of course, didn't like to lose the wages the girl earned: Amy used to give all her money to her mother. But there was in Foster a very genuine aversion to that match. He contended that the fellow was very good with sheep, but was not fit for any girl to marry. For one thing, he used to go along the hedges muttering to himself like a dam' fool; and then, these foreigners behave very queerly to women sometimes. And perhaps he would want to carry her off somewhere—or run off himself.

It was not safe. He preached it to his daughter that
the fellow might ill-use her in some way. She made no
answer. It was, they said in the village, as if the man
had done something to her. People discussed the matter. It was quite an excitement, and the two went on
'walking out' together in the face of opposition. Then
something unexpected happened.

"I don't know whether old Swaffer ever understood
how much he was regarded in the light of a father by
his foreign retainer. Anyway the relation was curiously
feudal. So when Yanko asked formally for an interview—'and the Miss, too' (he called the severe, deaf
Miss Swaffer simply *Miss*)—it was to obtain their per-
mission to marry. Swaffer heard him unmoved, dismissed him by a nod, and then shouted the intelligence
into Miss Swaffer's best ear. She showed no surprise,
and only remarked grimly, in a veiled blank voice, 'He
certainly won't get any other girl to marry him.'

"It is Miss Swaffer who has all the credit of the muni-
ficence: but in a very few days it came out that Mr.
Swaffer had presented Yanko with a cottage (the cottage you've seen this morning) and something like an
acre of ground—had made it over to him in absolute
property. Willcox expedited the deed, and I remember
him telling me he had a great pleasure in making it
ready. It recited: 'In consideration of saving the life
of my beloved grandchild, Bertha Willcox.'

"Of course, after that no power on earth could prevent them from getting married.

"Her infatuation endured. People saw her going out
to meet him in the evening. She stared with unblinking, fascinated eyes up the road where he was expected
to appear, walking freely, with a swing from the hip,
and humming one of the love-tunes of his country.
When the boy was born, he got elevated at the 'Coach

and Horses,' essayed again a song and a dance, and was again ejected. People expressed their commiseration for a woman married to that Jack-in-the-box. He didn't care. There was a man now (he told me boastfully) to whom he could sing and talk in the language of his country, and show how to dance by-and-by.

"But I don't know. To me he appeared to have grown less springy of step, heavier in body, less keen of eye. Imagination, no doubt; but it seems to me now as if the net of fate had been drawn closer round him already.

"One day I met him on the footpath over the Talfourd Hill. He told me that 'women were funny.' I had heard already of domestic differences. People were saying that Amy Foster was beginning to find out what sort of man she had married. He looked upon the sea with indifferent, unseeing eyes. His wife had snatched the child out of his arms one day as he sat on the doorstep crooning to it a song such as the mothers sing to babies in his mountains. She seemed to think he was doing it some harm. Women are funny. And she had objected to him praying aloud in the evening. Why? He expected the boy to repeat the prayer aloud after him by-and-by, as he used to do after his old father when he was a child—in his own country. And I discovered he longed for their boy to grow up so that he could have a man to talk with in that language that to our ears sounded so disturbing, so passionate, and so bizarre. Why his wife should dislike the idea he couldn't tell. But that would pass, he said. And tilting his head knowingly, he tapped his breastbone to indicate that she had a good heart: not hard, not fierce, open to compassion, charitable to the poor!

"I walked away thoughtfully; I wondered whether his difference, his strangeness, were not penetrating with repulsion that dull nature they had begun by irresistibly attracting. I wondered. . . ."

The Doctor came to the window and looked out at the frigid splendour of the sea, immense in the haze, as if enclosing all the earth with all the hearts lost among the passions of love and fear.

"Physiologically, now," he said, turning away abruptly, "it was possible. It was possible."

He remained silent. Then went on—

"At all events, the next time I saw him he was ill— lung trouble. He was tough, but I daresay he was not acclimatized as well as I had supposed. It was a bad winter; and, of course, these mountaineers do get fits of home sickness; and a state of depression would make him vulnerable. He was lying half dressed on a couch downstairs.

"A table covered with a dark oilcloth took up all the middle of the little room. There was a wicker cradle on the floor, a kettle spouting steam on the hob, and some child's linen lay drying on the fender. The room was warm, but the door opens right into the garden, as you noticed perhaps.

"He was very feverish, and kept on muttering to himself. She sat on a chair and looked at him fixedly across the table with her brown, blurred eyes. 'Why don't you have him upstairs?' I asked. With a start and a confused stammer she said, 'Oh! ah! I couldn't sit with him upstairs, sir.'

"I gave her certain directions; and going outside, I said again that he ought to be in bed upstairs. She wrung her hands. 'I couldn't. I couldn't. He keeps on saying something—I don't know what.' With the memory of all the talk against the man that had been dinned into her ears, I looked at her narrowly. I looked into her short-sighted eyes, at her dumb eyes that once in her life had seen an enticing shape, but seemed, staring at me, to see nothing at all now. But I saw she was uneasy.

"'What's the matter with him?' she asked in a sort of vacant trepidation. 'He doesn't look very ill. I never did see anybody look like this before. . . .'

"'Do you think,' I asked indignantly, 'he is shamming?'

"'I can't help it, sir,' she said, stolidly. And suddenly she clapped her hands and looked right and left. 'And there's the baby. I am so frightened. He wanted me just now to give him the baby. I can't understand what he says to it.'

"'Can't you ask a neighbour to come in to-night?' I asked.

"'Please, sir, nobody seems to care to come,' she muttered, dully resigned all at once.

"I impressed upon her the necessity of the greatest care, and then had to go. There was a good deal of sickness that winter. 'Oh, I hope he won't talk!' she exclaimed softly just as I was going away.

"I don't know how it is I did not see—but I didn't. And yet, turning in my trap, I saw her lingering before the door, very still. and as if meditating a flight up the miry road.

"Towards the night his fever increased.

"He tossed, moaned, and now and then muttered a complaint. And she sat with the table between her and the couch, watching every movement and every sound, with the terror, the unreasonable terror, of that man she could not understand creeping over her. She had drawn the wicker cradle close to her feet. There was nothing in her now but the maternal instinct and that unaccountable fear.

"Suddenly coming to himself, parched, he demanded

a drink of water. She did not move. She had not understood, though he may have thought he was speaking in English. He waited, looking at her, burning with fever, amazed at her silence and immobility, and then he shouted impatiently, 'Water! Give me water!'

"She jumped to her feet, snatched up the child, and stood still. He spoke to her, and his passionate remonstrances only increased her fear of that strange man. I believe he spoke to her for a long time, entreating, wondering, pleading, ordering, I suppose. She says she bore it as long as she could. And then a gust of rage came over him.

"He sat up and called out terribly one word—some word. Then he got up as though he hadn't been ill at all, she says. And as in fevered dismay, indignation, and wonder he tried to get to her round the table, she simply opened the door and ran out with the child in her arms. She heard him call twice after her down the road in a terrible voice—and fled. . . . Ah! but you should have seen stirring behind the dull, blurred glance of these eyes the spectre of the fear which had hunted her on that night three miles and a half to the door of Foster's cottage! I did the next day.

"And it was I who found him lying face down and his body in a puddle, just outside the little wicker-gate.

"I had been called out that night to an urgent case in the village, and on my way home at daybreak passed by the cottage. The door stood open. My man helped me to carry him in. We laid him on the couch. The lamp smoked, the fire was out, the chill of the stormy night oozed from the cheerless yellow paper on the wall. 'Amy!' I called aloud, and my voice seemed to lose itself in the emptiness of this tiny house as if I had cried in a desert. He opened his eyes. 'Gone!' he said, distinctly. 'I had only asked for water—only for a little water. . . .'

"He was muddy. I covered him up and stood waiting in silence, catching a painfully gasped word now and then. They were no longer in his own language. The fever had left him, taking with it the heat of life. And with his panting breast and lustrous eyes he reminded me again of a wild creature under the net; of a bird caught in a snare. She had left him. She had left him—sick—helpless—thirsty. The spear of the hunter had entered his very soul. 'Why?' he cried, in the penetrating and indignant voice of a man calling to a responsible Maker. A gust of wind and a swish of rain answered.

"And as I turned away to shut the door he pronounced the word 'Merciful!' and expired.

"Eventually I certified heart-failure as the immediate cause of death. His heart must have indeed failed him, or else he might have stood this night of storm and exposure, too. I closed his eyes and drove away. Not very far from the cottage I met Foster walking sturdily between the dripping hedges with his collie at his heels.

"'Do you know where your daughter is?' I asked.

"'Don't I!' he cried. 'I am going to talk to him a bit. Frightening a poor woman like this.'

"'He won't frighten her any more,' I said. 'He is dead.'

"He struck with his stick at the mud.

"'And there's the child.'

"Then, after thinking deeply for a while—

"'I don't know that it isn't for the best.'

"That's what he said. And she says nothing at all now. Not a word of him. Never. Is his image as utterly gone from her mind as his lithe and striding figure, his carolling voice are gone from our fields? He is no longer before her eyes to excite her imagination into a passion of love or fear; and his memory seems to have vanished from her dull brain as a shadow passes away upon a white screen. She lives in the cottage and works for Miss Swaffer. She is Amy Foster for everybody, and the child is 'Amy Foster's boy.' She calls him Johnny—which means Little John.

"It is impossible to say whether this name recalls anything to her. Does she ever think of the past? I have seen her hanging over the boy's cot in a very passion of maternal tenderness. The little fellow was lying on his back, a little frightened at me, but very still, with his big black eyes, with his fluttered air of a bird in a snare. And looking at him I seemed to see again the other one—the father, cast out mysteriously by the sea to perish in the supreme disaster of loneliness and despair."

FALK

A REMINISCENCE

FALK

A REMINISCENCE

SEVERAL of us, all more or less connected with the sea, were dining in a small river-hostelry not more than thirty miles from London, and less than twenty from that shallow and dangerous puddle to which our coasting men give the grandiose name of "German Ocean." And through the wide windows we had a view of the Thames; an enfilading view down the Lower Hope Reach. But the dinner was execrable, and all the feast was for the eyes.

That flavour of salt-water which for so many of us had been the very water of life permeated our talk. He who hath known the bitterness of the Ocean shall have its taste for ever in his mouth. But one or two of us, pampered by the life of the land, complained of hunger. It was impossible to swallow any of that stuff. And indeed there was a strange mustiness in everything. The wooden dining-room stuck out over the mud of the shore like a lacustrine dwelling; the planks of the floor seemed rotten; a decrepid old waiter tottered pathetically to and fro before an antediluvian and worm-eaten sideboard; the chipped plates might have been disinterred from some kitchen midden near an inhabited lake; and the chops recalled times more ancient still, They brought forcibly to one's mind the night of ages when the primeval man, evolving the first rudiments of cookery from his dim consciousness, scorched lumps of flesh at a fire of sticks in the company of other good fellows; then, gorged and happy, sat him back among the gnawed bones to tell his artless tales of experience— the tales of hunger and hunt—and of women, perhaps!

But luckily the wine happened to be as old as the waiter. So, comparatively empty, but upon the whole fairly happy, we sat back and told our artless tales. We talked of the sea and all its works. The sea never changes, and its works for all the talk of men are wrapped in mystery. But we agreed that the times were changed. And we talked of old ships, of sea-accidents, of break-downs, dismastings; and of a man who brought his ship safe to Liverpool all the way from the River Platte under a jury rudder. We talked of wrecks, of short rations and of heroism—or at least of what the newspapers would have called heroism at sea— a manifestation of virtues quite different from the heroism of primitive times. And now and then falling silent all together we gazed at the sights of the river.

A P. & O. boat passed bound down. "One gets jolly good dinners on board these ships," remarked one of our band. A man with sharp eyes read out the name on her bows: *Arcadia*. "What a beautiful model of a ship!" murmured some of us. She was followed by a small cargo-steamer, and the flag they hauled down aboard while we were looking showed her to be a Norwegian. She made an awful lot of smoke, and before it had quite blown away, a high-sided, short, wooden barque, in ballast and towed by a paddle-tug, appeared in front of the windows. All her hands were forward busy setting up the headgear; and aft a woman in a red hood, quite alone with the man at the wheel, paced the length of the poop back and forth, with the gray wool of some knitting work in her hands.

"German I should think," muttered one. "The skipper has his wife on board," remarked another;

and the light of the crimson sunset all ablaze behind the
London smoke, throwing a glow of Bengal light upon
the barque's spars, faded away from the Hope Reach.

Then one of us, who had not spoken before, a man
of more than fifty, that had commanded ships for a
quarter of a century, looking after the barque now
gliding far away, all black on the lustre of the river,
said:

This reminds me of an absurd episode in my life,
now many years ago, when I got first the command of
an iron barque, loading then in a certain Eastern seaport. It was also the capital of an Eastern kingdom,
lying up a river as might be London lies up this old
Thames of ours. No more need be said of the place;
for this sort of thing might have happened anywhere
where there are ships, skippers, tugboats, and orphan
nieces of indescribable splendour. And the absurdity
of the episode concerns only me, my enemy Falk, and
my friend Hermann.

There seemed to be something like peculiar emphasis
on the words "My friend Hermann," which caused one
of us (for we had just been speaking of heroism at sea)
to say idly and nonchalantly:

"And was this Hermann a hero?"

Not at all, said our grizzled friend. No hero at all.
He was a Schiff-führer: Ship-conductor. That's how
they call a Master Mariner in Germany. I prefer our
way. The alliteration is good, and there is something
in the nomenclature that gives to us as a body the
sense of corporate existence: Apprentice, Mate, Master, in the ancient and honourable craft of the sea. As
to my friend Hermann, he might have been a consummate master of the honourable craft, but he was
called officially Schiff-führer, and had the simple, heavy
appearance of a well-to-do farmer, combined with the

good-natured shrewdness of a small shopkeeper. With
his shaven chin, round limbs, and heavy eyelids he did
not look like a toiler, and even less like an adventurer
of the sea. Still, he toiled upon the seas, in his own
way, much as a shopkeeper works behind his counter.
And his ship was the means by which he maintained
his growing family.

She was a heavy, strong, blunt-bowed affair, awakening the ideas of primitive solidity, like the wooden
plough of our forefathers. And there were, about her,
other suggestions of a rustic and homely nature. The
extraordinary timber projections which I have seen in
no other vessel made her square stern resemble the tail
end of a miller's waggon. But the four stern ports of
her cabin, glazed with six little greenish panes each, and
framed in wooden sashes painted brown, might have
been the windows of a cottage in the country. The
tiny white curtains and the greenery of flower-pots
behind the glass completed the resemblance. On one
or two occasions when passing under her stern I had
detected from my boat a round arm in the act of tilting
a watering-pot, and the bowed sleek head of a maiden
whom I shall always call Hermann's niece, because as a
matter of fact I've never heard her name, for all my
intimacy with the family.

This, however, sprang up later on. Meantime in
common with the rest of the shipping in that Eastern
port, I was left in no doubt as to Hermann's notions of
hygienic clothing. Evidently he believed in wearing
good stout flannel next his skin. On most days little
frocks and pinafores could be seen drying in the mizzen
rigging of his ship, or a tiny row of socks fluttering on
the signal halyards; but once a fortnight the family
washing was exhibited in force. It covered the poop
entirely. The afternoon breeze would incite to a weird

and flabby activity all that crowded mass of clothing, with its vague suggestions of drowned, mutilated and flattened humanity. Trunks without heads waved at you arms without hands; legs without feet kicked fantastically with collapsible flourishes; and there were long white garments, that taking the wind fairly through their neck openings edged with lace, became for a moment violently distended as by the passage of obese and invisible bodies. On these days you could make out that ship at a great distance by the multi-coloured grotesque riot going on abaft her mizzen-mast.

She had her berth just ahead of me, and her name was *Diana*,—Diana not of Ephesus but of Bremen. This was proclaimed in white letters a foot long spaced widely across the stern (somewhat like the lettering of a shop-sign) under the cottage windows. This ridiculously unsuitable name struck one as an impertinence towards the memory of the most charming of goddesses; for, apart from the fact that the old craft was physically incapable of engaging in any sort of chase, there was a gang of four children belonging to her. They peeped over the rail at passing boats and occasionally dropped various objects into them. Thus, sometime before I knew Hermann to speak to, I received on my hat a horrid rag-doll belonging to Hermann's eldest daughter. However, these youngsters were upon the whole well behaved. They had fair heads, round eyes, round little knobby noses, and they resembled their father a good deal.

This *Diana* of Bremen was a most innocent old ship, and seemed to know nothing of the wicked sea, as there are on shore households that know nothing of the corrupt world. And the sentiments she suggested were unexceptionable and mainly of a domestic order. She was a home. All these dear children had learned

to walk on her roomy quarter-deck. In such thoughts
there is something pretty, even touching. Their teeth,
I should judge, they cut on the ends of her running
gear. I have many times observed the baby Hermann
(Nicholas) engaged in gnawing the whipping of the
fore-royal brace. Nicholas' favourite place of residence
was under the main fife-rail. Directly he was let loose
he would crawl off there, and the first seaman who came
along would bring him, carefully held aloft in tarry
hands, back to the cabin door. I fancy there must have
been a standing order to that effect. In the course of
these transportations the baby, who was the only pep-
pery person in the ship, tried to smite these stalwart
young German sailors on the face.

Mrs. Hermann, an engaging, stout housewife, wore
on board baggy blue dresses with white dots. When,
as happened once or twice, I caught her at an elegant
little wash-tub rubbing hard on white collars, baby's
socks, and Hermann's summer neck-ties, she would
blush in girlish confusion, and raising her wet hands
greet me from afar with many friendly nods. Her
sleeves would be rolled up to the elbows, and the gold
hoop of her wedding ring glittered among the soapsuds. Her voice was pleasant, she had a serene brow,
smooth bands of very fair hair, and a good-humoured expression of the eyes. She was motherly and moderately talkative. When this simple matron smiled,
youthful dimples broke out on her fresh broad cheeks.
Hermann's niece, on the other hand, an orphan and very
silent, I never saw attempt a smile. This, however,
was not gloom on her part but the restraint of youthful
gravity.

They had carried her about with them for the last
three years, to help with the children and be company
for Mrs. Hermann, as Hermann mentioned once to me.

It had been very necessary while they were all little, he had added in a vexed manner. It was her arm and her sleek head that I had glimpsed one morning, through the stern-windows of the cabin, hovering over the pots of fuchsias and mignonette; but the first time I beheld her full length I surrendered to her proportions. They fix her in my mind, as great beauty, great intelligence, quickness of wit or kindness of heart might have made some other woman memorable.

With her it was form and size. It was her physical personality that had this imposing charm. She might have been witty, intelligent, and kind to an exceptional degree. I don't know, and this is not to the point. All I know is that she was built on a magnificent scale. Built is the only word. She was constructed, she was erected, as it were, with regal lavishness. It staggered you to see this reckless expenditure of material upon a chit of a girl. She was youthful and also perfectly mature, as though she had been some fortunate immortal. She was heavy, too, perhaps, but that's nothing. It only added to that notion of permanence. She was barely nineteen. But such shoulders! Such round arms! Such a shadowing forth of mighty limbs when with three long strides she pounced across the deck upon the overturned Nicholas—it's perfectly indescribable! She seemed a good, quiet girl, vigilant as to Lena's needs, Gustav's tumbles, the state of Karl's dear little nose—conscientious, hardworking, and all that. But what magnificent hair she had! Abundant, long, thick, of a tawny colour. It had the sheen of precious metals. She wore it plaited tightly into one single tress hanging girlishly down her back; and its end reached down to her waist. The massiveness of it surprised you. On my word it reminded one of a club. Her face was big, comely, of an unruffled expression.

She had a good complexion, and her blue eyes were so pale that she appeared to look at the world with the empty white candour of a statue. You could not call her good-looking. It was something much more impressive. The simplicity of her apparel, the opulence of her form, her imposing stature, and the extraordinary sense of vigorous life that seemed to emanate from her like a perfume exhaled by a flower, made her beautiful with a beauty of a rustic and olympian order. To watch her reaching up to the clothes-line with both arms raised high above her head, caused you to fall a musing in a strain of pagan piety. Excellent Mrs. Hermann's baggy cotton gowns had some sort of rudimentary frills at neck and bottom, but this girl's print frocks hadn't even a wrinkle; nothing but a few straight folds in the skirt falling to her feet, and these, when she stood still, had a severe and statuesque quality. She was inclined naturally to be still whether sitting or standing. However, I don't mean to say she was statuesque. She was too generously alive; but she could have stood for an allegoric statue of the Earth. I don't mean the worn-out earth of our possession, but a young Earth, a virginal planet undisturbed by the vision of a future teeming with the monstrous forms of life, clamorous with the cruel battles of hunger and thought.

The worthy Hermann himself was not very entertaining, though his English was fairly comprehensible. Mrs. Hermann, who always let off one speech at least at me in an hospitable, cordial tone (and in Platt-Deutsch I suppose) I could not understand. As to their niece, however satisfactory to look upon (and she inspired you somehow with a hopeful view as to the prospects of mankind) she was a modest and silent presence, mostly engaged in sewing, only now and then, as I observed, falling over that work into a state of maidenly meditation. Her aunt sat opposite her, sewing also, with her feet propped on a wooden foot-stool. On the other side of the deck Hermann and I would get a couple of chairs out of the cabin and settle down to a smoking match, accompanied at long intervals by the pacific exchange of a few words. I came nearly every evening. Hermann I would find in his shirt-sleeves. As soon as he returned from the shore on board his ship he commenced operations by taking off his coat; then he put on his head an embroidered round cap with a tassel, and changed his boots for a pair of cloth slippers. Afterwards he smoked at the cabin-door, looking at his children with an air of civic virtue, till they got caught one after another and put to bed in various staterooms. Lastly, we would drink some beer in the cabin, which was furnished with a wooden table on cross legs, and with black straight-backed chairs—more like a farm kitchen than a ship's cuddy. The sea and all nautical affairs seemed very far removed from the hospitality of this exemplary family.

And I liked this because I had a rather worrying time on board my own ship. I had been appointed ex-officio by the British Consul to take charge of her after a man who had died suddenly, leaving for the guidance of his successor some suspiciously unreceipted bills, a few dry-dock estimates hinting at bribery, and a quantity of vouchers for three years' extravagant expenditure; all these mixed up together in a dusty old violin-case lined with ruby velvet. I found besides a large account-book, which, when opened, hopefully turned out to my infinite consternation to be filled with verses—page after page of rhymed doggerel of a jovial and improper character, written in the neatest minute hand I ever did see. In the same fiddle-case a photograph of my predecessor, taken lately in Saigon,

represented in front of a garden view, and in company of
a female in strange draperies, an elderly, squat, rugged
man of stern aspect in a clumsy suit of black broadcloth, and with the hair brushed forward above the
temples in a manner reminding one of a boar's tusks.
Of a fiddle, however, the only trace on board was the
case, its empty husk as it were; but of the two last
freights the ship had indubitably earned of late, there
were not even the husks left. It was impossible to say
where all that money had gone to. It wasn't on
board. It had not been remitted home; for a letter
from the owners, preserved in a desk evidently by the
merest accident, complained mildly enough that they
had not been favoured by a scratch of the pen for the
last eighteen months. There were next to no stores on
board, not an inch of spare rope or a yard of canvas.
The ship had been run bare, and I foresaw no end of
difficulties before I could get her ready for sea.

As I was young then—not thirty yet—I took myself
and my troubles very seriously. The old mate, who had
acted as chief mourner at the captain's funeral, was not
particularly pleased at my coming. But the fact is
the fellow was not legally qualified for command, and
the Consul was bound, if at all possible, to put a
properly certificated man on board. As to the second
mate, all I can say his name was Tottersen, or something like that. His practice was to wear on his head,
in that tropical climate, a mangy fur cap. He was,
without exception, the stupidest man I had ever seen
on board ship. And he looked it, too. He looked so
confoundedly stupid that it was a matter of surprise
for me when he answered to his name.

I drew no great comfort from their company, to say
the least of it; while the prospect of making a long sea
passage with those two fellows was depressing. And

my other thoughts in solitude could not be of a gay complexion. The crew was sickly, the cargo was coming very slow; I foresaw I would have lots of trouble with the charterers, and doubted whether they would advance me enough money for the ship's expenses. Their attitude towards me was unfriendly. Altogether I was not getting on. ﹣ I would discover at odd times (generally about midnight) that I was totally inexperienced, greatly ignorant of business, and hopelessly unfit for any sort of command; and when the steward had to be taken to the hospital ill with choleraic symptoms I felt bereaved of the only decent person at the after end of the ship. He was fully expected to recover, but in the meantime had to be replaced by some sort of servant. And on the recommendation of a certain Schomberg, the proprietor of the smaller of the two hotels in the place, I engaged a Chinaman. Schomberg, a brawny, hairy Alsatian, and an awful gossip, assured me that it was all right. "First-class boy that. Came in the *suite* of his Excellency Tseng the Commissioner—you know. His Excellency Tseng lodged with me here for three weeks."

He mouthed the Chinese Excellency at me with great unction, though the specimen of the "*suite*" did not seem very promising. At the time, however, I did not know what an untrustworthy humbug Schomberg was. The "boy" might have been forty or a hundred and forty for all you could tell—one of those Chinamen of the death's-head type of face and completely inscrutable. Before the end of the third day he had revealed himself as a confirmed opium-smoker, a gambler, a most audacious thief, and a first-class sprinter. When he departed at the top of his speed with thirty-two golden sovereigns of my own hard-earned savings it was the last straw. I had reserved that money in case my difficulties came to the worst. Now it was gone I felt as poor and naked as a fakir. I clung to my ship, for all the bother she caused me, but what I could not bear were the long lonely evenings in her cuddy, where the atmosphere, made smelly by a leaky lamp, was agitated by the snoring of the mate. That fellow shut himself up in his stuffy cabin punctually at eight, and made gross and revolting noises like a water-logged trombone. It was odious not to be able to worry oneself in comfort on board one's own ship. Everything in this world, I reflected, even the command of a nice little barque, may be made a delusion and a snare for the unwary spirit of pride in man.

From such reflections I was glad to make my escape on board that Bremen *Diana*. There apparently no whisper of the world's iniquities had ever penetrated. And yet she lived upon the wide sea: and the sea tragic and comic, the sea with its horrors and its peculiar scandals, the sea peopled by men and ruled by iron necessity is indubitably a part of the world. But that patriarchal old tub, like some saintly retreat, echoed nothing of it. She was world proof. Her venerable innocence apparently put a restraint on the roaring lusts of the sea. And yet I have known the sea too long to believe in its respect for decency. An elemental force is ruthlessly frank. It may, of course, have been Hermann's skilful seamanship, but to me it looked as if the allied oceans had refrained from smashing these high bulwarks, unshipping the lumpy rudder, frightening the children, and generally opening this family's eyes out of sheer reticence. It looked like reticence. The ruthless disclosure was, in the end, left for a man to make; a man strong and elemental enough and driven to unveil some secrets of the sea by the power of a simple and elemental desire.

This, however, occurred much later, and meantime I took sanctuary in that serene old ship early every evening. The only person on board that seemed to be in trouble was little Lena, and in due course I perceived that the health of the rag-doll was more than delicate. This object led a sort of "in extremis" existence in a wooden box placed against the starboard mooring-bitts tended and nursed with the greatest sympathy and care by all the children, who greatly enjoyed pulling long faces and moving with hushed footsteps. Only the baby—Nicholas—looked on with a cold, ruffianly leer, as if he had belonged to another tribe altogether. Lena perpetually sorrowed over the box, and all of them were in deadly earnest. It was wonderful the way these children would work up their compassion for that bedraggled thing I wouldn't have touched with a pair of tongs. I suppose they were exercising and developing their racial sentimentalism by the means of that dummy. I was only surprised that Mrs. Hermann let Lena cherish and hug that bundle of rags to that extent, it was so disreputably and completely unclean. But Mrs. Hermann would raise her fine womanly eyes from her needlework to look on with amused sympathy, and did not seem to see it, somehow, that this object of affection was a disgrace to the ship's purity. Purity, not cleanliness, is the word. It was pushed so far that I seemed to detect in this, too, a sentimental excess, as if dirt had been removed in very love. It is impossible to give you an idea of such a meticulous neatness. It was as if every morning that ship had been arduously explored with—with toothbrushes. Her very bowsprit three times a week had its toilette made with a cake of soap and a piece of soft flannel. Arrayed—I *must* say arrayed—arrayed artlessly in dazzling white paint as to wood and dark green as to ironwork the simple-minded

distribution of these colours evoked the images of
guileless peace, of arcadian felicity; and the childish
comedy of disease and sorrow struck me sometimes as
an abominably real blot upon that ideal state.

I enjoyed it greatly, and on my part I brought a little
mild excitement into it. Our intimacy arose from the
pursuit of that thief. It was in the evening, and Hermann, who, contrary to his habits, had stayed on shore
late that day, was extricating himself backwards out of
a little gharry on the river bank, opposite his ship, when
the hunt passed. Realizing the situation as though he
had eyes in his shoulder-blades, he joined us with a leap
and took the lead. The Chinaman fled silent like a
rapid shadow on the dust of an extremely oriental road.
I followed. A long way in the rear my mate whooped
like a savage. A young moon threw a bashful light on
a plain like a monstrous waste ground: the architectural
mass of a Buddhist temple far away projected itself in
dead black on the sky. We lost the thief of course; but
in my disappointment I had to admire Hermann's
presence of mind. The velocity that stodgy man
developed in the interests of a complete stranger earned
my warm gratitude—there was something truly cordial
in his exertions.

He seemed as vexed as myself at our failure, and
would hardly listen to my thanks. He said it was
"nothings," and invited me on the spot to come on
board his ship and drink a glass of beer with him. We
poked sceptically for a while amongst the bushes, peered
without conviction into a ditch or two. There was not
a sound: patches of slime glimmered feebly amongst
the reeds. Slowly we trudged back, drooping under
the thin sickle of the moon, and I heard him mutter
to himself, "Himmel! Zwei und dreissig Pfund!"
He was impressed by the figure of my loss. For a

long time we had ceased to hear the mate's whoops and yells.

Then he said to me, "Everybody has his troubles," and as we went on remarked that he would never have known anything of mine hadn't he by an extraordinary chance been detained on shore by Captain Falk. He didn't like to stay late ashore—he added with a sigh. The something doleful in his tone I put to his sympathy with my misfortune, of course.

On board the *Diana* Mrs. Hermann's fine eyes expressed much interest and commiseration. We had found the two women sewing face to face under the open skylight in the strong glare of the lamp. Hermann walked in first, starting in the very doorway to pull off his coat, and encouraging me with loud, hospitable ejaculations: "Come in! This way! Come in, captain!" At once, coat in hand, he began to tell his wife all about it. Mrs. Hermann put the palms of her plump hands together; I smiled and bowed with a heavy heart: the niece got up from her sewing to bring Hermann's slippers and his embroidered calotte, which he assumed pontifically, talking (about me) all the time. Billows of white stuff lay between the chairs on the cabin floor; I caught the words "Zwei und dreissig Pfund" repeated several times, and presently came the beer, which seemed delicious to my throat, parched with running and the emotions of the chase.

I didn't get away till well past midnight, long after the women had retired. Hermann had been trading in the East for three years or more, carrying freights of rice and timber mostly. His ship was well known in all the ports from Vladivostok to Singapore. She was his own property. The profits had been moderate, but the trade answered well enough while the children were small yet. In another year or so he hoped he would be

able to sell the old *Diana* to a firm in Japan for a fair
price. He intended to return home, to Bremen, by
mail boat, second class, with Mrs. Hermann and the
children. He told me all this stolidly, with slow puffs at
his pipe. I was sorry when knocking the ashes out he
began to rub his eyes. I would have sat with him till
morning. What had I to hurry on board my own ship
for? To face the broken rifled drawer in my state-
room. Ugh! The very thought made me feel unwell.

I became their daily guest, as you know. I think
that Mrs. Hermann from the first looked upon me as a
romantic person. I did not, of course, tear my hair
coram populo over my loss, and she took it for lordly
indifference. Afterwards, I daresay, I did tell them
some of my adventures—such as they were—and they
marvelled greatly at the extent of my experience.
Hermann would translate what he thought the most
striking passages. Getting upon his legs, and as if
delivering a lecture on a phenomenon, he addressed
himself, with gestures, to the two women, who would
let their sewing sink slowly on their laps. Meantime I
sat before a glass of Hermann's beer, trying to look
modest. Mrs. Hermann would glance at me quickly,
emit slight "Ach's!" The girl never made a sound.
Never. But she, too, would sometimes raise her pale
eyes to look at me in her unseeing, gentle way. Her
glance was by no means stupid; it beamed out soft and
diffuse as the moon beams upon a landscape—quite
differently from the scrutinizing inspection of the stars.
You were drowned in it, and imagined yourself to appear blurred. And yet this same glance when turned
upon Christian Falk must have been as efficient as the
searchlight of a battle-ship.

Falk was the other assiduous visitor on board, but
from his behaviour he might have been coming to see

the quarter-deck capstan. He certainly used to stare at it a good deal when keeping us company outside the cabin door, with one muscular arm thrown over the back of the chair, and his big shapely legs, in very tight white trousers, extended far out and ending in a pair of black shoes as roomy as punts. On arrival he would shake Hermann's hand with a mutter, bow to the women, and take up his careless and misanthropic attitude by our side. He departed abruptly, with a jump, going through the performance of grunts, hand-shakes, bow, as if in a panic. Sometimes, with a sort of discreet and convulsive effort, he approached the women and exchanged a few low words with them, half a dozen at most. On these occasions Hermann's usual stare became positively glassy and Mrs. Hermann's kind countenance would colour up. The girl herself never turned a hair.

Falk was a Dane or perhaps a Norwegian, I can't tell now. At all events he was a Scandinavian of some sort, and a bloated monopolist to boot. It is possible he was unacquainted with the word, but he had a clear perception of the thing itself. His tariff of charges for towing ships in and out was the most brutally inconsiderate document of the sort I had ever seen. He was the commander and owner of the only tug-boat on the river, a very trim white craft of 150 tons or more, as elegantly neat as a yacht, with a round wheelhouse rising like a glazed turret high above her sharp bows, and with one slender varnished pole mast forward. I daresay there are yet a few shipmasters afloat who remember Falk and his tug very well. He extracted his pound and a half of flesh from each of us merchant-skippers with an inflexible sort of indifference which made him detested and even feared. Schomberg used to remark: "I won't talk about the fellow. I don't

think he has six drinks from year's end to year's end
in my place. But my advice is, gentlemen, don't you
have anything to do with him, if you can help it."

This advice, apart from unavoidable business relations, was easy to follow because Falk intruded upon no
one. It seems absurd to compare a tug-boat skipper to
a centaur: but he reminded me somehow of an en-
graving in a little book I had as a boy, which represented
centaurs at a stream, and there was one especially, in
the foreground, prancing bow and arrows in hand, with
regular severe features and an immense curled wavy
beard, flowing down his breast. Falk's face reminded
me of that centaur. Besides, he was a composite
creature. Not a man-horse, it is true, but a man-boat.
He lived on board his tug, which was always dashing
up and down the river from early morn till dewy eve.
In the last rays of the setting sun, you could pick out
far away down the reach his beard borne high up on the
white structure, foaming up stream to anchor for the
night. There was the white-clad man's body, and the
rich brown patch of the hair, and nothing below the
waist but the 'thwart-ship white lines of the bridge-
screens, that led the eye to the sharp white lines of the
bows cleaving the muddy water of the river.

Separated from his boat, to me at least he seemed
incomplete. The tug herself without his head and
torso on the bridge looked mutilated as it were. But he
left her very seldom. All the time I remained in harbour I saw him only twice on shore. On the first
occasion it was at my charterers, where he came in
misanthropically to get paid for towing out a French
barque the day before. The second time I could hardly
believe my eyes, for I beheld him reclining under his
beard in a cane-bottomed chair in the billiard-room of
Schomberg's hotel.

It was very funny to see Schomberg ignoring him pointedly. The artificiality of it contrasted strongly with Falk's natural unconcern. The big Alsatian talked loudly with his other customers, going from one little table to the other, and passing Falk's place of repose with his eyes fixed straight ahead. Falk sat there with an untouched glass at his elbow. He must have known by sight and name every white man in the room, but he never addressed a word to anybody. He acknowledged my presence by a drop of his eyelids, and that was all. Sprawling there in the chair, he would, now and again, draw the palms of both his hands down his face, giving at the same time a slight, almost imperceptible, shudder.

It was a habit he had, and of course I was perfectly familiar with it, since you could not remain an hour in his company without being made to wonder at such a passionate and inexplicable gesture breaking some long period of stillness. He used to make it at all sorts of times; as likely as not after he had been listening to little Lena's chatter about the suffering doll, for instance. The Hermann children always besieged him about his legs closely, though, in a gentle way, he shrank from them a little. He seemed, however, to feel a great affection for the whole family. For Hermann himself especially. He sought his company In this case, for instance, he must have been waiting for him, because as soon as he appeared Falk rose hastily, and they went out together. Then Schomberg expounded in my hearing to three or four people his theory that Falk was after Captain Hermann's niece, and asserted confidently that nothing would come of it. It was the same last year when Captain Hermann was loading here, he said.

Naturally, I did not believe Schomberg, but I own

that for a time I observed closely what went on. All I discovered was some impatience on Hermann's part. At the sight of Falk, stepping over the gangway, the excellent man would begin to mumble and chew between his teeth something that sounded like German swear-words. However, as I've said, I'm not familiar with the language, and Hermann's soft, round-eyed countenance remained unchanged. Staring stolidly ahead he greeted him with, "Wie geht's," or in English, "How are you?" with a throaty enunciation. The girl would look up for an instant and move her lips slightly: Mrs. Hermann let her hands rest on her lap to talk volubly to him for a minute or so in her pleasant voice before she went on with her sewing again. Falk would throw himself into a chair, stretch his big legs, as like as not draw his hands down his face passionately. As to myself, he was not pointedly impertinent: it was rather as though he could not be bothered with such trifles as my existence; and the truth is that being a monopolist he was under no necessity to be amiable. He was sure to get his own extortionate terms out of me for towage whether he frowned or smiled. As a matter of fact, he did neither: but before many days went by he managed to astonish me not a little and to set Schomberg's tongue clacking more than ever.

It came about in this way. There was a shallow bar at the mouth of the river which ought to have been kept down, but the authorities of the State were piously busy gilding afresh the great Buddhist Pagoda just then, and had no money to spare for dredging operations. I don't know how it may be now, but at the time I speak of that sandbank was a great nuisance to the shipping. One of its consequences was that vessels of a certain draught of water, like Hermann's or mine, could not complete their loading in the river.

After taking in as much as possible of their cargo, they had to go outside to fill up. The whole procedure was an unmitigated bore. When you thought you had as much on board as your ship could carry safely over the bar, you went and gave notice to your agents. They, in their turn, notified Falk that so-and-so was ready to go out. Then Falk (ostensibly when it fitted in with his other work, but, if the truth were known, simply when his arbitrary spirit moved him), after ascertaining carefully in the office that there was enough money to meet his bill, would come along unsympathetically, glaring at you with his yellow eyes from the bridge, and would drag you out dishevelled as to rigging, lumbered as to the decks, with unfeeling haste, as if to execution. And he would force you, too, to take the end of his own wire hawser, for the use of which there was of course an extra charge. To your shouted remonstrances against this extortion this towering trunk with one hand on the engine-room telegraph only shook its bearded head above the splash, the racket and the clouds of smoke, in which the tug, backing and filling in the smother of churning paddle-wheels behaved like a ferocious and impatient creature. He had her manned by the cheekiest gang of lascars I ever did see, whom he allowed to bawl at you insolently, and, once fast, he plucked you out of your berth as if he did not care what he smashed. Eighteen miles down the river you had to go behind him, and then three more along the coast to where a group of uninhabited rocky islets enclosed a sheltered anchorage. There you would have to lie at single anchor with your naked spars showing to seaward over these barren fragments of land scattered upon a very intensely blue sea. There was nothing to look at besides but a bare coast, the muddy edge of the brown plain with the sinuosities of the river you had

left, traced in dull green, and the Great Pagoda up-
rising lonely and massive with shining curves and
pinnacles like the gorgeous and stony efflorescence of
tropical rocks. You had nothing to do but to wait fretfully for the balance of your cargo, which was sent out of
the river with the greatest irregularity. And it was
open to you to console yourself with the thought that,
after all, this stage of bother meant that your departure
from these shores was indeed approaching at last.

We both had to go through that stage, Hermann and
I, and there was a sort of tacit emulation between the
ships as to which should be ready first. We kept on
neck and neck almost to the finish, when I won the
race by going personally to give notice in the forenoon;
whereas Hermann, who was very slow in making up his
mind to go ashore, did not get to the agents' office till
late in the day. They told him there that my ship was
first on turn for next morning, and I believe he told
them he was in no hurry. It suited him better to go
the day after.

That evening, on board the *Diana*, he sat staring
with his plump knees well apart and puffing at the
curved mouthpiece of his pipe. Presently he spoke
with some impatience to his niece about putting the
children to bed. Mrs. Hermann, who was talking to
Falk, stopped short and looked at her husband uneasily,
but the girl got up at once and drove the children before her into the cabin. In a little while Mrs. Hermann had to leave us to quell what, from the sounds
inside, must have been a dangerous mutiny. At this
Hermann grumbled to himself. For half an hour
longer Falk left alone with us fidgeted on his chair,
sighed lightly, then at last, after drawing his hands
down his face, got up, and as if renouncing the hope
of making himself understood (he hadn't opened his

mouth once) he said in English: "Well . . . Good-
night, Captain Hermann." He stopped for a moment
before my chair and looked down fixedly, I may even
say he glared, and he went so far as to make a deep
noise in his throat. All this was so marked that for the
first time in our limited intercourse of nods and grunts
he excited in me something like interest. But next
moment he disappointed me—for he strode away
hastily without a nod even.

His manner was usually odd it is true, and I certainly did not pay much attention to it; but that sort of
obscure intention, which seemed to lurk in his noncha-
lance like a wary old carp in a pond, had never before
come so near the surface. He had distinctly aroused
my expectations. I would have been unable to say
what it was I expected, but at all events I did not expect the absurd developments he sprung upon me no
later than the break of the very next day.

I remember only that there was, on that evening,
enough point in his behaviour to make me, after he had
fled, wonder audibly what he might mean. To this
Hermann, crossing his legs with a swing and settling
himself viciously away from me in his chair, said:
"That fellow don't know himself what he means."

There might have been some insight in such a remark. I said nothing, and, still averted, Hermann
added: "When I was here last year he was just the
same." An eruption of tobacco smoke enveloped his
head as if his temper had exploded like gunpowder.

I had half a mind to ask him point blank whether he,
at least, didn't know why Falk, a notoriously unsociable
man, had taken to visiting his ship with such assiduity.
After all, I reflected suddenly, it was a most remarkable
thing. I wonder now what Hermann would have said.
As it turned out-he didn't let me ask. Forgetting all

about Falk apparently, he started a monologue on his plans for the future: the selling of the ship, the going home; and falling into a reflective and calculating mood he mumbled between regular jets of smoke about the expense. The necessity of disbursing passage-money for all his tribe seemed to disturb him in a manner that was the more striking because otherwise he gave no signs of a miserly disposition. And yet he fussed over the prospect of that voyage home in a mail-boat like a sedentary grocer who has made up his mind to see the world. He was racially thrifty I suppose, and for him there must have been a great novelty in finding himself obliged to pay for travelling—for sea travelling which was the normal state of life for the family—from the very cradle for most of them. I could see he grudged prospectively every single shilling which must be spent so absurdly. It was rather funny. He would become doleful over it, and then again, with a fretful sigh, he would suppose there was nothing for it now but to take three second-class tickets—and there were the four children to pay for besides. A lot of money that to spend at once. A big lot of money.

I sat with him listening (not for the first time) to these heart-searchings till I grew thoroughly sleepy, and then I left him and turned in on board my ship. At daylight I was awakened by a yelping of shrill voices, accompanied by a great commotion in the water, and the short, bullying blasts of a steam-whistle. Falk with his tug had come for me.

I began to dress. It was remarkable that the answering noise on board my ship together with the patter of feet above my head ceased suddenly. But I heard more remote guttural cries which seemed to express surprise and annoyance. Then the voice of my mate reached me howling expostulations to somebody at a distance. Other voices joined, apparently indignant; a chorus of something that sounded like abuse replied. Now and then the steam-whistle screeched.

Altogether that unnecessary uproar was distracting, but down there in my cabin I took it calmly. In another moment, I thought, I should be going down that wretched river, and in another week at the most I should be totally quit of the odious place and all the odious people in it.

Greatly cheered by the idea, I seized the hair-brushes and looking at myself in the glass began to use them. Suddenly a hush fell upon the noise outside, and I heard (the ports of my cabin were thrown open)—I heard a deep calm voice, not on board my ship, however, hailing resolutely in English, but with a strong foreign twang, "Go ahead!"

There may be tides in the affairs of men which taken at the flood . . . and so on. Personally I am still on the look-out for that important turn. I am, however, afraid that most of us are fated to flounder for ever in the dead water of a pool the shores of which are arid indeed. But I know that there are often in men's affairs unexpectedly—even irrationally—illuminating moments when an otherwise insignificant sound, perhaps only some perfectly commonplace gesture, suffices to reveal to us all the unreason, all the fatuous unreason, of our complacency. "Go ahead" are not particularly striking words even when pronounced with a foreign accent; yet they petrified me in the very act of smiling at myself in the glass. And then, refusing to believe my ears, but already boiling with indignation, I ran out of the cabin and up on deck.

It was incredibly true. It was perfectly true. I had no eyes for anything but the *Diana*. It was she that was being taken away. She was already out of her berth and shooting athwart the river. "The way this loonatic plucked that ship out is a caution," said the awed voice of my mate close to my ear. "Hey! Hallo! Falk! Hermann! What's this infernal trick?" I yelled in a fury.

Nobody heard me. Falk certainly could not hear me. His tug was turning at full speed away under the other bank. The wire hawser between her and the *Diana*, stretched as taut as a harpstring, vibrated alarmingly.

The high black craft careened over to the awful strain. A loud crack came out of her, followed by the tearing and splintering of wood. "There!" said the awed voice in my ear. "He's carried away their towing chock." And then, with enthusiasm, "Oh! Look! Look, sir! Look at them Dutchmen skipping out of the way on the forecastle. I hope to goodness he'll break a few of their shins before he's done with 'em."

I yelled my vain protests. The rays of the rising sun coursing level along the plain warmed my back, but I was hot enough with rage. I could not have believed that a simple towing operation could suggest so plainly the idea of abduction, of rape. Falk was simply running off with the *Diana*.

The white tug careered out into the middle of the river. The red floats of her paddle-wheels revolving with mad rapidity tore up the whole reach into foam. The *Diana* in mid-stream waltzed round with as much grace as an old barn, and flew after her ravisher. Through the ragged fog of smoke driving headlong upon the water I had a glimpse of Falk's square motionless shoulders under a white hat as big as a cart-wheel, of his red face, his yellow staring eyes, his great beard. Instead of keeping a look-out ahead, he was deliberately turning his back on the river to glare at his tow.

The tall heavy craft, never so used before in her life, seemed to have lost her senses; she took a wild sheer against her helm, and for a moment came straight at us, menacing and clumsy, like a runaway mountain. She piled up a streaming, hissing, boiling wave halfway up her blunt stem, my crew let out one great howl,— and then we held our breaths. It was a near thing. But Falk had her! He had her in his clutch. I fancied I could hear the steel hawser ping as it surged across the *Diana's* forecastle, with the hands on board of her bolting away from it in all directions. It was a near thing. Hermann, with his hair rumpled, in a snuffy flannel shirt and a pair of mustard-coloured trousers, had rushed to help with the wheel. I saw his terrified round face; I saw his very teeth uncovered by a sort of ghastly fixed grin; and in a great leaping tumult of water between the two ships the *Diana* whisked past so close that I could have flung a hair-brush at his head, for, it seems, I had kept them in my hands all the time. Meanwhile Mrs. Hermann sat placidly on the skylight, with a woollen shawl on her shoulders. The excellent woman in response to my indignant gesticulations fluttered a handkerchief, nodding and smiling in the kindest way imaginable. The boys, only half-dressed, were jumping about the poop in great glee, displaying their gaudy braces; and Lena in a short scarlet petticoat, with peaked elbows and thin bare arms, nursed the rag-doll with devotion. The whole family passed before my sight as if dragged across a scene of unparalleled violence. The last I saw was Hermann's niece with the baby Hermann in her arms standing apart from the others. Magnificent in her close-fitting print frock, she displayed something so commanding in the manifest perfection of her figure that the sun seemed to be rising for her alone. The flood of

light brought the opulence of her form and the vigour of
her youth in a glorifying way. She went by perfectly
motionless and as if lost in meditation; only the hem of
her skirt stirred in the draught; the sun rays broke on
her sleek tawny hair; that bald-headed ruffian, Nicholas,
was whacking her on the shoulder. I saw his tiny fat
arm rise and fall in a workmanlike manner. And then
the four cottage windows of the *Diana* came into view
retreating swiftly down the river. The sashes were up,
and one of the white calico curtains fluttered straight
out like a streamer above the agitated water of the
wake.

To be thus tricked out of one's turn was an unheard
of occurrence. In my agent's office, where I went to
complain at once, they protested with apologies they
couldn't understand how the mistake arose: but
Schomberg, when I dropped in later to get some tiffin,
though surprised to see me, was perfectly ready with an
explanation. I found him seated at the end of a long
narrow table, facing his wife—a scraggy little woman,
with long ringlets and a blue tooth, who smiled abroad
stupidly and looked frightened when you spoke to her.
Between them a waggling punkah fanned twenty vacant
cane-bottomed chairs and two rows of shiny plates.
Three Chinamen in white jackets loafed with napkins in
their hands around that desolation. Schomberg's pet
table-d'hôte was not much of a success that day. He
was feeding himself furiously and seemed to overflow
with bitterness. .

He began by ordering in a brutal voice the chops
to be brought back for me, and turning in his chair:
"Mistake they told you? Not a bit of it! Don't you
believe it for a moment, captain! Falk isn't a man to
make mistakes unless on purpose." His firm conviction
was that Falk had been trying all along to curry favour

on the cheap with Hermann. "On the cheap—mind you! It doesn't cost him a cent to put that insult upon you, and Captain Hermann gets in a day ahead of your ship. Time's money! Eh? You are very friendly with Captain Hermann I believe, but a man is bound to be pleased at any little advantage he may get. Captain Hermann is a good business man, and there's no such thing as a friend in business. Is there?" He leaned forward and began to cast stealthy glances as usual. "But Falk is, and always was, a miserable fellow. I would despise him."

I muttered, grumpily, that I had no particular respect for Falk.

"I would despise him," he insisted, with an appearance of anxiety which would have amused me if I had not been fathoms deep in discontent. To a young man fairly conscientious and as well-meaning as only the young be, the current ill-usage of life comes with a peculiar cruelty. Youth that is fresh enough to believe in guilt, in innocence, and in itself, will always doubt whether it have not perchance deserved its fate. Sombre of mind and without appetite, I struggled with the chop while Mrs. Schomberg sat with her everlasting stupid grin and Schomberg's talk gathered way like a slide of rubbish.

"Let me tell you. It's all about that girl. I don't know what Captain Hermann expects, but if he asked me I could tell him something about Falk. He's a miserable fellow. That man is a perfect slave. That's what I call him. A slave. Last year I started this *table d'hôte*, and sent cards out—you know. You think he had one meal in the house? Give the thing a trial? Not once. He has got hold now of a Madras cook—a blamed fraud that I hunted out of my cook-house with a rattan. He was not fit to cook for white

men.   No, not for the white men's dogs either; but see,
any damned native that can boil a pot of rice is good
enough for Mr. Falk.   Rice and a little fish he buys for
a few cents from the fishing-boats outside is what he
lives on.   You would hardly credit it—eh?   A white
man, too.   . . ."

He wiped his lips, using the napkin with indignation,
and looking at me.   It flashed through my mind in the
midst of my depression that if all the meat in the town
was like these *table-d 'hôte* chops, Falk wasn't so much
to blame.   I was on the point of saying this, but
Schomberg's stare was intimidating.   "He's a vegetar-
ian, perhaps," I murmured instead.

"He's a miser.   A miserable miser," affirmed the
hotel-keeper with great force.   "The meat here is not
so good as at home—of course.   And dear, too.   But
look at me.   I only charge a dollar for the tiffin, and
one dollar and fifty cents for the dinner.   Show me anything cheaper.   Why am I doing it?   There's little
profit in this game.   Falk wouldn't look at it.   I do it
for the sake of a lot of young white fellows here that
hadn't a place where they could get a decent meal and
eat it decently in good company.   There's first-rate
company always at my table."

The convinced way he surveyed the empty chairs
made me feel as if I had intruded upon a tiffin of
ghostly Presences.

"A white man should eat like a white man, dash it
all," he burst out impetuously.   "Ought to eat meat,
must eat meat.   I manage to get meat for my patrons
all the year round.   Don't I?   I am not catering for
a dam' lot of coolies: Have another chop, captain.   . . .   No?   You, boy—take away!"

He threw himself back and waited grimly for the
curry.   The half-closed jalousies darkened the room

pervaded by the smell of fresh whitewash; a swarm of
flies buzzed and settled in turns, and poor Mrs. Schomberg's smile seemed to express the quintessence of all
the imbecility that had ever spoken, had ever breathed,
had ever been fed on infamous buffalo meat within
these bare walls. Schomberg did not open his lips till
he was ready to thrust therein a spoonful of greasy
rice. He rolled his eyes ridiculously before he swallowed the hot stuff, and only then broke out afresh.

"It is the most degrading thing. They take the
dish up to the wheelhouse for him with a cover on it,
and he shuts both the doors before he begins to eat.
Fact! Must be ashamed of himself. Ask the engineer.
He can't do without an engineer—don't you see—and
as no respectable man can be expected to put up with
such a table, he allows them fifteen dollars a month
extra mess money. I assure you it is so! You just
ask Mr. Ferdinand da Costa. That's the engineer he
has now. You may have seen him about my place, a
delicate dark young man, with very fine eyes and a little
moustache. He arrived here a year ago from Calcutta.
Between you and me, I guess the money-lenders there
must have been after him. He rushes here for a meal
every chance he can get, for just please tell me what
satisfaction is that for a well-educated young fellow to
feed all alone in his cabin—like a wild beast? That's
what Falk expects his engineers to put up with for fifteen
dollars extra. And the rows on board every time a
little smell of cooking gets about the deck! You
wouldn't believe! The other day da Costa got the
cook to fry a steak for him—a turtle steak it was, too,
not beef at all—and the fat caught or something.
Young da Costa himself was telling me of it here in
this room. 'Mr. Schomberg'—says he—'if I had let
a cylinder cover blow off through my negligence Captain

Falk couldn't have been more savage. He frightened the cook so that he won't put anything on the fire for me now.' Poor da Costa had tears in his eyes. Only try to put yourself in his place, captain: a sensitive, gentlemanly young fellow. Is he expected to eat his food raw? But that's your Falk all over. Ask any one you like. I suppose the fifteen dollars extra he has to give keep on rankling—in there."

And Schomberg tapped his manly breast. I sat half stunned by his irrelevant babble. Suddenly he gripped my forearm in an impressive and cautious manner, as if to lead me into a very cavern of confidence.

"It's nothing but enviousness," he said in a lowered tone, which had a stimulating effect upon my wearied hearing. "I don't suppose there is one person in this town that he isn't envious of. I tell you he's dangerous. Even I myself am not safe from him. I know for certain he tried to poison . . . ."

"Oh, come now," I cried, disgusted.

"But I know for certain. The people themselves came and told me of it. He went about saying everywhere I was a worse pest to this town than the cholera. He had been talking against me ever since I opened this hotel. And he poisoned Captain Hermann's mind, too. Last time the *Diana* was loading here Captain Hermann used to come in every day for a drink or a cigar. This time he hasn't been here twice in a week. How do you account for that?"

He squeezed my arm till he extorted from me some sort of mumble.

"Falk makes ten times the money I do. I've another hotel to fight against, and there is no other tug on the river. I am not in his way, am I? He wouldn't be fit to run an hotel if he tried. But that's just his nature. He can't bear to think I am making a living.

I only hope it makes him properly wretched. He's like that in everything. He would like to keep a decent table well enough. But no—for the sake of a few cents. Can't do it. It's too much for him. That's what I call being a slave to it. But he's mean enough to kick up a row when his nose gets tickled a bit. See that? That just paints him. Miserly and envious. You can't account for it any other way. Can you? I have been studying him these three years."

He was anxious I should assent to his theory. And indeed on thinking it over it would have been plausible enough if there hadn't been always the essential falseness of irresponsibility in Schomberg's chatter. However, I was not disposed to investigate the psychology of Falk. I was engaged just then in eating despondently a piece of stale Dutch cheese, being too much crushed to care what I swallowed myself, let alone bothering my head about Falk's ideas of gastronomy. I could expect from their study no clue to his conduct in matters of business, which seemed to me totally unrestrained by morality or even by the commonest sort of decency. How insignificant and contemptible I must appear, for the fellow to dare treat me like this—I reflected suddenly, writhing in silent agony. And I consigned Falk and all his peculiarities to the devil with so much mental fervour as to forget Schomberg's existence, till he grabbed my arm urgently. "Well, you may think and think till every hair of your head falls off, captain; but you can't explain it in any other way."

For the sake of peace and quietness I admitted hurriedly that I couldn't; persuaded that now he would leave off. But the only result was to make his moist face shine with the pride of cunning. He removed his hand for a moment to scare a black mass of flies off the sugar-basin, and caught hold of my arm again.

"To be sure. And in the same way everybody is aware he would like to get married. Only he can't. Let me quote you an instance. Well, two years ago a Miss Vanlo, a very ladylike girl, came from home to keep house for her brother, Fred, who had an engineering shop for small repairs by the waterside. Suddenly Falk takes to going up to their bungalow after dinner and sitting for hours in the verandah saying nothing. The poor girl couldn't tell for the life of her what to do with such a man, so she would keep on playing the piano and singing to him evening after evening till she was ready to drop. And it wasn't as if she had been a strong young woman either. She was thirty, and the climate had been playing the deuce with her. Then— don't you see—Fred had to sit up with them for propriety, and during whole weeks on end never got a chance to get to bed before midnight. That was not pleasant for a tired man—was it? And besides Fred had worries then because his shop didn't pay and he was dropping money fast. He just longed to get away from here and try his luck somewhere else, but for the sake of his sister he hung on and on till he ran himself into debt over his ears—I can tell you. I, myself, could show a handful of his chits for meals and drinks in my drawer. I could never find out tho' where Fred found all the money at last. Can't be but he must have got something out of that brother of his, a coal merchant in Port Said. Anyhow he paid everybody before he left, but the girl nearly broke her heart. Disappointment, of course, and at her age, don't you know. . . Mrs. Schomberg here was very friendly with her, and she could tell you. Awful despair. Fainting fits. It was a scandal. A notorious scandal. To that extent that old Mr. Siegers—not your present charterer, but Mr. Siegers, the father, the old gentleman who retired

from business on a fortune and got buried at sea going
home, *he* had to interview Falk in his private office.
He was a man who could speak like a Dutch Uncle, and,
besides, Messrs. Siegers had been helping Falk with a
good bit of money from the start. In fact, you may say
they made him as far as that goes. It so happened that
just at the time he turned up here, their firm was
chartering a lot of sailing-ships every year, and it suited
their business that there should be good towing facili-
ties on the river. See? . . . Well—there's always
an ear at the keyhole—isn't there? In fact," he
lowered his tone confidentially, "in this case it was a
good friend of mine; a man you can see here any evening; only they conversed rather low. Anyhow my
friend's certain that Falk was trying to make all sorts of
excuses, and old Mr. Siegers was coughing a lot. And
yet Falk wanted all the time to be married, too. Why!
It's notorious the man has been longing for years to
make a home for himself. Only he can't face the
expense. When it comes to putting his hand in his
pocket—it chokes him off. That's the truth and no
other. I've always said so, and everybody agrees with
me by this time. What do you think of that—eh?"

He appealed confidently to my indignation, but having a mind to annoy him I remarked, "that it seemed to
me very pitiful—if true."

He bounced in his chair as if I had run a pin into him.
I don't know what he might have said, only at that
moment we heard through the half-open door of the
billiard-room the footsteps of two men entering from the
verandah, a murmur of two voices; at the sharp tapping
of a coin on a table Mrs. Schomberg half rose irresolutely. "Sit still," he hissed at her, and then, in an
hospitable, jovial tone, contrasting amazingly with the
angry glance that had made his wife sink in her chair,

he cried very loud: "Tiffin still going on in here, gentlemen."

There was no answer, but the voices dropped suddenly. The head Chinaman went out. We heard the clink of ice in the glasses, pouring sounds, the shuffling of feet, the scraping of chairs. Schomberg, after wondering in a low mutter who the devil could be there at this time of the day, got up napkin in hand to peep through the doorway cautiously. He retreated rapidly on tip-toe, and whispering behind his hand informed me that it was Falk, Falk himself who was in there, and what's more, he had Captain Hermann with him.

The return of the tug from the outer Roads was unexpected but possible, for Falk had taken away the *Diana* at half-past five, and it was now two o'clock. Schomberg wished me to observe that neither of these men would spend a dollar on a tiffin, which they must have wanted. But by the time I was ready to leave the dining-room Falk had gone. I heard the last of his big boots on the planks of the verandah. Hermann was sitting quite alone in the large, wooden room with the two lifeless billiard tables shrouded in striped covers, mopping his face diligently. He wore his best go-ashore clothes, a stiff collar, black coat, large white waistcoat, gray trousers. A white cotton sunshade with a cane handle reposed between his legs, his side whiskers were neatly brushed, his chin had been freshly shaved; and he only distantly resembled the dishevelled and terrified man in a snuffy night shirt and ignoble old trousers I had seen in the morning hanging on to the wheel of the *Diana*.

He gave a start at my entrance, and addressed me at once in some confusion, but with genuine eagerness. He was anxious to make it clear he had nothing to do with what he called the "tam pizness" of the morning.

It was most inconvenient. He had reckoned upon another day up in town to settle his bills and sign certain papers. There were also some few stores to come, and sundry pieces of "my ironwork," as he called it quaintly, landed for repairs, had been left behind. Now he would have to hire a native boat to take all this out to the ship. It would cost five to six dollars perhaps. He had had no warning from Falk. Nothing. . . . He hit the table with his dumpy fist. . . . Der verfluchte Kerl came in the morning like a "tam' ropper," making a great noise, and took him away. His mate was not prepared, his ship was moored fast—he protested it was shameful to come upon a man in that way. Shameful! Yet such was the power Falk had on the river that when I suggested in a chilling tone that he might have simply refused to have his ship moved, Hermann was quite startled at the idea. I never realized so well before that this is an age of steam. The exclusive possession of a marine boiler had given Falk the whip hand of us all. Hermann, recovering, put it to me appealingly that I knew very well how unsafe it was to contradict that fellow. At this I only smiled distantly.

"Der Kerl!" he cried. He was sorry he had not refused. He was indeed. The damage! The damage! What for all that damage! There was no occasion for damage. Did I know how much damage he had done? It gave me a certain satisfaction to tell him that I had heard his old waggon of a ship crack fore and aft as she went by. "You passed close enough to me," I added, significantly.

He threw both his hands up to heaven at the recollection. One of them grasped by the middle the white parasol, and he resembled curiously a caricature of a shopkeeping citizen in one of his own German comic

papers. "Ach! That was dangerous," he cried. I
was amused. But directly he added with an appearance of simplicity, "The side of your iron ship would
have been crushed in like—like this matchbox."

"Would it?" I growled, much less amused now;
but by the time I had decided that this remark was not
meant for a dig at me he had worked himself into a high
state of resentfulness against Falk. The inconvenience,
the damage, the expense! Gottferdam! Devil take
the fellow. Behind the bar Schomberg, with a cigar in
his teeth, pretended to be writing with a pencil on a large
sheet of paper; and as Hermann's excitement increased
it made me comfortingly aware of my own calmness and
superiority. But it occurred to me while I listened to
his revilings, that after all the good man had come up in
the tug. There perhaps—since he must come to town
—he had no option. But evidently he had had a drink
with Falk, either accepted or offered. How was that?
So I checked him by saying loftily that I hoped he
would make Falk pay for every penny of the damage.

"That's it! That's it! Go for him," called out
Schomberg from the bar, flinging his pencil down and
rubbing his hands.

We ignored his noise. But Hermann's excitement
suddenly went off the boil as when you remove a saucepan from the fire. I urged on his consideration that he
had done now with Falk and Falk's confounded tug.
He, Hermann, would not, perhaps, turn up again in
this part of the world for years to come, since he was
going to sell the *Diana* at the end of this very trip ("Go
home passenger in a mail-boat," he murmured mechanically). He was therefore safe from Falk's malice. All
he had to do was to race off to his consignees and stop
payment of the towage bill before Falk had the time to
get in and lift the money.

Nothing could have been less in the spirit of my advice than the thoughtful way in which he set about to make his parasol stay propped against the edge of the table.

While I watched his concentrated efforts with astonishment he threw at me one or two perplexed, half-shy glances. Then he sat down. "That's all very well," he said, reflectively.

It cannot be doubted that the man had been thrown off his balance by being hauled out of the harbour against his wish. His stolidity had been profoundly stirred, else he would never have made up his mind to ask me unexpectedly whether I had not remarked that Falk had been casting eyes upon his niece. "No more than myself," I answered with literal truth. The girl was of the sort one necessarily casts eyes at in a sense. She made no noise, but she filled most satisfactorily a good bit of space.

"But you, captain, are not the same kind of man," observed Hermann.

I was not, I am happy to say, in a position to deny this. "What about the lady?" I could not help asking. At this he gazed for a time into my face, earnestly, and made as if to change the subject. I heard him beginning to mutter something unexpected, about his children growing old enough to require schooling. He would have to leave them ashore with their grandmother when he took up that new command he expected to get in Germany.

This constant harping on his domestic arrangements was funny. I suppose it must have been like the prospect of a complete alteration in his life. An epoch. He was going, too, to part with the *Diana!* He had served in her for years. He had inherited her. From an uncle, if I remember rightly. And the future loomed big before him, occupying his thought exclusively with all its aspects as on the eve of a venturesome enterprise. He sat there frowning and biting his lip, and suddenly he began to fume and fret.

I discovered to my momentary amusement that he seemed to imagine I could, should or ought, have caused Falk in some way to declare himself. Such a hope was incomprehensible, but funny. Then the contact with all this foolishness irritated me. I said crossly that I had seen no symptoms, but if there were any—since he, Hermann, was so sure—then it was still worse. What pleasure Falk found in humbugging people in just that way I couldn't say. It was, however, my solemn duty to warn him. It had lately, I said, come to my knowledge that there was a man (not a very long time ago either) who had been taken in just like this.

All this passed in undertones, and at this point Schomberg, exasperated at our secrecy, went out of the room slamming the door with a crash that positively lifted us in our chairs. This, or else what I had said, huffed my Hermann. He supposed, with a contemptuous toss of his head towards the door which trembled yet, that I had got hold of some of that man's silly tales. It looked, indeed, as though his mind had been thoroughly poisoned against Schomberg. "His tales were—they were," he repeated, seeking for the word—"trash." They were trash, he reiterated and moreover I was young yet . . .

This horrid aspersion (I regret I am no longer exposed to that sort of insult) made me huffy, too. I felt ready in my own mind to back up every assertion of Schomberg's and on any subject. In a moment, devil only knows why, Hermann and I were looking at each other most inimically. He caught up his hat without more ado and I gave myself the pleasure of calling after him:

"Take my advice and make Falk pay for breaking up your ship. You aren't likely to get anything else out of him."

When I got on board my ship, the old mate, who was very full of the events of the morning, remarked:

"I saw the tug coming back from the outer Roads just before two P. M." (He never by any chance used the words morning or afternoon. Always P. M. or A. M., log-book style.) "Smart work that. Man's always in a state of hurry. He's a regular chucker-out, ain't he, sir? There's a few pubs I know of in the East-end of London that would be all the better for one of his sort around the bar." He chuckled at his joke. "A regular chucker-out. Now he has fired out that Dutchman head over heels, I suppose our turn's coming to-morrow morning."

We were all on deck at break of day (even the sick —poor devils—had crawled out) ready to cast off in the twinkling of an eye. Nothing came. Falk did not come. At last, when I began to think that probably something had gone wrong in his engine-room, we perceived the tug going by, full pelt, down the river, as if we hadn't existed. For a moment I entertained the wild notion that he was going to turn round in the next reach. Afterwards, I watched his smoke appear above the plain, now here, now there, according to the windings of the river. It disappeared. Then without a word I went down to breakfast. I just simply went down to breakfast.

Not one of us uttered a sound till the mate, after imbibing—by means of suction out of a saucer—his second cup of tea, exclaimed: "Where the devil is the man gone to?"

"Courting!" I shouted, with such a fiendish laugh
that the old chap didn't venture to open his lips any
more.

I started to the office perfectly calm. Calm with
excessive rage. Evidently they knew all about it
already, and they treated me to a show of consternation. The manager, a soft-footed, obese man, breathing short, got up to meet me, while all round the room
the young clerks, bending over their desks, cast
glances in my direction. The fat man, without waiting
for my complaint, wheezing heavily and in a tone as if
he himself were incredulous, conveyed to me the news
that Falk—Captain Falk—had declined—had absolutely declined—to tow my ship—to have anything to
to with my ship—this day or any other day. Never!

I did my best to preserve a cool appearance, but, all
the same, I must have shown how much taken aback
I was. We were talking in the middle of the room.
Suddenly, behind my back some ass blew his nose with
a great noise and at the same time another quill-
driver got up and went out on the landing hastily. It
occurred to me I was cutting a foolish figure there. I
demanded angrily to see the principal in his private
room.

The skin of Mr. Siegers' head showed dead white
between the iron gray streaks of hair lying plastered
cross-wise from ear to ear over the top of his skull in
the manner of a bandage. His narrow sunken face
was of an uniform and permanent terra-cotta colour,
like a piece of pottery. He was sickly, thin, and short,
with wrists like a boy of ten. But from that debile
body there issued a bullying voice, tremendously loud,
harsh and resonant, as if produced by some powerful
mechanical contrivance in the nature of a fog-horn. I
do not know what he did with it in the private life of

his home, but in the larger sphere of business it presented the advantage of overcoming arguments without
the slightest mental effort, by the mere volume of sound.
We had had several passages of arms. It took me all
I knew to guard the interest of my owners—whom,
nota bene, I had never seen—while Siegers (who had
made their acquaintance some years before, during a
business tour in Australia) pretended to the knowledge
of their innermost minds, and, in the character of "our
very good friends," threw them perpetually at my head.

He looked at me with a jaundiced eye (there was no
love lost between us), and declared at once that it was
strange, very strange. His pronunciation of English
was so extravagant that I can't even attempt to repro-
duce it. For instance, he said "Fferie strantch."
Combined with the bellowing intonation it made the
language of one's childhood sound weirdly startling,
and even if considered purely as a kind of unmeaning
noise it filled you with astonishment at first. "They
had," he continued, "been acquainted with Captain
Falk for very many years, and never had any
reason. . . ."

"That's why I come to you, of course," I interrupted.
"I've the right to know the meaning of this infernal
nonsense." In the half-light of the room, which was
greenish, because of the tree-tops screening the window,
I saw him writhe his meagre shoulders. It came into
my head, as disconnected ideas will come at all sorts of
times into one's head, that this, most likely, was the
very room where, if the tale were true, Falk had been
lectured by Mr. Siegers, the father. Mr. Siegers' (the
son's) overwhelming voice, in brassy blasts, as though
he had been trying to articulate words through a
trumpet, was expressing his great regret at conduct
characterized by a very marked want of discre-

tion . . . As I lived I was being lectured, too!
His deafening gibberish was difficult to follow, but it
was *my* conduct—mine!—that . . . Damn! I
wasn't going to stand this.

"What on earth are you driving at?" I asked in a
passion. I put my hat on my head (he never offered a
seat to anybody), and as he seemed for the moment
struck dumb by my irreverence, I turned my back on
him and marched out. His vocal arrangements blared
after me a few threats of coming down on the ship for
the demurrage of the lighters, and all the other expenses
consequent upon the delays arising from my frivolity.

Once outside in the sunshine my head swam. It
was no longer a question of mere delay. I perceived
myself involved in hopeless and humiliating absurdities
that were leading me to something very like a disaster.
"Let us be calm," I muttered to myself, and ran into
the shade of a leprous wall. From that short side-
street I could see the broad main thoroughfare ruinous
and gay, running away, away between stretches of decaying masonry, bamboo fences, ranges of arcades of brick
and plaster, hovels of lath and mud, lofty temple gates
of carved timber, huts of rotten mats—an immensely
wide thoroughfare, loosely packed as far as the eye
could reach with a barefooted and brown multitude
paddling ankle deep in the dust. For a moment
I felt myself about to go out of my mind with worry
and desperation.

Some allowance must be made for the feelings of a
young man new to responsibility. I thought of my
crew. Half of them were ill, and I really began to
think that some of them would end by dying on board if
I couldn't get them out to sea soon. Obviously I
should have to take my ship down the river, either
working under canvas or dredging with the anchor

down; operations which, in common with many modern sailors, I only knew theoretically. And I almost shrank from undertaking them shorthanded and without local knowledge of the river bed, which is so necessary for the confident handling of a ship. There were no pilots, no beacons, no buoys of any sort; but there was a very devil of a current for anybody to see, no end of shoal places, and at least two obviously awkward turns of the channel between me and the sea. But how dangerous these turns were I could not tell. I didn't even know what my ship was capable of! I had never handled her in my life. A misunderstanding between a man and his ship, in a difficult river with no room to make it up, is bound to end in trouble for the man. On the other hand, it must be owned I had not much reason to count upon a general run of good luck. And suppose I had the misfortune to pile her up high and dry on some beastly shoal? That would have been the final undoing of that voyage. It was plain that if Falk refused to tow me out he would also refuse to pull me off. This meant—what? A day lost at the very best; but more likely a whole fortnight of frizzling on some pestilential mudflat, of desperate work, of discharging cargo; more than likely it meant borrowing money at an exorbitant rate of interest—from the Siegers' gang, too, at that. They were a power in the port. And that elderly seaman of mine, Gambril, had looked pretty ghastly when I went forward to dose him with quinine that morning. *He* would certainly die—not to speak of two or three others that seemed nearly as bad, and of the rest of them just ready to catch any tropical disease going. Horror, ruin and everlasting remorse. And no help. None. I had fallen amongst a lot of unfriendly lunatics!

At any rate, if I must take my ship down myself it

was my duty to procure if possible some local knowledge. But that was not easy. The only person I
could think of for that service was a certain Johnson,
formerly captain of a country ship, but now spliced to
a country wife and gone utterly to the bad. I had
only heard of him in the vaguest way, as living concealed in the thick of two hundred thousand natives,
and only emerging into the light of day for the purpose
of hunting up some brandy. I had a notion that if I
could lay my hands on him I would sober him on board
my ship and use him for a pilot. Better than nothing.
Once a sailor always a sailor—and he had known the
river for years. But in our Consulate (where I arrived
dripping after a sharp walk) they could tell me nothing.
The excellent young men on the staff, though willing
to help me, belonged to a sphere of the white colony for
which that sort of Johnson does not exist. Their
suggestion was that I should hunt the man up myself
with the help of the Consulate's constable—an ex-
sergeant-major of a regiment of Hussars.

This man, whose usual duty apparently consisted in
sitting behind a little table in an outer room of Consular
offices, when ordered to assist me in my search for Johnson displayed lots of energy and a marvellous amount
of local knowledge of a sort. But he did not conceal an
immense and sceptical contempt for the whole business.
We explored together on that afternoon an infinity of
infamous grog shops, gambling dens, opium dens. We
walked up narrow lanes where our gharry—a tiny box of
a thing on wheels, attached to a jibbing Burmah pony—
could by no means have passed. The constable seemed
to be on terms of scornful intimacy with Maltese, with
Eurasians, with Chinamen, with Klings, and with the
sweepers belonging to a temple, with whom he talked at
the gate. We interviewed also through a grating in a

mud wall closing a blind alley an immensely corpulent Italian, who, the ex-sergeant-major remarked to me perfunctorily, had "killed another man last year." Thereupon he addressed him as "Antonio" and "Old Buck," though that bloated carcase, apparently more than half filling the sort of cell wherein it sat, recalled rather a fat pig in a stye. Familiar and never unbending, the sergeant chucked—absolutely chucked—under the chin a horribly wrinkled and shrivelled old hag propped on a stick, who had volunteered some sort of information: and with the same stolid face he kept up an animated conversation with the groups of swathed brown women, who sat smoking cheroots on the doorsteps of a long range of clay hovels. We got out of the gharry and clambered into dwellings airy like packing crates, or descended into places sinister like cellars. We got in, we drove on, we got out again for the sole purpose, as it seemed, of looking behind a heap of rubble. The sun declined; my companion was curt and sardonic in his answers, but it appears we were just missing Johnson all along. At last our conveyance stopped once more with a jerk, and the driver jumping down opened the door.

A black mudhole blocked the lane. A mound of garbage crowned with the dead body of a dog arrested us not. An empty Australian beef tin bounded cheerily before the toe of my boot. Suddenly we clambered through a gap in a prickly fence. . . .

It was a very clean native compound: and the big native woman, with bare brown legs as thick as bedposts, pursuing on all fours a silver dollar that came rolling out from somewhere, was Mrs. Johnson herself. "Your man's at home," said the ex-sergeant, and stepped aside in complete and marked indifference to anything that might follow. Johnson—at home—

stood with his back to a native house built on posts and
with its walls made of mats. In his left hand he held a
banana. Out of the right he dealt another dollar into
space. The woman captured this one on the wing, and
there and then plumped down on the ground to look at
us with greater comfort.

"My man" was sallow of face, grizzled, unshaven,
muddy on elbows and back; where the seams of his
serge coat yawned you could see his white nakedness.
The vestiges of a paper collar encircled his neck. He
looked at us with a grave, swaying surprise. "Where
do you come from?" he asked. My heart sank. How
could I have been stupid enough to waste energy and
time for this?

But having already gone so far I approached a little
nearer and declared the purpose of my visit. He would
have to come at once with me, sleep on board my ship,
and to-morrow, with the first of the ebb, he would give
me his assistance in getting my ship down to the sea,
without steam. A six-hundred-ton barque, drawing
nine feet aft. I proposed to give him eighteen dollars
for his local knowledge; and all the time I was speaking
he kept on considering attentively the various aspects
of the banana, holding first one side up to his eye, then
the other.

"You've forgotten to apologize," he said at last with
extreme precision. "Not being a gentleman yourself,
you don't know apparently when you intrude upon a
gentleman. I am one. I wish you to understand that
when I am in funds I don't work, and now . . ."

I would have pronounced him perfectly sober had
he not paused in great concern to try and brush a hole
off the knee of his trousers.

"I have money—and friends. Every gentleman
has. Perhaps you would like to know my friend? His

name is Falk. You could borrow some money. Try to remember. F-A-L-K. Falk." Abruptly his tone changed. "A noble heart," he said, muzzily.

"Has Falk been giving you some money?" I asked, appalled by the detailed finish of the dark plot.

"Lent me, my good man, not given me," he corrected, suavely. "Met me taking the air last evening, and being as usual anxious to oblige—— Hadn't you better go to the devil out of my compound?"

And upon this, without other warning, he let fly with the banana, which missed my head and took the constable just under the left eye. He rushed at the miserable Johnston, stammering with fury. They fell. . . . But why dwell on the wretchedness, the breathlessness, the degradation, the senselessness, the weariness, the ridicule and humiliation and—and—the perspiration, of these moments? I dragged the ex-hussar off. He was like a wild beast. It seems he had been greatly annoyed at losing his free afternoon on my account. The garden of his bungalow required his personal attention, and at the slight blow of the banana the brute in him had broken loose. We left Johnson on his back still black in the face, but beginning to kick feebly. Meantime, the big woman had remained sitting on the ground, apparently paralyzed with extreme terror.

For half an hour we jolted inside our rolling box, side by side, in profound silence. The ex-sergeant was busy staunching the blood of a long scratch on his cheek. "I hope you're satisfied," he said, suddenly. "That's what comes of all that tomfool business. If you hadn't quarrelled with that tugboat skipper over some girl or other, all this wouldn't have happened."

"You heard *that* story?" I said.

"Of course I heard. And I shouldn't wonder if the

Consul-General himself doesn't come to hear of it. How am I to go before him to-morrow with that thing on my cheek—I want to know. It's *you* who ought to have got this!"

After that, till the gharry stopped and he jumped out without leave-taking, he swore to himself steadily, horribly; muttering great, purposeful, trooper oaths, to which the worst a sailor can do is like the prattle of a child. For my part I had just the strength to crawl into Schomberg's coffee-room, where I wrote at a little table a note to the mate instructing him to get everything ready for dropping down the river next day. I couldn't face my ship. Well! she had a clever sort of skipper and no mistake—poor thing! What a horrid mess! I took my head between my hands. At times the obviousness of my innocence would reduce me to despair. What had I done? If I had done something to bring about the situation I should at least have learned not to do it again. But I felt guiltless to the point of imbecility. The room was empty yet; only Schomberg prowled round me goggle-eyed and with a sort of awed respectful curiosity. No doubt he had set the story going himself; but he was a good-hearted chap, and I am really persuaded he participated in all my troubles. He did what he could for me. He ranged aside the heavy matchstand, set a chair straight, pushed a spittoon slightly with his foot—as you show small attentions to a friend under a great sorrow— sighed, and at last, unable to hold his tongue:

"Well! I warned you, captain. That's what comes of running your head against Mr. Falk. Man'll stick at nothing."

I sat without stirring, and after surveying me with a sort of commiseration in his eyes, he burst out in a hoarse whisper: "But for a fine lump of a girl, she's a

fine lump of a girl." He made a loud smacking noise
with his thick lips. "The finest lump of a girl that I
ever . . ." he was going on with great unction, but
for some reason or other broke off. I fancied myself
throwing something at his head. "I don't blame you,
captain. Hang me if I do," he said with a patronizing
air.

"Thank you," I said, resignedly. It was no use
fighting against this false fate. I don't know even if I
was sure myself where the truth of the matter began.
The conviction that it would end disastrously had been
driven into me by all the successive shocks my sense of
security had received. I began to ascribe an extraordinary potency to agents in themselves powerless.
It was as if Schomberg's baseless gossip had the power
to bring about the thing itself or the abstract enmity
of Falk could put my ship ashore.

I have already explained how fatal this last would
have been. For my further action, my youth, my inexperience, my very real concern for the health of my
crew must be my excuse. The action itself, when it
came, was purely impulsive. It was set in movement
quite undiplomatically and simply by Falk's appearance
in the doorway of the coffee-room.

The room was full by then and buzzing with voices.
I had been looked at with curiosity by everyone, but
how am I to describe the sensation produced by the
appearance of Falk himself blocking the doorway?
The tension of expectation could be measured by the
profundity of the silence that fell upon the very click of
the billiard balls. As to Schomberg, he looked extremely frightened; he hated mortally any sort of row
(*fracas* he called it) in his establishment. *Fracas* was
bad for business, he affirmed; but in truth, this specimen of portly, middle-aged manhood was of a timid

disposition. I don't know what, considering my presence in the place, they all hoped would come of it. A
sort of stag fight, perhaps. Or they may have supposed
Falk had come in only to annihilate me completely. As
a matter of fact, Falk had come in because Hermann
had asked him to inquire after the precious white
cotton parasol which, in the worry and excitement of
the previous day, he had forgotten at the table where
we had held our little discussion.

It was this that gave me my opportunity. I don't
think I would have gone to seek Falk out. No. I don't
think so. There are limits. But there was an opportunity and I seized it—I have already tried to explain
why. Now I will merely state that, in my opinion, to
get his sickly crew into the sea air and secure a quick
despatch for his ship a skipper would be justified in
going to any length, short of absolute crime. He should
put his pride in his pocket; he may accept confidences;
he must explain his innocence as if it were a sin; he
may take advantage of misconceptions, of desires and
of weaknesses; he ought to conceal his horror and
other emotions, and, if the fate of a human being, and
that human being a magnificent young girl, is strangely
involved—why, he should contemplate that fate
(whatever it might seem to be) without turning a hair.
And all these things I have done; the explaining, the
listening, the pretending—even to the discretion—and
nobody, not even Hermann's niece, I believe, need
throw stones at me now. Schomberg at all events
needn't, since from first to last, I am happy to say
there was not the slightest "*fracas.*"

Overcoming a nervous contraction of the windpipe, I
had managed to exclaim "Captain Falk!" His start of
surprise was perfectly genuine, but afterwards he
neither smiled nor scowled. He simply waited. Then,

when I had said, "I must have a talk with you," and had pointed to a chair at my table, he moved up to me, though he didn't sit down. Schomberg, however, with a long tumbler in his hand, was making towards us prudently, and I discovered then the only sign of weakness in Falk. He had for Schomberg a repulsion resembling that sort of physical fear some people experience at the sight of a toad. Perhaps to a man so essentially and silently concentrated upon himself (though he could talk well enough, as I was to find out presently) the other's irrepressible loquacity, embracing every human being within range of the tongue, might have appeared unnatural, disgusting, and monstrous. He suddenly gave signs of restiveness—positively like a horse about to rear, and, muttering hurriedly as if in great pain, "No. I can't stand that fellow," seemed ready to bolt. This weakness of his gave me the advantage at the very start. "Verandah," I suggested, as if rendering him a service, and walked him out by the arm. We stumbled over a few chairs; we had the feeling of open space before us, and felt the fresh breath of the river—fresh, but tainted. The Chinese theatres across the water made, in the sparsely twinkling masses of gloom an Eastern town presents at night, blazing centres of light, and of a distant and howling uproar. I felt him become suddenly tractable again like an animal, like a good-tempered horse when the object that scares him is removed. Yes. I felt in the darkness there how tractable he was, without my conviction of his inflexibility—tenacity, rather, perhaps—being in the least weakened. His very arm abandoning itself to my grasp was as hard as marble—like a limb of iron. But I heard a tumultuous scuffling of boot-soles within. The unspeakable idiots inside were crowding to the windows, climbing over each other's backs behind the blinds, billiard cues and all. Somebody broke a window-pane, and with the sound of falling glass, so suggestive of riot and devastation, Schomberg reeled out after us in a state of funk which had prevented him from parting with his brandy and soda. He must have trembled like an aspen leaf. The piece of ice in the long tumbler he held in his hand tinkled with an effect of chattering teeth. "I beg you, gentlemen," he expostulated, thickly. "Come! Really, now, I must insist . . ."

How proud I am of my presence of mind! "Hallo," I said instantly in a loud and naïve tone, "somebody's breaking your windows, Schomberg. Would you please tell one of your boys to bring out here a pack of cards and a couple of lights? And two long drinks. Will you?"

To receive an order soothed him at once. It was business. "Certainly," he said in an immensely relieved tone. The night was rainy, with wandering gusts of wind, and while we waited for the candles Falk said, as if to justify his panic, "I don't interfere in anybody's business. I don't give any occasion for talk. I am a respectable man. But this fellow is always making out something wrong, and can never rest till he gets somebody to believe him."

This was the first of my knowledge of Falk. This desire of respectability, of being like everybody else, was the only recognition he vouchsafed to the organization of mankind. For the rest he might have been the member of a herd, not of a society. Self-preservation was his only concern. Not selfishness, but mere self-preservation. Selfishness presupposes consciousness, choice, the presence of other men; but his instinct acted as though he were the last of mankind nursing that law like the only spark of a sacred fire. I don't mean to say that living naked in a cavern would have satisfied him. Obviously he was the creature of the conditions to which he was born. No doubt self-preservation meant also the preservation of these conditions. But essentially it meant something much more simple, natural, and powerful. How shall I express it? It meant the preservation of the five senses of his body— let us say—taking it in its narrowest as well as in its widest meaning. I think you will admit before long the justice of this judgment. However, as we stood there together in the dark verandah I had judged nothing as yet—and I had no desire to judge—which is an idle practice anyhow. The light was long in coming.

"Of course," I said in a tone of mutual understanding, "it isn't exactly a game of cards I want with you."

I saw him draw his hands down his face—the vague stir of the passionate and meaningless gesture; but he waited in silent patience. It was only when the lights had been brought out that he opened his lips. I understood his mumble to mean that "he didn't know any card-games."

"Like this Schomberg and all the other fools will have to keep off," I said, tearing open the pack. "Have you heard that we are universally supposed to be quarrelling about a girl? You know who—of course. I am really ashamed to ask, but is it possible that you do me the honour to think me dangerous?"

As I said these words I felt how absurd it was and also I felt flattered—for, really, what else could it be? His answer, spoken in his usual dispassionate undertone, made it clear that it was so, but not precisely as flattering as I supposed. He thought me dangerous with Hermann, more than with the girl herself; but, as to quarrelling, I saw at once how inappropriate the word was. We had no quarrel. Natural forces are not quarrelsome. You can't quarrel with the wind that inconveniences and humiliates you by blowing off your hat in a street full of people. He had no quarrel with me. Neither would a boulder, falling on my head, have had. He fell upon me in accordance with the law by which he was moved—not of gravitation, like a detached stone, but of self-preservation. Of course this is giving it a rather wide interpretation. Strictly speaking, he had existed and could have existed without being married. Yet he told me that he had found it more and more difficult to live alone. Yes. He told me this in his low, careless voice, to such a pitch of confidence had we arrived at the end of half an hour.

It took me just about that time to convince him that I had never dreamed of marrying Hermann's niece. Could any necessity have been more extravagant? And the difficulty was the greater because he was so hard hit himself that he couldn't imagine anybody else being able to remain in a state of indifference. Any man with eyes in his head, he seemed to think, could not help coveting so much bodily magnificence. This profound belief was conveyed by the manner he listened sitting sideways to the table and playing absently with a few cards I had dealt to him at random. And the more I saw into him the more I saw of him. The wind swayed the lights so that his sunburnt face, whiskered to the eyes, seemed to successively flicker crimson at me and to go out. I saw the extraordinary breadth of the high cheek-bones, the perpendicular style of the features, the massive forehead, steep like a cliff, denuded at the top, largely uncovered at the temples. The fact is I had never before seen him without his hat; but now, as if my fervour had made him hot, he had taken it off and laid it gently on the floor. Something peculiar in the shape and setting of his yellow eyes gave them the provoking silent intensity which characterized his glance. But the face was thin, furrowed, worn; I discovered this through the bush of his hair, as you may detect the gnarled shape of a tree trunk in a dense undergrowth. These overgrown cheeks were sunken. It was an anchorite's bony head fitted with a Capuchin's beard and adjusted to a herculean body. I don't mean athletic. Hercules, I take it, was not an athlete. He was a strong man, susceptible to female charms, and not afraid of dirt. And thus with Falk, who was a strong man. He was extremely strong, just as the girl (since I must think of them together) was magnificently attractive by the masterful power of flesh and blood, expressed in shape, in size, in attitude—that is by a straight appeal to the senses. His mind meantime, preoccupied with respectability, quailed before Schomberg's tongue and seemed absolutely impervious to my protestations; and I went so far as to protest that I would just as soon think of marrying my mother's (dear old lady!) faithful female cook as Hermann's niece. Sooner, I protested, in my desperation, much sooner; but it did not appear that he saw anything outrageous in the proposition, and in his sceptical immobility he seemed to nurse the argument that at all events the cook was very, very far away. It must be said that, just before, I had gone wrong by appealing to the evidence of my manner whenever I called on board the *Diana*. I had never attempted to approach the girl, or to speak to her, or even to look at her in any marked way. Nothing could be clearer. But, as his own idea of—let us say—courting, seemed to consist precisely in sitting silently .for hours in the vicinity of the beloved object, that line of argument inspired him with distrust. Staring down his extended legs he let out a grunt—as much as to say, "That's all very fine, but you can't throw dust in *my* eyes."

As last I was exasperated into saying, "Why don't you put the matter at rest by talking to Hermann?" and I added, sneeringly: "You don't expect me perhaps to speak for you?"

To this he said, very loud for him, "Would you?"

And for the first time he lifted his head to look at me with wonder and incredulity. He lifted his head so sharply that there could be no mistake. I had touched a spring. I saw the whole extent of my opportunity, and could hardly believe in it.

"Why! Speak to . . . Well, of course," I proceeded very slowly, watching him with great attention, for, on my word, I feared a joke. "Not, perhaps, to the young lady herself. I can't speak German, you know. But . . ."

He interrupted me with the earnest assurance that Hermann had the highest opinion of me; and at once I felt the need for the greatest possible diplomacy at this juncture. So I demurred just enough to draw him on. Falk sat up, but except for a very noticeable enlargement of the pupils, till the irises of his eyes were reduced to two narrow yellow rings, his face, I should judge, was incapable of expressing excitement. "Oh, yes! Hermann did have the greatest . . ."

"Take up your cards. Here's Schomberg peeping at us through the blind!" I said.

We went through the motions of what might have been a game of écarté. Presently the intolerable scandalmonger withdrew, probably to inform the people in the billiard-room that we two were gambling on the verandah like mad.

We were not gambling, but it was a game; a game

in which I felt I held the winning cards. The stake,
roughly speaking, was the success of the voyage—for
me; and he, I apprehended, had nothing to lose. Our
intimacy matured rapidly, and before many words had
been exchanged I perceived that the excellent Hermann
had been making use of me. That simple and astute
Teuton had been, it seems, holding me up to Falk in
the light of a rival. I was young enough to be shocked
at so much duplicity. "Did he tell you that in so many
words?" I asked with indignation.

Hermann had not. He had given hints only; and
of course it had not taken very much to alarm Falk;
but, instead of declaring himself, he had taken steps to
remove the family from under my influence. He was
perfectly straightforward about it—as straightforward
as a tile falling on your head. There was no duplicity
in that man; and when I congratulated him on the
perfection of his arrangements—even to the bribing of
the wretched Johnson against me—he had a genuine
movement of protest. Never bribed. He knew the
man wouldn't work as long as he had a few cents in
his pocket to get drunk on, and, naturally (he said—
"*naturally*") he let him have a dollar or two. He was
himself a sailor, he said, and anticipated the view another sailor, like myself, was bound to take. On the
other hand, he was sure that I should have to come to
grief. He hadn't been knocking about for the last seven
years up and down that river for nothing. It would
have been no disgrace to me—but he asserted confidently I would have had my ship very awkwardly ashore
at a spot two miles below the Great Pagoda. . . .

And with all that he had no ill-will. That was evident. This was a crisis in which his only object had
been to gain time—I fancy. And presently he mentioned that he had written for some jewellery, real good

jewellery—had written to Hong-Kong for it. It would arrive in a day or two.

"Well, then," I said, cheerily, "everything is all right. All you've got to do is to present it to the lady together with your heart, and live happy ever after."

Upon the whole he seemed to accept that view as far as the girl was concerned, but his eyelids drooped. There was still something in the way. For one thing Hermann disliked him so much. As to me, on the contrary, it seemed as though he could not praise me enough. Mrs. Hermann, too. He didn't know why they disliked him so. It made everything most difficult.

I listened impassive, feeling more and more diplomatic. His speech was not transparently clear. He was one of those men who seem to live, feel, suffer in a sort of mental twilight. But as to being fascinated by the girl and possessed by the desire of home life with her—it was as clear as daylight. So much being at stake, he was afraid of putting it to the hazard of the declaration. Besides, there was something else. And with Hermann being so set against him . . .

"I see," I said, thoughtfully, while my heart beat fast with the excitement of my diplomacy. "I don't mind sounding Hermann. In fact, to show you how mistaken you were, I am ready to do all I can for you in that way."

A light sigh escaped him. He drew his hands down his face, and it emerged, bony, unchanged of expression, as if all the tissues had been ossified. All the passion was in those big brown hands. He was satisfied. Then there was that other matter. If there were anybody on earth it was I who could persuade Hermann to take a reasonable view! I had a knowledge of the world and lots of experience. Hermann admitted this

himself. And then I was a sailor, too. Falk thought
that a sailor would be able to understand certain things
best. . . .

He talked as if the Hermanns had been living all
their life in a rural hamlet, and I alone had been
capable, with my practice in life, of a large and indulgent view of certain occurrences. That was what my
diplomacy was leading me to. I began suddenly to
dislike it.

"I say, Falk," I asked quite brusquely, "you haven't
already a wife put away somewhere?"

The pain and disgust of his denial were very striking.
Couldn't I understand that he was as respectable as
any white man hereabouts; earning his living honestly.
He was suffering from my suspicion, and the low undertone of his voice made his protestations sound very
pathetic. For a moment he shamed me, but, my diplomacy notwithstanding, I seemed to develop a conscience, as if in very truth it were in my power to decide
the success of this matrimonial enterprise. By pretending hard enough we come to believe anything—anything to our advantage. And I had been pretending
very hard, because I meant yet to be towed safely down
the river. But, through conscience or stupidity, I
couldn't help alluding to the Vanlo affair. "You acted
rather badly there. Didn't you?" was what I ventured
actually to say—for the logic of our conduct is always at
the mercy of obscure and unforeseen impulses.

His dilated pupils swerved from my face, glancing at
the window with a sort of scared fury. We heard
behind the blinds the continuous and sudden clicking of
ivory, a jovial murmur of many voices, and Schomberg's
deep manly laugh.

"That confounded old woman of a hotel-keeper then
would never, never let it rest!" Falk exclaimed. Well,

yes! It had happened two years ago. When it came to the point he owned he couldn't make up his mind to trust Fred Vanlo—no sailor, a bit of a fool, too. He could not trust him, but, to stop his row, he had lent him enough money to pay all his debts before he left. I was greatly surprised to hear this. Then Falk could not be such a miser after all. So much the better for the girl. For a time he sat silent; then he picked up a card and while looking at it he said:

"You need not think of anything bad. It was an accident. I've been unfortunate once."

"Then in heaven's name say nothing about it."

As soon as these words were out of my mouth I fancied I had said something immoral. He shook his head negatively. It had to be told. He considered it proper that the relations of the lady should know. No doubt—I thought to myself—had Miss Vanlo not been thirty and damaged by the climate he would have found it possible to entrust Fred Vanlo with this confidence. And then the figure of Hermann's niece appeared before my mind's eye, with the wealth of her opulent form, her rich youth, her lavish strength. With that powerful and immaculate vitality, her girlish form must have shouted aloud of life to that man, whereas poor Miss Vanlo could only sing sentimental songs to the strumming of a piano.

"And that Hermann hates me, I know it!" he cried in his undertone, with a sudden recrudescence of anxiety. "I must tell them. It is proper that they should know. You would say so yourself."

He then murmured an utterly mysterious allusion to the necessity for peculiar domestic arrangements. Though my curiosity was excited I did not want to hear any of his confidences. I feared he might give me a piece of information that would make my assumed *rôle* of match-maker odious—however unreal it was. I was aware that he could have the girl for the asking; and keeping down a desire to laugh in his face, I expressed a confident belief in my ability to argue away Hermann's dislike for him. "I am sure I can make it all right," I said. He looked very pleased.

And when we rose not a word had been said about towage! Not a word! The game was won and the honour was safe. Oh! blessed white cotton umbrella! We shook hands, and I was holding myself with difficulty from breaking into a dance of joy when he came back, striding all the length of the verandah, and said doubtfully:

"I say, captain, I have your word? You—you—won't turn round?"

Heavens! The fright he gave me. Behind his tone of doubt there was something desperate and menacing. The infatuated ass. But I was equal to the situation.

"My dear Falk," I said, beginning to lie with a glibness and effrontery that amazed me even at the time—"confidence for confidence." (He had made no confidences.) "I will tell you that I am already engaged to an extremely charming girl at home, and so you understand . . ."

He caught my hand and wrung it in a crushing grip.

"Pardon me. I feel it every day more difficult to live alone . . ."

"On rice and fish," I interrupted smartly, giggling with the sheer nervousness of escaped danger.

He dropped my hand as if it had become suddenly red hot. A moment of profound silence ensued, as though something extraordinary had happened.

"I promise you to obtain Hermann's consent," I faltered out at last, and it seemed to me that he could not help seeing through that humbugging promise. "If there's anything else to get over I shall endeavour to stand by you," I conceded further, feeling somehow defeated and overborne; "but you must do your best yourself."

"I have been unfortunate once," he muttered, unemotionally, and turning his back on me he went away, thumping slowly the plank floor as if his feet had been shod with iron.

Next morning, however, he was lively enough as man-boat, a combination of splashing and shouting; of the insolent commotion below with the steady overbearing glare of the silent head-piece above. He turned us out most unnecessarily at an ungodly hour, but it was nearly eleven in the morning before he brought me up a cable's length from Hermann's ship. And he did it very badly, too, in a hurry, and nearly contriving to miss altogether the patch of good holding ground, because, forsooth, he had caught sight of Hermann's niece on the poop. And so did I; and probably as soon as he had seen her himself. I saw the modest, sleek glory of the tawny head, and the full, gray shape of the girlish print frock she filled so perfectly, so satisfactorily, with the seduction of unfaltering curves—a very nymph of Diana the Huntress. And *Diana* the ship sat, high-walled and as solid as an institution, on the smooth level of the water, the most uninspiring and respectable craft upon the seas, useful and ugly, devoted to the support of domestic virtues like any grocer's shop on shore. At once Falk steamed away; for there was some work for him to do. He would return in the evening.

He ranged close by us, passing out dead slow, without a hail. The beat of the paddle-wheels reverberating amongst the stony islets, as if from the ruined walls of a vast arena, filled the anchorage confusedly with the

clapping sounds as of a mighty and leisurely applause.
Abreast of Hermann's ship Falk stopped the engines;
and a profound silence reigned over the rocks, the shore
and the sea, for the time it took him to raise his hat
aloft before the nymph of the gray print frock. I had
snatched up my binoculars, and I can answer for it she
didn't stir a limb, standing by the rail shapely and
erect, with one of her hands grasping a rope at the
height of her head, while the way of the tug carried
slowly past her the lingering and profound homage of
the man. There was for me an enormous significance
in the scene, the sense of having witnessed a solemn
declaration. The die was cast. After such a manifestation he couldn't back out. And I reflected that it
was nothing whatever to me now. With a rush of
black smoke belching suddenly out of the funnel, and a
mad swirl of paddle-wheels provoking a burst of weird
and precipitated clapping, the tug shot out of the
desolate arena. The rocky islets lay on the sea like the
heaps of a cyclopean ruin on a plain; the centipedes and
scorpions lurked under the stones; there was not a
single blade of grass in sight anywhere, not a single
lizard sunning himself on a boulder by the shore. When
I looked again at Hermann's ship the girl had disappeared. I could not detect the smallest dot of a bird
on the immense sky, and the flatness of the land continued the flatness of the sea to the naked line of the
horizon.

This is the setting now inseparably connected with
my knowledge of Falk's misfortune. My diplomacy
had brought me there, and now I had only to wait the
time for taking up the *rôle* of an ambassador. My
diplomacy was a success; my ship was safe; old Gambril would probably live; a feeble sound of a tapping
hammer came intermittently from the *Diana*. During

the afternoon I looked at times at the old homely ship,
the faithful nurse of Hermann's progeny, or yawned
towards the distant temple of Buddha, like a lonely
hillock on the plain, where shaven priests cherish the
thoughts of that Annihilation which is the worthy reward of us all. Unfortunate! He had been unfortunate once. Well, that was not so bad as life goes.
And what the devil could be the nature of that misfortune? I remembered that I had known a man before who had declared himself to have fallen, years
ago, a victim to misfortune; but this misfortune, whose
effects appeared permanent (he looked desperately hard
up) when considered dispassionately, seemed indistinguishable from a breach of trust. Could it be something of that nature? Apart, however, from the utter
improbability that he would offer to talk of it even to
his future uncle-in-law I had a strange feeling that
Falk's physique unfitted him for that sort of delin-
quency. As the person of Hermann's niece exhaled the
profound physical charm of feminine form, so her
adorer's big frame embodied to my senses the hard,
straight masculinity that would conceivably kill but
would not condescend to cheat. The thing was obvious. I might just as well have suspected the girl of a
curvature of the spine. And I perceived that the sun
was about to set.

The smoke of Falk's tug hove in sight, far away at
the mouth of the river. It was time for me to assume
the character of an ambassador, and the negotiation
would not be difficult except in the matter of keeping
my countenance. It was all too extravagantly non-
sensical, and I conceived that it would be best to
compose for myself a grave demeanour. I practised
this in my boat as I went along, but the bashfulness
that came secretly upon me the moment I stepped on

the deck of the *Diana* is inexplicable. As soon as we
had exchanged greetings Hermann asked me eagerly if
I knew whether Falk had found his white parasol.

"He's going to bring it to you himself directly," I
said with great solemnity. "Meantime, I am charged
with an important message for which he begs your
favourable consideration. He is in love with your
niece. . . ."

"*Ach So !*" he hissed with an animosity that made
my assumed gravity change into the most genuine concern. What meant this tone? And I hurried on.

"He wishes, with your consent of course, to ask her
to marry him at once—before you leave here, that is.
He would speak to his Consul."

Hermann sat down and smoked violently. Five
minutes passed in that furious meditation, and then,
taking the long pipe out of his mouth, he burst into a
hot diatribe against Falk—against his cupidity, his
stupidity (a fellow that can hardly be got to say "yes"
or "no" to the simplest question)—against his outrageous treatment of the shipping in port (because he
saw they were at his mercy)—and against his manner
of walking, which to his (Hermann's) mind showed a
conceit positively unbearable. The damage to the
old *Diana* was not forgotten, of course, and there was
nothing of any nature said or done by Falk (even to
the last offer of refreshment in the hotel) that did not
seem to have been a cause of offence. "Had the cheek"
to drag him (Hermann) into that coffee-room; as though
a drink from him could make up for forty-seven dollars
and fifty cents of damage in the cost of wood alone—not
counting two days' work for the carpenter. Of course
he would not stand in the girl's way. He was going
home to Germany. There were plenty of poor girls
walking about in Germany.

"He's very much in love," was all I found to say.

"Yes," he cried. "And it is time, too, after making himself and me talked about ashore the last voyage I was here, and then now again; coming on board every evening unsettling the girl's mind, and saying nothing. What sort of conduct is that?"

The seven thousand dollars the fellow was always talking about did not, in his opinion, justify such behaviour. Moreover, nobody had seen them. He (Hermann) seriously doubted if Falk possessed seven thousand cents, and the tug, no doubt, was mortgaged up to the top of the funnel to the firm of Siegers. But let that pass. He wouldn't stand in the girl's way. Her head was so turned that she had become no good to them of late. Quite unable even to put the children to bed without her aunt. It was bad for the children; they got unruly; and yesterday he actually had to give Gustav a thrashing.

For that, too, Falk was made responsible apparently. And looking at my Hermann's heavy, puffy, good-natured face, I knew he would not exert himself till greatly exasperated, and, therefore, would thrash very hard, and being fat would resent the necessity. How Falk had managed to turn the girl's head was more difficult to understand. I supposed Hermann would know. And then hadn't there been Miss Vanlo? It could not be his silvery tongue, or the subtle seduction of his manner; he had no more of what is called "manner" than an animal—which, however, on the other hand, is never, and can never be called vulgar. Therefore it must have been his bodily appearance, exhibiting a virility of nature as exaggerated as his beard, and resembling a sort of constant ruthlessness. It was seen in the very manner he lolled in the chair. He meant no offence, but his intercourse was characterized by tha'

sort of frank disregard of susceptibilities a tall man,
living in a world of dwarfs, would naturally assume,
without in the least wishing to be unkind. But amongst
men of his own stature, or nearly, this frank use of his
advantages, in such matters as the awful towage bills
for instance, caused much impotent gnashing of teeth.
When attentively considered it seemed appalling at
times. He was a strange beast. But maybe women
liked it. Seen in that light he was well worth taming,
and I suppose every woman at the bottom of her heart
considers herself as a tamer of strange beasts. But
Hermann arose with precipitation to carry the news to
his wife. I had barely the time, as he made for the
cabin door, to grab him by the seat of his inexpressibles.
I begged him to wait till Falk in person had spoken with
him. There remained some small matter to talk over
as I understood.

He sat down again at once, full of suspicion.

"What matter?" he said, surlily. "I have had
enough of his nonsense. There's no matter at all, as
he knows very well; the girl has nothing in the world.
She came to us in one thin dress when my brother died,
and I have a growing family."

"It can't be anything of that kind," I opined. "He's
desperately enamoured of your niece. I don't know
why he did not say so before. Upon my word, I believe it is because he was afraid to lose, perhaps, the
felicity of sitting near her on your quarter-deck."

I intimated my conviction that Falk's love was so
great as to be in a sense cowardly. The effects of a
great passion are unaccountable. It has been known to
make a man timid. But Hermann looked at me as if
I had raved; and the twilight was dying out rapidly.

"You don't believe in passion, do you, Hermann?"
I continued, cheerily. "The passion of fear will make a

cornered rat courageous. Falk's in a corner. He will take her off your hands in one thin frock just as she came to you. And after ten years' service it isn't a bad bargain," I added.

Far from taking offence, he resumed his air of civic virtue. The sudden night came upon him while he stared placidly along the deck, bringing in contact with his thick lips, and taking away again after a jet of smoke, the curved mouthpiece fitted to the stem of his pipe. The night came upon him and buried in haste his whiskers, his globular eyes, his puffy pale face, his fat knees and the vast flat slippers on his fatherly feet. Only his short arms in respectable white shirt-sleeves remained very visible, propped up like the flippers of seal reposing on the strand.

"Falk wouldn't settle anything about repairs. Told me to find out first how much wood I should require and he would see," he remarked; and after he had spat peacefully in the dusk we heard over the water the beat of the tug's floats. There is, on a calm night, nothing more suggestive of fierce and headlong haste than the rapid sound made by the paddle-wheels of a boat threshing her way through a quiet sea; and the approach of Falk towards his fate seemed to be urged by an impatient and passionate desire. The engines must have been driven to the very utmost of their revolutions. We heard them slow down at last, and, vaguely, the white hull of the tug appeared moving against the black islets, whilst a slow and rhythmical clapping as of thousands of hands rose on all sides. It ceased all at once, just before Falk brought her up. A single brusque splash was followed by the long-drawn rumbling of iron links running through the hawse pipe. Then a solemn silence fell upon the Roadstead.

"He will soon be here," I murmured, and after that

we waited for him without a word. Meantime, raising
my eyes, I beheld the glitter of a lofty sky above the
Diana's mastheads. The multitude of stars gathered
into clusters, in rows, in lines, in masses, in groups,
shone all together, unanimously—and the few isolated
ones, blazing by themselves in the midst of dark
patches, seemed to be of a superior kind and of an inextinguishable nature. But long striding footsteps
were heard hastening along the deck; the high bulwarks of the *Diana* made a deeper darkness. We rose
from our chairs quickly, and Falk, appearing before us,
all in white, stood still.

Nobody spoke at first, as though we had been
covered with confusion. His arrival was fiery, but his
white bulk, of indefinite shape and without features,
made him loom up like a man of snow.

"The captain here has been telling me . . ."
Hermann began in a homely and amicable voice; and
Falk gave a low, nervous laugh. His cool, negligent
undertone had no inflexions, but the strength of a
powerful emotion made him ramble in his speech. He
had always desired a home. It was difficult to live
alone, though he was not answerable. He was domestic; there had been difficulties; but since he had seen
Hermann's niece he found that it had become at last
impossible to live by himself. "I mean—impossible,"
he repeated with no sort of emphasis and only with the
slightest of pauses, but the word fell into my mind with
the force of a new idea.

"I have not said anything to her yet," Hermann
observed, quietly. And Falk dismissed this by a
"That's all right. Certainly. Very proper." There
was a necessity for perfect frankness—in marrying,
especially. Hermann seemed attentive, but he seized
the first opportunity to ask us into the cabin. "And

by-the-by, Falk," he said, innocently, as we passed in,
"the timber came to no less than forty-seven dollars
and fifty cents."

Falk, uncovering his head, lingered in the passage.
"Some other time," he said; and Hermann nudged me
angrily—I don't know why. The girl alone in the
cabin sat sewing at some distance from the table.
Falk stopped short in the doorway. Without a word,
without a sign, without the slightest inclination of his
bony head, by the silent intensity of his look alone, he
seemed to lay his herculean frame at her feet. Her
hands sank slowly on her lap, and raising her clear eyes,
she let her soft, beaming glance enfold him from head to
foot like a slow and pale caress. He was very hot when
he sat down; she, with bowed head, went on with her
sewing; her neck was very white under the light of the
lamp; but Falk, hiding his face in the palms of his hands,
shuddered faintly. He drew them down, even to his
beard, and his uncovered eyes astonished me by their
tense and irrational expression—as though he had just
swallowed a heavy gulp of alcohol. It passed away
while he was binding us to secrecy. Not that he cared,
but he did not like to be spoken about; and I looked at
the girl's marvellous, at her wonderful, at her regal hair,
plaited tight into that one astonishing and maidenly
tress. Whenever she moved her well-shaped head it
would stir stiffly to and fro on her back. The thin
cotton sleeve fitted the irreproachable roundness of her
arm like a skin; and her very dress, stretched on her
bust, seemed to palpitate like a living tissue with the
strength of vitality animating her body. How good her
complexion was, the outline of her soft cheek and the
small convoluted conch of her rosy ear! To pull her
needle she kept the little finger apart from the others;
it seemed a waste of power to see her sewing—eternally

sewing—with that industrious and precise movement
of her arm, going on eternally upon all the oceans, under
all the skies, in innumerable harbours. And suddenly
I heard Falk's voice declare that he could not marry a
woman unless she knew of something in his life that had
happened ten years ago. It was an accident. An
unfortunate accident. It would affect the domestic
arrangements of their home, but, once told, it need not
be alluded to again for the rest of their lives. "I should
want my wife to feel for me," he said. "It has made me
unhappy." And how could he keep the knowledge of it
to himself—he asked us—perhaps through years and
years of companionship? What sort of companionship
would that be? He had thought it over. A wife must
know. Then why not at once? He counted on Hermann's kindness for presenting the affair in the best
possible light. And Hermann's countenance, mystified
before, became very sour. He stole an inquisitive
glance at me. I shook my head blankly. Some people
thought, Falk went on, that such an experience changed
a man for the rest of his life. He couldn't say. It was
hard, awful, and not to be forgotten, but he did not
think himself a worse man than before. Only he
talked in his sleep now, he believed. . . . At last
I began to think he had accidentally killed someone,
perhaps a friend—his own father maybe; when he went
on to say that probably we were aware he never touched
meat. Throughout he spoke English, of course on my
account.

He swayed forward heavily.

The girl, with her hands raised before her pale eyes,
was threading her needle. He glanced at her and his
mighty trunk overshadowed the table, bringing nearer
to us the breadth of his shoulders, the thickness of his
neck, and that incongruous, anchorite head, burnt in

the desert, hollowed and lean as if by excesses of vigils and fasting. His beard flowed imposingly downwards, out of sight, between the two brown hands gripping the edge of the table, and his persistent glance made sombre by the wide dilations of the pupils, fascinated.

"Imagine to yourselves," he said in his ordinary voice, "that I have eaten man."

I could only ejaculate a faint "Ah!" of complete enlightenment. But Hermann, dazed by the excessive shock, actually murmured, "Himmel! What for?"

"It was my terrible misfortune to do so," said Falk in a measured undertone. The girl, unconscious, sewed on. Mrs. Hermann was absent in one of the state-rooms, sitting up with Lena, who was feverish; but Hermann suddenly put both his hands up with a jerk. The embroidered calotte fell, and, in the twinkling of an eye, he had rumpled his hair all ends up in a most extravagant manner. In this state he strove to speak; with every effort his eyes seemed to start further out of their sockets; his head looked like a mop. He choked, gasped, swallowed, and managed to shriek out the one word, "Beast!"

From that moment till Falk went out of the cabin the girl, with her hands folded on the work lying in her lap, never took her eyes off him. His own, in the blindness of his heart, darted all over the cabin, only seeking to avoid the sight of Hermann's raving. It was ridiculous, and was made almost terrible by the stillness of every other person present. It was contemptible, and was made appalling by the man's overmastering horror of this awful sincerity, coming to him suddenly, with the confession of such a fact. He walked with great strides; he gasped. He wanted to know from Falk how dared he to come and tell him this? Did he think himself a proper person to be sitting in this cabin where his wife

and children lived? Tell his niece! Expected him to
tell his niece! His own brother's daughter! Shameless! Did I ever hear tell of such impudence?—he
appealed to me. "This man here ought to have gone
and hidden himself out of sight instead of . . ."

"But it's a great misfortune for me. But it's a great
misfortune for me," Falk would ejaculate from time to
time.

However, Hermann kept on running frequently
against the corners of the table. At last he lost a slipper, and crossing his arms on his breast, walked up with
one stocking foot very close to Falk, in order to ask him
whether he did think there was anywhere on earth a
woman abandoned enough to mate with such a monster. "Did he? Did he? Did he?" I tried to restrain him. He tore himself out of my hands; he found
his slipper, and, endeavouring to put it on, stormed
standing on one leg—and Falk, with a face unmoved
and averted eyes, grasped all his mighty beard in one
vast palm.

"Was it right then for me to die myself?" he asked,
thoughtfully. I laid my hand on his shoulder.

"Go away," I whispered, imperiously, without any
clear reason for this advice, except that I wished to
put an end to Hermann's odious noise. "Go away."

He looked searchingly for a moment at Hermann before he made a move. I left the cabin, too, to see him
out of the ship. But he hung about the quarter-deck.

"It is my misfortune," he said in a steady voice.

"You were stupid to blurt it out in such a manner.
After all, we don't hear such confidences every day."

"What does the man mean?" he mused in deep
undertones. "Somebody had to die—but why me?"

He remained still for a time in the dark—silent;
almost invisible. All at once he pinned my elbows to

my sides. I felt utterly powerless in his grip, and his voice, whispering in my ear, vibrated.

"It's worse than hunger. Captain, do you know what that means? And I could kill then—or be killed. I wish the crowbar had smashed my skull ten years ago. And I've got to live now. Without her. Do you understand? Perhaps many years. But how? What can be done? If I had allowed myself to look at her once I would have carried her off before that man in my hands—like this."

I felt myself snatched off the deck, then suddenly dropped—and I staggered backwards, feeling bewildered and bruised. What a man! All was still; he was gone. I heard Hermann's voice declaiming in the cabin, and went in.

I could not at first make out a single word, but Mrs. Hermann, who, attracted by the noise, had come in some time before, with an expression of surprise and mild disapproval depicted broadly on her face, was giving now all the signs of profound, helpless agitation. Her husband shot a string of guttural words at her, and instantly putting out one hand to the bulkhead as if to save herself from falling, she clutched the loose bosom of her dress with the other. He harangued the two women extraordinarily, with much of his shirt hanging out of his waistbelt, stamping his foot, turning from one to the other, sometimes flinging both his arms straight up above his rumpled hair and keeping them in that position while he uttered a passage of loud denunciation; at others folding them tight across his breast—and then he hissed with indignation, elevating his shoulders and protruding his head. The girl was crying.

She had not changed her attitude. From her steady eyes that, following Falk in his retreat, had remained fixed wistfully on the cabin door, the tears fell rapid, thick, on her hands, on the work in her lap, warm and gentle like a shower in spring. She wept without grimacing, without noise—very touching, very quiet, with something more of pity than of pain in her face, as one weeps in compassion rather than grief—and Hermann, before her, declaimed. I caught several times the word "Mensch," man; and also "Fressen," which last I looked up afterwards in my dictionary. It means "Devour." Hermann seemed to be requesting an answer of some sort from her; his whole body swayed. She remained mute and perfectly still; at last his agitation gained her; she put the palms of her hands together, her full lips parted, no sound came. His voice scolded shrilly, his arms went like a windmill—suddenly he shook his thick fist at her. She burst out into loud sobs. He seemed stupefied.

Mrs. Hermann rushed forward babbling rapidly.

The two women fell on each other's necks, and, with an arm round her niece's waist, she led her away. Her own eyes were simply streaming, her face was flooded. She shook her head back at me negatively, I wonder why to this day. The girl's head dropped heavily on her shoulder. They disappeared together.

Then Hermann sat down and stared at the cabin floor.

"We don't know all the circumstances," I ventured to break the silence. He retorted tartly that he didn't want to know of any. According to his ideas no circumstances could excuse a crime—and certainly not such a crime. This was the opinion generally received. The duty of a human being was to starve. Falk therefore was a beast, an animal; base, low, vile, despicable, shameless, and deceitful. He had been deceiving him since last year. He was, however, inclined to think that Falk must have gone mad quite recently; for no sane person, without necessity, uselessly, for no earthly reason, and regardless of another's self-respect and peace of mind, would own to having devoured human flesh. "Why tell?" he cried. "Who was asking him?" It showed Falk's brutality because after all he had selfishly caused him (Hermann) much pain. He would have preferred not to know that such an unclean creature had been in the habit of caressing his children. He hoped I would say nothing of all this ashore, though. He wouldn't like it to get about that he had been intimate with an eater of men—a common cannibal. As to the scene he had made (which I judged quite unnecessary) he was not going to inconvenience and restrain himself for a fellow that went about courting and upsetting girls' heads, while he knew all the time that no decent housewifely girl would think of marrying him. At least he (Hermann) could not conceive how any girl could. "Fancy Lena! . . . No, it was impossible. The thoughts that would come into their heads every time they sat down to a meal. Horrible! Horrible!"

"You are too squeamish, Hermann," I said.

He seemed to think it was eminently proper to be squeamish if the word meant disgust at Falk's conduct; and turning up his eyes sentimentally he drew my attention to the horrible fate of the victims—the victims of that Falk. I said that I knew nothing about them. He seemed surprised. Could not anybody imagine without knowing? He—for instance—felt he would like to avenge them. But what if—said I—there had not been any? They might have died as it were, naturally—of starvation. He shuddered. But to be eaten—after death! To be devoured! He gave another deep shudder, and asked suddenly, "Do you think it is true?"

His indignation and his personality together would have been enough to spoil the reality of the most authentic thing. When I looked at him I doubted the story—but the remembrance of Falk's words, looks, gestures, invested it not only with an air of reality but with the absolute truth of primitive passion.

"It is true just as much as you are able to make it; and exactly in the way you like to make it. For my part, when I hear you clamouring about it, I don't believe it is true at all."

And I left him pondering. The men in my gig lying at the foot of *Diana's* side-ladder, told me that the captain of the tug had gone away in his boat some time ago.

I let my fellows pull an easy stroke; because of the heavy dew the clear sparkle of the stars seemed to fall on me cold and wetting. There was a sense of lurking gruesome horror somewhere in my mind, and it was mingled with clear and grotesque images. Schomberg's gastronomic tittle-tattle was responsible for these; and I half hoped I should never see Falk again. But the first thing my anchor-watchman told me was that the captain of the tug was on board. He had sent his boat away and was now waiting for me in the cuddy.

He was lying full length on the stern settee, his face buried in the cushions. I had expected to see it discomposed, contorted, despairing. It was nothing of the kind; it was just as I had seen it twenty times, steady and glaring from the bridge of the tug. It was immovably set and hungry, dominated like the whole man by the singleness of one instinct.

He wanted to live. He had always wanted to live. So we all do—but in us the instinct serves a complex conception, and in him this instinct existed alone. There is in such simple development a gigantic force, and like the pathos of a child's naïve and uncontrolled desire. He wanted that girl, and the utmost that can be said for him was that he wanted that particular girl alone. I think I saw then the obscure beginning, the seed germinating in the soil of an unconscious need, the first shoot of that tree bearing now for a mature mankind the flower and the fruit, the infinite gradation in shades and in flavour of our discriminating love. He was a child. He was as frank as a child, too. He was hungry for the girl, terribly hungry, as he had been terribly hungry for food.

Don't be shocked if I declare that in my belief it was the same need, the same pain, the same torture. We are in his case allowed to contemplate the foundation of all the emotions—that one joy which is to live, and the one sadness at the root of the innumerable torments. It was made plain by the way he talked. He had never suffered so. It was gnawing, it was fire; it was there, like this! And after pointing below his breastbone, he made a hard wringing motion with his hands. And I assure you that, seen as I saw it with my bodily eyes, it was anything but laughable. And again, as he was presently to tell me (alluding to an early incident of the disastrous voyage when some damaged meat had been flung overboard), he said that a time soon came when his heart ached (that was the expression he used), and he was ready to tear his hair out at the thought of all that rotten beef thrown away.

I heard all this; I witnessed his physical struggles, seeing the working of the rack and hearing the true voice of pain. I witnessed it all patiently, because the moment I came into the cuddy he had called upon me to stand by him—and this, it seems, I had diplomatically promised.

His agitation was impressive and alarming in the

little cabin, like the floundering of a great whale driven into a shallow cove in a coast. He stood up; he flung himself down headlong; he tried to tear the cushion with his teeth; and again hugging it fiercely to his face he let himself fall on the couch. The whole ship seemed to feel the shock of his despair; and I contemplated with wonder the lofty forehead, the noble touch of time on the uncovered temples, the unchanged hungry character of the face—so strangely ascetic and so incapable of portraying emotion.

What should he do? He had lived by being near her. He had sat—in the evening—I knew?—all his life! She sewed. Her head was bent—so. Her head—like this—and her arms. Ah! Had I seen? Like this.

He dropped on a stool, bowed his powerful neck whose nape was red, and with his hands stitched the air, ludicrous, sublimely imbecile and comprehensible.

And now he couldn't have her? No! That was too much. After thinking, too, that . . . What had he done? What was my advice? Take her by force? No? Mustn't he? Who was there to stop him? For the first time I saw one of his features move; a fighting teeth-baring curl of the lip. . . . "Not Hermann, perhaps." He lost himself in thought as though he had fallen out of the world.

I may note that the idea of suicide apparently did not enter his head for a single moment. It occurred to me to ask:

"Where was it that this shipwreck of yours took place?"

"Down south," he said, vaguely, with a start.

"You are not down south now," I said. "Violence won't do. They would take her away from you in no time. And what was the name of the ship?"

"*Borgmester Dahl*," he said. "It was no shipwreck."

He seemed to be waking up by degrees from that trance, and waking up calmed.

"Not a shipwreck? What was it?"

"Break down," he answered, looking more like himself every moment. By this only I learned that it was a steamer. I had till then supposed they had been starving in boats or on a raft—or perhaps on a barren rock.

"She did not sink then?" I asked in surprise. He nodded. "We sighted the southern ice," he pronounced, dreamily.

"And you alone survived?"

He sat down. "Yes. It was a terrible misfortune for me. Everything went wrong. All the men went wrong. I survived."

Remembering the things one reads of it was difficult to realize the true meaning of his answers. I ought to have seen at once—but I did not; so difficult is it for our minds, remembering so much, instructed so much, informed of so much, to get in touch with the real actuality at our elbow. And with my head full of preconceived notions as to how a case of "Cannibalism and suffering at sea" should be managed I said—"You were then so lucky in the drawing of lots?"

"Drawing of lots?" he said. "What lots? Do you think I would have allowed my life to go for the drawing of lots?"

Not if he could help it, I perceived, no matter what other life went.

"It was a great misfortune. Terrible. Awful," he said. "Many heads went wrong, but the best men would live."

"The toughest, you mean," I said. He considered the word. Perhaps it was strange to him, though his English was so good.

"Yes," he asserted at last. "The best. It was everybody for himself at last and the ship open to all."

Thus from question to question I got the whole story. I fancy it was the only way I could that night have stood by him. Outwardly at least he was himself again; the first sign of it was the return of that incongruous trick he had of drawing both his hands down his face—and it had its meaning now, with that slight shudder of the frame and the passionate anguish of these hands uncovering a hungry immovable face, the wide pupils of the intent, silent, fascinating eyes.

It was an iron steamer of a most respectable origin. The burgomaster of Falk's native town had built her. She was the first steamer ever launched there. The burgomaster's daughter had christened her. Country people drove in carts from miles around to see her. He told me all this. He got the berth as, what we would call, chief mate. He seemed to think it had been a feather in his cap; and, in his own corner of the world, this lover of life was of good parentage.

The burgomaster had advanced ideas in the ship-owning line. At that time not everyone would have known enough to think of despatching a cargo steamer to the Pacific. But he loaded her with pitch-pine deals and sent her off to hunt for her luck. Wellington was to be the first port, I fancy. It doesn't matter, because in latitude 44° south and somewhere halfway between Good Hope and New Zealand the tail-shaft broke and the propeller dropped off.

They were steaming then with a fresh gale on the quarter and all their canvas set, to help the engines. But by itself the sail power was not enough to keep way on her. When the propeller went the ship broached-to at once, and the masts got whipped overboard.

The disadvantage of being dismasted consisted in

this, that they had nothing to hoist flags on to make themselves visible at a distance. In the course of the first few days several ships failed to sight them; and the gale was drifting them out of the usual track. The voyage had been, from the first, neither very successful nor very harmonious. There had been quarrels on board. The captain was a clever, melancholic man, who had no unusual grip on his crew. The ship had been amply provisioned for the passage, but, somehow or other, several barrels of meat were found spoiled on opening, and had been thrown overboard soon after leaving home, as a sanitary measure. Afterwards the crew of the *Borgmester Dahl* thought of that rotten carrion with tears of regret, covetousness and despair.

She drove south. To begin with, there had been an appearance of organization, but soon the bonds of discipline became relaxed. A sombre idleness succeeded. They looked with sullen eyes at the horizon. The gales increased, she lay in the trough and the seas made a clean breach over her. One frightful night, when they expected their hulk to turn over with them every moment, a heavy sea broke on board, deluged the store-rooms and spoiled the best part of the remaining provisions. It seems the hatch had not been properly secured. This instance of neglect is characteristic of utter discouragement. Falk tried to inspire some energy into his captain, but failed. From that time he retired more into himself, always trying to do his utmost in the situation. It grew worse. Gale succeeded gale, with black mountains of water hurling themselves on the *Borgmester Dahl*. Some of the men never left their bunks; many became quarrelsome. The chief-engineer, an old man, refused to speak at all to anybody. Others shut themselves up in their berths to cry. On calm days the inert steamer rolled on a leaden sea under a murky sky, or showed, in sunshine, the squalor of sea waifs, the dried white salt, the rust, the jagged broken places. Then the gales came again. They kept body and soul together on short rations. Once, an English ship, scudding in a storm, tried to stand by them, heaving-to pluckily under their lee. The seas swept her decks; the men in oilskins clinging to her rigging looked at them, and they made desperate signs over their shattered bulwarks. Suddenly her main-topsail went, yard and all, in a terrific squall; she had to bear up under bare poles and disappeared.

Other ships had spoken them before, but at first they had refused to be taken off, expecting the assistance of some steamer. There were very few steamers in those latitudes then; and when they desired to leave this dead and drifting carcase, no ship came in sight. They had drifted south out of men's knowledge. They failed to attract the attention of a lonely whaler: and very soon the edge of the polar ice-cap rose from the sea and closed the southern horizon like a wall. One morning they were alarmed by finding themselves floating amongst detached pieces of ice. But the fear of sinking passed away like their vigour, like their hopes; the shocks of the floes knocking against the ship's side could not rouse them from their apathy: and the *Borgmester Dahl* drifted out again, unharmed, into open water. They hardly noticed the change.

The funnel had gone overboard in one of the heavy rolls; two of their three boats had disappeared, washed away in bad weather, and the davits swung to and fro, unsecured, with chafed rope's ends waggling to the roll. Nothing was done on board, and Falk told me how he had often listened to the water washing about the dark engine-room where the engines, stilled for ever, were

decaying slowly into a mass of rust, as the stilled heart
decays within the lifeless body. At first, after the loss
of the motive power, the tiller had been thoroughly
secured by lashings. But in course of time these had
rotted, chafed, rusted, parting one by one; and the
rudder, freed, banged heavily to and fro night and day,
sending dull shocks through the whole frame of the
vessel. This was dangerous. Nobody cared enough to
lift a little finger. He told me that even now sometimes waking up at night, he fancied he could hear the
dull vibrating thuds. The pintles carried away, and it
dropped off at last.

The final catastrophe came with the sending off of
their one remaining boat. It was Falk who had
managed to preserve her intact, and now it was agreed
that some of the hands should sail away into the track
of the shipping to procure assistance. She was provisioned with all the food they could spare for the six
who were to go. They waited for a fine day. It was
long in coming. At last one morning they lowered her
into the water.

Directly, in that demoralized crowd, trouble broke
out. Two men who had no business there had jumped
into the boat under the pretence of unhooking the
tackles, while some sort of squabble arose on the deck
amongst these weak, tottering spectres of a ship's
company. The captain, who had been for days living
secluded and unapproachable in the chart-room, came
to the rail. He ordered the two men to come up on
board and threatened them with his revolver. They
pretended to obey, but suddenly cutting the boat's
painter, gave a shove against the ship's side and made
ready to hoist the sail.

"Shoot, sir! Shoot them down!" cried Falk—"and I
will jump overboard to regain the boat." But the

captain, after taking aim with an irresolute arm, turned
suddenly away.

A howl of rage arose. Falk dashed into his cabin
for his own pistol. When he returned it was too late.
Two more men had leaped into the water, but the fellows in the boat beat them off with the oars, hoisted the
boat's lug and sailed away. They were never heard
of again.

Consternation and despair possessed the remaining
ship's company, till the apathy of utter hopelessness
re-asserted its sway. That day a fireman committed
suicide, running up on deck with his throat cut from
ear to ear, to the horror of all hands. He was thrown
overboard. The captain had locked himself in the
chart-room, and Falk, knocking vainly for admittance,
heard him reciting over and over again the names of
his wife and children, not as if calling upon them or
commending them to God, but in a mechanical voice
like an exercise of memory. Next day the doors of
the chart-room were swinging open to the roll of the
ship, and the captain had disappeared. He must during
the night have jumped into the sea. Falk locked both
the doors and kept the keys.

The organized life of the ship had come to an end.
The solidarity of the men had gone. They became indifferent to each other. It was Falk who took in hand
the distribution of such food as remained. Sometimes
whispers of hate were heard passing between the languid
skeletons that drifted endlessly to and fro, north and
south, east and west, upon that carcase of a ship.

And in this lies the grotesque horror of this sombre
story. The last extremity of sailors, overtaking a small
boat or a frail craft, seems easier to bear, because of the
direct danger of the seas. The confined space, the close
contact, the imminent menace of the waves, seem to

draw men together, in spite of madness, suffering and despair. But there was a ship—safe, convenient, roomy: a ship with beds, bedding, knives, forks, comfortable cabins, glass and china, and a complete cook's galley, pervaded, ruled and possessed by the pitiless spectre of starvation. The lamp oil had been drunk, the wicks cut up for food, the candles eaten. At night she floated dark in all her recesses and full of fears. One day Falk came upon a man gnawing a splinter of pine wood. Suddenly he threw the piece of wood away, tottered to the rail, and fell over. Falk, too late to prevent the act, saw him claw the ship's side desperately before he went down. Next day another man did the same thing, after uttering horrible imprecations. But this one somehow managed to get hold of the broken rudder chains and hung on there, silently. Falk set about trying to save him, and all the time the man, holding with both hands, looked at him anxiously with his sunken eyes. Then, just as Falk was ready to put his hand on him, the man let go his hold and sank like a stone. Falk reflected on these sights. His heart revolted against the horror of death, and he said to himself that he would struggle for every precious minute of his life.

One afternoon—as the survivors lay about on the after-deck—the carpenter, a tall man with a black beard, spoke of the last sacrifice. There was nothing eatable left on board. Nobody said a word to this; but that company separated quickly, these listless feeble spectres slunk off one by one to hide in fear of each other. Falk and the carpenter remained on deck together. Falk liked the big carpenter. He had been the best man of the lot, helpful and ready as long as there was anything to do, the longest hopeful, and had preserved to the last some vigour and decision of mind.

They did not speak to each other. Henceforth no voices were to be heard conversing sadly on board that ship. After a time the carpenter tottered away forward; but later in the day Falk going to drink at the fresh-water pump, had the inspiration to turn his head. The carpenter had stolen upon him from behind, and, summoning all his strength, was aiming with a crowbar a blow at the back of his skull.

Dodging just in time, Falk made his escape and ran into his cabin. While he was loading his revolver there, he heard the sound of heavy blows struck upon the bridge. The locks of the chart-room doors were slight, they flew open, and the carpenter, possessing himself of the captain's revolver, fired a shot of defiance.

Falk was about to go on deck and have it out at once, when he remarked that one of the ports of his cabin commanded the approaches to the fresh-water pump. Instead of going out he stayed within and secured the door. "The best man shall survive," he said to himself —and the other, he reasoned, must at some time or other come there to drink. These starving men would drink often to cheat the pangs of their hunger. But the carpenter, too, must have noticed the position of the port. They were the two best men in the ship, and the game was with them. All the rest of the day Falk saw no one and heard no sound. At night he strained his eyes. It was dark—he heard a rustling noise once, but he was certain that no one could have come near the pump. It was to the left of his deck port, and he could not have failed to see a man, for the night was clear and starry. He saw nothing; towards morning another faint noise made him suspicious. Deliberately and quietly he unlocked his door. He had not slept, and had not given way to the horror of the situation. He wanted to live.

But during the night the carpenter, without even trying to approach the pump, had managed to creep
quietly along the starboard bulwark, and, unseen, had
crouched down right under Falk's deck port. When
daylight came he rose up suddenly, looked in, and
putting his arm through the round, brass-framed opening, fired at Falk within a foot. He missed—and Falk,
instead of attempting to seize the arm holding the
weapon, opened his door unexpectedly, and with the
muzzle of his revolver nearly touching the other's side,
shot him dead.

The best man had survived. Both of them had at
the beginning just strength enough to stand on their
feet, and both had displayed pitiless resolution, endurance, cunning and courage—all the qualities of classic
heroism. At once Falk threw overboard the captain's
revolver. He was a born monopolist. Then after the
report of the two shots, followed by a profound silence,
there crept out into the cold, cruel dawn of Antarctic
regions, from various hiding-places, over the deck of
that dismantled corpse of a ship floating on a gray sea
ruled by iron necessity and with a heart of ice—there
crept into view one by one, cautious, slow, eager, glaring, and unclean, a band of hungry and livid skeletons.
Falk faced them, the possessor of the only fire-arm on
board; and the second best man—the carpenter—was
lying dead between him and them.

"He was eaten, of course," I said.

Falk bent his head slowly, shuddered a little, drawing
his hands over his face, and said, "I had never any
quarrel with that man. But there were our lives between him and me."

Why continue the story of that ship, that story before which—with its fresh-water pump like a spring of
death, its man with the weapon, the sea ruled by iron

necessity, its spectral band swayed by terror and hope, its mute and unhearing heaven—the fable of the *Flying Dutchman* with its convention of crime and its sentimental retribution fades like a graceful wreath, like a wisp of white mist. What is there to say that everyone of us cannot guess for himself? I believe Falk began by going through the ship, revolver in hand, to annex all the matches. Those starving wretches had plenty of matches! He had no mind to have the ship set on fire under his feet, either from hate or from despair. He lived in the open, camping on the bridge, commanding all the after-deck and the only approach to the pump. He lived! Some of the others lived, too—concealed, anxious, coming out one by one from their hiding-places at the seductive sound of a shot. And he was not selfish. They shared all alike. But only three of them all remained alive when a whaler, returning from her cruising-ground, nearly ran over the waterlogged hull of the *Borgmester Dahl*, which, it seems, in the end had in some way sprung a leak in both her holds, but being loaded with deals could not sink.

"They all died," Falk said. "These three, too, afterwards. But I would not die. All died, all! under this terrible misfortune. But was I, too, to throw away my life? Could I? Tell me, captain? I was alone there, quite alone, just like the others. Each man was alone, Was I to give up my revolver? Who to? Or was I to throw it into the sea? What would have been the good? Only the best man would survive. It was a great, terrible, and cruel misfortune."

He had survived! I saw him before me as though preserved for a witness to the mighty truth of an unerring and eternal principle. Great beads of perspiration stood on his forehead. And suddenly it struck the table with a heavy blow, as he fell forward throwing his hands out.

"And this is worse," he cried. "This is a worse pain! This is more terrible."

He made my heart thump with the profound conviction of his cry. And after he had left me to go on board his ship I called up before my mental eye the image of the girl weeping silently, abundantly, patiently, and as if irresistibly. I thought of her tawny hair. I thought how, if unplaited, it would have covered her all round as low as the hips, like the hair of a siren. And she had bewitched him. Fancy a man who would guard his own life with the inflexibility of a pitiless and immovable fate, being brought to lament that once a crowbar had missed his skull! The sirens sing and lure to death, but this one had been weeping silently as if for the pity of his life. She was the tender and voiceless siren of this appalling navigator. He evidently wanted to live his whole conception of life. Nothing else would do. And she, too, was a servant of that life that, in the midst of death, cries aloud to our senses. She was eminently fitted to interpret for him its feminine side. And in her own way, and with her own profusion of sensuous charms she also seemed to illustrate the eternal truth of an unerring principle. I don't know though what sort of principle Hermann illustrated when he turned up early on board my ship with a most perplexed air. It struck me, however, that he, too, would do his best to survive. He seemed greatly calmed on the subject of Falk, but still very full of it.

"What is it you said I was last night? You know—" he asked after some preliminary talk. "Too—too—I don't know. A very funny word."

"Squeamish?" I suggested.

"Yes. What does it mean?"

"That you exaggerate things—to yourself. Without inquiry, and so on."

He seemed to turn it over in his mind. We went on talking. This Falk was the plague of his life. Upsetting everybody like this! Mrs. Hermann was unwell this morning. His niece was crying still. There was nobody to look after the children. He struck his umbrella on the deck. The girl would be like that for months. Fancy carrying all the way home, second class, a perfectly useless girl who is crying all the time. It was bad for Lena, too, he observed; but on what grounds I could not guess. Perhaps of the bad example. That child was already sorrowing and crying enough over the rag doll. Nicholas was really the least sentimental person of the family.

"Why does your niece weep?" I asked.

"From pity," cried Hermann.

It was impossible to make out women. Mrs. Hermann was the only one he pretended to understand. She was very, very upset and doubtful.

"Doubtful about what?" I asked.

He averted his eyes and did not answer this. It was impossible to make women out. For instance, his niece was weeping for Falk. Now he (Hermann) would like to wring his neck—but then . . . He supposed he had too tender a heart. "Frankly," he asked at last, "what do you think of what we heard last night, captain?"

"In all these tales," I observed, "there is always a good deal of exaggeration."

And not letting him recover from his surprise I assured him that I knew all the details. He begged me not to repeat them. His heart was too tender. They would make him feel unwell. Then, looking at his feet and speaking very slowly, he supposed that he need not see much of them after they were married. For, indeed, he could not bear the sight of Falk. On the other hand, it was ridiculous to take home a girl with her head turned. A girl that weeps all the time and is of no help to her aunt.

"Now you will be able to do with one cabin only on your passage home," I said.

"Yes, I had thought of that," he said brightly, almost. Yes! Himself, his wife, four children—one cabin might do. Whereas if his niece went . . .

"And what does Mrs. Hermann say to it?" I inquired.

Mrs. Hermann did not know whether a man of that sort could make a girl happy—she had been greatly deceived in Captain Falk. She had passed a very bad night.

Those good people did not seem to be able to retain an impression for a whole twelve hours. I assured him on my own personal knowledge that Falk possessed in himself all the qualities to make his niece's future prosperous. He said he was glad to hear this, and that he would tell his wife. Then the object of the visit came out. He wished me to help him to resume relations with Falk. His niece, he said, had expressed the hope I would do so in my kindness. He was evidently anxious that I should, for though he seemed to have forgotten nine-tenths of his last night's opinions and the whole of his indignation, yet he evidently feared to be sent to the right-about. "You told me he was very much in love," he concluded, slyly, and leered in a sort of bucolic way.

As soon as he had left my ship I called Falk on board by signal—the tug still lying at the anchorage. He took the news with calm gravity, as though he had all along trusted the stars to fight for him in their courses.

I saw them once more together, and only once—on the quarter-deck of the *Diana*. Hermann sat smoking with a shirt-sleeved elbow hooked over the back of his chair. Mrs. Hermann was sewing alone. As Falk stepped over the gangway, Hermann's niece, with a slight swish of the skirt and a friendly nod to me, glided past my chair.

Those two met in sunshine abreast of the mainmast. He held her hands and looked down at them, and she looked up at him with her candid and unseeing glance. It seemed to me they had come together as if attracted, drawn and guided to each other by a mysterious influence. They were a complete couple. In her gray frock, palpitating with life, generous of form, olympian and simple, she was indeed the siren to fascinate that dark navigator, this ruthless lover of the five senses. From afar I seemed to feel the masculine strength with which he grasped those hands she had extended to him with a womanly swiftness. Lena, a little pale, nursing her beloved lump of dirty rags, ran towards her big friend; and then in the drowsy silence of the good old ship Mrs. Hermann's voice rang out so changed that it made me spin round in my chair to see what was the matter.

"Lena, come here!" she screamed. And this good-natured matron gave me a wavering glance, dark and full of fearsome distrust. The child ran back, surprised, to her knee. But the two, standing before each other in sunlight with clasped hands, had heard nothing, had seen nothing and no one. Three feet away from them, in the shade, a seaman sat on a spar, very busy splicing a strop and dipping his fingers into a tar-pot, as if utterly unaware of their existence.

When I returned in command of another vessel some five years afterwards, Mr. and Mrs. Falk had left the place. I shouldn't wonder if Schomberg's tongue had succeeded at last in scaring Falk away for good; and, indubitably, there was some vague tale still going about the town of a certain Falk, owner of a tug, who had won his wife at cards from the captain of an English ship.

TO–MORROW

TO-MORROW

WHAT was known of Captain Hagberd in the little seaport of Colebrook was not exactly in his favour. He did not belong to the place. He had come to settle there under circumstances not at all mysterious—he used to be very communicative about them at the time —but extremely morbid and unreasonable. He was possessed of some little money evidently, because he bought a plot of ground, and had a pair of ugly yellow brick cottages run up very cheaply. He occupied one of them himself and let the other to Josiah Carvil— blind Carvil, the retired boat-builder—a man of evil repute as a domestic tyrant.

These cottages had one wall in common, shared in a line of iron railing dividing their front gardens; a wooden fence separated their back gardens. Miss Bessie Carvil was allowed, as it were of right, to throw over it the tea-cloths, blue rags, or an apron that wanted drying.

"It rots the wood, Bessie my girl," the captain would remark mildly, from his side of the fence, each time he saw her exercising that privilege.

She was a tall girl; the fence was low, and she could spread her elbows on the top. Her hands would be red with the bit of washing she had done, but her fore arms were white and shapely, and she would look at her father's landlord in silence—in an informed silence, which had an air of knowledge, expectation and desire.

"It rots the wood," repeated Captain Hagberd. "It is the only unthrifty, careless habit I know in you.

Why don't you have a clothes line out in your back yard?"

Miss Carvil would say nothing to this—she only shook her head negatively. The tiny back yard on her side had a few stone-bordered little beds of black earth, in which the simple flowers she found time to cultivate appeared somehow extravagantly overgrown, as if belonging to an exotic clime; and Captain Hagberd's upright, hale person, clad in No. 1 sail-cloth from head to foot, would be emerging knee-deep out of rank grass and the tall weeds on his side of the fence. He appeared, with the colour and uncouth stiffness of the extraordinary material in which he chose to clothe himself—"for the time being," would be his mumbled remark to any observation on the subject—like a man roughened out of granite, standing in a wilderness not big enough for a decent billiard-room. A heavy figure of a man of stone, with a red handsome face, a blue wandering eye, and a great white beard flowing to his waist and never trimmed as far as Colebrook knew.

Seven years before, he had seriously answered, "Next month, I think," to the chaffing attempt to secure his custom made by that distinguished local wit, the Colebrook barber, who happened to be sitting insolently in the tap-room of the New Inn near the harbour, where the captain had entered to buy an ounce of tobacco. After paying for his purchase with three half-pence extracted from the corner of a handkerchief which he carried in the cuff of his sleeve, Captain Hagberd went out. As soon as the door was shut the barber laughed. "The old one and the young one will be strolling arm in arm to get shaved in my place presently. The tailor shall be set to work, and the barber, and the candlestick maker; high old times are coming for Colebrook, they are coming, to be sure.

It used to be 'next week,' now it has come to 'next month,' and so on—soon it will be 'next spring,' for all I know."

Noticing a stranger listening to him with a vacant grin, he explained, stretching out his legs cynically, that this queer old Hagberd, a retired coasting-skipper, was waiting for the return of a son of his. The boy had been driven away from home, he shouldn't wonder, had run away to sea and had never been heard of since. Put to rest in Davy Jones's locker this many a day, as likely as not. That old man came flying to Colebrook three years ago all in black broadcloth (had lost his wife lately then), getting out of a third-class smoker as if the devil had been at his heels; and the only thing that brought him down was a letter—a hoax probably. Some joker had written to him about a seafaring man with some such name who was supposed to be hanging about some girl or other, either in Colebrook or in the neighbourhood. "Funny, ain't it?" The old chap had been advertising in the London papers for Harry Hagberd, and offering rewards for any sort of likely information. And the barber would go on to describe with sardonic gusto, how that stranger in mourning had been seen exploring the country, in carts, on foot, taking everybody into his confidence, visiting all the inns and alehouses for miles around, stopping people on the road with his questions, looking into the very ditches almost; first in the greatest excitement, then with a plodding sort of perseverance, growing slower and slower; and he could not even tell you plainly how his son looked. The sailor was supposed to be one of two that had left a timber ship, and to have been seen dangling after some girl; but the old man described a boy of fourteen or so—"a clever-looking, high-spirited boy." And when people only smiled at this

he would rub his forehead in a confused sort of way
before he slunk off, looking offended. He found nobody, of course; not a trace of anybody—never heard of
anything worth belief, at any rate; but he had not been
able somehow to tear himself away from Colebrook.

"It was the shock of this disappointment, perhaps,
coming soon after the loss of his wife, that had driven
him crazy on that point," the barber suggested, with
an air of great psychological insight. After a time the
old man abandoned the active search. His son had
evidently gone away; but he settled himself to wait.
His son had been once at least in Colebrook in pref-
erence to his native place. There must have been some
reason for it, he seemed to think, some very powerful
inducement, that would bring him back to Colebrook
again.

"Ha, ha, ha! Why, of course, Colebrook. Where
else? That's the only place in the United Kingdom
for your long-lost sons. So he sold up his old home in
Colchester, and down he comes here. Well, it's a
craze, like any other. Wouldn't catch me going crazy
over any of my youngsters clearing out. I've got eight
of them at home." The barber was showing off his
strength of mind in the midst of a laughter that shook
the tap-room.

Strange, though, that sort of thing, he would confess,
with the frankness of a superior intelligence, seemed
to be catching. His establishment, for instance, was
near the harbour, and whenever a sailorman came in
for a hair-cut or a shave—if it was a strange face he
couldn't help thinking directly, "Suppose he's the son of
old Hagberd!" He laughed at himself for it. It was a
strong craze. He could remember the time when the
whole town was full of it. But he had his hopes of
the old chap yet. He would cure him by a course of

judicious chaffing. He was watching the progress of the treatment. Next week—next month—next year! When the old skipper had put off the date of that return till next year, he would be well on his way to not saying any more about it. In other matters he was quite rational, so this, too, was bound to come. Such was the barber's firm opinion.

Nobody had ever contradicted him; his own hair had gone gray since that time, and Captain Hagberd's beard had turned quite white, and had acquired a majestic flow over the No. 1 canvas suit, which he had made for himself secretly with tarred twine, and had assumed suddenly, coming out in it one fine morning, whereas the evening before he had been seen going home in his mourning of broadcloth. It caused a sensation in the High Street—shopkeepers coming to their doors, people in the houses snatching up their hats to run out—a stir at which he seemed strangely surprised at first, and then scared; but his only answer to the wondering questions was that startled and evasive, "For the present."

That sensation had been forgotten, long ago; and Captain Hagberd himself, if not forgotten had come to be disregarded—the penalty of dailiness—as the sun itself is disregarded unless it makes its power felt heavily. Captain Hagberd's movements showed no infirmity: he walked stiffly in his suit of canvas, a quaint and remarkable figure; only his eyes wandered more furtively perhaps than of yore. His manner abroad had lost its excitable watchfulness; it had become puzzled and diffident, as though he had suspected that there was somewhere about him something slightly compromising, some embarrassing oddity; and yet had remained unable to discover what on earth this something wrong could be.

He was unwilling now to talk with the townsfolk.
He had earned for himself the reputation of an awful
skinflint, of a miser in the matter of living. He
mumbled regretfully in the shops, bought inferior
scraps of meat after long hesitations; and discouraged
all allusions to his costume. It was as the barber had
foretold. For all one could tell, he had recovered already from the disease of hope; and only Miss Bessie
Carvil knew that he said nothing about his son's return because with him it was no longer "next week,"
"next month," or even "next year." It was "to-
morrow."

In their intimacy of back yard and front garden he
talked with her paternally, reasonably, and dogmatically, with a touch of arbitrariness. They met on the
ground of unreserved confidence, which was authenti-
cated by an affectionate wink now and then. Miss
Carvil had come to look forward rather to these winks.
At first they had discomposed her: the poor fellow was
mad. Afterwards she had learned to laugh at them:
there was no harm in him. Now she was aware of
an unacknowledged, pleasurable, incredulous emotion,
expressed by a faint blush. He winked not in the least
vulgarly; his thin red face with a well-modelled curved
nose had a sort of distinction—the more so that when
he talked to her he looked with a steadier and more
intelligent glance. A handsome, hale, upright, capable
man, with a white beard. You did not think of his
age. His son, he affirmed, had resembled him amazingly
from his earliest babyhood.

Harry would be one-and-thirty next July, he declared.
Proper age to get married with a nice, sensible girl that
could appreciate a good home. He was a very high-
spirited boy. High-spirited husbands were the easiest
to manage. These mean, soft chaps, that you would

think butter wouldn't melt in their mouths, were the
ones to make a woman thoroughly miserable. And
there was nothing like home—a fireside—a good roof:
no turning out of your warm bed in all sorts of weather.
"Eh, my dear?"

Captain Hagberd had been one of those sailors that
pursue their calling within sight of land. One of the
many children of a bankrupt farmer, he had been
apprenticed hurriedly to a coasting skipper, and had
remained on the coast all his sea life. It must have
been a hard one at first: he had never taken to it; his
affection turned to the land, with its innumerable
houses, with its quiet lives gathered round its firesides.
Many sailors feel and profess a rational dislike for the
sea, but his was a profound and emotional animosity—
as if the love of the stabler element had been bred into
him through many generations.

"People did not know what they let their boys in for
when they let them go to sea," he expounded to Bessie.
"As soon make convicts of them at once." He did not
believe you ever got used to it. The weariness of such a
life got worse as you got older. What sort of trade was
it in which more than half your time you did not put
your foot inside your house? Directly you got out to
sea you had no means of knowing what went on at home.
One might have thought him weary of distant voyages;
and the longest he had ever made had lasted a fortnight,
of which the most part had been spent at anchor,
sheltering from the weather. As soon as his wife had
inherited a house and enough to live on (from a bachelor
uncle who had made some money in the coal business)
he threw up his command of an East-coast collier with
a feeling as though he had escaped from the galleys.
After all these years he might have counted on the
fingers of his two hands all the days he had been out

of sight of England. He had never known what it was
to be out of soundings. "I have never been further than
eighty fathoms from the land," was one of his boasts.

Bessie Carvil heard all these things. In front of
their cottage grew an under-sized ash; and on summer
afternoons she would bring out a chair on the grass plot
and sit down with her sewing. Captain Hagberd, in
his canvas suit, leaned on a spade. He dug every day
in his front plot. He turned it over and over several
times every year, but was not going to plant anything
"just at present."

To Bessie Carvil he would state more explicitly:
"Not till our Harry comes home to-morrow." And
she had heard this formula of hope so often that it only
awakened the vaguest pity in her heart for that hopeful
old man.

Everything was put off in that way, and everything
was being prepared likewise for to-morrow. There was
a boxful of packets of various flower-seeds to choose
from, for the front garden. "He will doubtless let you
have your say about that, my dear," Captain Hagberd
intimated to her across the railing.

Miss Bessie's head remained bowed over her work.
She had heard all this so many times. But now and
then she would rise, lay down her sewing, and come
slowly to the fence. There was a charm in these gentle
ravings. He was determined that his son should not
go away again for the want of a home all ready for him.
He had been filling the other cottage with all sorts of
furniture. She imagined it all new, fresh with varnish,
piled up as in a warehouse. There would be tables
wrapped up in sacking; rolls of carpets thick and
vertical like fragments of columns, the gleam of white
marble tops in the dimness of the drawn blinds. Captain Hagberd always described his purchases to her,

carefully, as to a person having a legitimate interest in them. The overgrown yard of his cottage could be laid over with concrete . . . after to-morrow.

"We may just as well do away with the fence. You could have your drying-line out, quite clear of your flowers." He winked, and she would blush faintly.

This madness that had entered her life through the kind impulses of her heart had reasonable details. What if some day his son returned? But she could not even be quite sure that he ever had a son; and if he existed anywhere he had been too long away. When Captain Hagberd got excited in his talk she would steady him by a pretence of belief, laughing a little to salve her conscience.

Only once she had tried pityingly to throw some doubt on that hope doomed to disappointment, but the effect of her attempt had scared her very much. All at once over that man's face there came an expression of horror and incredulity, as though he had seen a crack open out in the firmament.

"You—you—you don't think he's drowned!"

For a moment he seemed to her ready to go out of his mind, for in his ordinary state she thought him more sane than people gave him credit for. On that occasion the violence of the emotion was followed by a most paternal and complacent recovery.

"Don't alarm yourself, my dear," he said a little cunningly: "the sea can't keep him. He does not belong to it. None of us Hagberds ever did belong to it. Look at me; I didn't get drowned. Moreover, he isn't a sailor at all; and if he is not a sailor he's bound to come back. There's nothing to prevent him coming back. . . ."

His eyes began to wander.

"To-morrow."

She never tried again, for fear the man should go out of his mind on the spot. He depended on her. She seemed the only sensible person in the town; and he would congratulate himself frankly before her face on having secured such a level-headed wife for his son. The rest of the town, he confided to her once, in a fit of temper, was certainly queer. The way they looked at you—the way they talked to you! He had never got on with any one in the place. Didn't like the people. He would not have left his own country if it had not been clear that his son had taken a fancy to Colebrook.

She humoured him in silence, listening patiently by the fence; crocheting with downcast eyes. Blushes came with difficulty on her dead-white complexion, under the negligently twisted opulence of mahogany coloured hair. Her father was frankly carroty.

She had a full figure; a tired, unrefreshed face. When Captain Hagberd vaunted the necessity and propriety of a home and the delights of one's own fire-side, she smiled a little, with her lips only. Her home delights had been confined to the nursing of her father during the ten best years of her life.

A bestial roaring coming out of an upstairs window would interrupt their talk. She would begin at once to roll up her crochet-work or fold her sewing, without the slightest sign of haste. Meanwhile the howls and roars of her name would go on, making the fisher-men strolling upon the sea-wall on the other side of the road turn their heads towards the cottages. She would go in slowly at the front door, and a moment afterwards there would fall a profound silence. Presently she would reappear, leading by the hand a man, gross and unwieldy like a hippopotamus, with a bad-tempered, surly face.

He was a widowed boat-builder, whom blindness had

overtaken years before in the full flush of business. He behaved to his daughter as if she had been responsible for its incurable character. He had been heard to bellow at the top of his voice, as if to defy Heaven, that he did not care: he had made enough money to have ham and eggs for his breakfast every morning. He thanked God for it, in a fiendish tone as though he were cursing.

Captain Hagberd had been so unfavourably impressed by his tenant, that once he told Miss Bessie, "He is a very extravagant fellow, my dear."

She was knitting that day, finishing a pair of socks for her father, who expected her to keep up the supply dutifully. She hated knitting, and, as she was just at the heel part, she had to keep her eyes on her needles.

"Of course it isn't as if he had a son to provide for," Captain Hagberd went on a little vacantly. "Girls, of course, don't require so much—h'm—h'm. They don't run away from home, my dear."

"No," said Miss Bessie, quietly.

Captain Hagberd, amongst the mounds of turned-up earth, chuckled. With his maritime rig, his weather-beaten face, his beard of Father Neptune, he resembled a deposed sea-god who had exchanged the trident for the spade.

"And he must look upon you as already provided for, in a manner. That's the best of it with the girls. The husbands . . ." He winked. Miss Bessie, absorbed in her knitting, coloured faintly.

"Bessie! my hat!" old Carvil bellowed out suddenly. He had been sitting under the tree mute and motionless, like an idol of some remarkably monstrous superstition. He never opened his mouth but to howl for her, at her, sometimes about her; and then he did not moderate the terms of his abuse. Her system was never to answer him at all; and he kept up his shouting till he got attended to—till she shook him by the arm, or thrust the mouthpiece of his pipe between his teeth. He was one of the few blind people who smoke. When he felt the hat being put on his head he stopped his noise at once. Then he rose, and they passed together through the gate.

He weighed heavily on her arm. During their slow toilful walks she appeared to be dragging with her for a penance the burden of that infirm bulk. Usually they crossed the road at once (the cottages stood in the fields near the harbour, two hundred yards away from the end of the street), and for a long, long time they would remain in view, ascending imperceptibly the flight of wooden steps that led to the top of the sea-wall. It ran on from east to west, shutting out the Channel like a neglected railway embankment, on which no train had ever rolled within memory of man. Groups of sturdy fishermen would emerge upon the sky, walk along for a bit, and sink without haste. Their brown nets, like the cobwebs of gigantic spiders, lay on the shabby grass of the slope; and, looking up from the end of the street, the people of the town would recognize the two Carvils, by the creeping slowness of their gait. Captain Hagberd, pottering aimlessly about his cottages, would raise his head to see how they got on in their promenade.

He advertised still in the Sunday papers for Harry Hagberd. These sheets were read in foreign parts to the end of the world, he informed Bessie. At the same time he seemed to think that his son was in England—so near to Colebrook that he would of course turn up "to-morrow." Bessie, without committing herself to that opinion in so many words, argued that in that case the expense of advertising was unnecessary; Captain

Hagberd had better spend that weekly half-crown on himself. She declared she did not know what he lived on. Her argumentation would puzzle him and cast him down for a time. "They all do it," he pointed out. There was a whole column devoted to appeals after missing relatives. He would bring the newspaper to show her. He and his wife had advertised for years; only she was an impatient woman. The news from Colebrook had arrived the very day after her funeral; if she had not been so impatient she might have been here now, with no more than one day more to wait. "You are not an impatient woman, my dear."

"I've no patience with you sometimes," she would say.

If he still advertised for his son he did not offer rewards for information any more; for, with the muddled lucidity of a mental derangement he had reasoned himself into a conviction as clear as daylight that he had already attained all that could be expected in that way. What more could he want? Colebrook was the place, and there was no need to ask for more. Miss Carvil praised him for his good sense, and he was soothed by the part she took in his hope, which had become his delusion; in that idea which blinded his mind to truth and probability, just as the other old man in the other cottage had been made blind, by another disease, to the light and beauty of the world.

But anything he could interpret as a doubt—any coldness of assent, or even a simple inattention to the development of his projects of a home with his returned son and his son's wife—would irritate him into flings and jerks and wicked side glances. He would dash his spade into the ground and walk to and fro before it. Miss Bessie called it his tantrums. She shook her finger at him. Then, when she came out again, after he had parted with her in anger, he would watch out of the corner of his eyes for the least sign of encouragement to approach the iron railings and resume his fatherly and patronizing relations.

For all their intimacy, which had lasted some years now, they had never talked without a fence or a railing between them. He described to her all the splendours accumulated for the setting-up of their housekeeping, but had never invited her to an inspection. No human eye was to behold them till Harry had his first look. In fact, nobody had ever been inside his cottage; he did his own housework, and he guarded his son's privilege so jealously that the small objects of domestic use he bought sometimes in the town were smuggled rapidly across the front garden under his canvas coat. Then, coming out, he would remark apologetically. "It was only a small kettle, my dear."

And, if not too tired with her drudgery, or worried beyond endurance by her father, she would laugh at him with a blush, and say: "That's all right, Captain Hagberd; I am not impatient."

"Well, my dear, you haven't long to wait now," he would answer with a sudden bashfulness, and looking uneasily, as though he had suspected that there was something wrong somewhere.

Every Monday she paid him his rent over the railings. He clutched the shillings greedily. He grudged every penny he had to spend on his maintenance, and when he left her to make his purchases his bearing changed as soon as he got into the street. Away from the sanction of her pity, he felt himself exposed without defence. He brushed the walls with his shoulder. He mistrusted the queerness of the people; yet, by then, even the town children had left off calling after him, and the tradesmen served him without a word. The slightest allusion to his clothing had the power to puzzle and frighten especially, as if it were something utterly unwarranted and incomprehensible.

In the autumn, the driving rain drummed on his sailcloth suit saturated almost to the stiffness of sheet-iron, with its surface flowing with water. When the weather was too bad, he retreated under the tiny porch, and, standing close against the door, looked at his spade left planted in the middle of the yard. The ground was so much dug up all over, that as the season advanced it turned to a quagmire. When it froze hard, he was disconsolate. What would Harry say? And as he could not have so much of Bessie's company at that time of the year, the roars of old Carvil, that came muffled through the closed windows, calling her indoors, exasperated him greatly.

"Why don't that extravagant fellow get you a servant?" he asked, impatiently, one mild afternoon. She had thrown something over her head to run out for a while.

"I don't know," said the pale Bessie, wearily, staring away with her heavy-lidded, gray, and unexpectant glance. There were always smudgy shadows under her eyes, and she did not seem able to see any change or any end to her life.

"You wait till you get married, my dear," said her only friend, drawing closer to the fence. "Harry will get you one."

His hopeful craze seemed to mock her own want of hope with so bitter an aptness that in her nervous irritation she could have screamed at him outright. But she only said in self-mockery, and speaking to him as though he had been sane, "Why, Captain Hagberd, your son may not even want to look at me."

He flung his head back and laughed his throaty affected cackle of anger.

"What! That boy? Not want to look at the only sensible girl for miles around? What do you think I am here for, my dear—my dear—my dear? . . . What? You wait. You just wait. You'll see to-morrow. I'll soon——"

"Bessie! Bessie! Bessie!" howled old Carvil inside. "Bessie!—my pipe!" That fat blind man had given himself up to a very lust of laziness. He would not lift his hand to reach for the things she took care to leave at his very elbow. He would not move a limb; he would not rise from his chair, he would not put one foot before another, in that parlour (where he knew his way as well as if he had his sight) without calling her to his side and hanging all his atrocious weight on her shoulder. He would not eat one single mouthful of food without her close attendance. He had made himself helpless beyond his affliction, to enslave her better. She stood still for a moment, setting her teeth in the dusk, then turned and walked slowly indoors.

Captain Hagberd went back to his spade. The shouting in Carvil's cottage stopped, and after a while the window of the parlour downstairs was lit up. A man coming from the end of the street with a firm leisurely step passed on, but seemed to have caught sight of Captain Hagberd, because he turned back a pace or two. A cold white light lingered in the western sky. The man leaned over the gate in an interested manner.

"You must be Captain Hagberd," he said, with easy assurance.

The old man spun round, pulling out his spade, startled by the strange voice.

"Yes, I am," he answered, nervously.

The other, smiling straight at him, uttered very

slowly: "You've been advertising for your son, I believe?"

"My son Harry," mumbled Captain Hagberd, off his guard for once. "He's coming home to-morrow."

"The devil he is!" The stranger marvelled greatly and then went on, with only a slight change of tone: "You've grown a beard like Father Christmas himself."

Captain Hagberd drew a little nearer, and leaned forward over his spade. "Go your way," he said, resentfully and timidly at the same time, because he was always afraid of being laughed at. Every mental state, even madness, has its equilibrium based upon self-esteem. Its disturbance causes unhappiness; and Captain Hagberd lived amongst a scheme of settled notions which it pained him to feel disturbed by people's grins. Yes, people's grins were awful. They hinted at something wrong: but what? He could not tell; and that stranger was obviously grinning—had come on purpose to grin. It was bad enough on the streets, but he had never before been outraged like this.

The stranger, unaware how near he was of having his head laid open with a spade, said seriously: "I am not trespassing where I stand, am I? I fancy there's something wrong about your news. Suppose you let me come in."

"*You* come in!" murmured old Hagberd, with inexpressible horror.

"I could give you some real information about your son—the very latest tip, if you care to hear."

"No," shouted Hagberd. He began to pace wildly to and fro, he shouldered his spade, he gesticulated with his other arm. "Here's a fellow—a grinning fellow, who says there's something wrong. I've got more information than you're aware of. I've all the information I want. I've had it for years—for years—for years—enough to last me till to-morrow. Let you come in, indeed! What would Harry say?"

Bessie Carvil's figure appeared in black silhouette on the parlour window; then, with the sound of an opening door, flitted out before the other cottage, all black, but with something white over her head. These two voices beginning to talk suddenly outside (she had heard them indoors) had given her such an emotion that she could not utter a sound.

Captain Hagberd seemed to be trying to find his way out of a cage. His feet squelched in the puddles left by his industry. He stumbled in the holes of the ruined grass-plot. He ran blindly against the fence.

"Here, steady a bit!" said the man at the gate, gravely, stretching his arm over and catching him by the sleeve. "Somebody's been trying to get at you. Hallo! what's this rig you've got on? Storm canvas, by George!" He had a big laugh. "Well, you *are* a character!"

Captain Hagberd jerked himself free, and began to back away shrinkingly. "For the present," he muttered, in a crestfallen tone.

"What's the matter with him?" The stranger addressed Bessie with the utmost familiarity, in a deliberate, explanatory tone. "I didn't want to startle the old man." He lowered his voice as though he had known her for years. "I dropped into a barber's on my way, to get a twopenny shave, and they told me there he was something of a character. The old man has been a character all his life."

Captain Hagberd, daunted by the allusion to his clothing, had retreated inside, taking his spade with him; and the two at the gate, startled by the unexpected slamming of the door, heard the bolts being shot, the snapping of the lock, and the echo of an affected gurgling laugh within.

"I didn't want to upset him," the man said, after a short silence. "What's the meaning of all this? He isn't quite crazy."

"He has been worrying a long time about his lost son," said Bessie, in a low, apologetic tone.

"Well, I am his son."

"Harry!" she cried—and was profoundly silent.

"Know my name? Friends with the old man, eh?"

"He's our landlord," Bessie faltered out, catching hold of the iron railing.

"Owns both them rabbit-hutches, does he?" commented young Hagberd, scornfully: "just the thing he would be proud of. Can you tell me who's that chap coming to-morrow? You must know something of it. I tell you, it's a swindle on the old man—nothing else."

She did not answer, helpless before an insurmountable difficulty, appalled before the necessity, the impossibility and the dread of an explanation in which she and madness seemed involved together.

"Oh—I am so sorry," she murmured.

"What's the matter?" he said, with serenity. "You needn't be afraid of upsetting me. It's the other fellow that'll be upset when he least expects it. I don't care a hang; but there will be some fun when he shows his mug to-morrow. I don't care *that* for the old man's pieces, but right is right. You shall see me put a head on that coon—whoever he is!"

He had come nearer, and towered above her on the other side of the railings. He glanced at her hands. He fancied she was trembling, and it occurred to him that she had her part perhaps in that little game that was to be sprung on his old man to-morrow. He had come just in time to spoil their sport. He was entertained by the idea—scornful of the baffled plot. But all his life he had been full of indulgence for all sorts of women's tricks. She really was trembling very much; her wrap had slipped off her head. "Poor devil!" he thought. "Never mind about that chap. I daresay he'll change his mind before to-morrow. But what about me? I can't loaf about the gate till the morning."

She burst out: "It is *you*—you yourself that he's waiting for. It is *you* who come to-morrow."

He murmured. "Oh! It's me!" blankly, and they seemed to become breathless together. Apparently he was pondering over what he had heard; then, without irritation, but evidently perplexed, he said: "I don't understand. I hadn't written or anything. It's my chum who saw the paper and told me—this very morning. . . . Eh? What?"

He bent his ear; she whispered rapidly, and he listened for a while, muttering the words "yes" and "I see" at times. Then, "But why won't to-day do?" he queried at last.

"You didn't understand me!" she exclaimed, impatiently. The clear streak of light under the clouds died out in the west. Again he stooped slightly to hear better; and the deep night buried everything of the whispering woman and the attentive man, except the familiar contiguity of their faces, with its air of secrecy and caress.

He squared his shoulders; the broad-brimmed shadow of a hat sat cavalierly on his head. "Awkward this, eh?" he appealed to her. "To-morrow? Well, well! Never heard tell of anything like this. It's all to-morrow, then, without any sort of to-day, as far as I can see."

She remained still and mute.

"And you have been encouraging this funny notion," he said.

"I never contradicted him."

"Why didn't you?"

"What for should I?" she defended herself. "It would only have made him miserable. He would have gone out of his mind."

"His mind!" he muttered, and heard a short nervous laugh from her.

"Where was the harm? Was I to quarrel with the poor old man? It was easier to half believe it myself."

"Aye, aye," he meditated, intelligently. "I suppose the old chap got around you somehow with his soft talk. You are good-hearted."

Her hands moved up in the dark nervously. "And it might have been true. It was true. It has come. Here it is. This is the to-morrow we have been waiting for."

She drew a breath, and he said good-humoredly: "Aye, with the door shut. I wouldn't care if . . . And you think he could be brought round to recognize me . . . Eh? What? . . . You could do it? In a week you say? H'm, I daresay you could—but do you think I could hold out a week in this dead-alive place? Not me! I want either hard work, or an all-fired racket, or more space than there is in the whole of England. I have been in this place, though, once before, and for more then a week. The old man was advertising for me then, and a chum I had with me had a notion of getting a couple of quid out of him by writing a lot of silly nonsense in a letter. That lark did not come off, though. We had to clear out—and none too soon. But this time I've a chum waiting for me in London, and besides . . ."

Bessie Carvil was breathing quickly.

"What if I tried a knock at the door?" he suggested.

"Try," she said.

Captain Hagberd's gate squeaked, and the shadow of his son moved on, then stopped with another deep laugh in his throat, like the father's, only soft and gentle, thrilling to the woman's heart, awakening to her ears.

"He isn't frisky—is he? I would be afraid to lay hold of him. The chaps are always telling me I don't know my own strength."

"He's the most harmless creature that ever lived," she interrupted.

"You wouldn't say so if you had seen him chasing me upstairs with a hard leather strap," he said; "I haven't forgotten it in sixteen years."

She got warm from head to foot under another soft subdued laugh. At the rat-tat-tat of the knocker her heart flew into her mouth.

"Hey, dad! Let me in. I am Harry, I am. Straight! Come back home a day too soon."

One of the windows upstairs ran up.

"A grinning, information fellow," said the voice of old Hagberd, up in the darkness. "Don't you have anything to do with him. It will spoil everything."

She heard Harry Hagberd say, "Hallo, dad," then a clanging clatter. The window rumbled down, and he stood before her again.

"It's just like old times. Nearly walloped the life out of me to stop me going away, and now I come back he throws a confounded shovel at my head to keep me out. It grazed my shoulder."

She shuddered.

"I wouldn't care," he began, "only I spent my last shillings on the railway fare and my last twopence on a shave—out of respect for the old man."

"Are you really Harry Hagberd?" she asked, swiftly. "Can you prove it?"

"Can I prove it? Can any one else prove it?" he said, jovially. "Prove with what? What do I want to prove? There isn't a single corner in the world, barring England, perhaps, where you could not find some man, or more likely a woman, that would remember me for Harry Hagberd. I am more like Harry Hagberd than any man alive; and I can prove it to you in a minute, if you will let me step inside your gate."

"Come in," she said.

He entered then the front garden of the Carvils. His tall shadow strode with a swagger; she turned her back on the window and waited, watching the shape, of which the footfalls seemed the most material part. The light fell on a tilted hat; a powerful shoulder, that seemed to cleave the darkness; on a leg stepping out. He swung about and stood still, facing the illuminated parlour window at her back, turning his head from side to side, laughing softly to himself.

"Just fancy, for a minute, the old man's beard stuck on to my chin. Hey? Now say. I was the very spit of him from a boy."

"It's true," she murmured to herself.

"And that's about as far as it goes. He was always one of your domestic characters. Why, I remember how he used to go about looking very sick for three days before he had to leave home on one of his trips to South Shields for coal. He had a standing charter from the gas-works. You would think he was off on a whaling cruise—three years and a tail. Ha, ha! Not a bit of it. Ten days on the outside. The *Skimmer of the Seas* was a smart craft. Fine name, wasn't it? Mother's uncle owned her. . . ."

He interrupted himself, and in a lowered voice,

"Did he ever tell you what mother died of?" he asked.

"Yes," said Miss Bessie, bitterly: "from impatience."

He made no sound for a while; then brusquely: "They were so afraid I would turn out badly that they fairly drove me away. Mother nagged at me for being idle, and the old man said he would cut my soul out of my body rather than let me go to sea. Well, it looked as if he would do it, too—so I went. It looks to me sometimes as if I had been born to them by a mistake —in that other hutch of a house."

"Where ought you to have been born by rights?" Bessie Carvil interrupted him defiantly.

"In the open, upon a beach, on a windy night," he said, quick as lightning. Then he mused slowly. "They were characters, both of them, by George; and the old man keeps it up well—don't he? A damned shovel on the—— Hark! who's that making that row? 'Bessie, Bessie.' It's in your house."

"It's for me," she said with indifference.

He stepped aside, out of the streak of light. "Your husband?" he inquired, with the tone of a man accustomed to unlawful trysts. "Fine voice for a ship's deck in a thundering squall."

"No; my father. I am not married."

"You seem a fine girl, Miss Bessie dear," he said at once.

She turned her face away.

"Oh, I say,—what's up? Who's murdering him?"

"He wants his tea." She faced him, still and tall, with averted head, with her hands hanging clasped before her.

"Hadn't you better go in?" he suggested, after watching for a while the nape of her neck, a patch of dazzling white skin and soft shadow above the sombre line of her shoulders. Her wrap had slipped down to her elbows. "You'll have all the town coming out presently. I'll wait here a bit."

Her wrap fell to the ground, and he stooped to pick it up; she had vanished. He threw it over his arm, and approaching the window squarely he saw a monstrous form of a fat man in an armchair, an unshaded lamp, the yawning of an enormous mouth in a big flat face encircled by a ragged halo of hair—Miss Bessie's head and bust. The shouting stopped; the blind ran down. He lost himself in thinking how awkward it was. Father mad; no getting into the house. No money to get back; a hungry chum in London who would begin to think he had been given the go-by. "Damn!" he muttered. He could break the door in, certainly; but they would perhaps bundle him into chokey for that without asking questions—no great matter, only he was confoundedly afraid of being locked up, even in mistake. He turned cold at the thought. He stamped his feet on the sodden grass.

"What are you?—a sailor?" said an agitated voice.

She had flitted out, a shadow herself, attracted by the reckless shadow waiting under the wall of her home.

"Anything. Enough of a sailor to be worth my salt before the mast. Came home that way this time."

"Where do you come from?" she asked.

"Right away from a jolly good spree," he said, "by the London train—see? Ough! I hate being shut up in a train. I don't mind a house so much."

"Ah," she said; "that's lucky."

"Because in a house you can at any time open the blamed door and walk away straight before you."

"And never come back?"

"Not for sixteen years at least," he laughed. "To
a rabbit hutch, and get a confounded old shovel . . ."

"A ship is not so very big," she taunted.

"No, but the sea is great."

She dropped her head, and as if her ears had been
opened to the voices of the world, she heard beyond
the rampart of sea-wall the swell of yesterday's gale
breaking on the beach with monotonous and solemn
vibrations, as if all the earth had been a tolling bell.

"And then, why, a ship's a ship. You love her and
leave her; and a voyage isn't a marriage." He quoted
the sailor's saying lightly.

"It is not a marriage," she whispered.

"I never took a false name, and I've never yet told
a lie to a woman. What lie? Why, *the* lie——. Take
me or leave me, I say; and if you take me, then it
is . . ." He hummed a snatch very low, leaning
against the wall.

> Oh, ho, ho Rio!
> And fare thee well,
> My bonnie young girl,
> We're bound to Rio Grande.

"Capstan song," he explained. Her teeth chattered.

"You are cold," he said. "Here's that affair of
yours I picked up." She felt his hands about her,
wrapping her closely. "Hold the ends together in
front," he commanded.

"What did you come here for?" she asked, repressing
a shudder.

"Five quid," he answered, promptly. "We let our
spree go on a little too long and got hard up."

"You've been drinking?" she said.

"Blind three days; on purpose. I am not given that

way—don't you think. There's nothing and nobody
that can get over me unless I like. I can be as steady
as a rock. My chum sees the paper this morning, and
says he to me: 'Go on, Harry: loving parent. That's
five quid sure.' So we scraped all our pockets for the
fare. Devil of a lark!"

"You have a hard heart, I am afraid," she sighed.

"What for? For running away? Why! he wanted
to make a lawyer's clerk of me—just to please himself.
Master in his own house; and my poor mother egged
him on—for my good, I suppose. Well, then—so long;
and I went. No, I tell you: the day I cleared out, I was
all black and blue from his great fondness for me.
Ah! he was always a bit of a character. Look at that
shovel, now. Off his chump? Not much. That's
just exactly like my dad. He wants me here just to
have somebody to order about. However, we two were
hard up; and what's five quid to him—once in sixteen
hard years?"

"Oh, but I am sorry for you. Did you ever want
to come back home?"

"Be a lawyer's clerk and rot here—in some such place
as this?" he cried in contempt. "What! if the old man
set me up in a home to-day, I would kick it down about
my ears—or else die there before the third day was out."

"And where else is it that you hope to die?"

"In the bush somewhere; in the sea; on a blamed
mountain top for choice. At home? Yes! the world's
my home; but I expect I'll die in a hospital some day.
What of that? Any place is good enough, as long as
I've lived; and I've been everything you can think of
almost but a tailor or a soldier. I've been a boundary
rider; I've sheared sheep; and humped my swag; and
harpooned a whale. I've rigged ships, and prospected
for gold, and skinned dead bullocks,—and turned my

back on more money than the old man would have scraped in his whole life. Ha, ha!"

He overwhelmed her. She pulled herself together and managed to utter, "Time to rest now."

He straightened himself up, away from the wall, and in a severe voice said, "Time to go."

But he did not move. He leaned back again, and hummed thoughtfully a bar or two of an outlandish tune.

She felt as if she were about to cry. "That's another of your cruel songs," she said.

"Learned it in Mexico—in Sonora." He talked easily. "It is the song of the Gambucinos. You don't know? The song of restless men. Nothing could hold them in one place—not even a woman. You used to meet one of them now and again, in the old days, on the edge of the gold country, away north there beyond the Rio Gila. I've seen it. A prospecting engineer in Mazatlan took me along with him to help look after the waggons. A sailor's a handy chap to have about you anyhow. It's all a desert: cracks in the earth that you can't see the bottom of; and mountains—sheer rocks standing up high like walls and church spires, only a hundred times bigger. The valleys are full of boulders and black stones. There's not a blade of grass to see; and the sun sets more red over that country than I have seen it anywhere—blood-red and angry. It *is* fine."

"You do not want to go back there again?" she stammered out.

He laughed a little. "No. That's the blamed gold country. It gave me the shivers sometimes to look at it—and we were a big lot of men together, mind; but these Gambucinos wandered alone. They knew that country before anybody had ever heard of it. They had a sort of gift for prospecting, and the fever of it was on them, too; and they did not seem to want the gold very much. They would find some rich spot, and then turn their backs on it; pick up perhaps a little—enough for a spree—and then be off again, looking for more. They never stopped long where there were houses; they had no wife, no chick, no home, never a chum. You couldn't be friends with a Gambucino; they were too restless—here to-day, and gone, God knows where, to-morrow. They told no one of their finds, and there has never been a Gambucino well off. It was not for the gold they cared; it was the wandering about looking for it in the stony country that got into them and wouldn't let them rest: so that no woman yet born could hold a Gambucino for more than a week. That's what the song says. It's all about a pretty girl that tried hard to keep hold of a Gambucino lover, so that he should bring her lots of gold. No fear! Off he went, and she never saw him again."

"What became of her?" she breathed out.

"The song don't tell. Cried a bit, I daresay. They were the fellows: kiss and go. But it's the looking for a thing—a something . . . Sometimes I think I am a sort of Gambucino myself."

"No woman can hold you, then," she began in a brazen voice, which quavered suddenly before the end.

"No longer than a week," he joked, playing upon her very heartstrings with the gay, tender note of his laugh; "and yet I am fond of them all. Anything for a woman of the right sort. The scrapes they got me into, and the scrapes they got me out of! I love them at first sight. I've fallen in love with you already, Miss—Bessie's your name—eh?"

She backed away a little, and with a trembling laugh: "You haven't seen my face yet."

He bent forward gallantly. "A little pale: it suits some. But you are a fine figure of a girl, Miss Bessie."

She was all in a flutter. Nobody had ever said so much to her before.

His tone changed. "I am getting middling hungry, though. Had no breakfast to-day. Couldn't you scare up some bread from that tea for me, or——"

She was gone already. He had been on the point of asking her to let him come inside. No matter. Anywhere would do. Devil of a fix! What would his chum think?

"I didn't ask you as a beggar," he said, jestingly, taking a piece of bread-and-butter from the plate she held before him. "I asked as a friend. My dad is rich, you know."

"He starves himself for your sake."

"And I have starved for his whim," he said, taking up another piece.

"All he has in the world is for you," she pleaded.

"Yes, if I come here to sit on it like a dam' toad in a hole. Thank you; and what about the shovel, eh? He always had a queer way of showing his love."

"I could bring him round in a week," she suggested, timidly.

He was too hungry to answer her; and, holding the plate submissively to his hand, she began to whisper up to him in a quick, panting voice. He listened, amazed, eating slower and slower, till at last his jaws stopped altogether. "That's his game, is it?" he said, in a rising tone of scathing contempt. An ungovernable movement of his arm sent the plate flying out of her fingers. He shot out a violent curse.

She shrank from him, putting her hand against the wall.

"No!" he raged. "He expects! Expects *me*—for

his rotten money! . . . . Who wants his home?
Mad—not he! Don't you think. He wants his own
way. He wanted to turn me into a miserable lawyer's
clerk, and now he wants to make of me a blamed tame
rabbit in a cage. Of me! Of me!" His subdued
angry laugh frightened her now.

"The whole world ain't a bit too big for me to spread
my elbows in, I can tell you—what's your name—
Bessie—let alone a dam' parlour in a hutch. Marry!
He wants me to marry and settle! And as likely as not
he has looked out the girl, too—dash my soul! And do
you know the Judy, may I ask?"

She shook all over with noiseless dry sobs; but he was
fuming and fretting too much to notice her distress.
He bit his thumb with rage at the mere idea. A window rattled up.

"A grinning, information fellow," pronounced old
Hagberd, dogmatically, in measured tones. And the
sound of his voice seemed to Bessie to make the night
itself mad—to pour insanity and disaster on the earth.

"Now I know what's wrong with the people here, my
dear. Why, of course! With this mad chap going
about. Don't you have anything to do with him,
Bessie. Bessie, I say!"

They stood as if dumb. The old man fidgeted and
mumbled to himself at the window. Suddenly he
cried piercingly: "Bessie—I see you. I'll tell Harry."

She made a movement as if to run away, but stopped
and raised her hands to her temples. Young Hagberd,
shadowy and big, stirred no more than a man of
bronze. Over their heads the crazy night whimpered
and scolded in an old man's voice.

"Send him away, my dear. He's only a vagabond.
What you want is a good home of your own. That
chap has no home—he's not like Harry. He can't be

Harry. Harry is coming to-morrow. Do you hear? One day more," he babbled more excitedly: "never you fear—Harry shall marry you."

His voice rose very shrill and mad against the regular deep soughing of the swell coiling heavily about the outer face of the sea-wall.

"He will have to. I shall make him, or if not"—he swore a great oath—"I'll cut him off with a shilling to-morrow, and leave everything to you. I shall. To you. Let him starve."

The window rattled down.

Harry drew a deep breath, and took one step towards Bessie. "So it's you—the girl," he said, in a lowered voice. She had not moved, and she remained half turned away from him, pressing her head in the palms of her hands. "My word!" he continued, with an invisible half-smile on his lips. "I have a great mind to stop. . . ."

Her elbows were trembling violently.

"For a week," he finished without a pause.

She clapped her hands to her face.

He came up quite close, and took hold of her wrists gently. She felt his breath on her ear.

"It's a scrape I am in—this, and it is you that must see me through." He was trying to uncover her face. She resisted. He let her go then, and stepping back a little, "Have you got any money?" he asked. "I must be off now."

She nodded quickly her shamefaced head, and he waited, looking away from her, while, trembling all over and bowing her neck, she tried to find the pocket of her dress.

"Here it is!" she whispered. "Oh, go away! go away for God's sake! If I had more—more—I would give it all to forget—to make you forget."

He extended his hand. "No fear! I haven't forgotten a single one of you in the world. Some gave me more than money—but I am a beggar now—and you women always had to get me out of my scrapes."

He swaggered up to the parlour window, and in the dim light filtering through the blind, looked at the coin lying in his palm. It was a half-sovereign. He slipped it into his pocket. She stood a little on one side, with her head drooping, as if wounded; with her arms hanging passive by her side, as if dead.

"You can't buy me in," he said, "and you can't buy yourself out."

He set his hat firmly with a little tap, and next moment she felt herself lifted up in the powerful embrace of his arms. Her feet lost the ground; her head hung back; he showered kisses on her face with a silent and overmastering ardour, as if in haste to get at her very soul. He kissed her pale cheeks, her hard forehead, her heavy eyelids, her faded lips; and the measured blows and sighs of the rising tide accompanied the enfolding power of his arms, the overwhelming might of his caresses. It was as if the sea, breaking down the wall protecting all the homes of the town, had sent a wave over her head. It passed on; she staggered backwards, with her shoulders against the wall, exhausted, as if she had been stranded there after a storm and a shipwreck.

She opened her eyes after a while; and, listening to the firm, leisurely footsteps going away with their conquest, began to gather her skirts, staring all the time before her. Suddenly she darted through the open gate into the dark and deserted street.

"Stop!" she shouted. "Don't go!"

And listening with an attentive poise of the head, she could not tell whether it was the beat of the swell or his fateful tread that seemed to fall cruelly upon her heart. Presently every sound grew fainter, as though she were slowly turning into stone. A fear of this awful silence came to her—worse than the fear of death. She called upon her ebbing strength for the final appeal: "Harry!"

Not even the dying echo of a footstep. Nothing. The thundering of the surf, the voice of the restless sea itself, seemed stopped. There was not a sound—no whisper of life, as though she were alone, and lost in that stony country of which she had heard, where madmen go looking for gold and spurn the find.

Captain Hagberd, inside his dark house, had kept on the alert. A window ran up; and in the silence of the stony country a voice spoke above her head, high up in the black air—the voice of madness, lies, and despair—the voice of inextinguishable hope. "Is he gone yet—that information fellow? Do you hear him about, my dear?"

She burst into tears. "No! no! no! I don't hear him any more," she sobbed.

He began to chuckle up there triumphantly. "You frightened him away. Good girl. Now we shall be all right. Don't you be impatient, my dear. One day more."

In the other house old Carvil, wallowing regally in his armchair, with a globe lamp burning by his side on the table, yelled for her in a fiendish voice: "Bessie! Bessie! You, Bessie!"

She heard him at last, and, as if overcome by fate, began to totter silently back towards her stuffy little inferno of a cottage. It had no lofty portal, no terrific inscription of forfeited hopes—she did not understand wherein she had sinned.

Captain Hagberd had gradually worked himself into a state of noisy happiness up there.

"Go in! Keep quiet!" she turned upon him tearfully, from the doorstep below.

He rebelled against her authority in his great joy at having got rid at last of that "something wrong." It was as if all the hopeful madness of the world had broken out to bring terror upon her heart, with the voice of that old man shouting of his trust in an everlasting to-morrow.

THE END

NOTES

The Nigger of the 'Narcissus'

The Narcissus *and her journey*

On 17th April 1884, Conrad left the S.S. *Riversdale* at Madras and went to Bombay to find another berth. He told his biographer, G. Jean-Aubry, that 'he was sitting with other officers of the Mercantile Marine on the verandah of the Sailors' Home in Bombay, which overlooks the port, when he saw a lovely ship, with all the graces of a yacht, come sailing into the harbour'. (*The Life and Letters of Joseph Conrad*, I, p. 76.) This was the *Narcissus*. She was a full-rigged iron sailing ship of 1,336 tons, built at Glasgow in 1876 (cf. 'She was born in the thundering peal of hammers beating upon iron . . . on the banks of the Clyde'). The first mate and six members of the crew were discharged at Bombay and Conrad signed on as second mate on 28th April 1884. According to the ship's Agreement and Account of Crew, the master was Captain Archibald Duncan and there were twenty-five officers and crew. The ship sailed on 28th April, paying off on 16th October at Dunkirk at the end of a voyage of four and a half months via the Cape. The fictional voyage takes about the same time (cf. 'It was the first land seen for nearly four months', and 'A week afterwards, the *Narcissus* entered the chops of the Channel').

Conrad's account, given shortly before his death, of his use of this journey as the basis of his story suggests that the storm and the death of the negro seaman, both central to the tale, were part of his original experience:

> I remember . . . the last occasion I saw the Nigger. That morning I was quarter officer, and about five o'clock I entered the double-bedded cabin where he was lying full length. . . . I asked him how he felt, but he hardly made me any answer. A little later a man brought him some coffee in a cup provided with a hook to suspend it on the edge of the bunk. At about six o'clock the officer-in-charge came to tell me that he was dead. We had just experienced an awful gale in the vicinity of the Needles, south of the Cape, of which I have tried to give an impression in my book . . . (*L & L*, I, pp. 77–8.)

279

We can see how Conrad transferred to Podmore the cook the taking of the tin hook-pot of water to the Nigger: 'He saw the cook standing in the doorway, a brass key in one hand and a bright tin hook-pot in the other. "... I brought you a pot of cold tea for your night's drinking, Jimmy . . ." He came in, hung the pot on the edge of the bunk.' James Wait's death does not follow immediately after the storm as did the death of the actual negro on the *Narcissus*. *He* was able-seaman Joseph Barron, aged thirty-five and born at Charlton (Agreement and Account of Crew). He died on 24th September on board the *Narcissus* and his wages of £13. 2*s*. 0*d*. were paid to the Consul at Dunkirk.

Conrad further stated: 'Most of the personages I have portrayed actually belonged to the crew of the real *Narcissus*, including the admirable Singleton (whose real name was Sullivan), Archie, Belfast, and Donkin.' (*L & L*, I, p. 77.) Donkin, however, appears to have a mixed source. He is a Londoner, and of the two Londoners on board the *Narcissus* the older one, J. Wild who was thirty-eight, seems the likeliest source. He signed on eighteen days after Conrad and therefore Conrad could have witnessed his arrival on board as it is described in the story. Donkin had 'saved his inefficient carcass from violent destruction by running away from an American ship', and Wild's previous ship was the American *Pharos*. But Donkin's viciousness may well have been suggested by stories Conrad heard about another crew member, able-seaman Charles Dutton (and there is some similarity in the sound of the names), who had been imprisoned at Cape Town during the voyage of the *Narcissus* to Bombay.

The sources for Archie and Belfast ('A little fellow, called Craik and nicknamed Belfast') are surely Archibald McLean, twenty-three years old, from Scotland, and James Craig, twenty-one years old, from Belfast.

In spite of what Conrad says, there was no Sullivan or Singleton on the *Narcissus*, but it has been pointed out (by Jocelyn Baines and J. D. Gordan) that there was a Daniel Sullivan on the *Tilkhurst* when Conrad sailed in her to the Far East (24th April 1885 to 17th June 1886). But he was then fifty-four, and Singleton is described as a very old man: 'a sixty-year old child of the mysterious sea', 'Old as Father Time himself'. It is possible that Conrad had another sailor in mind when he was creating Singleton, and a passage in the story gives a clue: '"What kind of ship is this? Pretty fair? Eh?" Singleton didn't stir. A long while after he said, with unmoved face—"Ship! . . . Ships are all right. It is the men in them!"' It is this very reply which Conrad has an 'elderly seaman' give in the autobiographical *The Mirror of the Sea* (1906): '"Ships!" exclaimed an elderly seaman in clean shore togs. "Ships . . . Ships are all right; it's the men in 'em . . ."' (pp. 128–9).

Although Conrad makes no mention of the source of Mr Baker, the mate, a passage in *The Mirror of the Sea* suggests that he derives from the mate of the *Duke of Sutherland*, in which Conrad sailed in 1878–9. He was A. G. Baker, thirty-six when Conrad knew him, and he came from Norfolk (the fictional mate lost two brothers, Yarmouth fishermen, at sea), was 'bull-necked', had a sardonic expression and in spite of being 'a better chief officer than many a man who had never tasted grog in his life' could never manage to get on (cf. pp. 21 & 166–7 and *The Mirror of the Sea*, p. 126). 'I met him ten years afterwards [Conrad records], casually, unexpectedly, in the street, on coming out of my consignee office [in Sydney] . . . "What are you doing here?" he asked. "I am commanding a little barque," I said, "unloading here for Mauritius."' (*The Mirror of the Sea*, p. 127.) Baker dines on board Conrad's ship and he 'went over [her] conscientiously, praised her heartily, congratulated me on my command with absolute sincerity', and like the fictional Baker 'seemed as though he could not tear himself away from the ship'. (*The Mirror of the Sea*, p. 128.) It is possible to date this meeting fairly precisely since the *Otago*, Conrad's only command, arrived in Sydney from Bangkok on 7th May 1888 and departed on 7th August 1888 (*Sydney Morning Herald*). Baker and Conrad dined on board the *Otago* at some time between these two dates.

If it is accepted that A. G. Baker is the source for the fictional first mate, it becomes possible to speculate on the original of young Creighton, second mate of the fictional *Narcissus*, who is a gentleman and whom the fictional Baker thinks 'will get on'. It is likely that Creighton is Conrad, who was a gentleman and who did get on.

The text and its growth

Conrad began the novel, originally to be a short story, during his honeymoon on the Ile-Grande, in June 1896. On the wrapper of the manuscript he has written: 'Begun in 1896—June'. He wrote some ten pages and then went on to 'An Outpost of Progress' in July, and 'Lagoon' in August. He took up the novel again in his lodgings in Gillingham Street, London, in September, and on 25th October he wrote: 'it will be about 30,000 words . . . There are so many touches necessary for such a picture.' This would seem to indicate that

Conrad had a clear notion of what he intended. To Edward Garnett on 1st November 1896 he wrote: 'I am letting myself go with the *Nigger*. He grows and grows. I do not think it's wholly bad.' His involvement in the semi-fictional world of his 'Beloved Nigger' was complete. As he neared the end of his work he wrote again to Garnett: 'Nigger died on the 7th at 6.00 p.m.; but the ship is not home yet. Expected to arrive tonight and be paid off tomorrow. And the end! I can't eat—I dream—nightmares—and scare my wife. I wish it was over!' (10th January 1897). Its conclusion was followed by a bout of illness: 'A cheap price,' as he wrote, 'for finishing that story.' A letter to Edward Garnett on 29th November 1896 indicates that the novel's lack of incident is the result of a definite policy:

> As to lack of incident well—it's life. The incomplete joy, the incomplete sorrow, the incomplete rascality or heroism—the incomplete suffering. Events crowd and push and nothing happens . . . The opportunities do not last long enough. Unless in a boy's book of adventures. Mine were never finished. They fizzled out before I had a chance to do more than another man would.

Very little can be said here about the development of the novel from manuscript (housed in the Rosenbach Museum, Philadelphia) to final text. J. D. Gordan discovered that the manuscript had been worked over unceasingly by the author until 'some pages were almost solid black with rewriting' (Gordan, p. 132), each chapter, in ascending order, being corrected more heavily than its predecessor up to chapter four. And though the first seven pages are comparatively clean, these also were revised since they differ substantially from the serial version.

The nature of Conrad's revisions can be demonstrated by his treatment of Wait. In the manuscript, Wait is aware that he is dying, but this idea was removed so that the tension of uncertainty that surrounds the Nigger, and his dramatic end, could be introduced.

Often we see, in his first draft, Conrad giving an outline which is later filled in to give a much better reading. For example:

> Mr. Baker the chief mate of the ship *Narcissus* came out of his cabin on to the dark quarter deck. It was then just nine o'clock. (MS.)

> Mr. Baker, chief mate of the ship *Narcissus*, stepped in one stride out of his lighted cabin into the darkness of the quarter-

deck. Above his head, on the break of the poop, the night-watchman rang a double stroke. It was nine o'clock. (p. 3.)

The problem of language

This is the only novel in which Conrad found it necessary to make liberal use of dialects, technical sea-terms and seamen's slang, and invective. His realistic intention was behind this, and the result is a rich and varied texture, but he involved himself in some problems over it. For the dialects, he had to resort to phonetic spelling, which caused him some difficulties. 'Blooming imposyshun' (p. 110, *l.* 27) was 'bloomin ymposishun' in the MS. and then 'bloomin himposyshun' in the first edition. Conrad tried to get rid of all the initial aspirates for the cockney Donkin without success. C. S. Evans of Heinemann, while correcting the proofs, wrote to Conrad: 'I have queried the spelling of "minnyt" . . . it is spelt differently in different parts of the book . . . I have queried the spelling of "Hymposed" since Donkin would only adorn the word with an initial aspirate. On page 172 a number of you's appear in Donkin's speech,—he usually says "yer".' (2nd September 1920.) Conrad replied forcefully the following day: 'All the phonetics of Donkin's speech are wrong . . . A real cockney drops his aspirates—but he never adds one . . . What I ought to have done was to take *every* initial *h* out of his speeches, since I call him a cockney. But God only knows what Donkin is! It's too late now to chase all those h's out of the text, I fear.' (*L & L*, II, p. 248.)

The slang phrases ('I'll put a head on him if he comes near you' p. 122, *l.* 27; 'I will smash his mug', p. 122, *l.* 28) caused no difficulty, but invective which appeared in the text as the word 'bloody' led to problems. Conrad wrote to Garnett on 11th October 1897: 'Heinemann objects to the *bloody*'s in the book. That Israelite is afraid of women . . . So I struck 3 or 4 bloody's out. I am sure there is a couple left yet but, damn it, I am not going to hunt 'em up.' Conrad himself was sensitive to the effect of his novel on women readers, as his letter to Sanderson (May 1897) proves:

> I address it [the novel] rather to you than your dear Mother be-cause I want you to see it first. I know, my dear fellow, that *you* will never suspect me of ingrained coarseness of thought and language. But I want you to read and judge before you hand it over to Mrs. Sanderson . . . I want to spare to her . . . any unpleasant experience. (*L & L*, I, pp. 204–5.)

In spite of his having cleaned up the text ('bloody nigger', Rosen-bach, p. 69, became 'cursed nigger', p. 165), there are still a few 'bloody's' left in the Dent text—'An ye're a thing—a bloody thing' (p. 152)—and the novel was criticized on the grounds of the rough language of the sailors: 'Strong, brutal, and in many places absolutely repellent by reason of the robustness of the adjectives employed . . .' (*The Literary World*, 28th January 1898); 'Their [the sailors'] talk and their swearing, especially the latter, is absolutely natural . . .' (*Daily Mail*, 7th December 1897).

In a letter (wrongly dated 6th December 1897) to his friend R. B. Cunninghame Graham, Conrad wrote of the *Daily Mail* reviewer: 'The man complains of lack of heroism! and is, I fancy, shocked at the bad language. I confess reluctantly there is a swear here and there. I grovel in the waste-paper basket, I beat my breast.'

The Title

Jean-Aubry states in a footnote that Conrad suggested 'thirteen different titles' for *The Nigger of the "Narcissus"* to his publisher, Heinemann. The difficulty obviously arose from the word 'nigger' which could be, and today would be, used as a pejorative term. We recall Wait's retort to Belfast: 'You wouldn't call me nigger if I wasn't half dead, you Irish beggar.' (pp. 79–80.) Conrad sent Sidney Pawling the innocuous title, *The Forecastle. A Tale of Ships and Men*, on 21st January 1897, but soon changed it back to *The Nigger: A Tale of Ships and Men*. For the serial form (*New Review*, August–December 1897) the title had changed again: *The Nigger of the 'Narcissus': A Tale of the Forecastle*. Of the seven copies of the novel issued first for purposes of copyright on 29th July 1897, one was sent to Edward Garnett's mother in which the sub-title was altered from *A Tale of the Forecastle* to *A Tale of the Sea*. Until 1914, the American edition had the title, *Children of the Sea: A Tale of the Forecastle*, in deference to possible American prejudices. Conrad found this 'absurdly sweet' though it is derived from the text: 'They were the everlasting children of the mysterious sea' (p. 25).

There is no suggestion that for Conrad the word 'nigger' carried any overtone of abuse. He wrote to Garnett (28th August 1897): 'If then, there is the slightest chance of it [The Preface] doing some good to the Nigger it shall *not* go to the Saturday or any other Review. Hang the filthy lucre. I would do any mortal thing for Jimmy—you know'; and again (29th November 1896): 'I send you seventeen pages more . . . of my Beloved Nigger.'

The 1897 Preface

Conrad, after finishing the novel, wrote a Preface to it which is an important statement of his artistic purpose. He appears to have considered publishing this separately, but it was first published by W. H. Henley, editor of the *New Review*, at the end of the finsl instalment of *The Nigger of the 'Narcissus'* (pp. 628–31), in what was the last issue of the magazine. The Preface was entitled 'Author's Note'. It was published again alone in 1902 (Hythe and Cheriton, printed by J. Lovick) in an edition of 100 copies. It appeared as 'The Art of Fiction' in *Harper's Weekly* (13th May 1905), and then was published in 1914 by Doubleday, Page of New York with a specially written note by Conrad entitled 'To My Readers in America'.

Edward Garnett and The Nigger of the 'Narcissus'

'You are,' Conrad wrote to Edward Garnett, 'my "father in letters"'. Conrad owed a great deal to Garnett who until Pinker took over Conrad's work (1901–2) was his literary confidant and 'agent'. His influence was greatest during the writing of *An Outcast of the Islands* and *The Nigger of the 'Narcissus'*. Garnett, as reader for Fisher Unwin, recommended publication of Conrad's first two novels, and when the firm refused better terms for Conrad's third book (£50 advance on a 10 per cent royalty on the first 2,000 copies), it was Garnett who suggested finding another publisher and asking for an advance of £100. Reginald Smith, of Smith, Elder & Co., wanted to put the book into cold storage, but Conrad wrote: 'Nothing would induce me to go back to F.U. Still it worries me to think that my "nigger" would be locked up for a year or two.' (Letter to Garnett, 13th November.) Garnett, however, 'put the case frankly' before S. S. Pawling of Heinemann who offered to show part of *The Nigger* to Henley of *New Review*, who commented: 'Tell Conrad that if the rest is up to the sample it shall certainly come out in *New Review*.' Garnett was also responsible for introducing Conrad to *Blackwood's Magazine* of which Sir Hugh Clifford wrote: 'It was, I think, the ambition of all young writers in my day to find themselves in Blackwood' (Blackburn, p. xv).

After their initial meeting in the National Liberal Club in November 1894, Conrad and Garnett met 'in little Soho restaurants, in Newgate Street, St. Paul's Churchyard and in a Mecca cafe in Cheapside', their 'collaboration' taking on the aspect of 'humble conspiracy à deux'. A scattering of cryptic notes through Conrad's correspondence while he worked on *The Nigger* gives the flavour of their relationship: 'The Vienna at 1.30 Friday when I shall report' (16th November 1896); 'Will you lunch with me on Friday, 1.30. Ang-Am [Anglo-American Café]?' (2nd December 1896); 'Shall I meet you at Compton Street? I suppose it is the place where we had dinner together once or twice. At the back of the Palace music-hall' (7th December 1896) and a postscript to the same letter: 'I shall look for you downstairs first. But I will be in Monico's entrance-hall at 5.30 for a vermouth'; 'I shall be in the Mecca on Thursday between 2.30 and 3'.

'All the good moments—the real good ones in my new life I owe to you . . . You sent me to Pawling—you sent me to Blackwoods—when are you going to send me to heaven?' Conrad wrote to Garnett on 28th August 1897.

Notes on the text

p. 3. *l*. 17　*forecastle*　short raised deck in bows of a vessel; crew quarters in a merchant ship.

p. 4. *l*. 13.　*liberty-men*　established members of the crew who were free to go ashore.

p. 6. *l*. 19.　'*Pelham*'　Pelham (1828) was subtitled *The Adventures of a Gentleman*. This novel by Bulwer Lytton (1803–73) was his second and was immensely popular, as was the novelist himself.

p. 8. *l*. 31.　*bridge-stanchion*　stanchions are upright posts supporting the vessel's beams or bulwarks.

p. 10. *l*. 28.　*shellback*　shell-back, a sailor of full age, especially if tough and knowledgeable: 'It takes a sailor a long time to straighten his spine and get quit of the bold sheer that earns him the name of shell-back' (W. Clark Russell, *Jack's Courtship*, 1883).

p. 13. *l*. 27.　*square-head*　a Scandinavian. After the first World War it came to refer more especially to a German.

l. 33.　*Whitechapel*　a district in London once inhabited by low characters, a Londoner of the coster-monger kind.

p. 19. *l*. 19.　*doctor*　nautical slang for a ship's cook.

p. 21. *l*. 19.　*western ocean style*　a term applied to deep sea sailors as opposed to the coastal water sailor.

p. 23. *l.* 8.   *in the kids* a flat dish used to measure a sailor's food ration.

     l. 14.   *rampin' mad* raging violently.

p. 26. *l.* 35.   *incult* untrimmed.

p. 36. *l.* 13.   '*We hesitated*' the first narrator appears here. He is not the second mate, as Conrad was, but one of the crew who was involved in rescuing Wait in the storm. The use of the narrator is not consistent, and at the end of the story he becomes 'I'.

p. 40. *l.* 24.   *the yards* cross timber on the mast to spread the square-sails on.

p. 56. *l.* 3.   *goose-wing* one of the lower corners of a ship's mainsail or foresail when the middle part is furled or tied up to the yard, hence goose-winged.

     l. 13.   *ratlines* small lines fastened horizontally to the shrouds of a vessel and serving as steps to go up and down the rigging.

p. 58. *l.* 1.   *deadeyes* a round laterally flattened wooden block, pierced with three holes through which a lanyard is reeved, used for extending the shrouds.

     l. 19.   *scend* scend or send—the carrying or driving impulse of a sea or wave or the sudden plunge of a boat.

p. 79. *l.* 16.   *sticks* masts. *Sticks up* To set up a boat's masts.

p. 80. *l.* 15.   *Podmore* the cook of the *Narcissus*. The name of the cook on the original *Narcissus* was John Youlton, aged forty-six and probably the source for the cook in the fictional *Narcissus* who is a religious maniac. There was another cook on board, Alfred Harvey aged twenty-nine. The name is derived from Conrad's source for Lord Jim—Augustine Podmore Williams, first mate on the pilgrim ship *Jeddah* during her fateful voyage in 1880.

p. 81. *l.* 30.   *milch-cow* a cow kept for milking on board ship.

p. 84. *l.* 28.   *wear-ship* to put the ship about, bringing her stern to windward.

p. 86. *l.* 25.   *brace* one of the metal straps secured with bolts and screws to the stern post and bottom planks of a ship.

p. 92. *l.* 25.   *head-earrings* one of a number of small ropes employed to fasten the upper corner of a sail to the yard.

p. 93. *l.* 9.   *reeve clear* to fit a block with a rope by reeving.

l. 28.   *tally on to that gantline* gantline or girtline. A rope taken up to the mast-head from which the stay leads, and rove through a block to hoist up the rigging, or to catch hold or 'clap' on to a rope.

l. 33.   '*Do or die*' cf. 'Youth' p. 12: the words written on her stern: '*Judea*, London. Do or die.'

p. 100. *l.* 30.   *dorg's loife for two poun' ten a month* the A.B.s on the actual *Narcissus* were paid £3 per month, O.S. £2 and the cook £3.15*s*. Conrad's salary as second mate was £5 per month.

p. 105. *l.* 11.   *dog-watches* name of the two short watches, one from 4 to 6 p.m. and the other 6 to 8 p.m.

p. 107. *l.* 20.   *square mainsail coat* a frock coat.

l. 20.   *gaff-topsail hat* a silk 'topper'.

l. 25.   *beak* a magistrate. Originally in the 16th century the form was 'beck' and meant constable.

l. 29.   *coon* A man who is sly and shrewd. Also a negro.

p. 108. *l.* 11.   *chokey* (or *choky*) a lock-up or prison from Hindustani 'chauki'. First used in English in *Cruise of the Midge* (1836) by Michael Scott.

p. 109. *l.* 23.   *the spanker* a fore-and-aft sail.

p. 145. *l.* 27.   *island of Flores* most north-westerly of the Azores, a Portuguese group of islands in mid-Atlantic about 900 miles west of Lisbon.

p. 149. *l.* 9.   *Canton Street girl* a girl living in Canton street, near the East India Dock Road, London, well-known brothel area during the period when Conrad was at sea.

p. 158. *l.* 19.   *Yellow Jack* yellow fever. Derived from the yellow flag displayed from vessels or naval hospitals in quarantine to indicate a contagious disease.

p.161. ll.29–30.   *the chops of the Channel* the western entrance to the English Channel.

p. 171. ll. 27–8.   *before the Mint* Conrad has in mind here that area of London's sailortown known as Tiger Bay—Ratcliffe-Highway, Cable Street and alleys such as Ship Alley and the North-East Passage and Wellclose Square. The most famous bars were Prussian Eagle in Ship Alley and Old Mahogany Bar in the Square.

Typhoon

Sources

In his Author's Note of 1919 to *Typhoon*, Conrad states that his source was the story of 'a steamship full of returning coolies from Singapore to some port in northern China' which had been 'talked about in the East as a recent occurrence' years before. This relates *Typhoon* to his own experiences of the Far East, and there are suggestions in the story which incline one to relate it more closely to Conrad's period as mate on the S.S. *Vidar* as well as to his experience with the *Highland Forest*. After leaving the *Highland Forest* in July 1887, Conrad went to Singapore and served in the *Vidar* from 22nd August 1887 to 2nd January 1888, sailing out of Singapore round the islands of the Malayan Archipelago.

On three of the four occasions that the *Vidar* was in Singapore when Conrad served in her, a ship called the *Nan-shan* was also in port. On 30th September 1887 she arrived from Swatow with 546 Chinese passengers, her master being a Captain Blackburn, and on 28th October she arrived with 238 Chinese aboard. It was very likely that Conrad heard some story about Chinese coolies losing their money during a storm at this time, but, as he wrote: '. . . it was but a bit of a sea yarn after all. I felt that to bring out its deeper signifi-cance . . . something other, something more was required; a leading motive that would harmonize all these violent noises, and a point of view that would put all that elemental fury into its proper place.' (Author's Note.)

He concluded: 'What I needed . . . was Captain MacWhirr . . . he was the man for the situation.' Conrad goes on to suggest that MacWhirr had his origins in a general figure not a particular one. He never 'saw Captain MacWhirr in the flesh'. 'MacWhirr is not an acquaintance of a few hours, or a few weeks, or a few months. He is the product of twenty years of life. My own life.' (Author's Note.) But Captain MacWhirr can be related to one particular person. His name is taken from Captain John McWhirr who was master of the *Highland Forest*, which Conrad joined at Amsterdam on 16th February 1887 as first mate. McWhirr was from County Down, Ireland, and MacWhirr on the *Nan-shan* is said to be from Belfast. In *The Mirror of the Sea*, Conrad describes the master of the *Highland Forest*:

> the new captain . . . arrived the day after we had finished loading, on the very eve of the day of sailing. I first beheld him on the quay, a complete stranger to me . . . in a black bowler and a short drab overcoat. . . . This stranger was walking up and down absorbed in the marked contemplation of the ship's fore and aft trim; but when I saw him squat on his heels in the slush at the very edge of the quay to peer at the draught of water under her counter, I said to myself, 'this is the captain'. . . . Without further preliminaries than a friendly nod, he addressed me: 'You have got her pretty well in her fore and aft trim. Now, what about your weights?' (p. 52.)

This is a very close reflection of the fictional MacWhirr when he is provided with a new command by Messrs. Sigg & Co. (p. 8), and he is also described as wearing 'a brown bowler hat, a complete suit of a brownish hue, and clumsy black boots'.

Conrad experienced many gales in his life as a seaman and he describes some of them in *The Mirror of the Sea*, pp. 78–100, but as a result of loading the *Highland Forest*'s cargo 'one third above the beams', they had, as the original McWhirr cryptically put it, 'a lively time of it this passage' (*The Mirror of the Sea*, p. 53). The terrifying rolling of the ship in *Typhoon* which leads to some of the most horrific scenes described by Jukes (see pp. 62–3), may well have been an imaginative description of what Conrad himself experienced: 'Down south, running before the gales of high latitudes, she made our life a burden to us. There were days when . . . there was no position where you could fix yourself so as not to feel a constant strain upon all the muscles of your body. She rolled with an awful dislodging jerk and that dizzily fast sweep of her masts on every swing.' (*Mirror of the Sea*, p. 54.)

The story would seem to derive largely, therefore, from Conrad's experiences on two ships—the *Vidar* and the *Highland Forest*, and the reference in the story to 'poor Jack Allen' supports this idea. John Allen was not a member of the crew of the *Highland Forest* or the *Nan-shan*, but he was first engineer of the *Vidar* when Conrad sailed in her.

The growth of the story

Conrad suggests that he began writing *Typhoon* after finishing 'The End of the Tether' (Author's Note). In fact it was written soon after he had completed *Lord Jim*, when 'The End of the Tether' was still to be begun. The story seems to have been written during a four-month period. It was presumably started in September 1900 and the completion date is 'Midnight, 10–11 January, 1901'. To Meldrum, Conrad wrote on 1st September 1900: 'I must make a fresh start without further delay . . . I think I shall be ready in about six weeks' (*Joseph Conrad: Letters to William Blackwood and David S. Meldrum* ed. William Blackburn, U.S.A., 1958, p. 109). But a month later (3rd October) he had to tell Meldrum: 'I've not yet finished the *Typhoon*. . . . That infernal story does not seem to come off somehow' (Blackburn, p. 111), and later we learn, 'the end is not yet (though it is not far) and it's impossible to say till the thing is done'. And Conrad was right, for on 27th November: 'The typhoon is still blowing. I find it extremely difficult to express the simplest idea clearly.' And the last reference in a letter to Meldrum of 6th December comes in a postscriptum: 'The Typhoon is all but finished'.

According to Conrad, 'Typhoon' was to be his 'first attempt at treating a subject jocularly so to speak' (Letter to Pinker, 8th October 1900) and this was recognized in Quiller Couch's review in the *Bookman*, June 1903.

Publication

The story appeared first in *Pall Mall Magazine*, January to March 1902. It was published in book form by Heinemann on 22nd April 1902 and again serialized in the *Critic*, February to May 1902, in New York. Sixteen years after publication Conrad recalled that 'some critics' on its first appearance, classed it 'as a deliberately intended storm-piece'. He must be referring to the *Daily Mail*, 22nd April 1903, where the reviewer wrote that *Typhoon* was 'the most elaborate storm piece that one can recall in English Literature'.

Notes on the text

p. 5. l. 13.   *Talcahuano*   a town in Chile, near Concepción.

p. 6. l. 26.   *the treaty port of Fu-chau*   After the Opium Wars (1840–2) the Nanking Treaty of 1842 named Shanghai, Canton, Ning-po, Fu-chau and Amoy as treaty ports in which European merchants lived in special districts, enjoying extra-territorial rights and almost entirely self-governing.

p. 7. l. 27.   *built in Dumbarton*   The original *Nan-shan* was built at Glasgow in 1876. The only ship Conrad sailed in built at Dumbarton was the *Tilkhurst* in 1877.

p. 12. l. 33.   *seven-years'-men*   by 1895 contracts for Chinese labour had been reduced to three years.

p. 13. l. 15.   *pidgin-English*   a blend of English with Chinese pronunciations and idioms used in the Far East. Jukes's use of pidgin English catches the almost forgotten flavour of it.

p. 17. *ll.* 1–2.   [*Jukes*] *extolled . . . the easy life of the Far East*   cf. *Lord Jim*, p. 10: 'They were attuned to the eternal peace of Eastern sky and sea. They loved short passages, good deck-chairs, large native crews, and the distinction of being white' and *The Shadow-Line*: 'Too long out here. Easy life and deck-chairs more their mark.' (p. 31.)

l. 7.   *The black-squad*   usually black watch, i.e. stokers in coal burning ships.

p. 23. l. 12.   *their blanked heads down there*   an example here of the restraints placed on the writer by contemporary conventions.

p. 34. l. 33.   *old Captain Wilson of the 'Melita'*   Conrad travelled from Singapore to Bangkok in the *Melita*, a journey of four days, arriving 24th January 1888 to take over command of the *Otago*. The master's name at this time was Morck (also spelt Moretz) and Conrad describes him as 'the first really unsympathetic man I had ever come in contact with'. (*The Shadow-Line*, p. 47.)

p. 35. l. 31.   *gimbals*   a concentric metal suspension fitting for supporting nautical instruments in a horizontal position.

p. 70. *l.* 23.   *black as Tophet*   black as hell; originally the proper name of a place near Gehenna or the Valley of the Son or Children of Hinnom where the Jews made human sacrifices to strange gods (cf. Jeremiah, 19.6.).

p. 91. *l.* 24.   *quay of the Foreign Concession*   quay belonging to the country to whom the Chinese had conceded certain territory for the establishing of a trading community of foreign merchants.

'Amy Foster'

Sources

According to Jessie Conrad, Ford Madox Ford claimed the plot as his. Though she rejects this claim, she does admit that Ford pointed out to Conrad a grave in Winchelsea churchyard which 'bears on the head-stone no name', but records 'the fact that the bodies of one or two foreign seamen are buried there, after being washed ashore'. (*Joseph Conrad As I Knew Him*, pp. 117–8.) In the story Winchelsea churchyard becomes Brenzett Church where the drowned are 'to be laid out in a row under the north wall' of the church (p. 123).

The original of Amy Foster herself was a servant in the Conrad household: 'it was her animal-like capacity for sheer uncomplaining endurance that inspired Conrad', wrote his wife. (*Joseph Conrad As I Knew Him*, p. 118.)

Baines is surely correct is suggesting that it is 'easy to detect an autobiographical note in Conrad's description of Yanko Gooral "feeling bitterly as he lay in his emigrant bunk his utter loneliness; for his was a highly sensitive nature"'.

Growth of the text

'Amy Foster' was written very quickly. 'Falk' was completed by 24th May, and Conrad wrote to Galsworthy on 20th June: 'I've finished Falk and I've written another story since then.' (*L & L*, I, 300). The story was originally entitled, 'The Husband'.

The manuscript is at Yale University library and is written in pencil—100 folio pages. It was first serialized in the *Illustrated*

London News, 14th December, 21st December and 28th December 1901. In his Author's Note Conrad speaks of the illustration: 'a fine drawing of Amy on her day out giving tea to the children at her home, in a hat with a big feather'. The illustration was by Gunning King.

In 1903 the story was included in *Typhoon and other stories* (William Heinemann).

'Falk'

Sources

The 'suggestions' from which this story grew came to Conrad during a two weeks' stay in Bangkok (24th January 1888 to 9th February 1888), when he arrived from Singapore to take up his only command, the *Otago*. His experiences at this time produced not only 'Falk', but also 'The Secret Sharer' and *The Shadow-Line*.

The narrator in the story is 'not thirty yet', but Conrad was thirty-one when he took over the *Otago* in Bangkok, that 'Eastern seaport . . . the capital of an Eastern kingdom'. As in the story, the former master of the *Otago* had died and been buried at sea, probably off Cap St Jacques, Cochin China, and the mate, Charles Born, had brought her into Bangkok but was not given the command. 'The crew was sickly, the cargo was coming very slow; I foresaw I would have lots of trouble with the charterers,' says the narrator, and there was sickness among the *Otago*'s crew (one man had died of cholera before Conrad's arrival). But the narrator is unable to leave Bangkok ultimately because of Falk's refusal to tow his ship out. There *was* a bar at the mouth of the Meinam, and there was only one tug-boat, the *Bangkok*, owned by Windsor, Rose & Co., whose captain was called Saxtrop, but it is unlikely that he would have been allowed to refuse towage. The narrator suggests that he did not get on with the charterers, Messrs Siegers, particularly young Siegers with whom he dealt, and it is possible that a similar situation caused the delay of the *Otago*. This firm is most likely based on an actual firm. In a letter of 31st March 1917, Conrad wrote: 'In Bangkok when I took command, I hardly ever left the ship except to go to my charterers (Messrs. Jucker, Sigg and Co.)'. Messrs Jucker, Sigg & Co. were also teak merchants who had shares in the second tug on the Meinam which arrived after Conrad left. In the MS. of

'Falk', the firm is called 'Yucker' and this is cancelled and 'Siegers' substituted; in *Lord Jim* there is a firm of charterers in Bangkok called Yucker, with a partner named Siegmund Yucker; in *Typhoon*: 'the *Nan-Shan* was built for some merchants in Siam—Messrs. Sigg and Son'.

In 'Falk', the narrator takes on a Chinese 'boy' as steward, who departs with thirty-two golden sovereigns belonging to the narrator. The *Bangkok Times*, 1st February 1888, reports that a Chinese 'boy' employed by the *Otago* did steal fifteen gold mohurs (but from a sailor, not the captain) and that the captain (Conrad) and mate went in search of him, and arrested him in 'Mr. Clarke's compound'. He escaped, however, on the way to the police station.

The narrator in 'Falk' befriends Captain Hermann of the *Diana*. According to the *Bangkok Times* during Conrad's stay in Bangkok, there was no steamer called *Diana* in port. However, there was a German steamer called the *Hermann* and Conrad may be recalling this steamer in his description of the *Diana* and transferring the name of the ship to her fictional owner. The master of the *Hermann* was a Captain Traulsen and he may well be the original of Falk in terms of physical description and perhaps history, i.e. the story of cannibalism. But cannibalism on the high seas was not unknown then—accounts of it appeared in the Singapore newspapers during Conrad's stay in that port, though none was an obvious source.

The name 'Falk' may have been suggested by the firm of Falck and Beideck in Bangkok which ran two stores. Gustave Falck was in Bangkok during Conrad's stay, but the *Straits Times*, 3rd June 1888, reports his arrival in Singapore, and his death was recorded (of dysentery) the same day in the Singapore Register of Deaths. He was a German aged forty.

Many years earlier there had also been a Falck hotel in Bangkok, and reference was made to it in the *Bangkok Times* when Conrad was there, but at this time there were two hotels, the Universal and the Oriental. The smaller, the Universal, was owned and managed by Schumaker and Ulrich. Schomberg, it will be recalled, is 'the proprietor of the smaller of the two hotels in the place' (p. 155). His name may have been suggested by the firm of Brockers, Scomburgk & Co. The MS. of 'The End of the Tether' shows that Conrad knew the street in Singapore where this firm had its offices.

'Falk' shares with 'Heart of Darkness' and 'Youth', an introductory situation in which the narrator, Marlow, tells his story to a group of companions, all connected with the sea. In 'Falk' they are in a small river-hostelry, in 'Youth' at a mahogany table, in 'Heart of Darkness' on board the yawl *Nellie* on the Thames. This situation derives from Conrad's experiences on his friend G. F. W. Hope's yawl, *Nellie*. Hope's unpublished typescript, held by his daughter, entitled *My Life at Sea and Yachting*, describes occasions when he and Conrad and others once connected with the sea went yachting, and a typical journey was down the Thames and up the river Medway, stopping at various places such as the Bull Inn at Chatham or the Lobster Arms at Hole Haven (where it is known Conrad told the assembled ex-sailors the story of how he was as a youth smuggling arms into Spain for the Carlist cause), or the Fountain Hotel at Sheerness (facing the entrance to the Thames). Perhaps it was this last, where the 'dinner was execrable' (p. 145) that Conrad was recalling in this story.

Growth of the story and publication

'Falk' was begun in January 1901 soon after the completion of *Typhoon* on 11th January. It was completed four months later, for the MS. is dated 'Winchelsea, May 1901', and on 24th May Conrad wrote to William Blackwood: 'I have been in Winchelsea (returned yesterday) for a fortnight; finishing a story for Heinemann.' The MS. is 247 pages folio and is housed at the Yale University Library. The story was first published in *Typhoon and other stories* (William Heinemann, 1903).

'To-morrow'

Again Ford seems to have been useful to Conrad. In an undated letter Conrad wrote to Ford: 'All *your* suggestion and *absolutely my* conception.' Jessie Conrad wrote of the story: 'The last story in that volume we neither of us liked very much.' (p. 119.) Completed by 16th January 1902, Conrad described the story as '"Conrad" adapted down to the needs of a magazine' but 'by no means a pot-boiler'. It appeared in the *Pall Mall Magazine*, August 1902, and was included in *Typhoon and other stories* (William Heinemann, 1903). Conrad later dramatized 'To-morrow' under the title of *One Day More*. It was performed at the Court Theatre, London, 26th and 27th June 1905 by the Stage Society, and produced by Conrad's friend, Sir Sidney Colvin.